"Paul Scott is a novelist who understands how to employ image and scene to convey reality. . . . Climate and feeling thus complement each other. . . . Scott sees with an artist's eye and a humanist's understanding."
    MARTIN LAVIN, *New York Times Book Review*

"One of the best novelists to emerge from Britain's silver age."
    ROBERT TOWERS, *Newsweek*

"The author [of *The Chinese Love Pavilion*] handles his unusual situation well, writing with skill and restraint. He catches scene, emotion and action with effect. His dialogue is good and so is his perception of the telltale quirks of an exceedingly odd set of characters."
    MARK SAXTON, *New York Herald Tribune*

"Far more even than E. M. Forester, in whose long literary shadow he has to work, Paul Scott is successful in exploring the provinces of the human heart."
    Life

"Scott's vision is both precise and painterly. Like an engraver crosshatching the illusion of fullness, he selects nuances that will make his characters take on depth and poignancy."
    New York Times Book Review

"One has to admire Mr. Scott's gifts as a buttonholing storyteller, and his rich, close-textured prose; his descriptions of action and of certain kinds of relationships are superb."
    JEREMY BROOKS, *Guardian*

The Chinese Love Pavilion

PAUL SCOTT (1920–78) was a British novelist, play-wright, and poet, best known for his monumental work *The Raj Quartet* (1966–74) and for the Booker Prize–winning *Staying On* (1977). His other novels include *Johnnie Sahib, The Chinese Love Pavilion, The Birds of Paradise,* and *Six Days in Marapore.* During the Second World War, Scott was posted as an officer cadet to India, where he came to know and fall in love with that country. Scott's experiences in India emerge as themes in his novels: uneasy relationships between male friends or brothers; the representation of authority and social privilege in the British Raj; racial stratification and the oppression of local classes in the imperial context. His writing has been adapted for film and television series such as the 1980 film version of *Staying On* and the 1984 fourteen-part series known as *The Jewel in the Crown* (rebroadcast in 1997, then readapted by BBC in 2005). Before his death, Scott was visiting professor at the University of Tulsa, Oklahoma.

The
Chinese Love Pavilion

A Novel

PAUL SCOTT

THE UNIVERSITY OF CHICAGO PRESS

The University of Chicago Press, Chicago 60637
University of Chicago Press edition 2013
Printed in the United States of America

22 21 20 19 18 17 16 15 14 13   1 2 3 4 5

ISBN-13: 978-0-226-08843-3 (paper)
ISBN-13: 978-0-226-08857-0 (e-book)
DOI: 10.7208/chicago/9780226088570.001.0001

LIBRARY OF CONGRESS CATALOGING-IN-PUBLICATION DATA

Scott, Paul, 1920–1978, author.
   The Chinese love pavilion : a novel / Paul Scott.
      pages ; cm
   ISBN 978-0-226-08843-3 (pbk. : alk. paper) — ISBN 978-0-226-08857-0
(e-book) 1. British—India—Fiction. I. Title.
   PR6069.C596C48 2013
   823'.914—dc23

                                                             2013021657

♾ This paper meets the requirements of ANSI/NISO z39.48-1992
(Permanence of Paper).

TO
Carol and Sally
FOR LATER

AND TO
Penny
FOR NOW

Contents

7

The Door by which men enter –

HALF-WAY UP THE FORESTED HILL THAT LENDS ITS name to the town of Bukit Kallang the ground flattens into a grassy ledge one hundred yards wide and two hundred yards deep and on this ledge a Chinese merchant, who had sought and found his fortune in Malaya, built himself a house. He lived there in some splendour until the coming of the Japanese when having failed to convince them either of his good intentions towards Asian co-prosperity or of his innocence in a matter of sabotage he was taken one day into his own back garden and summarily executed. His head was fixed to the top of a pole and every day for two weeks the men, women, and children who lived in Bukit Kallang were marched up the hill into the garden to look upon his remains and learn by example.

The merchant was the first man to suffer death there but he was by no means the last. The daily parades ended but the executions continued with some monotony and because the Chinese are as ready as any to make a joke in adversity and because this was the place in which people could expect to lose their heads it became known locally as the garden of madness.

The merchant had built his house in the Eurasian style but behind it, looking towards it across the place of execution, he had erected a pavilion aggressively oriental in design and colour. It was the last building thirty-seven men and five women saw in this world. Those who were beheaded were made to kneel facing it while Japanese officers and important collaborators stood on the veranda to watch. As the victim bowed his head he must have carried an impression of the pavilion in his eyes, especially if the sun were shining because the tiles of the roof had once been painted gold and shabby as they were they still glowed.

The four corners of the roof curled up like the shoes of Aladdin and were supported by the main pillars of the veranda, each carved from a single block of wood in the shape of a dragon writhing round a post in an ecstasy of exhaled fire. The dragons like most of the exterior woodwork were painted dark green.

A flight of three steps led to the veranda. Facing the steps were two narrow doors, placed close together and painted scarlet. Sandwiched between the doors there was a single, narrow window, and this suggested not only that the doors led into the same room but that the room was dark. And so, after the first pleasurable shock of the pavilion's external appearance, curiosity about its interior was aroused.

*

Perhaps by now the house has been redecorated, the garden laid out and the gold of the pavilion roof restored. It would be interesting to know whether their legend remains, whether whoever lives there now can satisfy an inquisitive visitor who has heard the beginning of a tale but not its end.

Or perhaps the house is deserted, the garden gone to ruin, the jungle grown right up to the windows of the pavilion. There was in fact more than one window. Apart from the window facing south between the narrow doors there was one facing east, one north, and another west. If the jungle has encroached the sun coming up over the rim of the hills will no longer illuminate the Golden Room or at its height deflect through the north window the green light of trees into the Jade Room of Day Long Happiness, or as it sets expand through the west window into the third and last, the Scarlet Room.

The three rooms were each tiled and lacquered in their distinctive colour but in the ante-room these colours merged. It was the ante-room you entered first, having climbed the steps and pushed open the narrow door on the left of the south window. The walls of the ante-room were green, the ceiling gold, the doors scarlet. The floor was a mosaic of dragons, fish, and birds and after long looking at them they seemed to dance or swim or flutter their wings and the floor to undulate with their movement. Reeling a little, you pushed at the door on the other side of the window and came again on to the veranda.

Beyond the plateau the land tumbled down in frozen motion like the still picture of a waterfall into the valley that lay in the forested arms of the hills. Even if you closed your eyes you were aware of the hills and the way they had of shifting position, of coming nearer when they thought you weren't looking, of veiling themselves with violet mist on a sunny day to create an illusion of distance and safety, of advancing upon you on a grey day only half concealed by smoke-screen clouds trapped in their crests, and at night when they cupped their ears to their own silence and filled the darkness with their listening you could not forget them.

The Golden Room enslaved of the Rising Sun; the Jade Room of Day Long Happiness; the Scarlet Room wherein the Setting Sun lies sleeping: these were the names we gave the rooms. The ante-room had no name although I lay with Teena Chang all through one hot Malayan night and together we tried to think of one.

There were too many possible names for the ante-room, no name in itself definitive: the Room of the Dancing Dragons, of the Swimming Fish, of the Tongueless Birds. We found no lasting name for it but that was the night Teena christened the twin doors.

She said, "The little door that opens inwards, that is the door by which men enter in anticipation of desire. But the little door that opens outwards, that is the door by which men go in memory of loving."

When she said this she was sitting up on the mattress in the Scarlet Room, the sheet scarcely covering her thighs, moving a

13

palm-leaf fan gently to and fro. I lay back a little, supporting my weight on one elbow. Beyond the mosquito net our shadows were huge on the wall, cast there by the light of the oil-lamp set on the floor beside us. It amused us sometimes to watch our shadows, to see the gestures of love magnified.

Some men said that Teena Chang was the most beautiful woman in Malaya. I worked it out at the time from the information she gave me that she was half Chinese, one quarter Dutch and one quarter French. She was a Christian by upbringing, a prostitute by profession. She seldom exposed her skin to the sun. It was very pale. Her hair was black, as soft and shining as a child's. Her lips were large but firm and shapely. She applied make-up to suit her mood. In her Chinese mood she accentuated the slight almond shape of her eyes, heightened the prominence of cheekbone, pencilled her eyebrows theatrically upwards. In her European mood the brows were pencilled down, the slant of the eye balanced by a touch of pencil beneath, the rouge placed lower on the cheek.

She could match voice to mood; even her dresses, all the same in cut – high at the throat, sleeveless, tight to her body, slit on either side to just above the knee – subtly conveyed it. In her European mood she wore dresses of plain material but if you went into a room and she was in her Chinese mood you could detect it even if she had her back towards you because the dress would be intricately patterned with embroidered pagodas, dragons, bright stylized flowers. She might turn to you on such occasions and say in her higher-pitched voice, "Today I am Madame Ho. Please to inform Mac."

In this mood she seldom smiled and it took patience and experience to distinguish humour from seriousness in her. In her European mood she lowered her voice, spoke more quickly, broadened her gestures, slackened her whole body, smoked cigarettes, talked about the war and about herself. It was, in its way, superb mimicry and some cause for wonder because she had had few opportunities of meeting such women socially. I asked her once whether she had ever thought of becoming an actress but she said, "No, no. One day I shall go to Singapore."

"And what will you do there, Teena?"

She ran her fingers through the thick hair at the back of her neck, freeing it, shaking her head a little in the manner of occidental women.

"Do? The same as I do here. But it will be more expensive."

In her European mood she would undress in front of you, even demand help with the buttons at the back of her frock; but in her Chinese mood she would lower the oil-lamp and then lead you to the mattress, there with exquisite meekness to undress you first with hands that communicated a touching impression of shyness. Only when you lay in comfort would she attend to herself, undressing behind the screen or, if commanded, kneel submissively with her back towards you and allow you to help her.

But once in her arms the mood, whichever it had been, seemed to melt away and leave behind it a joy, a sadness the nature of which you never quite understood. I used to think of it as the third and final artifice, the professional mystery, the creation for you of Teena as a woman waiting for, capable of, love, ready to find it in you if you would find it in her.

Later, one of the moods would return. It was in her returned Chinese mood that she sat up that night, cooled me with the palm-leaf fan and found names for the doors of the pavilion.

*

The townspeople said that the pavilion was haunted, that on nights when the moon was full the souls of the dead came in procession down the steps of the veranda and formed a circle round the place of execution. One story had it that it was the sight of them which drove Lieutenant Hakinawa to suicide and not his love for Teena Chang. Hakinawa was a young Japanese officer remarkable for his physical beauty and his gentleness. These qualities were perhaps more legendary than actual. Teena would only talk about him in her European mood and in that mood she called him "Joe" and "poor boy", could be persuaded to show you his photograph and would do so with that air of expectation western women assume when their choice has been made but their confidence in it shaken. When she was in her Chinese mood it was less a matter of her refusing to talk about him than of your own unwillingness to intrude on her privacy by questioning her. In such silence you realized that her feelings for Hakinawa might have been deep or shallow or somewhere in between but that whatever the truth his death had intervened and made it of no present consequence.

Teena was sixteen when the Japanese invaded Malaya, nearly twenty when they surrendered and the British returned. She had come to Bukit Kallang from up-country in the second year of the Japanese occupation. She was then motherless. She had always been fatherless. Beyond explaining that her mother was Chinese, her father white, of Dutch and French parentage, she would seldom speak of them. Her mother, left alone either by his death or desertion, had worked as a servant to a European family on a rubber estate and Teena herself had been cared for by a Catholic mission. She lived in the priest's household, attended the mission school and taught the smaller children as she grew older. That much I gathered.

But again, she would only talk of these things in her European mood and she was expert in the occidental art of selective self-presentation, of communicating herself in a series of pictures that never quite interlocked to form a unified whole. It was never clear, for instance, what her father had been other than white, in what circumstances she had been sent to the mission or taken away from it. At some stage she had gone to Ipoh because it was from there that she had been brought to Bukit Kallang by a Japanese officer; but there were hints of other adventures before that in Taiping and Penang.

She had acquired wealth: not of cash but of personal possessions that made her as much admired as envied, as much held in esteem as in contempt. They were a two-fold adornment. They were proof too, if proof were needed, that in the midst of almost total world disaster energy and enterprise had been spent on the production and preservation of the things with which civilization is most concerned but least remembered by. There was both folly and beauty in this.

She possessed silks from Hong Kong, jewellery from Bangkok, silk stockings, some unworn and kept still in the flat cardboard boxes of their makers in New York, handbags from Rome, shoes from Paris, a shawl woven and embroidered in Kashmir, a gold watch from Switzerland, a Swan fountain-pen, lipsticks, creams and powders from Hollywood. You felt at the time that all she needed further were perfumes from Arabia and pearls from Bahrein, but the absence of the exotic and the permanently valuable was symptomatic.

It was possible to consider this hoard of blackmarketry, as she called it, and to be angry. It was possible to be amused by it. I wavered between the two extremes. Somewhere in the middle was respect. The collection of such things during total war, their appearance in the room of a prostitute in a small town in Malaya, had little to do with greed or callousness but everything to do with determination. Around herself Teena had built a small island of baubles. They were useless in themselves but when she wore or used them she announced herself as a woman of the world that had been fought for: she was clean and civilized and concerned with beauty. The only lasting wonder is of how they came to her. What route, for instance, had been taken to Bukit Kallang by the shoes that bore inside them the name of a shop in Paris? And through whose hands had they passed? And yet to satisfy that curiosity now would be to diminish the remembered magic of their presence.

*

If I unlock and open the top left-hand drawer of the desk at which I write these words I can take out and hold an object Teena held, an object I had bought long before I met her and which I gave to her.

The *kris* is the traditional Malayan dagger. Its blade is

curved like a flattened corkscrew. The *kris* in the drawer of my desk is perhaps an inch too short in the blade but it is by no means a toy. The workmanship of blade and handle was once described to me as impeccable. The handle is set with semi-precious stones. It looks more valuable than it is. Over the years the blade has grown dull, sheathed itself in a kind of skin so that it no longer flashes in so lively, so threatening a manner.

When I gave it to Teena she was in her Chinese mood. Would she, in her other mood, have smiled and returned it to me, pretending to shudder, and suggested I sell it and buy her something else with the money? Perhaps. As it was she looked at it for quite a long time as it lay between us, the handle towards her, the blade towards me as I had placed it, then said, "It is very beautiful. Very valuable. Why do you give it to me?"

"Because I love you, Teena."

In my mind there was an idea that through the *kris* I armed her with my love; that with it, symbolically, she would keep other men at distance. I had spoken half-jestingly of my growing jealousy. A game had been invented in which, although my desire for her was obvious, she went through a charade of laughingly proclaiming her innocence since last she lay with me, sealing each declaration with a kiss. It was a game she would not play, that I never felt the need to play myself, when she was in her Chinese mood. If she had been in her European mood when I gave her the *kris* we might have played the game then and the giving and acceptance of the gift been made part of the joke.

But I did not really intend it as a joke. If, on the evening I brought the dagger to the pavilion, she had not been in her Chinese mood I might not have given it to her at all. It was the Chinese mood that invited the gift and set the seal on the intention to offer it.

And when I said, "Because I love you, Teena," she lifted the dagger, kissed the handle and rose from the mattress to put it into the box where no doubt on other occasions she had temporarily put aside tributes men had paid her.

PART I

The God Hunter

I

THE STORY BEGINS NOT WITH TEENA CHANG BUT A
man called Brian Saxby, and it begins before the war in India,
not in Malaya.

India was of my bone.

The family tradition of service in that country had died with
my grandfather before I was born but, as a boy, I could hardly
imagine a life spent elsewhere and the house in Bayswater where
I lived until the age of seven when it was broken up by the
deaths of my renegade parents was full of Indian relics. Afterwards, as I moved from one distant relative to another, I
had only grandfather's yellowing photographs, his diaries and
papers and the pale, amateurish water-colours of the Punjabi
plains which he had painted himself and signed with a flourish:
Richard Warren Brent – the Warren, I liked to fancy, from
Warren Hastings. My parents left nothing behind them except
their own unused years and myself whom they had christened
plain Tom. The Indian tradition was my inheritance, my proof
of identity.

From early boyhood I had thought of a career in India in
terms of the army and brave actions against the hillmen of the
North-West Frontier; but at sixteen, forsaking Kipling for
Forster, as it were, the vision faded, ousted partly by a youthful
contempt for what I called the military mind (my parents would
have been pleased) and partly by the beginning of a new
vision: that of myself as a District Officer, following in grandfather's footsteps, wise, godlike, stern but just, administering
the law from under the peepul tree.

This vision was shorter lived than the first and at this stage I
had confirmation from an uncle, one of my mother's several

brothers (my father had none), that my father's failure to follow an Indian career was not a combination of circumstances, ill-luck, and marriage but as I had suspected for some time the result of a deliberate policy. He had spent much of his child-hood in India and his break with tradition had caused some unhappiness. My mother, according to this uncle, had been in "all the women's movements of her day". No doubt she had strengthened him in his resolve to have nothing to do with British Imperialism. They were schoolteachers.

I was torn between two loyalties. I admired my father and grandfather equally for keeping faith with what I assumed them to have believed in and yet I could not side with either of them. I too despised despotism, however benevolent, and yet I was bound to India emotionally and there was no point in denying it. For a while I considered the possibility of planting tea but the word "coolie" sat uncomfortably on my tongue. In the end, not unaware of anti-climax, acknowledging an urban upbringing, I plumped for commerce and became articled to a chartered accountant with the idea of qualifying and then applying for one of the jobs I used to see advertised by firms with offices in Bombay and Calcutta. It was a long-term project, too long for my patience. Within a year I approached a shipping line and after some weeks of waiting I was allowed, at the age of twenty, to work my passage out to Bombay in the purser's office of a small steamer carrying machinery and some hundred passengers. I had saved about eighty pounds and had the assurance of at least three months' work in the line's Bombay office. I felt rich beyond measure.

The year which followed fell into three distinct phases. The first, which lasted no more than a few weeks, at most a month, was a time of disappointment, even dismay. What had this city to do with me or I with it? It took young Brent by the scruff of his neck and rubbed his face in its own dirt as if to make sure the boy would be given a sharp lesson in reality. In a city where the white-skinned were usually rich, influential or favoured in some manner I quickly learned that I had chosen to live on the lowest level of sub-European society and that it needed more than half-baked notions to make it supportable.

In the shipping office I was an embarrassment to the executives, one of whom, in a chatty, probing interview, discovered the fact that we had gone to the same school. He offered me a job as his assistant, bed and board in his own house (he was careful to mention that he was married): social and financial security, the absence of which had hit me like a punch to the midriff within twenty-four hours of landing. I accepted his offer. He clapped me on the shoulder, said he was glad and a bit relieved because it would be awkward to have a chap like myself working as a temporary clerk with all the wogs. He added that it would involve a two-year contract of service. I began to raise objections which he brushed aside with the best good will. We were interrupted by an Indian clerk. He shouted at him, treated him like dirt. No, I thought, not two years, not two years. The office was cool, air-conditioned, the man himself young enough to speak the same language as I did. He would have been easy to work for and in two years I might not have noticed words like wog or irritable outbursts like: Get out and bloody well knock next time. But I noticed them now. I weighed them against the air-conditioned room and the sense of belonging which talking to him gave me; and went back to clerical grade B to work with the Eurasians and westernized Indians: the object of their curiosity and suspicion.

From the beginning I lived in a hostel run by a Mrs Ross, a dark-skinned Eurasian woman to whom I had been sent by the assistant purser. She catered mostly for male members of her own sad, rootless community. She was kind and gentle and I remember her and her guests with affection in spite of the hundred ways in which they conferred superior status on me because I was pure-bred white and came from that country most of them called home. Her own complexion was not light enough to let her pass as a European, even had she wanted to, but the others practised this deception even amongst themselves. Warm and motherly, she listened patiently to the imaginary tales of an English up-bringing with which they propped up their self-esteem. She worked far into the night at menial tasks they would have despised her for doing had they seen her at them. Every Monday great play was made of collecting laundry "for the man", filling in lists in duplicate, allotting marks; but I found her once, at two o'clock in the morning, in the room behind her kitchen, surrounded by those same bundles of ticketed clothes, ironing our white shirts and collars.

"Why?" I asked her, as she got me a cup of tea instead of the glass of water my sleeplessness had driven me downstairs to find. "Why don't you tell them there's no laundry, no man?"

"They know," she replied. "Now drink this down. I'll find you an aspirin."

"Yes," I said, "they know, so why not tell them?"

"Tell them yourself, Mr Brent."

"Tom. Call me Tom. For God's sake someone call me Tom and not always Mr Brent."

"All right, Tom. You tell them."

"I will."

But I didn't. That marked the end of the first month. I needed people to talk to, to be talked to by, to go out with, get drunk with, argue with. The next day I looked for another job. You can never be part of a city like Bombay but you can be whole within its walls. I wanted to work with my hands, to lift weights, heave crates, lay bricks, to sweat away the stench of ink and the airless smell of large rooms filled with paper, but that was as impossible for a white man, it seemed, as it was for a black one to swim in the pool of a European club.

I asked my fellow guests at Mrs Ross's to help me. They were puzzled. "But you're at the shipping office, Mr Brent." They suspected I had money, a private income, what in their idiom was referred to as "means". A job was a position. Holidays were vacs. To chuck a good position was a sign of instability, the supposed failing of half-castes. I longed to tell them to stop pretending but I couldn't. I could have tripped them up a score of times when they talked about home ("Our place in Shropshire"), but I had not the heart. There was an affinity between my dream of their country and theirs of mine.

But I was done for the moment with dreams, visions. I laid claim to my room by taking grandfather's paintings from my black tin trunk and hanging them on the wall. I gave notice at the office. That night at the hostel one of them took me aside and asked, "Would you work for an Indian?"

"Why not?" I asked.

The Indian was short and fat and ran what he described as an import and export business which meant that he handled on an agency basis anything that came his way. He wore brown suits, black shoes, and cream-coloured ties with gold threads in them. The palms of his hands were yellow and he smelt of garlic and lavender water. He gave me a job as what he called his right-hand man. This meant answering the telephone, taking messages, and generally looking after the one-roomed office when he was out. It also meant spending a lot of time at the docks, searching for, claiming and checking consignments of consumer goods from England, mostly novelties destined for the bazaars. We liked each other from the beginning because we set up no barriers of pretence. His grandfather had been a peasant who was born, lived, and died in hopeless debt to the local moneylender.

"And now I can fire you, isn't it, the grandson of a D.O.?"

"You haven't hired me yet," I reminded him. It was our first interview and we had not got round to anything definite.

He offered me something like half the market wage. We haggled. The Indians haggle, the English discuss the weather. Both are a sign of good manners.

"You youngsters," he exclaimed, mopping his forehead with a folded white handkerchief.

The wage settled, the job in my pocket, I left his office feeling that I had bridged the gap between my father and Richard Warren Brent. I would work in India but under and not over an Indian.

The job was never arduous, never began to represent a

fulfilment of ambitions, but I enjoyed it because so much of it was done in the open, on docks, in warehouses. Through it I established a circle of friends, none of them English, none of them close, all companionable. Time went quickly. I fell in love with a dusky Eurasian girl, if love is the word to describe what both of us recognized as a wholly physical attraction. It seemed that whatever she wore nothing would stop her nipples showing through.

I would have been a catch for her and she had the grace to admit it, and I, I'm glad to say, the grace to refuse a promise of marriage when she offered pre-marital rights in exchange for it. It was a sad, humorous, candid, lecherous business which led to a great deal of laughter on her part and, on mine, cold showers which I found over-rated.

Without the girl this second, gregarious phase might have ended sooner than it did: which was, appropriately, on my twenty-first birthday when there were three months to go to complete my first year out East. We had a beer party at Mrs Ross's: stag, because it was planned as a surprise for me and they had confused the celebration of a man's majority with that of his last night of bachelordom. It was wrong from the start, like the picnic arranged by the Indian in *A Passage to India*. I got drunk, my natural inclination to do so helped by their egging on of the Englishman to make a fool of himself. We did the thing in style: the sing-song, the bawdy solos (Brent the sole performer because they knew the tunes and titles but not the words), the feats of beer drinking and beer balancing, the rugger-scrum with the leather pouffe, which was ridiculous because I had played only soccer and they, I think, nothing but handball.

I went through it, good-humouredly at first, then sadly, finally angrily because through the beer haze – that not quite focused but deeply penetrating lens – I saw what I had not seen before: the communal resentment amounting to hatred which their individual good manners could not finally disguise. I had everything they most wanted in the way of background and

26

education. I *was* English, I *looked* English, I was the *raj*, the elusive father-image, and I insulted them by counting it all cheap when circumstances caused them to hold it dear.

At the end of the scrum, my dander up because someone's elbow had cracked me on the left eye, I rallied them like troops round a flag by shouting, "To the District Officer!" and led them upstairs. I barged into my room, raised my bottle of beer to the water-colours and bid them drink to "Grandad, the old sod", and then hurled the bottle at one of the pictures, shattering the glass that had preserved it for fifty years.

In the morning all they said was, "Good show, Brent old man," and were solicitous over the eye which had turned a splendid purple. I apologized to Mrs Ross for the noise and the damage and she said that it was not to bother me because we were only young once. The place seemed to vibrate with our doing and saying what was expected of us. It was a Sunday. I walked alone to the Gateway of India, that triumphal arch so placed that it leads nowhere, and from the stone parapet I stared out at the shipping anchored in the roads and thought about birth, copulation and death, and living your life in the station allotted to you. What have I to do with these people or they with me? I asked myself.

During the two months which followed I came to the conclusion that my escapade had been a failure and that I must go back to England. The inheritance was an illusion: I could never be stern father, loving mother to grown men and women, never sit under the peepul tree or stand on the parade ground or enjoy the luxury of the air-conditioned office, but that was all the inheritance seemed to amount to. My father's rebellion had bred these tastes out of me but it had not bred into me a compensating taste for self-identification with the under-privileged.

Without telling anyone of my plans I went back to the shipping office. The prospects looked dim. Several weeks went by. A letter came at last. I was offered a passage home on the S.S. —— which was due to leave Bombay in ten days' time.

Nothing was said about the nature of the work beyond a cryptic instruction to report to the Chief Steward. It sounded suspiciously like washing up. I glanced at the water-colours (the damaged one since repaired) and wondered what grandfather would have made of it all.

*

That night I sat up late. The others had gone to bed and Mrs Ross had retired into the back room to set up her ironing board. I stayed in the sitting-room reading and re-reading the letter and trying to make up my mind, but the thunder and rain made it impossible to concentrate. I decided to turn in.

When I was half-way up the stairs I heard a rapping on the frosted pane of glass in the front door. The door looked on to a courtyard and was normally left on the latch but Mrs Ross had locked up and the bell did not work. I went down, unbolted the door and opened it. At the same time I switched on the light that illuminated the porch and the steps leading up to it.

There were two of them, a white man and a Sikh. The effect was rather startling. They stood shoulder to shoulder, broad, large-boned men with beards, the white man's red, the Sikh's grey. The white man was hatless, the Sikh turbanned. Both were coatless and wore their grubby shirts hanging loose outside crumpled cotton trousers. The white man, like the Sikh, wore sandals on his bare wet feet, sandals of the kind that are held on by suction and a single strap over the big toe. They reminded me of visitors likely to be encountered otherwise only in a story by Conan Doyle.

"Is this Mrs Ross's?" the white man asked. He was unmistakably English.

"Yes, I'll call her."

I crossed the hall, opened the door to her kitchen and called through that there was someone to see her. The Sikh remained in the porch but the Englishman came into the hall. His shirt was soaked and clung to his chest. His hair was plastered across his scalp. Water glittered in the spade-shaped beard and

28

trickled down his smooth bronzed face and from the end of his aquiline nose. He did not seem bothered by it. I told him that Mrs Ross would be out in a moment and made my way to the foot of the stairs.

"Do you know whether she's got a room?" he asked.

"I don't, I'm afraid."

"They said up the road they thought she had."

"Up the road?"

"The smug little hotel on the corner," he explained.

"Are they full then?" I knew they weren't usually.

"They pretended to be," he said. "I expect I made an unfavourable impression."

I could not help glancing down at his shirt and trousers.

He said, "My friends always told me I had a genius for looking disreputable."

I smiled, began climbing the stairs, pondering on his use of the past tense, wondering whether the implication was that he had no friends left or that they had given up telling him.

"I've been away for a time," he called. "In Sumatra."

I paused, looked down at him. There was so much to look at on the outside that his eyes were the last things you noticed. I was noticing them now but, doing so, was uncertain what they told me, if anything.

"My name is Brian Saxby," he said.

"Tom Brent."

"Is Mrs Ross a Scotswoman?"

I said, "Her father may have been."

"Ah."

A puddle was forming round his feet. Through the open door came the monotonous sound of the rain. The Sikh was leaning against the door-jamb watching us.

"He's the taxi-driver," Saxby explained. "He doesn't trust me. Every time I get out he follows me to make sure I don't get away without paying him."

The kitchen door opened.

"Here's Mrs Ross," I told him, and leaving them to it

continued on up the stairs. His voice was deep and penetrating. Above, on the landing, I stopped and listened, my attention caught.

"I've nothing suitable," she was saying. "It's only a box-room. There's hardly room for a camp-bed. It wouldn't do at all."

"It would do for me," he said. "I think the only question is whether you think I would do for it."

I waited.

Presently she said, "You're welcome to it for the night, Mr Saxby." That meant she liked him and that her objection to the box-room as a suitable place for him was genuine. She had an instinct for people. "But," she went on, "you'd never stand it for more than that. How long did you want to stay?"

"Three months."

"Oh, well. That settles it. It would never do."

"Is there anything falling vacant?"

"Not for a month. I couldn't have you in the box-room for a month."

He said, "I'd pay in advance, Mrs Ross."

I knew that she could do with the money. In Mrs Ross's world rent tended to be something you waited for.

"I'm sorry, Mr Saxby. I'd like to accommodate you but I can't offer anything decent for at least a month. Come and have a look at the box-room and then if you're willing to put up with it for a night or two you can have it while you look for something else."

"I don't need to look at it. I'll get my luggage in."

His sandals clacked across the tiled floor. Going back down the stairs I saw him disappear into the rain taking the driver with him. "Mrs Ross," I said.

"Yes, Tom?"

"It's a good let."

"Well, it would have been." She smiled up at me.

"Not would have been. Will be. He can have my room next week. I'm going back to England."

I turned and climbed back to the landing. Later she came to my room and probably drew her own conclusions from the fact that I was still fully dressed, just sitting on the edge of the bed.

"Are you sure, Tom?"

"Yes, sure."

"It's what you want?"

"Absolutely." I grinned at her but she was not deceived.

"I'll miss you," she said.

The next day I gave my Indian employer a week's notice. He mopped his brow with the folded handkerchief and said that he supposed he'd have to pull on without me, wasn't it? I called at the shipping office and filled in forms under the supervision of an Indian clerk who showed his contempt for what I was letting myself in for by giving me no more than a quarter of his attention. He had nothing to lose. I thought of Forster's phrase: Only connect. But connect what to what?

"We need photographs," the Indian said.

"You've got those from last year," I said. "I still look the same."

Our eyes met.

"We need photographs," he repeated.

So I went to the studio of a Muslim photographer and sat in the little passport cubicle: front face, click; turn round, profile, click. "Half-hour," he said and I stepped out of the cubicle feeling like a magician's stooge emerging from a box at the climax of an illusion.

A lot can happen in half an hour, I told myself. But nothing did. Back at the shipping office I gave them the photographs and signed on the dotted line: Tom Brent; stubby, uncompromising. There was nothing to be introduced by way of flourish.

In the hostel that evening I dragged my tin trunk from under the bed and opened it. My old worsted suit was green with damp decay. I used a brush on it. The smell caught the back of my throat. I tried it on and found the sleeves and trousers were too short. The explanation for the trousers, perhaps, was that I'd grown a tail and tucked it between my legs.

There was a knock at the door.

"Come in."

I looked up, expecting Mrs Ross. It was Saxby. I had not seen him since the night before and had almost forgotten his existence. Apart from the fact that he was dry he looked much the same. His shirt and trousers were clean and pressed but they were old, bleached nearly colourless by the sun: the shirt in particular, which must once have been butcher blue; he still wore it loose outside his trousers in the manner affected by Indians; and he was still sockless, scuffling about in sandals. His dark red hair was surprisingly soft and silky, though, and the beard only a degree or two coarser in texture and gingerish in shade. He did not stand more than an inch or two taller than I but close together as we were I was conscious of his bigness, of his body as a vessel displacing air in the way a ship displaces water.

"Hello," I said, "have you come to see your room? If you smell anything funny it's this suit I've got on."

I began to initiate him into the mysteries of cupboards, shelves, uncertain window catches, the position of light and fan switches, the view he would have of the inner courtyard in daylight. I fancied he was only half listening. When I had finished he asked about the pictures.

"Oh, those are mine," I said casually. "I'll be taking 'em with me."

He crossed to the wall and examined them.

"Richard Warren Brent," he read out.

"My grandfather."

"Was he a soldier?"

"No, civil service."

"He's caught the Punjab well."

The pictures were only described on their backs.

I said, "D'you know it then?"

"Very well."

"What's he caught exactly?"

He looked at me over his shoulder. His eyes were dark brown, almost black in the artificial light. "You've not been there?"

"I haven't been anywhere. I only know Bombay."

He looked back at the pictures. "That's a pity. Bombay isn't India. Nor for that matter is the Punjab but at least the Punjab is part of India. I expect it was the only part that mattered to your grandfather, judging by what's gone into these. He's caught the sense of its intimate distances."

He seemed then to lose interest, to remember what he had come for. He looked at his watch. I couldn't help noticing that it was a very expensive one.

"Do you like curry?" he asked.

"Well, not much. Why?"

"Mrs Ross isn't exactly a dab-hand at it. She seems to specialize in European-style dishes. But tonight's a curry night as far as I'm concerned. I plan to eat out. Have you ever had a real curry?"

"No. I don't think I have."

"Then why don't you join me?"

I had been in India a year. I had never been outside Bombay. I had never eaten a proper curry. I felt pretty useless. It did not help to have my wrists sticking out of my sleeves. I saw that it would have been in character to refuse his invitation so I accepted it, if only for the honour of the family.

"Good," Saxby said. "I'll see you downstairs in ten minutes. That'll give you time to change."

*

Mercifully it was not raining. I say mercifully because the taxi-driver refused to take us beyond a certain point.

"He's afraid of getting his windows smashed," Saxby explained. "Come on, we'll have to walk."

He paid the man off and we stepped out into the ill-lit street that had marked the limit of the driver's courage. Apart from the stink of open drains there was nothing untoward and I said as much.

Saxby said, "The interesting bit's to come."

The interesting bit was a network of alleyways and thorough-fares of considerable squalor. We kept to the brighter lit of these, Saxby assured me. It seemed to me that all the cut-throats and beggars of Bombay were congregated there and I kept a hand on my wallet. If you have ever seen a Bombay beggar you will understand the trepidation with which I followed Saxby across the fouled pavements, through the gauntlet of their armless, legless bodies. I would swear that one of them was no more than a living head on a bed of straw. They howled at us and, if they had hands, clawed at us, but Saxby drove through them with a kind of relentless goodwill that brooked no nonsense.

From what I call the street of beggars we came to another, brighter lit street of open shops. There we encountered a sacred white Brahmini bull with black eyes as big as saucers. There was music from a first-floor window and Saxby turned to me and said, "That's the music of Rajputana," and then left me to follow again, my back cold of a sudden as if touched by a wind from the north where Rajputana lay. The air was hot, choked with the fumes of charcoal, the smell of spice and of the sweat-impregnated cotton clothes worn by passers-by.

We entered from an open doorway into what looked like the shop of a corn-chandler. There was a young man behind the counter smoking a *bidi* – the yellow-papered conical cigarettes which Indians smoked – and what looked like a corpse in a winding sheet on the floor. Saxby said it was probably the nightwatchman. He said something to the man with the *bidi* who jerked his head at the inner doorway. Parting glass-bead curtains which tinkled icily Saxby entered ahead of me and then stood aside.

The room was small, lantern-lit, empty. There was a low table in the middle, a wicker-chair and a divan covered with a dingy but, I discovered later, clean white counterpane. On the floor, which was tiled in black and white, was a large brass bowl that contained of all things an aspidistra. To one side a narrow staircase led upwards. Saxby went to the foot of it and called out. A man answered and Saxby called again. They spoke the kind of Hindustani I could just follow. "What! Is it you, Brianji?" "Yes." "But you are in Sumatra!" "No, no, Debi. I am in Bombay, here, below. I have brought a friend."

Debi came down, a mountain of a man, dressed in white homespun cotton dhoti and shirt. He stood with his bald head held well back to counterbalance the enormous weight of his belly and facing you he gave the impression of thrusting himself at you in greeting so that the hand, when it came, was more like an afterthought.

They switched to English.

"So you are back. For how long?"

"Three months, Debi."

"And then?"

"Assam, perhaps. For orchids."

Debi winked at me. "What it is to be rich, eh? Are you also a rich young man?"

"No. Far from it."

"You do it for a living then? But is there money in collecting plants?"

Saxby said, "Mr Brent doesn't collect plants, Debi. At the moment the only thing we have in common is a man-sized thirst. Have your boys been lucky recently?"

Debi laid a finger to his nose. "White Horse?"

"That'll do. Oh, and Debi –"

Saxby pulled a tiny cloth bag out of his trouser pocket and threw it on to the table. The Indian picked it up, loosened the string and upended it. The stones tumbled out and lay glittering.

"So. Sapphires. You came by way of Ceylon?"

"I promised you I would."

"Did you pay duty?"

"No," Saxby said. "I forgot. In any case I suspect the man I bought them from didn't come by them honestly."

"Rogues," Debi said, putting the stones back in the bag with his chubby brown fingers, "vagabonds. The world is full of thieves. Are you hungry?"

"Very."

"In one hour. Upstairs. Meanwhile I will send down someone nice with the whisky. She comes from Manipur but hasn't learned to dance, which is a pity."

When he had gone Saxby said, "Now let's get comfortable. There aren't any civilized amenities like punkahs so I advise you to take off your shirt. It gets very hot." He found two paper fans on the lower shelf of the table and gave me one. Solemnly he stripped to the waist and sat on the divan, leaving the wicker-chair for me.

"But what about mosquitoes?" I asked him, slapping at my arm.

"They don't bite me any more."

"No, they're concentrating on me." I kept my shirt on but pulled it loose outside my belt. It was, I discovered, remarkably comfortable that way.

"Who is he?" I asked, indicating the ceiling where Debi's heavy footsteps could be heard walking to and fro.

"He calls himself a merchant and that's as good a description as any, I suppose."

"Is the whisky we're waiting for pinched from somewhere?"

"The docks."

"By him?"

"No. His contacts. Ninety per cent of the trade in this area is in stolen goods."

"Have you known him long?"

"Oh, yes," Saxby said. "Years. How old would you say he is?"

"He's so fat it's difficult to tell. Forty?"

"He must be sixty if he's a day. Love keeps him young."

I grinned. Saxby looked at me quizzically. He said, "I meant love in the broader sense. Love of his God and his fellows. He's very rich but he gives half his annual profits to the Brahmins.

36

They cultivate him excessively because everything he touches turns to gold. It wasn't always like that with him. No, no. His father was rich but Debi was a bit of a prodigal son. In those days his enterprises usually ended in disaster."

"What changed his luck?"

"He seems to think I had something to do with it."

"Had you?"

"Perhaps. Does it matter? It's his point of view that counts."

"What happened?"

"We spent two days together in an open boat. This is what? oh, nine years ago. I'd been out East a year. How old are you?"

"Twenty-one," I said, rather proud to be able to.

"And you've been out how long?"

"A year."

Saxby nodded, thought for a bit. "We both came out when we were twenty then. Ah, looking for what? Life, adventure? Was that it? I had money. I've never been repressed by lack of funds. I went to Sumatra first, then to Borneo, then to Ceylon. In Ceylon I wanted it tough. I shipped before the mast in a steamer that was only fit for the graveyard. Old Debi's steamer. He owned it. He'd had it in cargo from Bombay to Colombo and came along for the ride. So he said. Now he was going back in ballast which meant a nett loss all round. Half the crew had gone adrift in Colombo which is why they took me on. I didn't know an anchor from a marlin-spike but I was young, and strong, and willing. It was a sieve that boat and we ran into squalls in the Arabian sea. The ballast shifted and some of her plates caved in; don't ask me how or why – ships are one of the big mysteries as far as I'm concerned. The skipper was a Muslim, a long-shore Arab old Debi called him. His answer to any tight spot was to drag out his prayer mat and knock his head on the deck. They said we were settling fast. Who was I to argue? We lowered a boat and abandoned her. There were a dozen or so of us and I'm not sure to this day whether or no old Debi scuttled her to collect the insurance. We stayed off about a mile and sure enough she sank within the hour. The skipper said we'd make the coast in a day but his navigation must have been lousy. We were picked up by a tramp and that was the end of my beating-round-the-horn phase."

"And those two days?" I asked.

"Well, they marked the turning point in Debi's luck, he always said, because they brought him back to God."

"What had that got to do with you?"

Saxby hesitated. "I sang," he said at last. "I sang every dirty song I knew and when I'd exhausted the ones I knew I sang dirty songs I'd made up. You see I wasn't a scrap worried. I was pretty sure they'd scuttled her and the long-boat was well stocked. I had water to wet my whistle and food in my stomach and I just sang and sang for pure joy. It's not every day a man gets shipwrecked and to be shipwrecked safely is even rarer. I sang for two days and after a bit I had most of the crew singing too, ah, not the words you understand, but the tunes, their own words. When Debi asked me what we were singing I said, 'Hymns.' I've never told him the truth since. I expect his luck changed because he gave half the insurance money to the Brahmins, but he swears it changed because he was brought back to the love of God and man by the sight of a young British seaman praising the Lord in the midst of adversity."

Saxby paused, then added, "Perhaps yelling bawdy songs in an open boat on the limitless sea *is* a way of praising the Lord. Ah, yes. Perhaps it is."

We were interrupted by the arrival of the whisky. The Manipuri girl was handsome, her eyes dark with kohl. She was small boned but well developed and wore nothing beneath the fine red-silk sari. She asked us each to say when, poured two glasses, then left us with the bottle and a clay *chatti* of cool water.

Saxby raised his glass.

"Well, then, to you," he said.

"To you," I replied. We drank and lit cigarettes. Saxby's body was coloured by exposure, not tanned the way his face was, but darkened, and mottled by areas of freckles. His chest and stomach were protected by a thick matting of chestnut-coloured hair. He was well fleshed and this, with his breadth of bone, gave the impression of great physical strength even though he lacked muscular definition. He had really begun to run to fat and he pouched over at the waistband of his trousers. According to the facts he had given me he was then thirty-one, but he looked forty.

"And after?" I prompted him. "After the shipwreck?"

"My life to date, what else? The story of my life," he replied, not very helpfully: but expanded, "Is that your question, Tom? That's your name isn't it? May I use it?"

"Of course." I was flattered. He was senior in years and experience, possessor it seemed of a great fund of knowledge of the way of the world: the particular world, I told myself at that second, I surely aspired to. For an instant my heart leapt at the thought of two endless days on the endless ocean and my own voice raised in a fervour of singing.

"Is that your question?" he repeated. "By after, did you mean all after?"

"I meant as much as you want to tell."

He was silent. He drank his whisky and poured himself another glass. I shook my head at his gesture towards mine.

He leaned back on the divan. "You and I," he said when he was comfortable, "yes, you and I speak the same language. As much as I want to tell you, you say. You imagine secrets, periods of activity best left to silence. Ah well. You are a romantic. You're probably capable of anything. Of falling in love with intimate distances, let's say, falling in love with something you've never set eyes on. Oh, that's the best kind of romanticism. The very best."

"Why?" I asked. He cocked an eye at me. The other appeared more concerned with the rim of the glass held near his nose.

"Why?" He drank, eased himself further back on the divan. "Because it's easier to romanticize things you've known or seen, things that have happened. To romanticize the unknown, to fall in love with the unseen is not often done."

"I'd have thought otherwise. People do it all the time, surely."

"They don't often travel three thousand miles as a result," he said, looking full at me. "They don't heave coal in the bowels of a ship."

"Heave coal?"

"Mrs Ross said you worked your passage out."

I laughed. "Yes, but snug in the purser's office."

"It doesn't matter a tittle. In your heart you were heaving coal. Why not admit it?"

I took a drink. "And now three thousand miles back, washing dishes. Real dishes," I said.

He said, "Yes, so I gather. Well, even a romantic makes stupid mistakes."

"Why do you call it a mistake?"

He made a gesture with the glass of whisky. "Because life is a business, isn't it, a business of going from peak to peak, not trough to trough. Is? I should say, ought to be. If you're a romantic your peaks will be romantic peaks. Turning tail and washing dishes is a mistake. Realistic maybe, but a mistake. A trough. Don't fall into it."

I shook my head. "It's settled. Besides I can't see any peaks."

"They're there. All the time."

"Where, for instance?"

"On the wall of your room."

"The Punjab?"

"The land. India. Not here. This is just a city and all cities are so much dead stone. Bombay was never part of your dream. You knew the way evening came to the Punjab long before you watched the way it comes in Bombay, if it can ever be said to do so. Am I right?"

"I suppose so."

"Tell me about the pictures. Tell me why you heaved coal."

He poured me another whisky. I told him, skirting round the edges at first, but then plunging into my whole history. When I had finished I felt a bit drunk. In the process of telling him he had replenished my glass once, perhaps twice.

40

"You've read Conrad?" he asked.

"No."

"He was a Pole who wrote in English."

"Well yes. I did know that."

"He said that directly a man is born he's flung into his dream as if into a sea, that he would suffocate if he tried to climb out of his dream, out of the sea into the air. Commit yourself, he said, commit yourself to the destructive element and by the exertion of your arms and legs keep yourself up. To that effect. Words like that. You'll notice he said men, any men. The realist may swim in the sea but he won't find a dream in it or recognize it as a dream at all. Your romantic will. What dream were you flung into?"

"Or you?" I countered.

"Ah," he said, "I sometimes think I was flung into no dream at all. Perhaps my exertion is to scramble *into* it. Will it suffocate me? I mean if I find a dream to keep myself up in?"

Debi announced curry.

*

He talked all through dinner, rising sometimes between plateful, pacing the floor, talking of people and places, seldom of himself.

"I'm a remittance man," he told me when pressed. "The last of the international beachcombers." He would say no more of his position in regard to others. Without committing himself to a categorical statement he succeeded in leaving you with the impression that he had no family. His money came from – what? private, and I assumed ample funds. Their origin? That was and remained a mystery.

I asked him what his interests were.

"People and plants," he replied. "People because they are articulate. Plants because they are not. I'm never bored. I enjoy spectacular good health. I have been anywhere in the Far East that you care to mention. I was born and bred west of Suez and can only breathe east of it. Which perhaps is proof that my dream is in these longitudes. My interest in plants began in Sumatra. I lent money to a botanist whose funds had dried up and he took me along for the ride. Now I'm a botanist too, a complete amateur, but Kew Gardens has heard of me."

It was not very satisfactory. Sometimes when he moved about the room I sensed a curious lack of balance in him, a kind of weightlessness as though he had cut himself adrift from moorings, thrown overboard whatever urge it is we have that acts as earthly ballast and keeps us from soaring heavenwards before our time. I blinked and concentrated on holding my liquor like a man.

The table was scattered with the remnants of the meal. My eyes watered from the hot green chillis Saxby himself ate as refreshers. My naked upper body – now offered to the mosquitoes as the lesser of two evils – ran with a luxurious, salt-warm sweat. I was drunk enough to give rein to fancies inspired by his tales. We were in the warm, close cabin of a schooner, a pearling lugger, two sailors afloat on the vast magic of the Pacific: we were in a ramshackle hut, two cast-aways bewitched by the pounding of surf and the cries of parrots: we were at ease, old hands, half intent on the yarns we spun, but with knowledgeable ears on the drums which moaned and beat their breasts in the jungle from which our lamp-lit room protected us.

But we were Brian Saxby and Tom Brent on the upper floor of the house of a Bombay merchant who had fed us and given us whisky and now plainly offered us women: two of them: the Manipuri, and another, even younger, girl who had smelt of musk as she cleared away the dishes. They stood together in the doorway making *namaska* and then disappeared.

"Do we make a night of it then?" Saxby asked, jerking my attention from the doorway. "It's not obligatory, but they'll be clean. Clean now, you understand, not later. Later the bloom goes. Disease enters."

"Does he sell them too?"

"To us first. Honoured guests. Then to others. He's a rogue

but the Brahmins forgive all. Well, is it to your taste? *Or does only white do?"*

I stared at him.

"Is *that* what you think?" I asked.

"Ah, well. I ask, that's all. *These* intimate distances are peopled by men and women with skins *that* colour. Since you're turning your back, I wondered; on the skins? Was that it?" He approached me, took my face in one hand and raised it. "You have the face of a *sahib,*" he said. I grasped his wrist, disliking the contact, but he was too strong for me. "You have the face of a sahib," he repeated, "but then in your heart you heave coal. I see your problem."

He released me. Automatically I rubbed away the feel of his hand on my chin. Looking up I thought I caught in his eyes a swift here-and-gone expression of sadness, a glimpse of a far down brooding look that left an echo, if a look can be said to do so, sounding behind his sudden laughter.

"You are confused by people," he said. He produced it like a rabbit from a hat. "Like your father and grandfather. I expect they had the faces of sahibs too."

"*They* weren't confused by people."

"They were confused by people," he insisted. "But they never heaved coal. That is where you are different. That is why you have come back."

"Come back to what?"

"India. Not here. Not this room. This isn't India. This isn't the India your grandfather explored for forty years. Think of that. Forty years. And all those people getting in his way, confusing him with a sense of duty and delusions of grandeur under the peepul tree. Forty years! He had to resort to water-colours to get anywhere near it. He had to go foraging about with a paintbrush and a box of paints to get near what was right under his nose. When it came to your father all *he* could see was the people, but he kept the pictures, and so revealed a side of him that could *not* rebel? His heart, ah, yes, that was it, his heart. Only his intellect said no. He kept the pictures long

43

enough to hand them down to you. And he kept other things too, littered all over a house in where did you say, Pimlico?"

"Bayswater."

"Bayswater! What an odd place to be born and fall into a dream." He punched me on the ribs, none too lightly. "Listen! Think of this! A man chucking coal into a furnace is down there, isn't he, deep down there by himself with a shovel. Don't crowd him. Give him shoulder room. Don't confuse him with people."

I got to my feet, swaying a bit. He steadied me by gripping my arm. "The world's full of people," I said.

"Not in the dream," he said, "they're not there in the dream."

We seemed to draw near, fall apart, draw near again. "You're drunk," I said. "You don't know anything about my dream. Besides, I like people. The dream's lonely without people."

He said, "Well, that's how it is." He released my arm and added, "And the other way round, people and no dream. God, that's lonely too." He rubbed his forehead, slid his hand down his face as if removing its outer skin and stared at me. He said, "You'd learn that, you'd be a fool to go. But it's your life. Muck it up if you like. Settle for what's easy. You've got the face of a sahib and it'll see you through."

He turned his back, lifted the whisky bottle. There wasn't much left in it. He divided it equally into our empty glasses.

I said, none too coherently because I had never drunk so much hard liquor in my life, "What's so important about a dream?"

He faced me, handed me the glass. Sweat had dampened down his hair: a lock of it hung wetly over his glistening forehead. He said, "It's only in dreams you get anywhere near the truth. Near it, I said, not at it, not to it. Let's say within spitting distance. Even touching distance of the outer shell. Nearer than that even, yes, hitting distance. But hammer at it through the longest night and you won't break it. Only God cracks that particular nut. He's got your soul tucked up inside it, you see."

44

I drank whisky. He shouted with laughter and sat down suddenly on his chair. "Oh yes! You've got the face of a sahib all right! Can't you even hear that word? Soul? Can't you say it, can't you admit it? What would you find to say to an animist who'd believe even this table had a soul?" Grinning, he lifted the cloth and tapped on the bare wood. "A bit of a soul anyway, a bit chipped off from the soul of the tree it was made from."

"I'd say he was loopy."

"Ah, would you? There are tribes in Malaya would tell you you had at least five souls. One in your head and one in your heart, one in your breath and one in your eyes. And one in your liver. That would be a nut to crack! How many thicknesses of dream would you have to enter to get within spitting distance of a nut like that?" He raised his hand, thumb and fingers spread. "Think of it! Five souls. And you can't admit one without hiding your face in a glass. There's Christian arrogance for you! You take your soul for granted but would no more think of discussing it than you would of unbuttoning in the street. You keep it tucked away like an extra private part."

In the centre of the table there was a potted fern, tender, feathery green. Saxby stretched his hand towards it, dug his fingers into the bowl and scattered dark, wet crumbs of earth over the cloth.

"There's your dream," he said. "Earth. That's where your instinct tells you to go searching, that's what you heaved coal for. What a romantic you are! And when it comes to it, how lucky!"

2

WHEN HE SCATTERED THE CRUMBS OF EARTH WITH A
gesture recalling the way he had emptied the bag of sapphires,
our relationship seemed to change from that of men met
casually, by chance, and – as he said – speaking the same
language, to that of men in whose meeting destiny had taken a
hand. I don't mean that I felt us destined to meet as men then
committed to firm, lasting friendship, the give and take of
mutual affection and esteem, for there was a quality in him
which always touched in me a nerve of resistance and from the
beginning I felt that what he opened my eyes to and what I
actually saw were not quite the same thing. The destiny I had
in mind was one that had set my foot in a certain direction and
Saxby's in another which, at a given place, must meet my own,
provide a point of illumination so that thereafter I travelled
less blindly. There was never a suggestion that from this meeting-place we should travel together, and I entirely failed to
notice as I left the meeting-place behind and continued along
the road he had lighted for me that his own way forward was
lost in darkness.

"There's your dream!" he said, pointing at the particles of
earth he had thrown, prophetically, like dirt under my nose. I
stared at them, not meeting his eyes.

He said I must learn not to wince from words like dream
and soul, learn not to let their work-a-day sense overawe, let
alone embarrass, me. "Show me any man," he insisted, "there's
always a canker in him, the worm of curiosity eating its way
outwards from the core to confound the chemist who can
explain everything except that last ounce of fret and wonder,
that seed of mystery, that final querulous plus in the equation.

But show me a romantic, ah, there's a man who puts the plus at the beginning of the equation. My body plus what? What plus my body? *He* works inwards to meet the worm, he can't wait for the worm to work outwards. He heaves coal. He's always fighting his way through the layers of dream which seem to promise sight of something inside. But no dream's transparent. You can't stand outside your dream and look through it at your own image, give a nod of recognition and say ah, so *that's* my soul, that's *it*. No you've got to enter the dream and it's not sure that *you'll* get through, that *you'll* crack the nut. You're simply committed to the act of trying."

I brushed my hands across the crumbs of earth. "Then where does this come in?"

"It comes in because I think your dream springs from a mystical conception of land."

"I'm not aware of it."

"Why should you be? You don't have to know the nature of your dream to move inexorably towards it. Ask the tides what they know of the moon and what answer will you get? But the pull is there." He pointed at the crumbs of earth. "There's your pull. How do I know? Oh, I don't *know*. But there are pointers, aren't there? Intimate distances preserved behind glass. Landscapes without figures. The dream is lonely without people you said. *That* slipped out. Ah yes, that rose up from the little worm-filled kernel."

"Why India though? Why India?"

"Because for a romantic land has shape and texture. It seems, doesn't it, to have a soul of its own? Does one acre please you as much as another? Don't you carry in your mind's eye a kind of perfection of landscape your actual eye is always searching to match? It might be swamp or waste, a configuration of rock and earth or a green fertile plain. Find it, come close to it, there'll be no other quite to come up to it. And your mind's eye being what it is it's just as likely you'll preconceive its whereabouts as not. That's why. That's why India for you. That's the dream you were flung into in Bayswater."

They say that a victim of hypnosis must be willing and hypnotized I undoubtedly was.

"If you do turn tail," he said, "you'll come back one day. You'll come back when you realize you never gave it a chance."

"A year. That's chance enough. How much chance does it need?"

"It hasn't been a chance. You've been confused by people. You didn't come to India to sit on your backside in Bombay. You've wasted a whole year. Wasted it. Thrown it away. At least, it'll be wasted if you turn tail. Not if you don't."

"Everything's fixed."

"Then unfix it. Go to the shipping office tomorrow and tell them you've changed your mind."

"And then?"

He leaned forward, putting his beard close to my face. "You come with me," he said, "and talk to a man called Greystone."

*

When I went to the shipping office to tell them I'd changed my mind they asked me what I was going to do instead. I replied truthfully that I had not the faintest idea. I was waiting for Saxby to tell me more about the man called Greystone and the good that might come of talking to him. Saxby promised me he would, but later – later.

"Pack your things. Be ready. I'll not give you much notice."

Now that I had burned my boats he seemed deliberately mysterious and there were moments when I suspected myself the victim of an elaborate practical joke. Without telling me he was doing so he went away for three days. I felt deserted, led into a tough situation and left to cope with it alone. He came back bringing with him an old but serviceable car which he said he had bought for our journey. I asked him whether he didn't think it was time he told me more because I could hardly be expected to set off with all my luggage and very little money without knowing where I was going or how long it would take to get there and what he supposed I should find to do there that would have a connexion with what he called my dream.

He looked at me rather sadly and handed me a small blue-bound book stamped with the name of the Imperial Bank of India. He had opened an account there in my name and deposited a sum of money, enough to pay my passage home if, as he now explained, I had reason in the next few weeks to regret staying. He said that I was not to feel embarrassed, far less insulted, because depositing the money was a sop to his own conscience and if I refused to recognize its existence he would worry. It would be silly to pretend that its presence did not at once produce a feeling of security and presently enable me to embark on the journey with a new lightheartedness. I admitted as much to him and at that he smiled and said that acts of faith were easier to make on a full belly.

When the journey began, a week to the day after our curry supper, I had no idea that the car, laden with my luggage and a suitcase of his own, would be our home from home for close on three weeks. We set off in a northerly direction, heading for Rajputana and the Punjab although the end of the journey lay, I discovered, to the east. We stayed the first night in a fairly respectable European-style hotel and thereafter rang the changes from the upper-class luxury of places like Faletti's in Lahore through a succession of variedly squalid Indian lodging houses to sleeping in tents or in the car in wild and rugged country far from habitation.

It was a voyage on which he officially invited me to join him the first night out from Bombay, a voyage of discovery and rediscovery; for "Greystone can wait", he said, "Greystone is used to waiting."

I pressed him to tell me about Greystone and he promised to do so later, later. I had to be content with that and I came to be content, to want nothing in the present beyond what I had, an unrolling map of the land and the feeling that time kept no other pace than that of our journey. Bombay receded, until it was no more than a speck, insubstantial as a cloud that had run before yesterday's wind.

Mud-spattered the car now entered regions where the rains had not yet penetrated, where the sky was milk white and the earth cracked and parched as if it were centuries old and had no memory of water. On flat endless plains distant and minareted towns glimmered like mirages, and yellow mud-walled villages loomed and were gone, hidden in the dust to crumble away invisibly behind us, forgotten. As the sun fell to the western edge of such plains the violet pigment of its rays would settle low in the air like the lees of wine leaving the sky above us clear, as pink as sea-shells.

On three successive nights we camped out and cooked supper over an open fire, watched from the perimeter of the circle of light it shed by children from the village where we had begged water. I would lie awake long after Saxby had fallen asleep and the last ember had ceased glowing, and listen to the melancholy, reed-thin music of a flute far off, and the baying of scavenging dogs and jackals whose otherwise silent progress to and fro I mapped from the changing direction of their cries in the darkness. Waking, I learnt the bitter-sweet scent of Indian mornings, those layers of freshness interwoven with layers of yesterday's heat and staleness, and the dry, barn-smell of smoke from dung-fuel fires.

We came again to regions where the wet monsoon had filled the muddy streams and brown rivers, where rain water stood in rice-fields and turned them into vast mirrors reflecting the swollen grey-yellow sky and sometimes the chance, lone figure of a man standing like a brown statue on a raised bank, or a single file of women carrying burdens on their heads.

It was a land's land, too vast, too beautiful to harbour well the designs men sought to carve upon it. The feeling grew in me that in the next hour, on the next day, I should find that matching image Saxby had spoken of, that configuration of rock and earth which matched the mind's eye image of shape and texture. But there was no known mind's eye image, only

50

an expectation that when the actual scene came into view the mind would claim it as its own conception. In the Punjab we found places so like the scenes my grandfather had painted that it was a temptation to say: Ah, yes, this is where he sat, this is where he turned aside from duty and expressed his love. But time had weathered away the degree of exactness looked for and the Punjab never yielded my matching image. We turned south, again, towards the arid centre, and at the end of our journey entered Greystone's valley.

It is time to explain Greystone, but difficult to reconjure the picture I had of him from Saxby when Saxby no longer fobbed me off with "later – later", because my own picture of him has interposed itself. He was a small, wiry man, greying, in his fifties. Saxby told me on the last few days of our voyage that Greystone had fought authority most of his life. I liked him instinctively for that.

Two years before I met him he had resigned from the civil service and persuaded one of the minor Indian princes to lease him a stretch of parched, unfertile land in order to cultivate it by the special methods he had preached in vain for years. He thought he might have better luck in areas not directly governed by the crown. As a servant of that crown he had been respected, even loved. When he begged peasants not to burn dung for fuel but to put it to its proper use as manure they said, "Sahib, you are our father and our mother and your words are the words of wisdom," but they continued to burn dung and Greystone came to feel that all his words, all his deeds, wise or not, were suspect because the authority behind them could never be seen wholly as his own. It was the crown that spoke and the crown was cunning. Who was there to swear that the laying of dung upon the earth had no Christian significance? And so Greystone abandoned the crown and devoted himself to the rehabilitation of a valley so barren that from the beginning it looked like a hopeless task.

He sank every penny he possessed into this enterprise and before the first year was out when his savings had gone and he faced ruin he travelled miles to beg, borrow, cajole and threaten. It was on this tour that he met Saxby. Perhaps they ate curry and got drunk together. Be that as it may Saxby went to look at the valley and then joined him on his money-raising expedition. It was Saxby who succeeded in persuading the ruling prince to award Greystone a small annual grant. He gave money himself but I did not know about that until later. Perhaps Greystone promised him a favour in exchange and had little alternative but to take me on as his assistant. God knows I had nothing to offer him in the way of experience.

"He's an odd bird," Saxby warned me before we arrived.

"With a mystical conception of land?" I asked, smiling.

"Oh, I think so. But different from your own."

"How different?"

But all Saxby would say was, "You'll see."

We churned our way along roads whose surfaces drought had pulverized into dust so deep it boiled behind us like the wake of a ship. "Greystone will be waiting for rain," Saxby said, "waiting for water as well as for his assistant." He had written in advance, he told me, and seemed to take it for granted that in order to be employed I had but to arrive. His conviction, like nearly everything else about him, was hypnotic, and I watched the new land take shape with eyes already critical, possessive.

It was hard, scarred by erosion and at first, when Saxby said, "We're getting near," I felt nothing but desolation. There were too many villages that were empty, abandoned; yellow ruins in an ochre landscape. The earth was shrunken, stretched tight, and the hills showed their bones like old, old men dying of hunger; but from this evidence of failure and failing, I found myself turning to discover all the signs I could of what was indestructible, man's need to hang on and take and take, and the land's own will, desire almost, to give and give until it could offer nothing but its own skeleton to the sky to look at and to the wind to feed on.

We turned at last on to a track which led us through the low humped hills enclosing Greystone's valley and so into the valley itself: a shallow, flat-bottomed basin of chequered fields. In the distance I could see the open framework of a barn, squat wooden huts and, perched on higher ground, a small bungalow Saxby pointed out as my future home. The valley was a world within a world, a microcosm of the land we had journeyed through. If here the bones did not show they were, I felt, close to the surface.

If I had never met Saxby, if by pure chance I had arrived in Greystone's valley, I suppose I should not have felt about it the way I did. But the thing happened, the recognition of a place whose image I had always carried with me because it had fallen with me, as Saxby would have it, into the dream, so that for a while I almost thought my eyes saw what he had opened them to: myself as a man who sought mystical union with earth for the promise it held of leading him straight to the truth, the querulous plus revealed – *this* plus my body, my body plus *this*.

But the plainer fact was, I suppose, that I recognized the valley as nothing more than the end of a journey during which piece by piece I had thrown away the clutter of the past and bit by bit revealed to myself, like a lost mosaic gradually uncovered, a sense of vocation. The dust of India sat in my nostrils, lay caked on my skin. Sweat stung my eyeballs and every muscle in my body ached from the rough jolting we had endured. I knew that my strong attachment to a land I had not seen had not after all been idle, and I knew what I wanted to do: work in the valley with my hands and somehow repay a debt I had inherited.

Greystone was waiting for us outside his bungalow, a nondescript figure in soiled khaki shirt and trousers: his face hidden from me by the shade of his wide-brimmed, old-fashioned solar topee.

"This is young Brent," Saxby said as we came up to him. I put out my hand but he did not take it. Instead he took the topee off, flung it on the ground and stared at me. His head was tiny, the features sharp, his eyes bright blue. Suddenly he turned to Saxby and cried, "But this lad's no good to me! Look at him! He's fallen in love with it!" Then he took me by the arms and shook me, small as he was. "You've got to hate it, lad. Hate it! Hate it!"

He left us abruptly, returning to the veranda of the bungalow by a set of wooden steps. The bungalow was built on a slope and the front was higher off the ground than the back. I looked at Saxby and found him watching me with an expression partly grave, partly amused.

"That is the difference," he said. "Greystone *hates* earth, you love it. But the conception is mystical in both cases. Come on. He wants to show you your room."

Greystone had climbed the steps and was watching us. He made a brief gesture, commanding us to follow.

"But he said I was no good to him."

Saxby propelled me forward. "It's his way," he said. "The job's yours. He's taken you."

Saxby was right. The job was mine. I was shown my room, already prepared with a narrow wooden bed, clean sheets, bookcase, wardrobe. I was shown where I could bathe, introduced to the kitchen staff of two Indian boys who cooked curry in the Madrassi manner. I was shown over the farm buildings and the constructional work in progress: irrigation ditches which were being dug by hand. I was taken over the cattle sheds, shown the pits of manure lovingly preserved, the thin pasture, the vegetable garden watered by kitchen and bathhouse waste. And at the end of the tour Greystone put his hand on my shoulder and said, "Try it then, lad. What one of us can't do with hate the other might do with love."

3

I WORKED WITH GREYSTONE FOR FOUR YEARS AND during them saw Saxby on three occasions. The first was when he visited us on his way to Assam, three months after he had brought me to the valley.

This first visit was quite unexpected. I was at work in the fields, swinging a pick-axe, helping the men to extend the system of irrigation ditches. I had taken to wearing nothing but an old pair of shorts during the day and the sun had burned my skin to the colour of copper. I was hard, proud of newly and painfully acquired muscle, fine-set, sharp with hungers I could lay no names to. Whenever we worked we sang meaningless, rhythmic songs and I did not hear Saxby's car approach. Suddenly the familiar voice said behind me, "So there you are! Still heaving coal!"

He had not changed a scrap and I was so surprised to see him I simply stood there, a couple of feet below him, the axe raised and my breath coming short. I said, "Good Lord!" and then, as I had when I wiped the feeling of his hand from my face, I caught an echo of disappointment behind his laughter. I climbed out of the ditch and pumped his hand up and down.

Greystone and I had never discussed Saxby except in the most general terms but there had been a feeling right from the beginning that Greystone disliked him and after this particular visit, which lasted no more than a few hours, he said, "The trouble with Saxby is that he's got nothing to *do* and won't let you get on."

"I thought we had a jolly good time," I said, seeing what he meant but defending Saxby stoutly, still annoyed with Greystone for having been morose enough for Saxby to have asked me when we were alone whether Greystone and I were hitting it off. I wasn't sure that we were but as I suspected any reservations Greystone had about me were due to my being Saxby's protégé I told him that everything was fine.

Presently when the ripples of unrest caused by Saxby's arrival and departure had settled I again applied myself to the business of standing on the two feet he had helped me to find. If Greystone resented me because of whatever it was he had against Saxby it was up to me to show that I was my own man, neither Greystone's nor Saxby's, and that the circumstances of my arrival could be forgotten. Through Saxby I had discovered a sense of vocation and through Greystone I was able to follow it. It was as simple as that. It was not always easy though.

Apart from the two houseboys and the overseer who slept in a hut near the barn, we had no workers of our own. We depended on men and women from nearby villages. They were attracted by the wages offered but they had their own meagre fields as well as those of their landlords to tend and we could never tell from one day to the next how many would turn up. When they had been paid and had set off for home leaving the five of us alone the feeling of isolation sometimes hung so heavily I thought I should never stand it. At night Greystone liked me to sit with him while he pored over the blue-prints of the village he said he hoped to build and after my body had got used to the demands I had to make of it and I no longer sat there with leaden eyes and aching shoulders the monotony of one man's companionship stretching out into the future threatened to become intolerable. We took to quarrelling over trivial matters but he usually had the last word by fixing me with his blue eyes and shouting, "So it's beaten you already, lad! You're learning to hate it too!"

For Greystone, earth was the great demon man must fight to survive. I have seen him stoop and gather a handful of it when he did not know I was near, fling it from him and shake both fists in the air. It was a fight in which he gave no quarter and expected none. In a year when the rains failed completely he sat on the veranda of the bungalow and watched the slow ruin of the season's work with a grim smile. "You wait," he seemed to be saying, "just you wait."

But hard and barren as the valley was I never learned to share his hate, and it came as near as anything ever did in those days to making me see what Saxby was getting at. There were times, particularly towards evening, when my more practical mind succumbed to the fancies he had stirred up in it so that I could pause in the middle of the field I had sweated in and feel alarmingly close to something, as if my hands which had been in contact with the earth all day felt now, in the fading light, capable of sweeping away, even of breaking by main strength, whatever it was which when parted, opened, would reveal a picture of my immortality.

But those times were rare enough and I was not cut out to be a hermit. Greystone had a ramshackle old truck in which, every three months, he used to send the overseer seventy-five miles into the nearest town to collect quarterly supplies. I persuaded him to let me strip it down and get it into better working order in return for which I should do the collections myself. I spent hours at it, night after night, working in the light of oil-lamps, developing a passion, a possessiveness which almost matched the daytime passion for the fields. Greystone rewarded me by telling me I could be away for three days, "to let off steam" as he put it. He even remembered to pay me three months' wages. The town proved to be squalid, with no European community. I drove a hundred miles farther north to the next town which had a rather down-at-heel club where I got mildly tight and sat, as the woman said afterwards, with my libido showing. She was a grass widow, lived in a small bungalow, and lent me her husband's pyjamas which smelt of moth-balls and needed buttons sewing on.

When I got back to the valley I had spent all my three months' pay and even found, to my shame, that I couldn't account for the whole of the money I had drawn from Greystone's bank to pay for the supplies. The situation was just ridiculous enough for me to ask him straight out whether he didn't think it would be better for us to employ an Indian girl to help in the kitchen and share my bed. He said, "Of course. Why didn't you say so before?" and at once interested himself in the business because, as he put it, he knew how these things could best be arranged, having had, in other days, a great deal of experience.

From there on Greystone's attitude towards me changed although he still called me lad, because that was his way of cutting down to size someone who stood a foot taller than himself. He began to lend me books from his library, books on husbandry, on the nature of soil and soil pests, on land reclamation. Eventually he gave me the pamphlet he had written on land improvement in his civil service days. I found these subjects absorbing and one day when I was asking him questions he blurted out, "You're really interested then? You're a perfectly ordinary young man who likes digging, tinkering with engines and finding out about things?"

I stared at him and then began to laugh. I hadn't been aware of providing evidence to the contrary and told him that any different impression he had gained must have been Saxby's fault. I was, as Greystone said, a perfectly ordinary young man neither more nor less romantic than others. I did not really have a mystical conception of land or turn the soil over in the expectation of laying my soul bare like an old white bone, or if I did then so did other young men with a bent for farming. I liked working in the valley because the work was useful and kept me physically fit. It was life I had been flung into in Bayswater, not a dream, and life was a perfectly ordinary business which ought not to be made complicated by people like Saxby. Every so often, thinking back on that brief exchange with Greystone, I would become quite annoyed with Saxby and when I was in this mood it looked as if he had brought Greystone and myself together mainly for the pleasure of watching, from a distance, the spectacle provided by two men whose dreams, as he would call them, being in opposition so far as their attitude to land was concerned, would clash and cause sparks to fly. But in that case the laugh was on him because quite apart from my own ordinariness Greystone was ordinary too: a bit eccentric perhaps but fundamentally a simple, practical man whose store of knowledge was being put to simple, practical use.

Saxby's second visit coincided with the drought of 1936, late in August or early in September it must have been. There had been some rain in July but nothing since and Greystone was at work on a plan for bringing more water to the valley. One well had been sunk but it had yielded nothing and he was talking about getting hold of a water diviner.

Saxby announced his arrival on a postcard which preceded him by scarcely twenty-four hours. Greystone's reaction was unexpectedly vehement.

"Oh, God, Saxby, Saxby! What's *he* poking his nose in for? What can *he* bring except *imaginary* rain?"

"It's only for one night, according to his card. He's on his way to Malaya."

Greystone shrugged and stamped out on to the veranda to glare at the sun. He called from the door, "It rains every day in Malaya, blast it!"

I laughed and went to find the girl to tell her to get the spare room ready. I was getting tired of her by now and thinking of telling her go but this wasn't a thing I felt I could arrange without Greystone's approval because he had gone to a lot of trouble to provide her. On the other hand he was in a nervous, excitable state and my domestic problems were scarcely relevant to the main business in hand: the drought.

Saxby had spent a year in the hills of Assam gathering tree orchids. He expected to be in Malaya for some time. The day he arrived Greystone went to bed soon after dinner and we were up late drinking the bottle of Scotch he had brought with him. I did most of the talking. He sat opposite me at the table on the veranda, no different physically, a little thinner perhaps, still cleanly but untidily dressed in loose shirt, crumpled trousers, and those peculiar, uncomfortable-looking sandals. I told him all about the valley, the success of one season, the failure of another, the difficulty of organizing an efficient or even adequate labour force, our plans for a model village, our search for water, the importance of the right amount of rain, the perils of drought, the no lesser peril of floods which swept away the precious topsoil. Eventually I had told him everything I knew and everything I thought Greystone knew.

"You're happy then?" he asked when a pause suggested I might have finished.

"As a sandboy," I said.

He said, "Would you like to come to Malaya with me?"

I was too surprised to find an immediate answer but he waited and presently I said, "For a holiday you mean?"

"No, I meant leave this and join me in Malaya."

"Collecting plants?"

"Yes."

"But I don't know one plant from another."

He smiled to himself. "Neither do they," was his reply.

"Neither do who?" I asked stupidly.

"The plants. The plants can't distinguish themselves from each other. They grow blindly, out of the earth towards the sun, as high as nature allows them. When you've worked with plants for a long time you sometimes wonder whether they're conscious of the struggle."

"What struggle?"

"To get out of the dark into the light and the air. I've sometimes caught myself thinking, ah, this one, let it break free from whatever encumbers it and it would shoot up and up, reaching as high as it could, higher, right up to touch the sun."

"Why on earth would it want to do that?"

He smiled again. "To find whether that's where God had put its soul. Why else?" He kept his eyes fixed on mine. He was waiting for me to react to the word, studying the face that was the face of a sahib and had once flushed with embarrassment, hidden itself in the glass of whisky. But I was tougher now,

60

tremendously tough and resilient. The word bounced back in his own face. I felt sorry for him. He was still on the same old tack, still complicating matters that were straightforward.

I said, "Don't say *you've* become an animist?"

"You haven't said yes or no," he reminded me.

"But I'm happy here," I replied.

He refilled our glasses. As he handed me mine he said, "But will you continue to be happy? Doesn't it depend too much on Greystone?"

"We get on splendidly." I hesitated, and then came out with it. "*Did* you expect us to quarrel?"

"Yes."

His frankness appalled me. He went on, "I expected you to quarrel at first. But I expected you finally to be a good influence on him. What do I find? That he's been a bad influence on you. Your face is more than ever a sahib's face. You've bowed to so-called practical wisdom, his, you've accepted so-called authority, his, you treat that little girl like dirt during the day and no doubt expect her favours at night. You're getting the mind of a sahib to go with the face. You think you and Greystone are engaged in something called farming. You think Greystone is a decent old stick who acts a bit oddly but has his feet firm on the ground and is as sound as a bell when it comes to ordinary matters. You can't see he's mad. He's mad because he's spent a lifetime resisting his own dream, refusing to acknowledge his love, twisting it so that he can make it feel like hate. That's how you'll end up if you stay here. You'll wake up one morning and look at this place and hate it because your love for it hasn't made it any different. Isn't it doomed to failure? How can you and Greystone make it fertile with all your technical knowledge and physical effort? It's dying. It was dying when Greystone came, dying when you came. It's still dying. No amount of love or hate will stop it dying. Is it to die unloved by either of you?"

"Greystone isn't mad," I said, controlling my temper.

"What about this water diviner?"

"What about him?"

"He'll come. He'll say, try here, and Greystone will sink a well expecting a miracle. Nothing. You'll try somewhere else. Nothing. The water diviner will be kicked out of the valley as a charlatan and Greystone will brood and sink more wells and brood again and curse the valley for hiding its water when all the time there's no water and if you're not careful you'll be cursing the valley too and then you'll be a sahib with the face of a sahib, the mind of a sahib and the madness of a sahib, trying to beat into submission something that submitted years before you arrived like a tin-pot king bringing peace and plenty. Ah, why can't you just love it, make Greystone love it and let it reflect your image at the moment that it dies?"

"Oh, for Pete's sake," I said, "talk like that's all right if you've got nothing to do and no living to earn. We're simply trying to do a job."

He looked at me, half-smiling. "How shallow you've become," he said. "And what a short time it's taken you to stop heaving coal and put the querulous plus in its proper place at the end of the equation. How did you complete it? In the usual way?"

"I don't know what the usual way is."

"Of course you do. The usual way is a five-letter word called faith. Just the word. Not even an act of faith is necessary. The word, the idea is enough. You say: I have faith in the existence of God and the presence of my soul, and you draw a line under the equation in the belief that it's finished and can be put away tidily so that you can get on simply doing your job and earning what you call your living."

"Well, yes. As you say. That's enough."

"You kid yourself."

"Let's call it the short cut," I said. "Faith has to be there at the end, doesn't it? You're never going to *see* what you have faith in. Well, there's no time to go the long way round. You'd spend your life at it."

He was silent for a while; staring into his glass. Eventually

62

he said, "As you say, you'd spend your life at it. Unless faith were given to you. Given to you in a vision as it was to Saul on the road to Damascus." He looked at me. "How gratifying that must have been. Perhaps a vision is only granted these days when you've tried and tried and given up hope."

Abruptly he drained his glass and stood up.

"I've got an early start in the morning," he said, and put out his hand. I began to stand up too but he pressed down on my shoulder and said, "No, no, formalities only disturb us." We shook hands awkwardly and then he said, "Drop me a line if ever you want to join me in Malaya. We are bad correspondents, aren't we, but you will always be welcome."

I thanked him and let him go, calling to him that I'd arranged an early breakfast and that I'd see him then. I sat for a while. Fitful light, forerunner of that which was to illuminate them in the next few years, played on the signposts that had been erected for me but gone unnoticed. I recollected the cry, "And people but no dream, ah! that can be lonely too," and for the first time understood it as a cry of unhappiness. And I remembered him saying, "Sometimes I think I was flung into no dream at all," and this time knew better what he meant.

I poured myself another drink and examined our friendship from this new angle. His having no dreams of his own would explain the earnestness with which he applied himself to foster them when he thought he found them in others. Perhaps he shared vicariously their pain and pleasure; perhaps he hoped that he would be present when a dream revealed the dreamer's image so that the moment of truth could be shared too and the belief in the existence of images vindicated.

I felt sorry for him but I still resented his attitude to Greystone, his preaching against him, his criticism of myself. I felt even more strongly that what Saxby wanted me to see was not at all what I actually saw. I could not have said exactly what it was that I did see and Saxby was right in suggesting I had completed the equation with the word if not an act of faith. I saw and loved the valley and was prepared to admit that my love for it was expressed through bodily exertion. If pressed I would have admitted to not minding whether the exertion proved profitable in the term in which the world understood the word, and this I thought was the difference between myself and Greystone, the difference Saxby could not see. I offered Greystone everything I could muster physically and mentally in the way of enthusiasm, but to the valley itself I offered something deeper. Perhaps offered is the wrong word. It was more as if the valley, like Greystone, had its own cause, its own demands, and found in me a willing servant. If the valley, in this sense, brought me close to God it seemed more fitting that I should simply believe in it, have faith in it. The equation had to end on such a note and Saxby's dogged search, his nosing through the undergrowth of a forest all of us were lost in became ludicrous, pitiful.

So why, I asked myself, does Saxby so much impinge on the darkness, the emptiness? I turned out the lamp and made my way across the creaking floorboards to my room, undressed in the dark, and climbed naked into bed.

In the morning I was woken by Greystone. Saxby had gone without saying good-bye to either of us. He had left a post-card, but no message; simply an address c/o a bank in Port Swettenham.

"What d'you think of that, lad? He's mad, of course, always was. Now you've seen for yourself."

But Saxby was right. Within six months of his departure the water diviner had come and gone and left Greystone in the grip of a deep melancholy that sometimes erupted in fits of violent anger. When those fits were on him he was impossible to live with and to show my independence I would take the truck and drive out of the valley, staying away for several days. It was on one of these self-granted leaves of absence that I met an English girl whose parents lived in Darjeeling but who, wanting to do something useful, was training as a nurse in the general hospital of the town where I had slept in borrowed pyjamas.

64

It is likely that without this outside distraction I should have quarrelled with Greystone irreparably.

It was quite some time before I allowed myself to be convinced that those fits of his were signs of madness. The valley was now pitted with the sites of abortive wells but still he went on, spending money we could not afford on special equipment which would enable him to drive deeper and deeper for the water only he continued to believe was there. The planning and administration of the valley project, with the sole exception of the wells, fell squarely on my shoulders and this became the main cause of dispute. Having paid no attention to husbandry as such for weeks at a time he would suddenly round on me and accuse me of subverting the labour, plotting against him with the overseer, with the houseboys, even with the Prince whom I had never seen. He had taken to using a stick, ostensibly to help himself along, but more I thought for the pleasure of hitting the earth with it and waiting for signs of moisture. During one particularly angry exchange he raised it against me. Securing it, I broke it over my knee and threw the pieces at his feet. I stayed away for ten days that time, telling myself that our association was at an end, but the girl, whose name was Millicent, persuaded me I was simply running away from a difficult situation and so I went back and found Greystone embattled within the walls of a self-imposed silence. We did not speak for a month, or rather he refused to respond to all my efforts to make even the simplest conversation. At the end of the month he came up to me and said, without warning, "You must get more money out of Saxby."

"*More* money?" I asked him.

Greystone smiled. "It's because he gave me money that I was originally able to afford an assistant." He laid heavy emphasis on the word "originally".

"So that's why you dislike him. You hate being beholden. But you'll be more beholden if he gives you money again."

"Will you write to him?"

"Write to him yourself."

"It would be unseemly," he said. "It's you who must ask him for the money. *You* like him, and after all you think the valley belongs to you now, don't you?"

I turned away. But then, knowing that the whole situation had become next to impossible, I turned back and said, "Look, either we talk to each other like ordinary civilized people or I muck off out of it."

He flushed and looked at the ground between our feet. When he raised his eyes I caught a glimpse of cunning in them and that, more than the violence, the raging, the imprecations, made me believe him mad as Saxby had said.

"I'm sorry, lad," he said, softly. "But you do provoke me with your tantrums."

"Tantrums!"

"Going off," he said, mildly, "going off and leaving me as you do when things get a bit tough. You ought not to have got rid of little Kamala. Wouldn't it be better if we got you another girl to live in the bungalow? It *is* a girl you go off to see, isn't it?"

"Yes," I said. "It's a girl I go off to see," and I left him there, furious because he had twisted things round, put them in such a way that there was no actual denying them. In the evening he chatted away as if nothing had happened to disrupt our relationship. He didn't mention the money again and he kept off the subject of water. I decided to give him the benefit of the doubt and take it that he had come through to the end of a bad patch. We lived in something like our old harmony for several weeks, and then the rains of 1938 broke, on time for once.

Throughout the monsoon and for several months afterwards Greystone was eminently reasonable. I saw Millicent every so often and one day she came to the valley for a brief holiday. Greystone was a charming and thoughtful host and as I drove her back to town she said, "But he's a poppet. What a bear you must be to live with if you quarrel with *him*." We laughed, but the warning note was there – not for the first time. There was unlikely to be a future for us.

66

"Well that was Millicent was it, lad?" he said, greeting me on the veranda.

"Yes, that was Millicent."

He said no more but the criticism was plain enough. That night over supper he said casually, "We must start on a new well soon."

I think he had deliberately enticed me by his almost year-long tractability into a state of passive co-operation. With his older man's wisdom he recognized that a young man knows better what he wants if he's made to fight every inch of the way. At the back of my mind there was an understanding that I was coming to the end of a period in my life during which nothing had been accomplished. If I had examined myself for an attitude I should have found none. This must have been clearer to Greystone than to myself. He guessed that he could use what was left of me. He could not have hoped to use me forever and must have known that if given sufficient time I would be off.

He went about the business of the well cleverly and carefully. "Where shall we sink it, lad?" he would say and say it often enough for me to react to the idea that my opinion was sought and respected. I found myself looking at the valley and almost willing it to disclose where it hid water.

"What about here?" he would say as we trudged the length and breadth of that dying bowl of earth, and then he would grasp my arm, digging his fingers in as if to suggest that I had but to flex the muscle to wrest the truth from the most closely guarded secret. It was not long before I had said, "I suppose there's no harm in trying here," and before he was able to say, "I think you were close to it that time, lad."

With half my mind I applied myself to the finding of water: the other half lay in limbo, critical, and uncaring by turns. But the half was all he wanted. He worked on that and on the natural pride of a man younger than himself. He had none of his own. He had discarded pride along with reason. He sought my advice at every turn. He wanted me to feel sufficiently committed to fight the last fight. Eventually the real shaft was loosed.

"We're by way of being broke, lad," he said one hot February night. It was 1939. The future was even physically uncertain. I would be a soldier for sure. Sometimes I studied my hands and wondered what metamorphosis was required to make them at home with a rifle or machine-gun. The trigger finger-to-be was extraordinarily innocent-looking.

"O.K.," I said, "so we're broke."

"If the rains fail this year we're done," he said.

"And if they don't we're done, too, aren't we?"

He narrowed his eyes.

"Not if we can get more money," he said.

He let the idea germinate. I never believed in the benefits to accrue from money but the idea of money was linked with the idea of Saxby and I became more and more obsessed with the notion that I ought to go and see him. Light that had played fitfully on the signposts now illuminated them strongly and I found his determined, single-minded search in the wilderness moving rather than foolish. I wondered how he had made out. He had always had a positive approach, if only to an abstraction. My own approach to what I thought of as hard reality was negative in comparison.

Since our last meeting we had not exchanged a single post-card and I did not even know whether he was still in Malaya. Greystone kept off the subject for a week but watched me with a shrewdly calculating look. Eventually he said over supper, "Have you written to Saxby yet?"

"Not yet."

"Which means you're going to?"

"Perhaps."

"To ask for some money?"

"No."

"Why then?"

"To see if he's still in Malaya. I might go and see him. You owe me some long leave."

He said, "You can have a couple of months whenever you want them."

I thanked him. My mind was made up. I wrote to Saxby the next morning. At the same time I wrote to shipping offices in Calcutta and Madras inquiring about passages. The trip to Malaya had caught fire, and I thought I might go even if Saxby did not reply. I wanted a holiday, a change of scene. I had saved enough money to have a fairly comfortable time.

In March Saxby's reply came. The message was on a postcard, typically short and to the point, like all his written communications. I would be welcome to stay if I did not object to primitive conditions. If I would reply giving details of my passage I would be met at Port Swettenham.

I had already heard from the shipping offices and wrote at once booking from Calcutta to Port Swettenham for the outward voyage. For the homeward journey I booked from Singapore because I hoped to persuade Saxby away from his botanical specimens to show me the sights of that city. As soon as I had confirmation I wrote again to Saxby, and then told Greystone of my plans. He had watched the arrival and departure of postcards and letters with studied unconcern. Now he merely said he hoped I would enjoy the break. But on the morning when I set out he put his hand on my shoulder and said, "If you can bring yourself to mention the money I'd be grateful. Without it we're really done for you know."

Alarmingly his eyes filled with tears and a wave of affection for him swept over me. We had fought the same fight, whatever else might be said. We shook hands rather solemnly and his last words, called from the veranda, were, "You'll come back, won't you, lad?"

I assured him I would. As the overseer drove us down the track I thought, Poor old beggar, he's got nothing but *this*.

*

Saxby's assistant, a young Malay who spoke good English and wore European clothes was at Port Swettenham to meet the boat. It docked early one morning and he came aboard, helped me with the formalities of landing and explained that

Saxby was up-country in a village called Singaputan which we could reach by night-fall if we set off without too much delay. He had come in an ancient truck and when my luggage had been safely stowed away we drove off together.

After the valley, the green of Malaya was nothing short of astonishing. The air hung thickly and as we drove along seemingly interminable metalled roads with rubber or coconut on either side I had a gradual sense of being smothered, of drowning in a sea where the weed grew tall and stiff. Sometimes the bed of the sea rose, broke the surface with islands of scarred hills which the Malay told me were tin workings. Above these hills the sky was restless with grey and golden clouds. You could smell the rain in the air: the rain that came every day of the year, borne by winds from the Indian Ocean and the South China Sea. It struck me as a bit unfair.

The Malay was a pleasant man but rather reserved and all my questions about *Tuan* Saxby as he called him were answered very briefly. The only picture I was able to draw of Saxby was one of a busy man, always in the forest looking for special types of orchid and lily. They had been in Singaputan for a year. The Malay said that he himself had originally trained as a doctor but had decided plants were more interesting than people. He said, "And I did not like to witness death." He had abandoned his studies and taken up botany, met Saxby on an expedition eighteen months before and been with him ever since.

We lunched in Kuala Lumpur. Afterwards I offered to drive but the Malay carried on himself and I settled down to doze fitfully. Apart from the several villages we passed through – or kampongs as I knew by now to call them – the road was taking us through pretty remote territory and the rubber had given way to jungle. At four o'clock the rain swished down as if a sluice had been opened. It streamed down the windscreen, danced on the bonnet, drummed on the roof of the cabin. After an hour it ended as abruptly as it had begun. The sun came out again, bright and fire-hot, steaming the moisture up.

I dozed again and finally slept. When I woke it was dark and the headlamps were glaring through a kampong. The Malay had touched my arm and now he said, "We are here, *tuan*. This is Singaputan."

On either side of the road there were atap-thatched huts, built on stilts and reached by ladders. Men and women shaded their eyes and watched us from the compounds. They wore the sarong, and some of them had little velvet caps on their heads.

At the end of the kampong we turned left on to a narrow track, churned slowly through mud, moving always, because the track curved continuously, head on to a dense curtain of undergrowth whose foetid smell came through the open window and mixed with the sweet odour of petrol. The headlamps then disclosed a rough, four-posted shelter made of bamboo and the Malay drove the truck under it.

When the engine was cut off the forest came alive, and behind the pulsing croaking noises in the undergrowth there was another sound, distant, tinny, vibrating, and musical like the clash of cymbals, which lent magic to the moment of arrival.

I followed the Malay along a track which struck off at right angles to the way we had come. Ahead of us there was a building with lighted windows and an open doorway. Like the huts in the kampong it was built up on stilts and he told me that this was a precaution against flooding. He said, "You will find *Tuan* Saxby waiting. I will arrange for your luggage." He put out his hand and as I shook it I said, "Don't you live here too?"

"No, *tuan*. The *tuan* likes to be alone. There are of course – servants."

He bowed slightly and then left me. I stood for a moment or two half expecting Saxby's deep voice to call: Well, are you there, is it you, coal-heaver? But the bungalow stayed resolutely silent, and presently, as I put my hand on the rail to climb the few steps to the veranda, I noticed the smell – a rich, heady mixture of perfumes and the warm smell of green things growing from dark, moist earth. It was coming from the open doorway.

It is the greenhouse smell and the sight of the plants I remember now as my first impression on entering although I must in fact have seen Saxby before I actually took in his background. All round the walls of the room there were tiers of benches on which stood trays of potted plants which hung, climbed, convoluted or stood spikily erect in a riot of leaf and stem with here and there an occasional white or scarlet flower.

The room was lighted by a pressure-lamp. The floor was laid with fibre matting. The bamboo-plaited walls – where they could be made out behind and above the plants – bulged with age and damp. In the middle of the room there was a low square table, empty except for a bottle of whisky and a glass. At the table were two wicker chairs softened by grubby cretonne cushions. In one of them Saxby sat, his upper body bare and glistening with sweat, his legs sheathed in a red and white patterned sarong. His skin looked unhealthily pale in the hard light, the chest and stomach hair, once thick and crisp as fibre, now limp and almost colourless. Only the hair of his head and his beard had retained richness and by comparision the rest of him looked diminished almost beyond recognition.

His flesh hung loosely on his large frame and when he did not get up and only slowly raised his hand to take mine I thought, because the hand was cold and damp, that he was ill or just recovering from illness. In his eyes burned a cold bright flame like that of fever.

"It's good to see you," I said, hoping my voice didn't betray too much anxiety. "How are you after all this time?"

"How long has it been?" he asked. The voice was unchanged but now seemed too big for his body.

"Over two years, nearly three." There was no answering pressure from his hand.

He smiled, took his hand away and let it rest on the arm of his chair. "In that case, you'd better pour yourself a drink. Just treat the bottle as yours."

"As mine? What's happened? Have you been warned off by the local quack?"

"No. I have simply abandoned it. There are a lot of things I have abandoned."

"But not plants," I said, pretty worried, not believing he would give up liquor on any grounds but those of health. I looked round the room. "You're surrounded by 'em! Drowning in 'em! What do you do with 'em all? Crate 'em up and send 'em to old professors to look at through microscopes?"

"No," he said. "Only the seeds and the bulbs are of interest. After that the plant is waste."

"It's a lot of waste," I said and then, catching his eye, blurted out, meaning it, "It's good to see you again. Thanks for letting me come." I thought I knew something about waste too. I wanted to sit with him again, talking about the things men usually ponder only in silence. I pointed at the whisky. "You mean it?"

"Go ahead."

I poured myself a moderate peg. He was looking straight ahead of him through half-closed eyes, his head pulled back. I thought, Poor chap! He's resisting temptation. I chatted away. I told him about the boat and the journey, my first impressions of Malaya, asked him questions about his work which he answered briefly. At last he opened his eyes fully, turned them on me and asked, "And the valley?"

"Oh, a dead loss. It's eroded to hell. Greystone leased a pup, didn't he?"

"He knew it," Saxby said. "A man like Greystone would never be content to work fertile land. Such men embrace destruction. It is a kind of necrophilia. Have you learned to embrace it yet?"

I laughed. This was more like the old Saxby I knew. I said, "I don't know what I've learned."

"Never mind. Are you hungry?"

I grinned. "Curry?"

"Yes. It will be curry. But you'll want to bathe first. I'm afraid your room is very small." He looked at me carefully – almost as though measuring me for it. "I'll have you shown to it."

73

He clapped his hands. There was a click of bead curtains and, looking in that direction, I saw a young girl standing there, a South Indian by the look of her, a Tamil. In Telegu he told her to take the sahib to his room and then to the bath-house and to see that all his wants were seen to.

I said, "I'll see you soon, then," and began to cross to the curtains which the girl held back for me.

"I have some work to do, I'm afraid. I'll see you tomorrow."

"But –"

"But what?"

"But we'll eat together, won't we?"

"I've already eaten and the work I have to do won't wait. Think no more of it. There is liquor, there are cigarettes. And the curry. The woman who prepares it will have taken special care because she seldom has the opportunity of showing off her culinary expertise. I eat next to nothing."

"Brian, you've become an ascetic!" I laughed and wondered as I had after my first meeting with him whether I was the victim of an elaborate joke.

"Not quite an ascetic," he said. "The woman is my mistress. Not that I love her, you will understand. The body can dispense with its enchantments but not its functions. The little one holding the curtain so patiently, is for you. She is an untouchable, and, I am told, virgin."

I looked from Saxby to the girl and back to Saxby. "That was very thoughtful of you."

He smiled.

He said, "I have always been accommodating to my friends," and then turned his head away, half-closed his eyes and watched the darkness beyond the open door.

Puzzled, but not unduly worried by his behaviour – for it was, in a sense, in character – I followed the girl into the ill-lit passage. She led the way to its end, opened a door and stood aside. The room was certainly very small, as he had warned me. It was lighted by a single hurricane lantern. I began to undress and the girl to collect my clothes, turning away when

74

I reached for the towel that lay ready for me to put round my waist. She crouched and gathered up my briefs.

Taking the lantern she led me back to the passage, down some steps at the back to a compound. In one corner there was a tarpaulin enclosure. There I bathed to the drone of the mosquitoes and the sound which she told me was that of ceremonial Chinese gongs from a settlement not far distant. She stood just outside the enclosure holding my sandals and clean socks ready.

Back in the room she offered me a brightly coloured sarong. At first I declined it and pointed to my open suitcase where a spare bush-shirt lay folded on the top but she smiled, shook her head and held the sarong in front of her, covering her face with the spread fingers of one hand, a gesture which seemed to indicate she thought I would look fetching in it. I let her help me. Her fingers were cool, pitifully thin. Her hair shone blue-black. She smelled of garlic and musk and when I raised her head with my hand beneath her chin the little ring in her left nostril glinted.

The plant room was empty when I returned but the table was laid ready for the meal. I sat down, half-expecting Saxby to come in roaring with laughter and crying, What? You thought I meant it? You didn't know I was kidding? But the one who entered was a middle-aged Malay woman. She was plump, ugly. Her hands were big-jointed, unshapely but clean; and she cooked magnificently. There were mounds of boiled rice, white and fluffy, pulao rice dyed with saffron and seasoned with bay leaves, curried chicken, and the green chillis Saxby had remembered my eventual liking for. During the meal the little Tamil girl sat outside on the veranda pulling the rope of the punkah and when I had finished she sang to me. I leaned back with my eyes closed and let the gentle melancholy pressure of the tune expand behind them.

*

I awoke refreshed and invigorated and the discovery that Saxby had gone out for the day leaving a message that he

75

would not be back until evening left me proportionately disappointed. But books had been put out for me, a choice of cigarettes, cigars and pipe tobacco, a fresh bottle of whisky, playing cards for patience, a solitaire board.

And yet I could not settle. In daylight the plants gave an impression of having fought their way in from the jungle to take possession of the bungalow. There were so many of them and, I discovered, no two alike. Some had shiny, deep green leaves and others leaves so pale, tender and velvety that you almost feared to touch them for fear of bruising them. Smooth and rough, round and spiky the leaves curled out of the stems like snake-tongues hissing for your attention.

I threw down the book I had tried to read and walked down the track to the kampong to smile and be smiled at by the velvet capped villagers. None of them seemed to understand English or any of the Indian languages I knew and I knew no Malayan. I bargained with a wrinkled old woman for fruit by signs and gestures and then made my way back to the bungalow hoping that I had misunderstood the message and would find Saxby waiting for me on the veranda.

But he was not. I questioned the Malay woman who had some English. No, the *tuan* was not ill. To her knowledge the *tuan* had never been ill. He went into the forest nearly every day with *doctor tuan*. Sometimes they brought back plants. Sometimes they went away for days together. Sometimes he drew pictures of the plants. Sometimes he would sit at his desk in his room and write for long hours in his book. What kind of book? She did not know. These matters were beyond her. She asked how long I was staying. It was good to cook food for a young man with a big stomach. Had the young girl pleased me? Was I married? Had I children? The tables were turned and it was I who broke away from the interrogation, not she.

I drank, ate well and slept. Towards evening the little Tamil girl again prepared my bath, dressed me in a clean sarong, and came to the veranda with me where she lighted my cigar, knelt by my side and waved a fan in the air to keep the mosquitoes off. To all my questions she had but one answer: a smile, a shake of the head. She seemed to have embarked on a private dream game of her own.

Night fell. In the distance the gongs sounded again. The pressure-lamp in the room behind me kept up its monotonous sibilant exhalation; and Saxby came out of the darkness when least I expected him, dressed in sweat- and mud-stained khaki, up the steps and past me without even a greeting.

I called after him, rose and followed, believing he could not have seen me and yet wondering how that could have been. He must have gone straight through to his bedroom. I called again but still got no answer. I returned to the veranda to drink what whisky remained in my glass and then went in to replenish it. Again I called. Silence. Now that it came to it I did not know where his bedroom was. I went through the bead curtains and found myself face to face with him.

"Did you have a good day?" he asked.

I said, "Yes. But you cut me dead out there. Didn't you see me?"

"Yes, I saw you. You said hello. I'll join you in a while."

His eyes burned cold. There were dark rims under them and his cheeks looked sunken, paler than ever. He turned, opened the door behind him, went into the room and slammed the door in my face.

I went back to the plant room, poured whisky thoughtfully and then returned to the veranda where the girl sat fanning the empty air. There I waited until that old familiar sound of clacking sandals warned me he had come into the room. One of the wicker chairs creaked. I turned round. He was in the same chair as the night before. I went in but did not sit.

"What's wrong?" I asked him.

"Nothing is wrong. What should be wrong?"

"I don't know. Unless it's that I'm not welcome after all."

"You have all the amenities you want?"

"I came here to see you, not to enjoy amenities."

77

"I know." He closed his eyes, cutting me off. When he opened them his expression was bitter.

"You came," he said, "for money. You came because you promised Greystone you'd try and cadge money. Or –" he held up a hand silencing me – "you came for what I am no longer here to give you. Renewed belief in your spiritual existence."

"The first, no," I said. "The second, who knows? But there's another reason. I came to see an old friend."

Of course, it sounded hollow. I poured myself a stiff whisky, and sat down. "You were friendly enough last night. What have I done since?"

He said, "It's no good asking this kind of question. What have you done, why do I do this, why do I do that? I'm no longer here to be explored in that way, to be examined, to be questioned, to be listened to for all the world as though there were something *here*, ah yes, sitting in this chair, except what you can see, touch, smell, hear – taste even, yes taste should you come within licking distance."

"Then why did you let me come and bother you at all?"

"Because," he said, "to have said that you couldn't, to have *denied* you, to have put obstacles in your way would have required, wouldn't it, an emotional response in myself? I am no longer here with emotional responses, with desires, wishes. My body has its functions but no enchantments. It has stopped wasting its time. It stands committed to nothing but its own inevitable waste, like a plant; yes, like a plant, you understand. It grows, produces seed, withers and dies, and the seed grows, blossoms, withers and, in turn, dies. The seed is the seed of waste."

"If you feel like that why do you bother with *anything*? Why do you still *collect* plants?"

He looked at me. "It represents, what? the glowing ember in the dying fire? But it is a physical commitment only. Waste – myself – committed to the collection of other waste, plants; a mechanism set in motion and running its time out. I collect plants, that is true, but I don't *explore* them. I don't touch them

78

with my hands and wait for my hands to reveal the manner, the exact manner, in which I am linked with eternity, with God. Oh, no. I used to. Yes, I used to explore them. They were the last things I seriously explored. I used to explore people too. You for instance, Greystone, Debi, oh, and many others – most of them people so obviously looking for their souls, looking for their images, some, a few of them, *not* obviously looking for their souls but all of them people not prepared to swear they had none. I explored people and plants. You are still exploring people and what, what was it, coal?"

"Earth you said."

"Yes, earth. It was coal you heaved. Time has gone. That has wasted away too. But you are still exploring. Perhaps you've never cottoned on to how mercilessly we all explore each other, endlessly and mercilessly, greedy for the smallest sign that God has touched somebody or something in a greater degree than he seems to have touched ourselves. You kid yourself he's capable of touching and must therefore have touched *you*. That's what you look for, an image of yourself that shows clearly how and where you've been touched by God, in what manner He has wrought you to make you more than mortal, more than a speck of waste in a wilderness of waste; ah, yes, waste flung further than the eye can see or the mind imagine."

"You've changed your tack at last, then. Why?"

His eyes were closed again, his head lolling back. For an instant the possibility of his having had some kind of seizure occurred to me, but when I started up his head came down and round and he watched me warily as if he suspected me of having been on the point of attacking him. I relaxed again in my chair and repeated the question, "Why, Brian?"

"Why I've changed tack as you call it? I should have thought it self-evident. I no longer *believe*. Once I thought there was God, a heaven, a kind of emotional continuum after death in which we would recognize ourselves as the people we felt ourselves to be in life. I say I *thought* this. But it was more. I felt.

As you do still, no doubt. And this seemed, what? oh, such a tremendous, awful, terrible, blessed thing, such a reward, do you see, such an unfathomable state of grace that I never thought it enough to say, Yes, it is so, I believe; because if it were so then what less, yes, what less could be asked of us than to explore, to examine, to ferret it out, to spend all our short mortal time in consideration, in preparation, in pursuit of it, the idea of it, not expecting to see or actually to prove but to prepare, to establish a condition of readiness, to see all that was allowed to be seen, prove all that it was permitted to prove here on earth of what existed beyond it? I thought, how bare, how puny, how defeated to solve the equation only with faith. For life was, what? like a maze with each of us in the middle and waiting for death to lift us up over the hazards and show us the point of exit. I was always prepared, yes, don't misunderstand, always prepared to accept that the man who said, I believe, I have faith, and then settled down comfortably to wait for death would find himself, when he died, at the same exit as a man like myself who had said, I believe, but had stumbled his way through the maze, round and round, searching, penetrating, mortifying his mind and body because he wanted to *deserve* his soul, *deserve* the grace that was coming to him. And then I thought that there was yet another way, the way of the vision. The vision that would reveal all, that would lift me up in the manner of death but before my death and there it would be, the whole maze beneath me, showing clearly what happened at the exit; the proof, the *smell* of eternity. Then I could say, I have faith, and this would not be puny or bare or defeated, because it would have been God who had given me faith directly, as you might give a jujube to a child to stop him from fretting."

I said, "And of course there hasn't been a vision, so you've chucked the whole thing, lock, stock, and barrel. Why? In the hope of provoking one?"

He smiled. "And why do you use that somewhat critical tone? In the hope of provoking *me*? I have told you I am no longer here to be used, to be worked on. When you've got used to the idea that you don't exist except in the physical sense, the sense of flesh, flesh like those, mere plants, there's no limit to the amount of provocation you can withstand, no limit to the amount of hate you can ignore or of love you can reject. I tell you, coal-heaver, yes, that's what I called you, isn't it? The only result of your heaving coal will be smoke issuing from a funnel and dissipating itself into fragments of matter. And one day you may wake up as I did and realize that for as many years as you can remember you've spent every day looking for your non-existent soul. You will say, being logical for once, Why, if I look for it, surely this means I haven't got it with me. A soul isn't a thing you could ignore, *have*, you know, and not notice. And well, you'll say, if I haven't got it with me, why then, I must have lost it. But when? Do I actually remember losing it, remember having it and losing it? And the answer will be no, you do not remember losing it. You're searching for it but can't remember losing it. And if you look that situation squarely in the eye you'll come to the same conclusion I did, and that's that you have *never* had it. You've never had it because there's no such thing, only the illusion of it brought about by what we might call the misunderstood mechanical or chemical processes of our bodies. The body requires, for instance, fuel, and we think, I am hungry, I want to eat. *Want*, you understand, with all the subtle ramifications of that word evolved by a million years use of it or its equivalents."

"And," I said, "the body requires to duplicate itself. *That's* a subtle ramification of want. What kind of want is that when it's at home?"

"Why," he said, "not a spiritual one. Want, you're trying to say, want love, tenderness –"

"Or continuation –"

"– of waste! Like the seed of plants. Not love, not tenderness, not continuation. These are words, dreams built up round processes. Finally they don't disguise them. For me the processes are no longer disguised. I face them, admit them. And do you know, once they are faced their pressure seems to lessen. Perhaps you think I mortify the flesh by denying it whisky or that stuff you're smoking, but mortification doesn't enter into it. The machine gets as much as its processes require and no more. And do you know another thing? I have a feeling, an impression, a kind of whispering in my blood which is probably a physical sensation brought about by its cooling, the fractional fraction of a degree fall in its temperature, that tells me that once you've stripped the processes of their dreams, the processes begin to slow down. It's almost, yes, almost as if they need the dreams to keep going, as if they are kept going only by that kind of excitation. Perhaps the animal is the real freak of nature, the throwback, the one mechanism that got chemically out of hand. Perhaps some chance amalgamation of substances and cells caused it to feel it felt, to think it thought, and if it were a man to say: I think, therefore I am. And, ah! isn't that a monstrosity! A tree that talks, a plant that weeps, a rock that moves of its own volition."

He moved himself, suddenly, rising to his feet, passing his hand over his face as I had seen him do before, that very first night of all. Then it had been like a wiping away of the outer skin but now it looked as if he touched his face to gauge how the flesh was faring in a slow but inevitable process of disintegration.

He said, not looking at me, but round the room as though the idea of escape might always come to plague him, "Well, you are here. You will stay as long as you will or go as soon as you must. I have no feelings in the matter, you understand."

"Yes, you have feelings," I said. "There was no need to answer my postcard. You wanted me to come, didn't you? Why, for God's sake? So that you could punish me in this childish way? What else am I to think?"

He stared at me, his arms hanging loose, swinging slightly. "Punish you?" he repeated. "You're aware perhaps of deserving punishment? Would the word have come to you otherwise? But then you were always an arrogant man, and only arrogant men can conceive of their sins being big enough, sinful enough, to invite retribution."

"You're evading my question," I said, angrily. "Why did you answer my postcard?"

"I've told you. To have put obstacles in your way would have called for an emotional response."

"That's no answer." I got to my feet, poured another glass of whisky. "That's no answer. You wanted me to come. You wanted to see me pay for all the times I took what you offered without giving you anything worthwhile in return. You wanted me to come for what you thought would be the kick you'd get when I asked for money for Greystone or something for myself, something, anything, even if it was only the opportunity to beef. So, you've got your kick, Greystone *does* want money. The fact that I didn't promise I'd ask you is neither here nor there. And I came prepared to beef, don't ask me what about. Just beef. Let off steam. Give my bloody soul a bit of an airing. But I came for something else too. The opportunity of telling you a bit late in the day that I read the signposts. The pennies dropped. It took 'em a long time but they dropped. You've never had a dream of your own to fall into. You tagged along after mine and Greystone's and how many others I don't know. You had lots of time. Too much time. You had it too easy, Brian. You may have had a stoker's heart but you travelled too long on a first-class ticket and the trouble with men travelling on first-class tickets is that they start believing people never give anything to them but only take things from them, and when a man believes *that* it hangs round his neck like a label. *Don't feed this animal, it's not used to it and feeds itself.* You were wearing it the first time I met you. You're still wearing a label, only now it says, *This animal doesn't need feeding because it no longer exists.* Well, you might fool yourself, but you don't fool me and you certainly won't fool God. He's not going to come up with a vision on the strength of *that.*"

For once I had been articulate. I wanted him to share my

pleasure. "Come on, Brian. Have a drink and praise the Lord *that* way. We might even sing a dirty song or two. And tomorrow to hell with everything and come to Singapore with me."

Throughout, he had been standing perfectly still but now his right hand moved up to his bare chest where it bunched into a fist, clutching the body-hair, crushing whatever it was that hung invisible from his neck. Then, without saying a word to me, he turned his back and walked out of the room. I stared at the bead curtains as they swayed and crackled. Then I sat down.

I lit a cigarette, poured myself more whisky. Ten minutes later his ugly Malayan mistress came in with trays of food. She did not look at me but arranged bowls and plates in front of me as if laying the table in an empty room. Only the swaying punkah acknowledged my presence, but tonight the little Tamil girl did not sing. I ate and drank and when I had finished stayed on to smoke a cigar. The monotonous, sibilant exhalation of the pressure-lamp and the *woof* of the punkah were my only companions and presently the lamp coughed. When the light died away and left me in darkness I rose and went to my room.

The hurricane lantern was turned low. I undressed, turned it out and got into bed. The pillow smelt of the jasmine oil with which the little Tamil girl sleeked her raven hair. I leaned up on one elbow and called softly, *Ayie, ayie*; and she came, her bare feet gentle on the floor so that there was scarcely a sound from the tinkling silver rings on her ankles. *Ayie, ayie*, I whispered. With my fingers I traced the shape of the small, sad smile on her lips and the tiny frown of interrogation between her eyebrows.

In the morning I rose early but he had already gone for the day. He had left a note: "There is no point in your staying. You will only decide that you dislike me, not that that would bother me. But it would bother you. My assistant has instructions to drive you, after breakfast, should you so wish, to Kuala Lumpur. From there you can take a train to Singapore which, I am told, abounds still with people in search of their souls."

I returned to my room, packed my things and thought: To hell with him then.

*

Wandering the streets of Singapore alone I found a shop that grew to have an irresistible fascination for me. I returned to it time and again. It was owned by a white-haired old Tamil whom I called the impeccable *makan-walla* because impeccable was the word he invariably used to describe the goods he had for sale.

On the face of it we were bargaining over a length of scarlet brocade that had attracted me from the beginning. Thereafter he used to clear a space on the counter as soon as I went in and bring the bale of brocade out for me to inspect. I think he judged correctly the moment I realized that Millicent, for whom the cloth was half-intended as a present, would find it unsuitable, even vulgar. Our eyes met above it and his head jerked to one side in an involuntary spasm of sympathy.

On subsequent visits I pretended a continued interest in it, but he saw through this and took to using it as a background against which to display the merits of other goods, a carved Kashmiri box, a set of ivory chessmen, a string of jade beads, a Tibetan silver brooch, a statue of the dancing Shiva or of Ganesh the elephant god. My hands would smell of sandal wood for the rest of the day.

On the last day there were so many other things to attend to that it was not until eight o'clock at night that I entered the shop for the last time. I was almost sorry that I had come because in the artificial light the place looked rather squalid. I had found the door open but the impeccable *makan-walla* was not to be seen and for a few moments I stood, apparently alone, and more than a bit put off by a powerful smell of cooking.

He came out of the shadows as I was on the point of leaving,

85

the *kris* held flat on the palm of his hand. The light from the single naked bulb kindled microscopic fires in its handle.

He said, "I was at the door and saw the sahib coming. I went to fetch him this."

I followed him to the counter. He took down the brocade and spread it out to receive the *kris*.

*

I suppose that in that grubby shop I was looking for a symbol of what I felt but could not then express in words.

It was all very well to say of Saxby: To hell with him. But which Saxby did I mean? Not the red-bearded, rain-soaked giant to whom I had opened the door of Mrs Ross's hostel. Of that Saxby I could never say, To hell with him, because part of me at least was bound to him: if only that previous self, that boy whose worsted suit showed his bony wrists.

At the time I only meant the Saxby I was about to leave behind in his remote Malayan jungle, but were we really divisible in this way? I was conscious of having involuntarily wished us to hell together. In my association with Saxby there had always been a slight sense of guilt for sins of omission not wholly to be excused by youth or inexperience; and for sins of commission not utterly absolved by a young man's need to be his own man in his own world. But guilty as I might feel, in Singapore, every time the guilt threatened to look me in the eye, I blinded it by throwing anger in its face. He had wasted my time, spoiled the beginning of my holiday, cast a shadow on all the better times we had had together.

When I think of the brocade now, I see it as a symbol of the richness, the variety, the sensuous magic of the world of which I wanted my share. Poor Millicent! She would have paled to insignificance in a dress made from that cloth, not because she was plain or colourless but because quite simply I did not love her, nor she me. The brocade, in that sense, was love and perhaps the old Tamil saw that I had a capacity for it if not yet an occasion.

When he laid the jewelled *kris* on the brocade I reacted only to its beauty, its hard symmetrical precision, the dormant power my hand could waken just by holding it. I knew that I had to possess it. It was more than I could really afford and I had to beat him down by several dollars. When he cut off a piece of the brocade in which to wrap the *kris* I suspected that even so he had cheated me and threw the brocade in as a makeweight.

When I gave the *kris* to Teena I remembered the piece of brocade in which it had been wrapped but could not recall just how or when it had been lost. It may have been discarded even before I sailed from Singapore. The old Tamil would have been concerned had he known. I no longer believe he threw it in as a sop to his conscience but gave it to me, out of the kindness of his heart, as a talisman against despair, because the weapon he had offered me, the weapon I had bought was one which men used when they could no longer endure the prison of their flesh, and ran amok.

PART II

The Garden of Madness

I

THE KRIS WAS WITH ME CONSTANTLY FOR SIX YEARS.
It hung on the walls of my bedroom for the few months I
continued to live with Greystone and it was in my suitcase
when I drove out of the valley for the last time in the September
of 1939. It was with me in countless huts and tents, on trucks
and lorries and trains, on endless marches, in desolate rain-
sodden rest camps. It was with me when I went back to
Malaya in the September of 1945, shortly after the surrender of
the Japanese who had occupied the country for over three years.

It was at the request of a Major Turner that I went back to
Malaya. I had met him only once before, some four or five
months previously, when we shared a room at the Grand Hotel
in Calcutta which, in those days, was used as an officers' hostel.
I had been staying there in connexion with a series of lectures
on the post-war rehabilitation of Indian troops and Turner had
come to Calcutta for a conference of his own, but of this he
would say nothing.

He was of medium height, compactly built, with light brown
hair and a mole high on his left cheek. His face was broad, his
eyes penetrating, and in the skin of his face and hands there was
the ingrained dirt I recognized as that which a man collected by
living in the jungle. It had taken me nearly six months to get
rid of it in my own.

We seemed to like each other instinctively and he did not
automatically assume because I then wore khaki instead of
jungle green and carried a brief-case instead of a revolver that
I had always done so. He was observant, too. It took him
no more than ten minutes to realize I was not naturally left-
handed. Perhaps it was this that really drew me to him. I had

become used to the superior, slightly contemptuous attitude my G.H.Q. appearance provoked in active-service officers, particularly those grimy, green-clad subalterns of the efficient new war who had their pistols strapped to their thighs and no experience of defeat, or of being whipped from one end of Burma to the other. I also had trouble with senior officers who stopped me in the street to inquire why I had given them an eyes right or an odd combination of a crookedly raised cane and lowered head instead of a proper salute.

The difficulty was that, dressed, I looked as capable as the next man and it was only when I was shirtless that the truth came out. Early in 1944 a shell splinter had carved a piece out of my right shoulder and left me finally unable to raise the arm much above chest level or straighten my right wrist from the peculiar angle it had got itself into. This was a legacy of the Arakan where the Indian regiment into which I was commissioned in 1940 fought after the retreat from Burma. Afterwards, I was unable to fire a weapon with any accuracy except in the direction of someone's knees. I practised hard with my left hand but seemed to acquire skill only with a glass and although I returned to my battalion as welfare officer they left me behind when they went back into the field at the end of 1944. Someone heard that I had worked with Greystone before the war and decided I might as well spend the rest of it telling Indian soldiers in training battalions how they could improve their fields and villages if they were ever lucky enough to go back to them. Greystone had died in 1941 and there was a nostalgic pleasure to be had out of teaching husbandry to others if only because at that time I doubted I should ever go back to farming.

Turner's stay in Calcutta coincided with mine by only twenty-four hours, but in one long after-dinner session we drank a great deal of Carew's gin and apparently I got on to the subject of Saxby of whom I had heard nothing for six years, nothing, in fact, since the note he left for me that morning in Singaputan.

Turner let me run on, indeed deliberately kept me talking,

but betrayed no familiarity with Saxby's name, no clue to the excitement he must have felt, and afterwards I had no real recollection of what I had told him. I even had difficulty in remembering who Turner was when some five months later, two weeks after the Japanese in Malaya had obeyed their Emperor's instructions to surrender and allowed our troops to go peacefully ashore, my colonel in Delhi, throwing a signal across his desk, told me I was instructed to fly to Malaya at once to report to a Major Turner in Kuala Lumpur in connexion with a man called Saxby.

The room in the house in Kuala Lumpur in which Turner and I had our second talk was cool, darkened on one side by slatted blinds. The doors giving on to the porticoed veranda were open and outside in the hard sunshine Japanese soldiers were sweeping the yard. They were the first I had seen for nearly eighteen months and it was curious to think that if I stepped out now and walked amongst them they would probably straighten up, hold their brooms to their sides and bow from the waist.

Turner said, "When you mentioned Saxby in Calcutta you could have knocked me down with a feather. Did it show?"

"We were doing some serious drinking, that's all I really remember."

Turner grinned. He said, "I must take up poker," and before I could ask him why he added, "Saxby is a bit of an obsession of yours, isn't he?"

"Why should you think that?"

"I made an *aide-memoire* next day. Listen." He glanced at an open pad and read out: "Saxby. Singaputan, 1939. Plants. Accepts physical existence but not spiritual. Signposts not seen by Major Brent. People and no dream. Earth. Greystone. Dream to keep yourself up in. The face of a sahib but in his heart heaves coal."

He closed the pad and smiled at me in an open, friendly manner. In Calcutta I had assumed he was engaged in something out-landish, something cloak-and-daggerish and coming to this particular headquarters I had proof of it, but the smile, his attitude, the *aide-memoire* were proof of more than military nonconformity. He was a man who understood the oddity, the eccentricity of life, and he would always respond to whatever it was in a situation that promised to make it greater than its circumstances.

I was not sure that I wanted him responding to Saxby though. For an instant I regretted ever having mentioned Saxby's name, but then my curiosity revived.

"I must have been drunk," I said.

"You were."

"Why the *aide-memoire*, why the interest? Why this summons?"

"Because," Turner said, "Saxby's been an obsession of mine too. For three years."

I said, "Oh," being unable for the moment to produce a more adequate reaction. It seemed to me so unlikely it could be the same Saxby. "You said nothing in Calcutta about knowing him."

"Knowing isn't quite the right word," he said. "And in Calcutta it was a question of security. I was due to drop into a place called Kampong Malim the week after I saw you."

I accepted a cigarette and leaned back.

"You'd better tell me from the beginning," I suggested.

*

Turner was in the army in Malaya at the time of the Japanese invasion. He was put in charge of one of the stay-behind parties. Their job was to hide out in the jungle, let the advancing enemy overrun them, but keep in touch with Singapore by radio. At that time the Japanese success was believed to be only a temporary set-back because Singapore was considered impregnable. From it, in due course, our own troops were expected to push back up the peninsula. Stay-behind parties therefore had two functions: they were to signal information about the enemy to Singapore and harry the retreating Japanese when the time came. But Singapore fell and the whole country was in enemy hands. Turner decided to stay in hiding for three months, find out as much as he could about the Japanese and the way the civil population reacted to them, then try to make his way back to India.

He joined a guerrilla camp up in the north. For years attempts had been made to suppress the Malayan communist party. When the war came its members had an underground movement made to measure. They took to the jungle and, as the Malayan People's Anti-Japanese Army, "anti-ed" the Japanese from jungle hideouts from one end of the country to another. At least, that was the intention. The camps communicated with each other by messengers and contact men. The jungle villages were full of fifth columnists. Directly a camp was known or thought to be compromised they had to move elsewhere. Some camps had to move so many times, they never gave the enemy's tail what Turner called a single tweak. In some other camps political indoctrination and the study of Marx took pride of place in the operational programme.

In the camp he lived in Turner was the only white man. Few of his companions spoke intelligible English. He grew lonely to the point of laughing at his own jokes. When he heard rumours of another white man in a camp not more than three or four days' journey away he begged leave to visit him but the camp commander refused. In the end permission was given for a letter to be written.

Turner had forgotten just what he wrote. "Something," he said, "to the effect of well, here I am, and there you are, isn't it all a cock-up and what about getting together?" He had not forgotten the reply though. How could he? He still had the note preserved in a cellophane envelope which he showed to me then and there. For weeks, reading it had been his only contact with a man of his own race. It read:

Dear Lieutenant Turner,
    Thank you for your letter. It is unlikely that we shall meet, if only because the situation here needs to be carefully

controlled. I have a great deal to do. I fancy from the tone of your letter you may not have appreciated the opportunity given to you. But good luck.

Yours sincerely,
B. Saxby.

I recognized the handwriting. It was the same Saxby and yet even in that short message the change in him was apparent. He had become committed to something. Saxby had always struck Turner as "something of a fire-eater" and he had been fascinated by what I told him in Calcutta that suggested the opposite. Turner, taking back the letter, said, "Something had happened, hadn't it? He believed in something again, didn't he?"

At the end of three months Turner set out on his perilous journey back to India. He crossed the Malacca Straits in a fishing junk. In Sumatra he teamed up with some other men making their way home. One of them was a man called Frisby. Frisby had actually met Saxby. Like Turner, Frisby had been on his own for a long time. The Japanese had caught him once but he escaped and was befriended by a Chinese who put him in touch with a band of guerrillas. It happened to be the band with whom Saxby was working. Frisby, starved of company of his own kind, hearing that another white man lived with the guerrillas, could scarcely believe his good fortune. But he got out as soon as he could. He hated Saxby. He described him to Turner as "a bloody hulk of a man with a flaming red beard who seemed to think he was God and made you feel like dirt".

When Frisby first arrived at the camp the guerrillas were planning a raid on a Japanese outpost. He said Saxby bullied him into taking part. The raid was carried out at night. The telephone wire was cut, the four Japanese soldiers captured, bound, gagged, soaked in petrol and set alight. Frisby was sick. He smelt roast Jap for days afterwards. The thing that stuck in his mind was the thought that the gags stopped the soldiers shrieking. He seemed to think being able to shriek would have helped them die easier.

Frisby himself died of cerebral meningitis in India shortly after the survivors of the escaping party reached there. He always swore it was Saxby who planned the raid. He had accused him of acting like a barbarian. Saxby had laughed at that, said that it was only a question of an eye for an eye and proceeded to tell Frisby a story.

When the war in Malaya began, Saxby was living with the Sakai, aboriginal tribes of the interior. The Japanese disliked going deep into the forest. There were probably some tribes who did not know to this day that the Japanese had come and gone. But the tribe Saxby was with were close enough to the outside world for the Japanese to hear that they had a white man with them and close enough for them to be warned that a Japanese patrol was coming to look for him. They abandoned their settlement. When they returned some days later they found everything burned to the ground. At first Frisby assumed that some of the old, feeble members of the tribe had been left behind and burned along with the settlement. He said, "Is that what you mean by an eye for an eye?" Saxby was evasive. In the end all he would say was, "Five were burned that couldn't be moved."

Saxby must first have gone into the jungle shortly after I left him in 1939. He went looking for a rare species of orchid and, having found it, returned to civilization some time in 1940. There was some mystery about the orchid. According to an article in a magazine Saxby had found it in what he simply told the reporter were "unusual circumstances". Turner was shown an old copy of this article by an expatriate rubber-estate manager when he got back to India. The manager was an amateur botanist himself. He had never met Saxby but at once recognized his name and remembered what he called the business about the orchid. It was the last botanical article he read before the invasion of Malaya at the end of 1941. By then, Saxby must have been back in the jungle, living with the Sakai.

In 1943 the organization to which Turner belonged sent a small party into Malaya by submarine. They took wireless equipment with them. Their job was to make contact with the guerrilla forces, lay down the foundations of a scheme of assistance and co-operation, and establish regular radio contact with Ceylon.

They found that Saxby had become something of a legend. The Japanese had put a price on his head. There was a wealth of stories about his exploits against them. The Chinese called him Sax Bee. The submarine party discovered that it was very difficult to get in touch with him, however. Their messages to him were always acknowledged eventually but no report of the kind they wanted was ever forthcoming. The impression gained was that of a man who liked to run his own show. He was known to be in the south, in the jungle above a town called Kampong Malim. Towards the end of 1944 there were reports of an escapade against the Japanese that had led to bloody reprisals and he was then reported to have moved to the jungle above the neighbouring but smaller town of Bukit Kallang.

At the end of 1944, with things going well in Burma, and the re-invasion of Malaya more than ever an early possibility, Turner's organization set to work to get the guerrilla forces better organized. They decided to send more officers into the country and Turner himself elected to be dropped into the Kampong Malim area. At the same time they decided to invite Saxby to come out by submarine. If he could be persuaded to leave Malaya his knowledge of Japanese troop conditions, of guerrilla organization and psychology would be invaluable. A message was sent through to him early in January. His reply reached them in March. He pin-pointed a dropping zone for Turner, suggested the night of May the second and third because of moon conditions and, to everyone's somewhat surprised delight, selected a beach for his own pick-up and asked to be taken off from there on the night of the fourth and fifth of June.

Turner assumed from Saxby's time-table that he would meet him at the dropping-zone and then set out for the submarine rendezvous. In this he was disappointed. Saxby did not meet him but sent a note welcoming Turner back to Malaya, wishing him luck and apologizing for not being there in person to greet him. He explained that as he had forty miles to go to the coast and would only march at night he was leaving Bukit Kallang straight away.

Turner soon forgot his disappointment. Getting the guerrillas organized was up-hill work. He found them sullen, suspicious, and unco-operative. Then, on the twelfth of June a message came from Ceylon. The submarine had stood off the beach on the night of June the fourth and fifth, and again on the following night, and flashed its recognition signals. But no reply had come from the dark shore and Saxby had not been heard of again.

*

Was he dead? Captured by the Japanese and killed? I visualized the shore-line where the jungle would grow right to the water's edge, the uninterrupted darkness from which a lamp should have flashed an answer to the winking light out to sea. Had he been betrayed by someone on the way to the coast?

When Turner sent a message to Bukit Kallang to ask the guerrilla leader what had happened the answer was that Saxby had set out on the appointed day with a Chinese boy called Ah Choong whose job it would be to buy food. Neither of them had come back. Turner showed me the note of welcome. It was genuine, the handwriting still recognizable over the years as Saxby's.

Saxby's journey was to have been on a camp-to-camp basis and Wan Lo Ping, the guerrilla leader, promised Turner he would send inquiries along the chain. In July he reported that Saxby and Ah Choong had failed to turn up at even the first camp. They had disappeared between there and Bukit Kallang.

Was he ill? Dying? Had Ah Choong betrayed him? Had there been a quarrel?

"What do we know about Ah Choong?" I asked.

"Nothing really. Wan Lo Ping wrote that he'd always found him reliable."

"Is Wan Lo Ping reliable?"

Turner leaned back in his chair. "Basically they're all the same. Young toughies with guns. I don't know how much Wan Lo conforms to type, I've never met him face to face. Before the Japs surrendered I never had time to go to Bukit Kallang and after they surrendered I had my hands full." He hesitated. "It's only recently I decided someone had better go and see Mister Wan and I thought that someone had better be you."

"So that's why you've brought me out here."

He smiled. "I've brought you here to find Saxby. You see, apart from the guerrillas there's nobody I know who'd be sure to recognize him if they saw him, except you." He stood up. "Now let's have lunch."

The mess was laid out with separate tables like an hotel dining-room. He took me to one tucked away in a corner. There were about a dozen altogether, each occupied. A pale, glutinous curry was served.

"You're a remarkable chap," Turner said suddenly. "You've not registered any kind of surprise. You're the least exclamatory fellow I've met, except of course when you're drunk. You lay it on the table then. You know I had to put you to bed round about three in the morning?"

"I'd forgotten."

"Don't you remember anything you told me about Saxby?"

"None of the details."

"About the labels, for instance? The ones he wore round his neck?"

"Oh, I told you as much as that did I?"

"There were two, but the one that sticks in my mind is the one you realized afterwards had two sides to it. 'This animal no longer exists' on one side, and 'This animal is in need of care and attention' on the back."

"Is he, you think? It sounds as if he'd learned how to take care of himself."

"Physically, yes. That's why I'm sure he's not dead. Spiritually's a different matter, isn't it? Mightn't he still be looking for a dream to fall into? Mightn't he have found one and be suffocating in it?"

He smiled, coped with a spoonful of soggy rice.

"I seem to have told you everything. Is that why're you're positive I'll help you look for him?"

Turner pushed his plate away to make room for his folded arms and looked at me, as if weighing up how much he should say.

"When you were well into the second bottle," he began, "you told me Saxby was the only man you'd ever known who spent his whole life fighting and kicking against the rot. Waste, you said, what you called waste and futility. I knew what you meant. I saw that. You said Saxby didn't deceive you in Singaputan when he protested he was committed to waste himself. You said he was daring God to prove they both existed and that this was plain bloody tragic because if there were a God you were sure he'd always found Saxby's soul too big for comfort, too much of a bloody nuisance, and wouldn't take any notice until Saxby turned the label round and admitted he wanted help. You said God had got so used to coping with what you called chaps who sludged around like a lot of namby-pambys saying 'I believe, I really do' that he wouldn't know what to do about Saxby. And you said you'd come to the conclusion that what felt like our souls was really God's hand pressing down on us and that Saxby had made the mistake of thinking he was entitled to push back. You said he'd pushed back so hard God had got fed up and taken his hand away so that Saxby would see what it felt like to have no pressure at all. And you said you'd give anything to retract what you did in 1939, which was leave Saxby wandering around defying what you called the law of spiritual gravity; give anything to tell Saxby about the wild orchid *you* saw in the Arakan. Don't you remember that? About it growing higher than it was allowed to?"

I shook my head, but saw the orchid there, close to the hand that seemed to be mine but which I could not feel because below my neck my whole body was numb. The delicate, creamy petals trembled, and far away, in another dimension entirely, was the roar and shock of bombardment. I willed the hand to move, to touch the satin-smooth, frilled and convoluted flower because I wanted it to touch what was alive, and suddenly, whining and shrieking through the air, the plant reached up and up because there was nothing to stop it. When I regained consciousness pain had entered and the orchid was in danger of being crushed by the boot of the medical orderly. I thought: If it's crushed it'll feel nothing. It doesn't even feel the hand that lets it grow so high, no higher.

Turner was saying, "You said that seemed to be the whole point: so high, no higher; that Saxby had gone further than was allowed, to find out how high, and that this was another aspect of his tragedy because at least he'd bothered to try and find out and hadn't been content just to sit back and get the pressure eased a bit by saying he believed. He'd tried to *show* that he believed and had simply failed to recognize that showing you believed was essentially a one-sided business. He'd got round to expecting God to exert himself to deserve *him*, a sort of spiritual tit-for-tat, a celestial *quid pro quo*." Turner paused, wondering, perhaps, how I was taking it. I nodded at him and said, "Go on."

"Finally you said that if someone didn't do something Saxby would compensate by inventing the *quid pro quo*, that's to say by producing a vision all on his own so that he could go round pretending God had been forced to relent and give him a special mission. Well, I think you were right. I think that's exactly what he *has* done, and I think he's carrying out his mission now. I expect the vision was something to do with finding the orchids in unusual circumstances. And then five being burned that couldn't be moved probably comes into it somewhere. Why 'that'? Why not 'who'. Five what? And why five?"

The Malay waiter took away our empty plates and brought tinned pears.

Turner said, "He's not dead, I'm sure of that. The Japanese certainly never caught him. I've checked the records and had a word with the Jap major who used to command troops in the Kampong Malim area. He said he'd have heard if Saxby had been nabbed. They were on the look-out for him and guessed he was still in the area – even though nothing happened after the lorry incident in August last year. Saxby was sent to Bukit Kallang after the lorry incident."

"All right, I'll ask. What was the lorry incident?"

"The Kampong Malim guerrillas ambushed a Jap lorry. After killing the driver they set fire to it. That was the Saxby hall-mark. Fire. The Japs retaliated by burning a couple of Chinese alive. The guerrillas didn't like that. It didn't always suit their book to have the Japs anti-ed in the way Saxby liked to anti them."

"So Saxby was sent to Bukit Kallang as a kind of punishment?"

"The guerrillas don't admit it. They don't like to be thought not to have been in complete control of things. I reckon the lorry incident was the last straw. It led to the reprisals and the guerrilla commander got himself killed. A chap called Lieu Lim. From our point of view that's a pity because he could have told us a lot about Saxby. They'd worked together once in a traitor-killing camp."

"Is that what its name implies?"

"Yes. Camps whose job was to anti the collaborators as well as the Jap. I got all this information from the central committee boys when Saxby disappeared and I started to ask questions. I got it bit by bit, squeeze by squeeze. I didn't get answers so much as a picture, a picture of Saxby beginning as an asset when everything was death and glory and ending as a liability when the party had to formulate a long-term policy without being sure what it was to be in aid of. Up to a few months ago there wasn't any special reason for believing the Japs would be kicked out of Malaya, was there?"

"No," I said, "but Saxby disappeared at a time when things were obviously looking up again, didn't he?"

"Yes, but looking up for whom? For us, yes. For the Chinese, yes. But for Saxby? What writing did he see on the wall? The writing that said: Law and Order? The Japs beaten and the British coming back to interrupt unfinished business? Where was his eye for an eye then? He knew we wouldn't come back to Malaya waving a sword of vengeance. We'd come back nice and polite because the natives had seen the Jap whip the pants off us. We couldn't call people collaborators simply because they'd gone on living with the Japs after we'd left them in the lurch."

"You're bent by it, Turner."

"Bent by what?"

"The whole situation."

I believed him but, sober, was not fully prepared to admit it. I had to maintain a reserve of what was dull and ordinary, so that when the going got too tough, the upper air too rare, the pursuit of intimations of immortality too exhausting, I could fall back on it, feed from it like a camel drinking from its hump, and there was in this particular desert always a mirage to walk towards, the consolation-prize of physical pleasures.

"Have I got to get you drunk then?" Turner asked. "You want to help him, you know. The better side of you wants that."

"Who's to say which is the better side? Why can't you just let him disappear? Perhaps when he heard you were coming he said, Ah well, the war's nearly over, let 'em get on with it. He's probably gone back to Singaputan to collect plants."

"I've checked Singaputan," Turner said. "I went up there a few days ago. They hadn't seen him since nineteen-forty when he went back to live with the Sakai."

"Who did you talk to?"

"His mistress. The one you told me was ugly. She was."

"You mean you breezed into Singaputan and asked for *Tuan* Saxby's old mistress?"

"I asked to be taken to his house. She was there. But alone."

"Had even the plants gone?"

"Even the plants. I was disappointed. After what you told me in Calcutta I had this picture of Saxby sitting in the middle of them as mad as a hatter."

"Perhaps he's turned up since."

"I'd have been told. I asked the local military police to keep an eye open."

"The police?"

"Yes."

"You've no right to persecute him. He's a civilian. He's not under our jurisdiction."

"That's right, Brent. He's not under our jurisdiction. In fact there's not a solitary bugger to care what happens to him. Except you and me."

"Then he'll be all right. Whatever his reasons were for what he did he's had his fun. He's anti-ed the Jap. Now he's gone into the jungle to find more orchids."

Turner hesitated, playing for a moment with spoon and fork. "Up to ten days ago I'd have agreed, I'd have accepted that. I'd got enough to do without getting steamed up about Saxby. But ten days ago something happened in Bukit Kallang. That's odd enough in itself because nothing ever happened in the Kampong Malim area after the lorry incident. In some districts where blood was thicker than politics the guerrillas clubbed traitors to death in broad daylight, between the Japs going and us coming back. But not everywhere. Not in Kampong Malim, for instance. Nor in Bukit Kallang until ten days ago. But ten days ago, Brent, they found the body of a Chinese merchant called Cheong Poh Kwee. He was the biggest local collaborator going. He'd made himself scarce when the Japanese threw in the towel, but with everything so quiet and peaceful I suppose he decided to come back. A couple of days later someone stabbed him, dragged his body into a clump of bamboo, poured petrol over his clothes and *set him alight.*"

Turner stood up. "Come and have some coffee. Then we'll go back to the office."

*

In Turner's office there was a large-scale map of Malaya.

Staring at it I seemed to see Saxby's face. I thought: Always turning up, aren't you, turning up, coming at me out of the dark, as if *we've* got unfinished business.

I said to Turner, "If I decide to go, how would I get there?"

"I'll show you. This is us. Up there's Kampong Malim. Carry on another three or four miles and there's Bukit Kallang. I'll give you a jeep. You can drive it in a couple of hours. You *can* drive with that arm?"

I nodded. "Did you want me to go tonight?"

"Tomorrow would do."

"Where would I stay when I got there?"

"I'll ring the battalion at Kampong Malim and ask them to fix you up with the company they've got detached at Bukit Kallang."

Coming away from the map I said, "It could have been anyone who killed Cheong Poh Kwee. Who would I see for a start?"

"Wan Lo Ping, I should think."

"That's the guerrilla leader?"

"Yes. You'll find him quartered in the town I expect. The commander of the rifle company will be able to put you on to him because the guerrillas are under us now for pay and admin. The pukka guerrillas, anyway. There are still bands of men who haven't come out of the jungle but the M.P.A.J.A. doesn't recognize them and they rank as bandits."

"M.P.A.J.A. meaning Malayan People's Anti-Japanese Army?"

"Yes. Wan Lo Ping's bunch."

"What are we doing about the bandits? Anything?"

Turner shrugged. "It depends what they get up to. If they

106

stay quiet in the jungle nobody minds but we have to go after them if they get up to hanky-panky like raiding villages for food."

"Or stabbing collaborators."

"Cheong Poh Kwee wasn't robbed," Turner said. "And bandits aren't interested in settling scores. It's enough for them trying to keep their bellies full."

"Wouldn't that depend on who led them?"

Turner said, "I've thought of that. But my guess is Saxby's on his own, with Ah Choong as his right-hand man."

"Killing collaborators? It's absurd."

"Is it?" Turner asked.

After a moment I said, "And after Wan Lo Ping? Whom do I see then?"

"I don't know, Brent. You follow your nose. You let things develop. You watch. You listen. And you do it discreetly because this is private between you and me and my department. We don't want it generally spread around that an Englishman is suspected of knocking off collaborators as part of a private vendetta. It'll be best if Wan Lo Ping is made to feel you suspect *him* of something. You present yourself as an old friend of Saxby."

"And what does the old friend do, Turner? What does he do if he finds Saxby?"

Turner watched me. Presently he said, "Would you rather we waited for the next body, and the next, and then sent the police after him with rifles?"

"It might never come to that."

"Would you like to risk it?"

He took me by the arm. "You look shagged out. Get in some kip and tell me this evening what you've decided."

*

During lunch my kit had been taken upstairs to a small, narrow-bedded room. Here, with the shutters at half-mast, a table-fan blowing a bulge into the white mosquito netting that festooned the bed like a nightmare spider web I lay back and considered things.

The curry, bad as it had been, had made me sleepy and I had been up at an early hour to fly from Penang. I turned on my left side to try to sleep, but whenever I closed my eyes he was standing there in the sarong, clutching the invisible label so that nobody, not even God, should turn it over and read what was on the back: *This animal is in need of care and attention.* He was always standing there, or moving to pass through the bead curtains but never going, always giving me the chance to retract my monumental selfishness of six years ago.

I should not have left him in Singaputan. On the narrow bed in the narrow room of a house in Kuala Lumpur whose ghosts tapped and sang, and cried: *Is anybody there?* I did not know what I should have done had I stayed, I simply knew in the marrow of the bones of my conscience that you do not leave such men alone with their thoughts, you do not abandon them, you do not leave them to the mercy of plants.

I had known this in Singapore, and at any one of a thousand moments of comprehension since. The knowledge had been with me, like the *kris*, all the years of the war. I knew it again now, and Turner knew it. And it was not for either of us simply a question of solving a puzzle, of finding Saxby in the flesh, of what would happen then, if he were found. It was really a question of pursuing him, of not letting him go for want of a word or an act, of not shrugging him away or of saying, To hell with him!

One man, wandering from his tribe, diminishes it. And even if he could be seen thereafter to walk with God, that would not make acceptable the empty hut and the cold ashes on the hearth.

2

THE INDIAN RIFLE COMPANY DETACHED BY THE battalion at Kampong Malim to control the situation in Bukit Kallang was commanded by a Major Reid.

I estimated him to be about forty, old for command of a company. He was broad, heavy looking. His hair was beginning to go grey but it was wiry and close packed and he wore it rather long for a soldier. There was a thin film of sweat on his face. The cheeks were ruddy but this was due to thread-like veins that lay broken and intricately patterned just beneath the skin.

He had a trick of closing his eyes, leaning his head to the left and stroking the outer edge of his left eyelid with the forefinger of his left hand as though trying to dislodge a piece of grit.

Beside Reid, Calthrop, his second-in-command, was noticeably young, not more than twenty-two or three. His fair gingerish hair lay crinkled in little waves close to his skull. His skin was of the kind that reddens and does not tan. It had a dry flaky look and his neat little nose was dusted with freckles. He was clean shaven and had a small cleft like a dimple in his chin.

The company office was at one end of a low wooden hut which was divided into sections. The doors and windows were wide open so that what breeze came would blow through. There was a resinous smell of pine needles and sun-warmed creosote. Sunlight filtered through the tops of the trees outside and was cast into the room through the panes of glass in the windows acting together as reflectors. It caught Reid's and Calthrop's faces at unusual angles. When a small wind disturbed the trees the reflection was disrupted so that momentarily discs and half-moons of butter yellow light played on their throats and cheeks.

Each of them sat at a small square table. On Calthrop's there were two field-service telephones, in and out trays, notepads, a circular cigarette tin now used for pencils, a field service cap, revolver, holster and lanyard. On Reid's there was only a map-case, a crushed slouch hat and a paper carton of revolver cartridges. You could tell that he left the paper work to Calthrop.

He pretended they had never heard of Saxby although it seemed unlikely to me that they would not have asked Kampong Malim what I was coming to see them about. Keeping strictly to the military facts and making no mention of Turner's suspicion I told them the story of Saxby's disappearance as briefly as possible and also why we felt the obvious place to begin investigations was in Bukit Kallang.

Reid, not looking at me because he was trying to dislodge the piece of grit, said, "What kind of investigations?"

"Into the question of whether he's alive and if so, where?"

He finished rubbing the eyelid, glanced at me, looked at the paper carton of cartridges and then began to finger it, to feel the way the cartridges rolled against each other inside.

He said. "The answer's obvious, isn't it? He's dead."

"And Ah Choong?"

"Well, he must be dead too."

"In that case it's a question of how and why."

He shrugged. "Kuala Lumpur must want something to do. Why is Saxby so important? Wan Lo's never mentioned him."

He moved his hand, flicked real or imaginary dust from the carton. "Has Wan Lo ever mentioned Saxby to you, Bill?"

Calthrop said, "No, sir."

"There you are then. The chap on the spot's written him off. Why can't Delhi?"

I fell back on the line Turner and I had agreed upon. "I knew Saxby personally."

"I see. So it's really a private inquiry?"

"Partly. But there's an official side to it. Where can I find Wan Lo Ping?"

Reid looked at Calthrop. "He's with Mac, isn't he?"

"Yes, sir. Mac was picking him up on the way."

Reid nodded. "You won't get him today. He's out with one of my officer patrols, so there's no telling when he'll be back."

"What are you patrolling for?"

"We've been having bandit trouble," Reid said.

"Much?"

"Oh, here and there. They raided a place called Sungei Malim last night. That's where we're patrolling today. We always take along one or two of Wan Lo's men, because they know the tracks." He paused. "Can you come back tomorrow?"

Calthrop began to doodle with a pencil.

I said, "The idea was that I'd be staying for a bit. Didn't your battalion tell you?"

"I don't know. Did they, Bill?"

"I didn't quite understand it that way, sir," He was a bad, perhaps an unwilling liar.

"You'd better ring them," I suggested.

"Oh, come," Reid murmured. "We don't have to be *ordered* to show hospitality. Bill, take Major Brent up to the house and make him as comfortable as you can, not that we can offer him G.H.Q. amenities."

Calthrop blushed slightly. The interview had been rehearsed and "G.H.Q. amenities" was the pay-off line.

"Not," Reid said, standing as soon as Calthrop and I were on our feet, "that we haven't made ourselves comfortable as these things go in Bukit Kallang. Eh, Bill?"

Calthrop's blush deepened. He reached for his cap.

"We manage to sort it out, sir."

*

The company was camped on the lower slopes of a forested hill. A narrow, metalled lane came up from the main road in a series of slow S-bends so that between the curves there were sloping triangular areas of ground. In these, before the war, the forestry commission had built huts to house labour for a project the war then forced them to abandon. The tree-trunks stood straight, bare and tall, but their top branches interlocked and hid the place from aerial reconnaissance. The Japanese and now Reid found it an ideal situation.

An hour before, turning off the main road into the lane a few hundred yards short of the town and directed by a military sign, I had come first to the check point that sealed the whole company area off from general traffic, and there I had shown my identity card to an armed sentry and driven on slowly, passing a transport harbour first. The low wooden hut in which my first meeting with Reid and Calthrop had taken place was at the highest point of the camp but the lane continued past it up the hill.

I drove along it now with Calthrop in the seat next to me. He took out a flat tin of cigarettes and offered me one. It may have been a peace overture because when I told him I wouldn't smoke for the moment he stuck a cigarette in the corner of his mouth and snapped the tin shut very ungraciously as if he had been rebuffed. The effect was spoiled by his discovery that he had left his lighter behind. I lent him my own lighter. It was gold, the gift of my battalion when they went back into Burma.

The lane came abruptly to an end, turning between a gap in high rhododendron bushes into a gravel drive. The drive sloped upwards, flanked by rough, weed-tossed grass which must once have been lawn. The house faced us, square, rather ugly, its red roof like a hat several sizes too large for it. The walls were stuccoed, washed with a cream distemper that had gone dirty yellow. The porch stuck out several feet from the front supported by round stone pillars. The upper storey of the porch was timbered to form a deep rectangular veranda and above it a subsidiary roof extended from the main roof.

On the left, as you faced the house, there was a garage attached to it by a high wall in which there was a wooden gate.

The whole was backed by the upward sweeping height of the hill.

It was when I had driven the jeep to a stop under the porch and looked to my right across the garden that I saw how high and open the place was. The jungle-covered hills stretched away to the horizon like a sea that had been petrified at a moment of turbulent motion. The green hills faded distantly to blue and violet. A soft breeze, wood-warmed and scented, came whispering in from the west.

Calthrop said, "You can see the Malacca Straits sometimes, sir, but a clear morning's best."

The interior struck dark and cool and was permeated by the smell of ripe, squashed fruit. It was a smell I associated with the presence of Japanese troops, from there having been, perhaps, ripe fruit nearby when I first saw them in Burma.

Calthrop said I would find the ante-room upstairs. He went through an archway into what looked like the mess and disappeared from sight calling for someone named Prabhu Singh. The hall was square and empty. The walls were whitewashed, the floor was made of stone. I climbed the stairs which took two turns. Built round the well of the stairs on the first floor was a large room open to the elements at the front where it extended above the porch in the three-sided veranda. The balustrade around the stair-well was of dark-stained wood. Twin potted palms stood sentinel in Victorian brass bowls at each side of the stair head. The uncarpeted floorboards were scratched, the walls like those below bare and whitewashed but a yellowing, large-scale map of Malaya shiny with varnish and stretched between black rods relieved their monotony. There was an assortment of ill-matched easy chairs, sofas, hard chairs, and coffee-tables. From the high ceiling two three-bladed fans were suspended. I found a panel of switches and set them both revolving.

There were voices below, one of them Calthrop's. In stilted but adequate Urdu he was telling Prabhu Singh to unload the jeep and bring the stuff up to the empty room next to Lieutenant

Holmes Sahib's room. I went on to the veranda, an island of blue shadow above the sunlit garden, and listened to the soft grating sound of Prabhu Singh's plimsolls on the gravel.

Calthrop's heavy booted footsteps came up the stairs.

"I'll show you your room, sir."

The room was hot and dark. He had some difficulty with the shutters. I turned the ceiling fan on. Here again the walls were bare and whitewashed, the floor-boards uncovered. There was a pedestal washbasin in one corner with a spotted mirror above it. The room was much larger than I should find comfortable. It looked on to the garage at the side of the house and we had entered it directly from the veranda room through the middle of three doors. Calthrop said my room was next to the bathroom and so I deduced that it lay between the bathroom and Lieutenant Holmes's room, whoever Holmes might be. On the other side of the veranda room there were three more doors; one no doubt led to Reid's room, one to Calthrop's, and the other to Mac's, who was out on patrol.

"Prabhu Singh's bringing your stuff up, sir."

"Thank you. Who's Prabhu Singh?"

"Lieutenant Holmes's orderly, sir."

"Will he be looking after me generally?"

"Yes, sir. I'll show you the ablution bandobast, shall I?"

"Don't bother. I'll find it. Did the Japanese use this house?"

"Yes, sir. It once belonged to a Chink but they cut his head off." He went out, leaned over the stair-well and shouted to Prabhu Singh to get on with it.

"There's no need to wait," I told him.

"Well, if it's all right, sir. I've got some stuff to clear up."

Presently I heard his footsteps on the stone floor below. I stood alone in the empty room and waited for Prabhu Singh.

*

Prabhu Singh had a face pitted from smallpox, bright brown lascivious eyes and teeth stained red with betel juice.

I helped him to finish putting up the camp-bed and to unstrap and open out my bedroll which contained not only sheets, blankets, mosquito-net, but also my spare clothes and the *kris*. He mistook the stones in the handle for real jewels and handled it with great respect. My status leapt upwards. He brought a coffee-table in from the ante-room to put by the bedside and promised to make some arrangements for my clothes. My spare uniform although clean was limp and creased. He said he would get one of the Chinese to run an iron over it while I had a shower.

"You have some Chinese?"

He said there were three, a woman and two men, but they were confined to the kitchen. The major sahib only allowed the company's own orderlies and the mess staff the freedom of the house. The Chinese lived in the compound at the back. The woman was old and fat and boasted of having been raped by the Japanese, but Prabhu Singh thought no man would ever lie with her, she was too ugly. She would be ugly even in the dark, even to a drunken man.

He had reverted from his army English into Mahratti. I answered him in it, suggesting to him that perhaps she was not ugly to a Japanese. He wagged his head from side to side and insisted that she was ugly to all men, that some Chinese women were beautiful and if he could tell when a Chinese woman was beautiful then he could tell when one was ugly.

"But does she iron well?" I reminded him.

Yes, she ironed very well, although she was very disagreeable and would complain in a high-pitched voice in a language he could not understand and he would have to shout at her and tell her in Mahratti that she was as ugly as a pig with its face on its backside and after they had shouted at each other for a long time she would iron the sahib's trousers.

"Don't let her forget the jacket," I said.

No, he wouldn't let her forget the jacket. But she would iron the trousers first. He had seen her iron trousers and could tell that when she ironed them she was thinking of what was going to be inside them, not that she would ever have much chance of enjoying what was inside them, but she ironed them like this: and he put on his face an expression of imbecile ecstasy.

I assumed Prabhu Singh and the Chinese laundress were engaged in some kind of abusive flirtation based on a mutual fascinated repulsion. Having bathed and changed and drunk the tea Prabhu Singh served me, I went into the veranda room, sat for a while, studied the map of Malaya and searched out Singaputan. To get there I would need to go part of the way back to Kuala Lumpur and then come north again but on a road which lay to the east of the rolling range of hills.

*

They returned just after it got dark, Reid, Calthrop, and a young man I had not met who turned out to be Holmes. They flooded the veranda .room with the glare of unshaded light bulbs reclaiming it in manly solidarity from the velvet shadows in which I had sat alone listening nostalgically for the sound of ceremonial gongs.

Holmes banged doors, yelled for his orderly. He was a big, clumsy youth with a pink fleshy face, and a penetrating voice. He moved about the house insulated from its atmosphere by his own noise. Calthrop was the first to finish bathing and changing. When Holmes joined us Reid was still in his room.

The telephone rang in the hall downstairs.

"I'll cope," Holmes shouted. "It might be Mac."

He went down the stairs two at a time. Presently he came back to the second bend.

"It's Sergeant Hamsher at the police station, Bill. He's had a call from Mac."

Reid's door had opened.

"I've got Hamsher on the line, sir," Holmes repeated for him. "Mac called him a few minutes ago from the police post at Sungei Malim. They've dropped a bandit and Hamsher's sending the beef wagon. Mac's asking for a thirty-hundred-weight to bring the patrol in."

Reid said to Calthrop, "Who's duty V.C.O.?"

"Rajendra Singh."

"Right, tell Hamsher to let Mac know the truck's laid on. Then get through to Rajendra Singh and tell him to get cracking."

"Right, sir."

"Does Mac report any casualties?"

"No, sir."

Reid nodded, came to join us. His attention was drawn by Calthrop to the bottle of Scotch I had presented to the mess. He thanked me civilly and asked if I had settled in comfortably. Holmes came back. He said he had warned the kitchen Mac would be in for dinner.

"He'll be an hour," Reid said, "we'd better not wait for him." He was sitting with his back to the veranda rail. Now he turned his head and looked out into the dark garden, a gesture with which he appeared to isolate himself from us.

Holmes said, "Prabhu Singh says you speak Mahratti, sir."

"Yes. I found him very entertaining in it."

"He says you've got a dagger covered in precious stones."

"They're not precious, I'm afraid. It's an ornamental *kris*."

Calthrop said, "That's a Malayan weapon, isn't it?"

"Yes. I bought it in Singapore."

Holmes tried to catch Calthrop's eye. All I needed now was a Japanese sword, one purchased in a bazaar as distinct from one taken in the field.

I said to Holmes, "What's a beef wagon?"

"That's what we call Sergeant Hamsher's fifteen-hundred-weight when we use it to collect dead bodies, sir."

"It sounds as if you use it a lot."

"Only a couple of times before tonight, sir."

"Bandits?"

"One of 'em. The other was a Chink called Cheong Poh Kwee that got himself done about two weeks ago."

"Done by whom?"

"Someone with a grudge, I suppose, sir. The Chink was much too pally with the Japs, they say."

117

"Is Hamsher a military policeman?"

"Yes, sir. The civil police made themselves scarce when the Jap pulled out. And no wonder, the population took a beating from them during the occupation. They were mostly Sikhs. They used to help the Kempetai work prisoners over in the jail here."

Reid leaned into the group. He put down his glass. "We won't wait for Mac."

In the hall downstairs an open archway on the right led directly into the mess: a large bare room with a stone floor and white walls. A ceiling fan revolved above the makeshift trestle-table but the room was lighted by hurricane lanterns, three on the table itself and two on a side table near the door that led to the kitchen. No explanation of the absence of electric light was given but after a moment or two I saw that the lights had been in the form of wall brackets, since dismantled. There were jagged holes in the plaster with bits of insulated wire poking through.

The meal was served by Reid's mess-waiter, a squat brown-skinned man with mongoloid cheekbones who padded round the table in plimsolls. From where I sat on Reid's right hand I could see into the kitchen. There was electric light there, glistening on the edge of the white-enamelled refrigerator. A Chinese boy wearing cotton singlet and khaki shorts was helping with plates and dishes.

Reid sat at the head of the table facing the open archway into the entrance hall. Calthrop was on his left hand opposite me, and next to him sat Holmes. There was a place laid on my right and one at the other end of the table opposite Reid. Seeing it reminded me that apart from Mac who had yet to come there must be a fifth member of the mess if Reid's company had its full complement of three platoons and each was commanded by a King's commissioned officer.

When the soup was in front of us Reid turned towards me and said, "Don't let it embarrass you but this company always says grace when it messes on its own. We used to find it helped."

118

He inclined his head slightly and said, in a low clear voice, "You have walked with us in the valley and stood with us on the hill. We ask for Your blessing on the living and for Your mercy on the dead, amen."

His spoon was poised over the soup. Now he dipped it and carried it casually to his mouth. "It needs more salt," he said and pushed the salt-cellar towards me.

"Did Hamsher say whether Wan Lo Ping identified the body?" he asked Holmes.

"No, sir."

I passed the salt back and drank soup with my left hand. The waiter came back to clear away the soup plates. On his last journey he removed the knife, fork, and spoons from the other end of the table.

Reid said, "As you see we're an officer short, we lay a place for him, the one that's gone." He looked at me. "His name was Ballister. You don't replace men like Ballister." I made a gesture intended to be non-committal. "You don't replace men like Ballister. All you get's a reserve or a substitute." He turned to Calthrop. "Does Rajendra Singh know yet about this chap Sutton who's supposed to be coming?"

"Yes. I told him today, sir."

"Did he say anything?"

"He said he once knew a Colonel Sutton and wondered whether this would be his son."

Holmes butted in. "It's the first thing Rajendra'll ask him when he gets here and he'll probably have to say his old man's a draper in Purley. Mac's Jemadar's never really forgiven him for not being the grandson of a Lieutenant MacAndrews who went bats in the Khyber Pass. Indian soldiers are fearful bloody snobs." He looked across at me. "Don't you agree, sir? Mind you," he went on before I had time to answer, "show me thirty pasty-faced erks from Surrey or Middlesex and thirty black-faced beggars from Rajputana I'd choose the Rajputs any day when it comes to a scrap. Wouldn't you, sir?"

"I suppose it's a question of what you're used to."

He winked at Calthrop, became reminiscent over the stew; told me about "the old man, the old Jap-Yap, the day they pasted 'em in Shwebo, the day they caught 'em with their pants down in the *chaung*, the night Mac had it with the Burmese bint behind the pagoda". Calthrop contributed nothing except an occasional wandering smile. In Calthrop a capacity for holding his own council was noticeable right from the beginning.

The waiter served sliced tinned peaches with what Holmes called the old milk evap.

"Ballister was killed, was he?" I asked Reid.

The question created a kind of vacuum. Eventually Reid said, "You could call it that. My officers came through the last campaign in Burma with no more than a scratch. But we reckoned without the bloody intelligence. When we came ashore in Malaya and nobody firing, mark you, nobody slinging the muck at you, we found we reckoned without them. They landed Ballister's platoon on a sandbank. He was leading the way, wading ashore, weighed down with equipment. When he got to the other side of the sandbank he sank like a stone."

"Like a stone," he repeated presently. "Yes, that's hard to forgive. Drowned. A soldier should bleed."

I caught Calthrop's eye, not intentionally but, looking in his direction casually, found him watching me.

Holmes said, "That's Mac, isn't it? Wasn't that the truck?"

We listened. Down the hill the gears of a lorry were shifted. Reid looked at his watch.

"He's moved. It's barely fifty minutes."

He shouted towards the kitchen. The mess-waiter looked in, glanced at our plates to see what was wrong.

"MacAndrews Sahib has returned," Reid told him in Urdu.

The waiter went back into the kitchen calling for Mac's orderly. The lorry, from the sound of it, had reached the end of the lane. A door slammed. The engine revved. The lorry was being reversed and driven away. When the sound had faded we could hear heavy ammunition boots crunching on the gravel.

Holmes said, "Old Mac sounds like a herd of elephants."

"You can talk, Nick," Reid said.

Abruptly the gravel-crunching noise was succeeded by the firm resistant clang of studded boots on stone. MacAndrews appeared at the open archway and came into the lamp-lit room.

He was a stocky lad with thick curly black hair. A red weal slantwise across his forehead showed where the inner rim of his soft slouch hat had pressed all day. Slung over his right shoulder was his sten-gun. His green cotton uniform was dark with sweat, and in open disregard of anti-malaria precautions he wore it with sleeves rolled up and jacket unbuttoned to the waist. He stank of cordite and rifle oil. There was dirt on his face and a deep scratch on his left cheek painted over with iodine. From above his knees to the toes of his boots his legs were plastered with dried mud. Reid introduced us and I stood to shake hands. He steadied the gun to stop it falling forward as he extended his right arm.

Reid said, "You had a party, Mac?"

"You couldn't call it a party, sir. There was only one." His accent was gently Scottish.

"Where?"

"In the river about two miles due north of Sungei Malim."

"*In* the river?"

"Aye. He was having a bath."

"And so – ?"

"He'd got a sten-gun propped on the rock behind him. When he saw us watching him he grabbed it so I dropped him."

"Chinese?"

"Yes, sir."

"How old?"

"Oh, eighteen, nineteen."

"What did Wan Lo Ping say?"

"Said he'd never seen him before."

"Was there a camp nearby?"

"Just the place this Chink had slept. He was on his jack."

"Anything in his clothes?"

"A dollar or two. Nothing to identify him though."

"Your men all right?"

"Tails up."

"What happened to your face, Mac?"

"Thorn, sir."

"And Wan Lo Ping's boys?"

"They're all right. They don't exactly extract it but they're useful for carrying the bag."

"O.K., Mac. We'll wrap it up in the morning."

MacAndrews nodded, went to the door, looked back at Holmes.

"You're duty officer tonight aren't you, Nick?"

"That's it."

"Is the green in my room?"

Holmes laughed. "You'll find it there."

"Everything as usual then?" Mac's eyes flicked in my direction.

Reid said, "Why not? You'd better get a move on." He touched my arm. "Come upstairs and have a drink if you're finished, Brent. The boys have a few chores, not business, but we take our pleasures just as seriously."

I followed him into the hall. From the mess came a loud, suddenly suppressed laugh.

Upstairs Reid said, "I'll join you in a minute." He went to MacAndrews' door, tapped and went in.

"Mac – " he began, but I heard no more. He came out presently and sat near me at the drinks table. Footsteps crunched on the gravel, fading quickly.

"I'll fill your glass," Reid said when he returned. "Which was it?"

"That one, I think."

Mac came out of his bedroom whistling Colonel Bogey. He crossed to the bathroom. That end of the veranda room behind the well of the stairs was in shadow. Below, Calthrop's voice reached us directing an activity amongst the servants the nature of which I could not fathom. From the bathroom came a steady hiss of water.

Reid was leaning forward in his chair, his arms supported by his knees which were spread. He held his glass between them in both hands. He said, "Well, what do you think of them?"

"Think of them?"

"My officers."

"They seem able enough."

"Oh, they're that. More than that, though. They've been through it together. It makes a difference." He paused to drink and then resumed the leaning position. "Now I make concessions. You understand."

I was not sure that I did, but I nodded. His eyes had lost their dullness. They were, I saw, directed at my right hand.

He jerked his head. "Have you hurt it?"

"It's a bit stiff."

"Accident?"

"That's it."

He leaned back, considered me in silence for a bit, quite unembarrassed to be watched doing so. "There's more in you than meets the eye, isn't there? Are you Field Security?"

"No."

"What are you then?"

"I work in Welfare."

He frowned. "Welfare?" and then, "What's Welfare got to do with this chap Saxby?"

"Nothing. I happen to be an old friend of his. So I was chosen for the job."

"I see. I don't believe a word you say of course. You don't look like a chap who's in Welfare."

"You thought I did this afternoon. And one of your officers has been taking the piss most of the evening. Not that it bothers me."

"No," he said. "I saw that it didn't. It's what made me wonder. And that hand of yours, that's not the result of writer's cramp, is it?"

"No. Of an accident." I changed the subject. "Has Wan Lo Ping never mentioned Saxby?"

123

"Not to me."

"And you didn't send him off on patrol just to muck me about a bit?"

Reid smiled. "I might have done if I'd known," he admitted. "But he'd already gone when battalion rang and told us about you."

"But they mentioned Saxby surely?"

"Yes. All right. They mentioned Saxby. We were pulling your leg to see how you took it. But there's no real harm in us, Brent. You see that, I think. You're really one of us, aren't you? You don't mind sitting at table with a ghost, do you? You don't really think it's odd to say grace. You know what things are about, you know what bends us, what's important and what isn't. You've been through it too." He narrowed his eyes a bit. "You'll like Wan Lo. He's no more than a kid but he's got the stuff. I hope he's not suspected of anything."

"He isn't."

"I thought he might be, by you, or rather by Kuala Lumpur. Take it from me, if Wan Lo says Saxby just disappeared then that's what he did, and if Wan Lo says Saxby's dead then he likely is. You see. It'll be as I say. You're wasting your time, but forget that, don't bother about that. You're welcome to waste it here."

The irritation started up again in his left eye. Calthrop came up to join us and as he arrived at the head of the stairs Mac-Andrews came out of the bathroom wearing a flamboyant green dressing-gown of shot silk, and sandals on his bare feet.

"Aren't you eating, Mac?" Reid asked him.

"I've told 'em to send me up a sandwich. I'll have some of that Scotch. Who's been clever?"

"Our guest."

He nodded at me and poured himself a glass. Sipping it he looked up at Calthrop. "Aren't you going to get comfortable, Bill?"

Reid said, "You might as well."

Calthrop left us.

In this light MacAndrews looked younger, slighter. The loosely cut sleeves of the gown fell away to his elbows and revealed slender forearms. The long iodine painted scratch on his now clean cheek emphasized his face's immaturity. He could not have been more than twenty. The mess waiter came up with his plate of sandwiches. He sat munching them.

Calthrop came back wearing a dressing-gown identical in cut to MacAndrews', but bright yellow. He said to MacAndrews, "Coming down?" and avoided looking at me.

MacAndrews stuffed the last bit of sandwich into his mouth and got out of his chair. "Aye. You'll be along, sir?" he asked Reid.

"Yes, Mac. We'll both be along."

Green and yellow they disappeared together round the bend of the stairs. Reid was watching me to see how I was taking it.

"We'll have another whisky, shall we?" He poured carefully, sipped his own drink and then got up. He went to his room. When he came out he had a scarlet gown over his arm and a torch in his hand. He came back to the table, picked up his glass, drained it, set it down. He used liquor as casually as a clothes-brush.

He held the dressing-gown up a little and said, "You're my guest tonight so you're entitled to wear this. But I expect you'd rather wait a bit before you put it on."

"Yes," I said. "I think I should."

"I'll lead the way then. There's not far to go."

*

He switched the torch on when we turned into the pitch black at the side of the house. Its unsteady circular beam fell on the gate in the wall connecting house to garage. He opened the gate, went through and stood aside to let me pass.

"You've not been in the back garden have you?"

"No."

I could see nothing at first. But when I looked up there was the outline of the high hill against the dark blue sky. It was a clear night and the stars looked very close. We were walking on gravel along the side of what I took to be the servants' compound. There was a spicy smell of cooking.

When the compound wall was behind us I felt underfoot the soft springiness of turf. In the darkness, although distinguishing nothing, I was aware of openness and a hundred yards away there were lights.

"The Chinese," Reid said, walking towards them slowly, "call this the garden of madness because it's where they used to lose their heads during the occupation. What do you think of that for a sense of humour? They say the first victim was the man who lived here. They stuck his head on a pole and made the population queue up to see it. The garden's supposed to be haunted now but there's no moon tonight and they say you can't see the ghosts except when the moon's full."

"Then we haven't come to see the ghosts?"

"No, not the ghosts."

I stopped because I had heard the tinny, vibrating sound of Chinese gongs.

"It's only the gramophone," he said. "They're playing it in the pavilion. Come on. Let's see what you think of it."

MacAndrews and Calthrop were sitting on the veranda. Two hurricane lanterns were suspended from the roof but cast only a pale gleam. There was a window facing us and light in the room behind it. As Reid motioned me up the steps Calthrop and MacAndrews rose. The gramophone was on the floor.

MacAndrews said, "Greetings and welcome to our humble pavilion, sir."

He had his hands tucked into the folds of his sleeves and bowed three times mandarin fashion. I bowed back once, gravely, mystified but oddly pleased, anticipation of some unexpected diversion blowing faintly at the back of my neck.

"If His Excellency pleases, this scrofulous undeserving chair is at the disposal of his exquisite backside."

"Can't I see inside first?"

Reid said, "I'll show you. It's something, I tell you."

He pushed the wall on the left of the window. Light developed rectangularly as a door opened inwards: yellow light shining on scarlet lacquer. I followed him through into the ante-room. It was lit by an old-fashioned oil-lamp with a tall glass funnel which was set on a bamboo table under the window. The green lacquer on the walls shone like satin and in each of them a closed scarlet door guarded mysteries yet to be discovered. Four wicker chairs were set out in the shape of a half-moon as if in preparation for an entertainment and, beside them, on the mosaic floor, red, green, and yellow cushions.

He said, "It's hot, isn't it? We'd better prop the doors open."

He did so with bricks kept there for that purpose, explaining and demonstrating how one of the doors only opened inwards and the other outwards. Dusting his hands he said, "Now I'll show you the rest."

He went on to the veranda and came back with a hurricane lantern. He opened the first of the red doors and holding the lantern high led the way in. Walls and ceiling were painted with gold and its particles glittered like frost. Cool tiles of creamy yellow paved the floor and on these, in one corner, was laid a white sheeted mattress with fine woven muslin suspended from a ring in the ceiling enclosing it in a gossamer bell. A four-sided screen, head high and covered in yellow silk that matched Calthrop's gown, stood opposite the bed, intimate, revelational. In another corner there was a gold lacquered chest holding a carafe of water and a tumbler.

Reid was watching me. He moistened his lips. "We call it the golden room. I'll show you the other two."

As he lowered the lantern the shadow of the screen leapt up the wall and expanded on the ceiling there to be lost in the darkness we left behind. We crossed the ante-room diagonally. He opened the next red door, raised the lantern high again so that the shadow, surprised, ran from where it lay on the ceiling and hid behind a screen similar to the one next door: but this screen was covered in green silk that matched the green walls and ceiling, the green tiles of the floor. Here, too, there was a mattress, a chest, a carafe of water.

"The green room?"

"Jade."

Reid was studying me carefully, his head tilted a bit to one side. In the light from the lantern I saw that his face was covered in minute beads of perspiration.

"I'll show you the other room."

I said. "The other room's red, isn't it?"

He smiled. "Now, how did you guess? But scarlet. Call it scarlet."

The scarlet room was the same in every detail, but Reid moved the lantern from side to side as if there were more to see, as if I should take a special interest in it. There was in this room a subtly elusive scent that reminded me of crushed rose petals, soft and delicate, yet clinging.

"You can see the sunset from the window," he said, "and you can watch it rise from the golden room. There's a sort of bathroom over there."

He led the way past the screen and pushed a panel which opening inwards revealed a shower, a pedestal basin, a mirror, and a water closet. There were clean towels and soap.

"There's another one on the other side for the green and gold room but this one's private. There's everything you could want."

There was a renewed crash of gongs.

"Or rather, there will be. Come on. It's time."

He led the way back to the veranda. The music was shrill, angular, even to my Indianized ear. On the other side of the dark garden blobs of light moved jerkily. Calthrop or Mac-Andrews, I wasn't sure which, put a glass into my hands. The liquor burned my dry lips. The music, thin as reeds, discordant, insistent, accompanied the lights on their journey towards the pavilion.

My arm was touched and Reid said, "It's time to go in."

I followed him into the ante-room where Calthrop and MacAndrews were already seated. Reid indicated that I should sit on his right. He still had the scarlet gown on his arm but now he leaned over and put it on the cushions at our feet.

The oil-lamp on the table obscured the view through the narrow window: a mirror now, more than a window, reflecting the funnel of the lamp, Reid's face and my own, but, hearing the soft tap of shoes on the wooden steps and glancing from one door to the other, I saw through it a pair of almond-shaped eyes in an oval, chalk-white face.

The girl came to the opening of the right-hand door and stood for a few seconds; doll-like, the skirt of her long green brocade dress gathered infinitesimally between the delicately curved finger and thumb of each of her hands which rested close together a few inches above her knees. Her arms were slender, white, bare to the shoulder, her face covered thickly with dead white powder except where patches of rouge showed prominently on her cheekbones. Her dark brows were drawn together in a frown but this was denied by the dimpled corners of her bright red lips. Her eyes were cast down, and her body, encased stiffly in the brocade, was subtly bent to prove its flexibility, its warmth and softness, so that in one economical attitude she excitingly communicated knowledge, experience and modesty. The front panel of the skirt was an inch or two higher than the back and separated from it by a knee-high slit on either side. Her tiny feet were strapped into low-heeled green satin shoes with rounded toes.

Still holding the skirt between fingers and thumbs she came a few steps into the room.

Reid said, "This is Green Lotus."

She dipped her body in a gesture half bow, half curtsy; first towards Reid and myself, then to Calthrop and finally to MacAndrews for whom she stayed down noticeably longer as though in recognition that he wore her colour. Her straight black hair was coiled loosely in the nape of her neck outside the high mandarin collar. Rising, she moved to the other side of the table by the window.

Reid said, "Yellow Blossom."

The girl who entered next wore a dress of yellow satin embroidered in gold and yellow thread. Like Green Lotus's dress it reached to her ankles and to her neck and left her arms bare to the shoulder. The palms of her hands as well as her cheeks were rouged. She displayed them as she made obeisance, first to Reid and myself again, then to MacAndrews, lastly to Calthrop. Yellow Blossom's hair was cut short and fringed her forehead. Her black, tight-skinned eyes were bright and liquid and through them, in her gestures, in the way she looked from one to the other of us and at the room as if she had never seen it before, she filled you with a sense of her own shining, happy wonder.

She went now to stand next to her colleague and I watched the doorway for the appearance of the third girl. The room was heavy with heat and scent.

*

She came. The yellow and green of Calthrop's and Mac-Andrews' dressing-gowns shimmered as they got to their feet. I rose instinctively to mine.

The light from the oil-lamp gilded her right cheek, gleamed on her right shoulder and shone on her soft black hair. She did not pause on the threshhold but came directly in, carrying her handbag on her left arm, her hands clasped lightly in front of her. Her dress of crimson shantung silk was calf-length but cut high to a mandarin collar. Her feet were arched into crimson high-heeled court shoes and her slender rounded legs had a smooth absorbent look. She was wearing one of her pairs of stockings. I did not know it then but she was in her European mood. Reid and his officers knew nothing of these moods. As yet they were undiscovered: blank charts which I would fill in.

She gave me the briefest of glances, smiled at MacAndrews and Calthrop, gave her attention to Reid. The two boys treated her with deference, Reid with the ease of one equal for another. He said, "This is Major Brent who's staying with us for a day or two. Brent, I'd like you to meet Madame Chang."

We shook hands. She did not ask my Christian name. He had not given me hers. Her smile was warm and friendly: no more than that. I offered her a cigarette which she took with a gesture only faintly Eurasian. Her nails extended sufficiently beyond the tips of her fingers to excite the senses in anticipation of the feel of them on your bare skin. They were lacquered evenly in a colour complementary to the colour of her dress. The same tone existed in the lipstick that had been applied meticulously, richly but not over-generously, and no attempt had been made to alter the shape of her full lips. It was only in the area of her eyes that a note of artifice had been deliberately introduced. A line drawn skilfully beneath the lower lids and outwards towards the edges widened them, counterbalanced their tendency to slant upwards. Pencil subtly changed the shape of her brows. Tracing their original curve with your eyes concern grew to do likewise with your finger-tips.

She had put the cigarette into a short jade holder which she now held in her right hand, supporting the elbow with her cupped left hand, bending back slightly from the waist, chin high.

The three of us went out on to the veranda where Reid had offered to mix drinks. On her way she said a few words to Calthrop. MacAndrews was winding the gramophone and changing the record. She said nothing to her two girls and for a fleeting second, seeing how they effaced themselves, half diffidently, half envious perhaps of her easy western manners, I was a bit annoyed with her. As Reid began to pour she said, "Don't let the boys give them too much to drink, Teddy."

"They like it," he said.

"I know, but they feel awful next day."

"Well, you're the boss, Teena."

I imagined it spelt Tina.

A quickstep started up scratchily inside.

Reid called, "Bill, Mac. Drinks."

But the girls came first, laughing, fluttering, the rouge on their cheeks like high flushes of excitement.

"Gin and lem-on," they chanted as Bill and Mac appeared. "Gin and ol-ange. Whis Kee So Da."

Mac's hair was tousled. He caught Green Lotus from behind, clasped his arms round her waist.

"Belt up, Green Lotus," he said. "Dance first, gin later."

She beat at his arms with her tiny white hands. Removing one he twisted her round and she was still.

"All right," he said, "say it, say it and you can have it."

"Gin and ol-ange."

"Again."

"Gin and ol-ange."

"Now my name."

"Mac."

He shook her gently from side to side.

"No. All of it."

"Mac-and-lews."

"What?"

"Mac-and-lews. Lieutenant Mac-and-lews." Pointing at each of us she said, "Captain Calth-lop, Major Leid, Lieutenant Mac-and-lews, Major –"

"Brent," MacAndrews prompted.

"Major Blent."

"Now. What are you going to have?"

"I am going to have a gin and ol-ange."

He released her. When she had sipped and choked and had her back slapped she leant over and kissed him on his scratched cheek, then let herself be led inside to dance, and Mac called Bill and Yellow Blossom to join them.

Reid said, "Will you dance, Teena?"

She was leaning against one of the carved dragons. She nodded, was guided by him past the drinks table where she set down her glass and stubbed out her cigarette. I perched myself on the veranda rail. Presently the music began again: a foxtrot. The garden was suddenly incandescent. Thunder rumbled. A cool draught of air swayed the hurricane lanterns and then was gone leaving behind it an increased humidity. I stared up into the sky waiting for the next jagged blue-white streak. The stars had disappeared. The foxtrot ended. One of the girls was laughing. I waited for Reid and Teena to come back but a quickstep was put on and half-way through it Reid came out alone with the red gown over his arm.

He said, "I'm going now, unless of course *you* don't want to stay."

I said, "You're very hospitable."

The garden glowed behind us. Thunder rumbled at once. Reid's mouth had opened but his words were lost.

I inclined my head. "I'm sorry, I missed –"

He held the dressing-gown out. I took it.

"I'll see what I can do about Wan Lo Ping in the morning," he said.

"Thank you, I'd forgotten him."

"Good night, then."

I said good night. He lowered his head, raised a hand in an abrupt gesture of farewell and went down the steps.

I watched him pass beyond the arc of light shed from the pavilion. A few moments later the third flash came showing him as a blue-grey spectre thrown by the white fire of the lightning.

The quickstep came to its end, was followed by a waltz. I watched the lightning and waited for Teena.

3

THE RAIN CAME WITH COOL SPURTS OF AIR AND spray, drove me from the edge of the veranda, drummed on the roof. Calthrop coming out had to raise his voice to make himself heard.

"The lanterns," he repeated and pointed at them.

I took one down while he took the other. The music had stopped. Holding one lantern he held out his hand.

"It's Mac's," he said, taking the other lantern.

I followed him inside. The ante-room was deserted. He crossed the mosaic floor to the jade room, put the lantern down outside the door and knocked. "Your lantern, Mac," he called.

The door of his own room opened. Yellow Blossom peeped out but seeing me with him shrank back into the darkness.

Calthrop said, "Anything you want, sir?"

"A lantern?"

"It's already in there."

He looked at the dressing-gown over my arm.

"Help yourself to drinks, won't you, sir? Can I leave you to turn the lamp down in here?"

"Of course."

"We leave it low."

The door of the jade room opened. With a bare arm Mac reached down for the lantern. He winked at us and went back inside.

Calthrop said, "The duty officer takes the girls back about half-past five, sir."

"Do they live in Bukit Kallang?"

"Yes, sir."

"All together?"

134

"Yes, sir. Teena Chang's got a bungalow there. It belongs to her, I think. Anyway, she's the boss." He lowered his voice further. "She's a stickler over the health angle, sir. There's nothing to worry about."

"Thanks. Don't let me keep you."

He said good night.

I put the gown on a chair and went back to the veranda to fetch the drinks tray in. I found two clean glasses, mixed drinks and then went to the door of the scarlet room with one of the glasses. I knocked and opened it.

"I've brought you a drink. I hope it's right. Gin and lemon."

There must have been a scarlet silk dressing-gown in the chest or behind the screen because this is what she now wore. She was sitting on cushions in front of the chest rubbing cream into her face. A mirror was propped up with the lantern placed strategically a bit to one side of it. I carried the glass over. She smiled up at me and took it.

She said, "Thank you. You've caught me."

"Shall I come back presently?"

"Only if that's what you'd prefer."

"No. I'll bring my drink in."

The rain had lessened but came down steadily. I took away the bricks from the doors, letting them swing to on their springs, lowered the oil-lamp until a faint blue-yellow flame rose from the wick. I went back to the scarlet room.

"Could you raise the window?" she said. "It's a bit stuck."

Above it there was a narrow grill. It was a sash window and there were shutters folded back against the walls. The veranda, extending all round the pavilion, protected us from driving rain. I managed to shift the window higher. Then we toasted each other silently. She had wiped the cream from her face and with it all traces of make-up. She had nothing to fear from exposing her natural complexion.

I went to the mattress, loosened the mosquito net and sat down. Her shadow moved on the wall.

"What did you mean I'd caught you?"

"Oh." She twisted further towards me and held a bare ankle in one hand. "I was doing repairs." She inclined her head to look in the mirror. "Shall I go on?"

"No. Don't go on."

She continued looking in the mirror for three or four seconds before turning her head towards me again.

"What is your first name?"

"Tom."

She repeated it, lingering over the vowel. She raised her chin a fraction. "Sometimes Tommy?"

"Sometimes."

She smiled gravely, raised her glass.

We drank again, our eyes unmoving from each other until lowering her glass to her lap she let her eyelids fall, but only to raise them almost at once and look at me again with a kind of frankness and a kind of modesty: neither exactly distinguishable from the other.

"Would you like to get comfortable?" she asked.

"I will in a minute. I've left my dressing-gown outside."

"I'll get it for you."

"No, it's dark and I know which chair I left it on. Shall I get you another drink?"

She shook her head.

"Not unless you want one too."

She took my empty glass and put it on the chest. Her own was still half-full.

When I returned with the gown over my arm she was in the shower cubicle running water into the hand-basin. She came out from behind the screen. Without her shoes she looked younger, childlike.

"There's a lamp in there," she said. "I've lighted it for you."

She went back to the chest and sat down on the cushions. As I left her she began to comb her hair and when I returned wearing the dressing-gown she still sat there, cooling herself with a palm-leaf fan.

I knelt behind her, lowered my head and pressed my lips to

the back of her neck, parting the hair first to find the soft warm skin. The fan moved to and fro gentling the air on my cheeks. My fingers found the cord of her gown, eased it out of its slack knot. My thumbs touched the base of each firm, bare breast as I raised my hands to discover them. In her hair was the smell of rose-petals.

I slipped the gown from her shoulders, leaned towards her again and saw her reflection in the mirror. Her nipples were red, tinged with rouge, her breasts and stomach powdered lightly.

Our eyes met and she smiled.

"Do I please you, Tommy?"

"Yes, Teena."

She twisted round slowly and placed her hands one on each side of the collar of my gown but with my left hand I covered the hand that lay on my right shoulder, knowing her purpose. A tiny frown of perplexity appeared above the bridge of her nose and she raised her eyes to look at me, taking her free hand from the collar and placing it on my chest. She twisted her fingers into the hair, watching me the while.

*

The rain had stopped. Echoes of it lingered in the drops that fell from the roof into puddles. I felt her sit up in the close darkness and presently swift little currents of cool air moved to and fro above me. I sought and found her waist, her shoulder blade, her arm and finally her wrist, pulled it closer to me, directed the palm-leaf fan until it fluttered just above my forehead.

"Teena?"

"Yes?"

"I'd like a cigarette."

"Where are they?"

"In my jacket behind the screen."

I helped her make an opening in the net. In a moment the room came up slowly like the auditorium of a theatre. She straightened up from the lantern, walked naked, barefooted behind the screen and returned with the jacket.

"The left pocket. There's a lighter there too."

Laying the jacket on the cushions in front of the chest she rejoined me inside the net, sat back on her heels, gave me the cigarettes, the lighter, an ashtray, reached again for the fan.

I lighted two and gave her one. Flat on my back, the gown open but covering arms and shoulders I watched the rhythmic movements of her hand as she cooled the air about us. The movement flowed back through her arms to her breasts.

I said, "You arrange things very well, Teena."

"Thank you."

"Where did you get the idea for the dressing-gowns?"

"The colours, you mean? The colours are for the rooms."

"No, I meant the idea of our wearing them. Is that a Chinese tradition?"

"I don't think it's Chinese."

"Well it wasn't Major Reid's idea, was it? He couldn't have thought of that."

"No, it wasn't Major Reid's idea."

The fanning changed tempo.

"Whose, then? Yours?"

"It is my idea."

"Am I asking too many questions?"

"No." She put the fan down. "But I should like another drink."

I thought she had put the fan down so that she could go for it but she made no further move. It was a command. I stubbed out the cigarette. On my knees I was close to her. She held my right shoulder.

"Why do you hide it?" she asked.

"Because it's not very pretty."

She frowned. "Were you a prisoner?"

"No. Just wounded."

She still held me. She leaned forward and kissed me on the mouth, holding my head between her hands. She said, "Silly boy. You can't wear a dressing-gown for the rest of your life."

"I might have to."

"What about your wife?"

"I'm not married."

"But when you are?"

"Perhaps I shan't be."

"Because of your shoulder?"

"Perhaps. It depends."

"What on?"

"The girl."

"A special girl?"

"No, girls, the girl."

"They might like it."

"It. Not me. Or me and not it. Me in spite of it would be different. I'd have to marry her. If I wanted to that is. It's very complicated, isn't it?"

"How will they tell?"

"Tell what?"

"What it's like if they haven't seen it."

"I'll have its picture taken and ask 'em round to look at it. Now I'll get that drink."

She called, "What kind of picture?"

"A snap'll do. Or a polyfoto. Do you know what a polyfoto is?"

"Yes."

I came back with the drinks tray. She was wrapped in her own gown and seated on the cushions.

"You've brought the whole tray but the others might want some." She cleared a space on the chest.

"They'll have to knock then. I'll put it outside before we go back to bed."

I went out for more cushions.

When we were settled she said, "You look nice in red."

"Do I? I'm glad. What would happen if I wore green tomorrow?"

"I should wear green too."

"What about Green Lotus?"

"She is only Green Lotus when she wears green."

"What's her real name, then?"

"Lily. When Mac wears the green dressing-gown it means he wants her to be Green Lotus. If he wore the yellow gown she would be Yellow Blossom."

"Supposing he wore this gown?"

"Then she would be Red Jade."

"Are you Red Jade tonight?"

"No."

"Why?"

"I am never any of these names. Tonight I am not even Madame Ho."

"What is Madame Ho?"

She said, "It is one of Mac's jokes. When he saw the three rooms he said one belonged to Madame Chin, one to Madame Cha and one to Madame Ho. *Chin cha ho* is the only bit of Chinese he knows."

"I don't even know that."

"It means very good."

"*Chin cha ho*. Very, very good?"

"Yes."

"When are you Madame Ho?"

"When I feel like it."

"And when Mac feels like it?"

She smiled. "No, no. It is just his name for me. Sometimes I feel like Madame Ho. But it is nothing to do with him. He does not even know whether I feel like Madame Ho or not."

"Lily is always Mac's girl, is she?"

"Yes, Lily is Mac's girl."

"How does she know when he's going to wear green?"

"The duty officer tells her." She shook her head to loosen the hair at the back of her neck.

"What's Yellow Blossom's name?"

"Anna is Yellow Blossom tonight. She is Bill Calthrop's girl. Nick Holmes's girl is called Suki but he is duty officer today. Duty officer has to make all the arrangements and then sleep

140

by himself in the house in a special room downstairs with the telephone at his ear." She smiled. "In case someone declares war."

"And his girl gets the night off?"

She nodded.

"Is Major Reid ever duty officer?"

"No, he is too important."

"Are you Major Reid's girl?"

"I suppose so."

"Why only suppose?"

She sipped her drink, looked at me over the edge of the glass. She said, "He only talks to me." She rested the glass on her lap and having fallen silent gave a slight shrug as an after-thought.

"What does he talk about?"

"Oh." She frowned. "The war. Old battles. These things."

"Doesn't that bore you?"

"No." She tapped ash from her cigarette. "Some men make love. Some act little plays. Some talk. I'm not bored."

"What gave you the idea of our wearing the dressing-gowns?"

"We used to bring the dressing-gowns with us and put them on our cushions. When a man picked one of them up we would know which of us he had chosen. Now they keep the gowns. That's the only difference."

"Who thought of keeping the gowns? Young MacAndrews?"

She looked at me steadily.

"No," she said, "a Japanese officer called Hakinawa."

It was an honest reply to a question that had not deserved one. Now would have been the time for the hard-luck story, rape, perhaps, compulsory service in a brothel, enforced con-cubinage; but she offered none and this seemed like honesty too. I took her hand, explored the pointed ends of her finger-nails and she did not take this as a signal that I required some form of further excitation as she might have done had she been already regretting her admission and anxious to take the first oppor-tunity of helping me forget it.

But I was anxious. I carried her hand to my chest and ran the nail of her index-finger up and down it slowly and then she leaned closer and, when I released her hand, continued to move it of her own accord. The word collaborator had written itself, invisible to the actual eye and only just distinguishable to that of the mind, in the narrow space between our bodies. I did not want it glowing there, rewriting itself in characters of fire; I did not want Saxby coming at me here. With my forefinger I traced an imaginary line from the cavity at the base of her throat down between breasts and gradually Saxby and the word collaborator melted away in the pleasurable male feeling of blood converging, flesh expanding. She leaned over and kissed me and I held her close, laughing happily because she was a mystery, an astonishment, an enigma, and in my arms.

"You're not full Chinese are you?"

She drew back her head to look at me and placed one finger on my nose. "My mother was Chinese. My father was French but his mother was Dutch."

"Then you're not Chang. You're Dupont or something like that."

"My mother was Chang. She wasn't Dupont or anything like that. Sometimes I feel I should like to be full Chinese and know a lot about China. It is when this happens that I feel like Madame Ho. Why are we talking about me again?"

"Because it's more interesting."

"For you it's more interesting, maybe. When were you wounded?"

"Last year."

"Where?"

"In Burma."

"What were you doing?"

"Ducking."

"Ducking?" She frowned, and suddenly smiled. "You're hopeless," she said.

"Yes. I know. Hopeless, hopeless."

"I'll take the drinks tray back," she said, and rose.

I returned to the mattress and waited for her.

When she came back she lowered the light and joined me, drew me towards her, slipped the gown from my shoulders and explored the nature of my disfigurement with her lips.

*

There was a man's voice saying, sir, and a hand that had nudged my hip once, now moved it again. I opened my eyes to daylight and saw Holmes. He was shaved and brushed and held the net above his head with one hand, nudged me gingerly with the other.

I lay on my stomach. The sheet came no higher than my waist. He kept his eyes fixed on mine, but as he straightened up from his kneeling position his eyes flickered down to my shoulder. He pushed the red dressing-gown through the net.

"Sorry to disturb you, sir, but it's eight o'clock."

"Thanks."

I sat up. He stood watching me through the net, pretending not to. I put the gown on, wiped the sleep from my eyes.

"Anything I can get you, sir?"

"No, thanks."

He said, "If you leave everything here Prabhu Singh'll cope with it. He's laid clean stuff out in your room."

"Have I missed breakfast?"

"We've had ours, sir. I've told the kitchen to save something."

"Thanks."

I got out of the net to tie the cord.

He said, "Major Reid'll be in his office until ten, sir. He asked me to let you know. If you want to go and see Wan Lo Ping."

"Right. I'll be there about half-nine."

Holmes waited.

"You didn't make much noise, any of you," I told him.

"You were dead off, sir."

"What time did they go?"

"Usual time, sir. About half-five."

"And Bill and Mac?"

"About six, sir. Breakfast's at 0700 and first parade at eight. I've just come off duty." He looked at his watch, coloured up a bit, nodded at my right shoulder. "Did you get that in Burma, sir?"

"Yes."

I told him I'd go over to the house presently.

When I came out of the shower cubicle he had gone. I was alone in the pavilion. I put my shoes on.

Her smell was in the room still. In the chest I found a mirror, her red silk dressing-gown, the palm-leaf fan, some cold cream, and a box of tissues. The cushions on the floor were as we left them, flattened, unresilient, with that morning after look about them. I plumped them up so that the new day should not begin without me.

I picked up jacket and trousers leaving underwear and socks for Prabhu Singh to give to the Chinese laundress, clumped out of the room in unlaced shoes. In the ante-room the chairs had been pushed to one side and piled with cushions. I stared down at the mosaic of dragons, fish, and birds and as I watched them those which felt themselves but in the corner of my eye moved their heads, flicked their tails, beat their wings, held themselves stiff and breathless when I tried to catch them at it. I shut my eyes and heard the tin rustle of scales, the miniature exhalations of fire, the green pool ripplings, the tick-tock of beak on beak. "Got you!" I said and opened my eyes again to the flat, two-dimensional surface of unbreathing fragments of cemented stone. I walked over them, pushed at the door that only opened outwards and at once screwed my face against the glare. A hundred yards away was the house. The walled compound hid the ground floor from view and apart from the higher-than-head row of windows in the bathroom the back of the house was blind upstairs. Perhaps the man who built it had wanted the pavilion to come as a surprise, a pleasure to be walked towards not dissipated by constant watching.

I went down the steps into the hot world of sun that burned

144

through the thin silk of the scarlet gown and arrived at a place in the middle of the trodden-down grass more trodden than the rest; it was the place of execution. Turning to look back at the pavilion I cried out involuntarily. I had not expected that final touch of sorcery, that gleaming, molten roof.

Behind the pavilion the hill climbed, jungle-covered and precipitous, with bare rock at its base, unscalable. Against it the pavilion looked no larger than a box, a toy, and presently I resumed my journey across the garden, turning every so often to make sure that neither my eyes nor the night had deceived me.

The turf underfoot gave way to gravel. In a few moments I was at the gate in the wall, opening it, passing through it, shutting it carefully, coming round to the front of the house to reality and the long view over the hills, the pale gleam of the Malacca straits on the horizon.

4

SERGEANT HAMSHER WHO COMMANDED THE MILITARY police detachment in Bukit Kallang was lean and tough with slim hips, broad shoulders, and mad, pale blue eyes. In another room of the police station, a two-storey stuccoed building in the centre of the town, a woman was wailing. Another woman shouted. When she shouted a man shouted back at her. They were quarrelling in Chinese. I had begun to distinguish its rhythm from Malayan speech. Outside the building the crowd still waited: curious but patient, docile. They had made way for the jeep as soon as they had sighted us.

"We were on our way to Wan Lo Ping when your message came," Reid said. "What's the grief?"

Hamsher jerked his thumb in the direction of the wailing. "Her, sir. She claims the Chink you dropped yesterday is her nephew."

"Does she now? How does she explain him having a sten-gun?"

"She doesn't know about that. I thought you'd want me to save that up, sir."

"Does anyone corroborate her story?"

"Yes, sir. There's three others with her. Her daughter for one and a man and his wife who say they're neighbours."

"Has she a husband?"

"No, sir. The Japs chopped him."

"And the boy's parents?"

"They're both dead, sir. There's only the question of what the boy was up to, as I see it."

"It wasn't a boy called Ah Choong, was it?" I asked.

Hamsher said, "No, sir. Who's Ah Choong?"

Reid broke in. "We'll tell you later. Let's get this over. Have you got Loy Boy?"

"Yes, sir. He's in there with them."

"Loy Hock Long's our interpreter," Reid told me. "He probably interpreted for the Japs too. We'll have to go into this if you don't mind. But it won't take long."

The room was low-ceilinged. Sunlight shafted in at a high angle, projected a foreshortened shadow on the floor of the unglazed barred window the shutters of which were hooked back on the inner wall. A revolving table-fan cooled our faces every few seconds, buzzing like a wasp trapped in a bottle. The papers on Hamsher's neat desk, at which Reid sat, were weighted with stones. Hamsher was smart in starched jungle-green. His webbing gaiters, belt, and holster were white, blancoed so thickly that the texture of the webbing was lost. He went to the door and opened it. The noise stopped abruptly. He was in no hurry.

"Right," he said at last, and came away leaving the door open.

A young man, immaculate in grey cotton trousers and white cotton shirt, his black hair shining with oil, appeared in the doorway.

Reid said, "This is our interpreter. Mr Loy, this is Major Brent."

I nodded. Loy Hock Long smiled and bowed elegantly from the waist.

"O.K., Loy Boy," Hamsher said, "wheel 'em in."

The woman came first. Loy Hock Long took a chair from the wall, placed it in the middle of the room, bowed to us again as though for permission, then made her sit down. She sat with slack shoulders, her gnarled, old woman's hands loosely curled, palms uppermost on her knees. Her head was canted to one side and she didn't look at us.

The daughter and the two neighbours stood with their backs to the wall. The daughter wore black trousers and a short black tunic. Her eyes were bright and liquid and reminded me of Yellow Blossom's. The man and his wife were elderly, nondescript. Having bowed to us they watched the floor at their feet.

Reid said, "Tell them we accept their claim. They can have the body to bury."

Loy Hock Long spoke at some length. The two women kept still but the man jerked his head constantly to signify his understanding of the situation. When Loy Hock Long had finished the man asked him a question.

"They bring up the question of compensation."

"Quite," Reid said.

"The woman is very poor. Her husband was beheaded. Her nephew was strong and willing. Now her daughter is her only support. There is a man in Taiping who is ready to buy her but this would bring dishonour on the house."

"What did the boy do?"

"He hired himself out to the fish merchant Cheong Poh Kwee."

"The man who was murdered?"

"Yes. And to other merchants. They say he did not mind what work he did. Even menial work."

"What does the woman do?"

"Her husband was a shopkeeper. She and her daughter run the shop. But there is little to sell and people have little money to buy."

"What sort of shop?"

"Fuel. Lamp oil, wood. The boy chopped wood."

"Tell her that we are very sorry for her misfortune."

She gave no sign that she had heard when Loy Hock Long put Reid's message into Chinese. She might have been listening, or not.

"Now ask her what her nephew was doing in the jungle."

"They say he had gone foraging."

"No. Let her speak."

"She finds it difficult."

"To speak or to say why he was in the jungle?"

148

Loy Hock Long turned to her. I fancied he said something like: Won't you, won't you? or Can't you, can't you? The man behind her interrupted and presently Loy Hock Long said, "In some of the jungle kampongs they hoard food. The boy had gone to buy rice."

"There is plenty of rice. The British Military Administration sees to that."

Loy Hock Long spoke again to the man.

"They say perhaps he had gone to buy pork. There are wild pig in the jungle."

"We know there are wild pig in the jungle. How did he expect to get wild pig? Buy it with money, or kill it? If kill it, kill it with his bare hands?"

We waited while this point was discussed at length.

"They don't know why exactly he had gone into the jungle, but he was a good boy."

"Ask them *when* he went into the jungle."

Loy Hock Long asked them.

"They say he often went into the jungle."

"Then you would have thought they knew why. Never mind. Ask them when they saw him last."

"They say the day before yesterday."

There was silence. Reid made no attempt to break it. He sought the grit in his left eye.

"All right, Sergeant," he said at last, "we'll have it now."

Hamsher went out. He came back with the sten-gun. He put the gun on the desk in front of Reid. For a moment the woman's eyes flickered up. The three witnesses looked at the ground.

"Tell them," Reid said, "that we are sorry for the misfortune of this family, repeat that they may take the body, but tell them that unlike the Japanese we don't punish the families of men who take up arms against us. Tell them that this boy was in the jungle armed with this gun and that when he saw our patrol he fired at them. Our patrol fired back and the boy was killed."

I looked at Reid. He raised his hand an inch or two to indicate to Loy Hock Long that he had not yet finished, and to

149

indicate to me, perhaps, that I had better keep my mouth shut.

"Tell them that we shall ask no further questions. It's our belief that the boy was a member of a group of bandits, or a contact man for bandits. Tell them that if a man, other than a British or Indian soldier, or a uniformed guerrilla, enters the jungle, *armed*," and he tapped the sten-gun with his forefinger, "and uses those arms to threaten or attack us, then he is outside the law and liable to get shot. There can't be any question of compensation, but it might be possible for us to make a local contract with the woman for a supply of fuel. You'd better take them into the other room and tell them there."

Loy Hock Long went to the woman, spoke to her, helped her up.

"I'll put it back in the arms-kot, sir," Hamsher said when we were alone again. He picked up the sten and went out into the passage.

Reid said, "You have to simplify things if you're going to make your point clear."

"But he didn't fire."

"He was going to. Mac happened to fire first, that's all. What was he supposed to do? Wait until the fellow pulled the trigger?"

When Hamsher came back Reid told him why I was in Bukit Kallang. While he was doing so the door opened and the woman came out supported by her daughter and her neighbour's wife. They passed through the room into the corridor, followed by the man who paused to bow to each of us in turn. Loy Hock Long closed the door.

"Do they understand?" Reid asked him.

"Yes, they understand," Loy Hock Long said. He went out after them.

*

In the days of the Japanese occupation two white lines had been painted on the road outside the police-station, twenty yards apart, and at a point midway between them a Japanese sentry used to stand. The sentry was there to protect the Sikh policemen and invest them with additional authority. It was prohibited to ride a bicycle between the two lines. You had to dismount at the first line, wheel your machine forward, pause, bow to the sentry and then, if he motioned you on, walk to the other white line, mount and ride away. If he did not motion you on you stayed at attention and awaited his pleasure.

I got this story from Hamsher while standing with him at the front entrance waiting for Reid who had gone to relieve himself. A short flight of steps led down to the street. The road was metalled but there were no pavements. Deep open drains ran along either side of the road. Opposite, there was an even row of terraced, open-fronted shops, stuccoed and whitewashed, with living quarters above and signs in English, Malayan, Indian, and Chinese characters. Most of the shops were shuttered. Flagstones laid across the drains gave access to them when they were open. The white of the stucco was faded, the paint peeling and weathered. Above the roof-line silver grey clouds bulged. The sun had gone in and drained the colour from everything.

This road, Hamsher explained, continued westward to the coast, about forty miles away. The fish lorries used it and the body of a fish merchant called Cheong Poh Kwee had been found about half a mile away in a clump of bamboo. The guerrillas denied knowledge of the crime, but, Hamsher said, Cheong Poh Kwee was the biggest collaborator in Bukit Kallang and it was certain he was executed by a man or men who had sworn revenge on him.

"When was this?" I asked.

"Couple of weeks ago, sir, and maybe he won't be the last either. I expect there's others pretty worried about their health right now."

I told him that I supposed there might be.

Reid joined us.

"We're patrolling up from Sungei Malim tomorrow, Sergeant, so have the beef wagon ready."

"Right, sir." Hamsher stamped to attention on the stone steps.

We had come in my jeep.

"Which way to Wan Lo Ping?"

"Go back to the main road and turn left. It's just out of town."

Bukit Kallang was built in the shape of an inverted letter L, thus: ⅂. The vertical stroke was part of the main road running south to Kampong Malim and north to the Ipoh region. The police station was on the north side of the horizontal stroke. The white stuccoed shops were built in two terraces, one on the south side of the horizontal stroke and the other on the west side of the vertical stroke. On the east side of the vertical stroke there was an atap-thatched hut, a petrol pump and a large compound littered with rusting coachwork and stacks of old tyres. Teena's bungalow, which Reid had pointed out to me on the way to Hamsher's, screened from the road by trees and bushes, was adjacent to it. Behind, the land erupted to the high hill above the garden of madness. Low jungle encroached upon both strokes of the inverted L with here and there tall, emaciated palms bent by random variable winds.

North of the junction of the two strokes, at the exit from the town, we passed beneath a makeshift triumphal arch, a duplicate of one at the entrance to it, a wooden framework with a banner across the road bearing the legend: Welcome To The Malayan People's Anti-Fascist Army. I had been amused to see that the original description "Anti-Japanese" had been redefined to give it a wider post-war significance.

Just beyond the arch Reid told me to slow down. On the left framed by the jungle, there was a bungalow separated from the road by an unwalled compound. Chickens tore at the thin grass and a sentry stood at the foot of the steps. He was armed and uniformed and wore a cloth cap with a red star on the front. As I drove the jeep off the road, scattering the chickens, the sentry stood upright. He gave us the clenched-fist salute when we approached him and Reid good-naturedly returned the compliment.

Another guerrilla appeared at the open doorway as we began to climb the steps. He went in again quickly, shouting something that sounded like, "Hoy-yoy!"

Reid said, "We wait on the veranda."

We did so. I was glad to. There was a powerful stench coming from the dark interior. A third guerrilla appeared. He spoke to us in Chinese and Reid said, "All right, we go in now."

In the middle of the room we entered there was a plain deal table with forms drawn up to it. The table was littered with arms and equipment. The third guerrilla indicated that we should stay where we were and then left us alone. There were heaps of blankets on the floor, tin mugs, mess tins, and discarded clothing. The windows were unglazed. Atap-thatch shutters that opened upwards and outwards were propped open by sticks. On one wall there was a garishly coloured poster of a handsome peasant-type soldier, sleeves rolled up on thick arms, chest straining at the buttons of his uniform jacket, holding a banner which drifted back in slow, stiff ripples. Behind him an equally muscular girl soldier held a sub-machine gun. The words were in Chinese characters but looked exclamatory.

The place stank of sweat, damp decay and urine, and it was stiflingly hot. A fourth guerrilla entered.

"Wan Lo," Reid said, "I want you to meet Major Brent."

The first thing I noticed about Wan Lo Ping was his extreme youth and extreme thinness. His uniform stood away from his body and achieved contours quite unconnected with it. When we were close to each other shaking hands I realized that the thinness was an illusion created partly by a uniform several sizes too big for him, and badly overstarched, and partly by his having not an ounce of superfluous fat on a body made up of small, tough bones and articulated by a system of wiry muscles. His face was delicately formed, the mouth firm, the eyes black and hard, the skin smooth and bronzed. He smelt faintly of eau-de-Cologne. His uniform was freshly laundered, the sleeves of the tunic rolled up into flat, neat turn-backs to just above the elbow. On his feet he wore brown plimsolls and white socks. On his left wrist there was a watch on a chromium expanding strap and on his right a chromium bracelet and identity plate. His teeth were white and even.

"Please sit down," he said.

He cleared a space on the table by pushing the arms and equipment over to one side, went to the door and shouted to somebody at the back. Reid and I sat opposite one another. Wan Lo came and sat between us at the head of the table.

"We're patrolling from Sungei Malim tomorrow, Wan Lo. Will you join us again?"

"Yes. I'll send two men."

"Will they speak English?"

"A bit. Yes, they will speak a bit."

He offered a tin of English cigarettes.

"Good," Reid said. "Can they be ready at nine? The patrol will pick them up on the way."

"Yes, nine o'clock."

"We'll go to Sungei Malim in the thirty-hundredweight and foot it from there."

"Yes, yes."

"It'll be Lieutenant Holmes in charge again. But I've a new officer coming next week, Wan Lo."

"Ah, good."

"Chap called Sutton. I don't know about good. He'll be green."

"Green?"

The "r" was scarcely pronounced, neither "r" nor "l" but something in between.

"No experience. Straight from India."

"Ah, yes, I see. Student soldier." He grinned.

Tea was brought in three tin mugs by a young man with the flattest face I had ever seen. Reid and I had to keep wiping the sweat from our foreheads but Wan Lo stayed miraculously cool.

"Wan Lo," Reid said, "Major Brent is in Bukit Kallang on a special assignment from Kuala Lumpur. He's an old friend of a man called Saxby."

Wan Lo nodded. I was disappointed because his reaction seemed so mild, so anti-climactic. "Ah, Sax Bee. Friend of Sax Bee."

"You've had no further news of him?" I asked.

"No, no. You have seen Major Turner?"

"Yes. I've talked to Major Turner. Is Ah Choong still missing?"

"Ah Choong and Sax Bee both are still missing."

Reid said, "You never told me about Saxby, Wan Lo."

"No, no. It is a long time ago. I did not know you were still looking for him, Major Reid."

"I'm not. I'd never heard of the man until Major Brent told me about him." Reid nodded at me, smiled, as if to say; You see? Wan Lo's in the clear.

I said, "You think they must be dead?"

Wan Lo sipped his tea. "You do not think they are dead, Major Brent?"

"I don't know what to think. Saxby is one of my oldest friends and I don't like to think of him lying ill somewhere. Major Turner seems sure he wasn't captured by the Japanese and killed. I wondered whether you might have any ideas."

He sipped more tea, blowing into the cup between each sip.

"I have not thought about it," he said, "since reporting to Major Turner."

"Tell me about him, then. He was with you for quite a while, wasn't he?"

"He came about one year, one year ago. He was in Kampong Malim for a long time, then he came to Bukit Kallang."

"And you were here then?"

"Not here. In the jungle. I meant he came to the jungle."

"Yes, but you were in charge of the Bukit Kallang group?"

"Oh, yes."

"What did he come to Bukit Kallang to do?"

"He was liaison."

"Liaison with what?"

"With me."

"He helped in training your young soldiers?"

"I was in charge of training."

"But he helped?"

"No. We discussed things together sometimes."

"What sort of things? Methods of training?"

"Yes, sometimes."

"And operations?"

"Sometimes."

"You planned operations together?"

"No. I was in charge of operations."

"What else did he do sometimes?"

"He put things down in his book."

"He took the book away with him, I suppose?"

"Yes. He liked his book."

"Did he ever show it to you?"

"No."

"Or tell you what was in it?"

"Accounts of things."

"Accounts? Not money accounts?"

"Accounts of things that had happened. Like a journal."

"He said it was a journal?"

"No, no. He did not talk about his book. I thought only that it was a journal. It was in his satchel."

"I see. What about Ah Choong?"

"We know nothing of Ah Choong."

"But you told Major Turner he was thought to be reliable, and you chose him as Saxby's companion, didn't you?"

"I did not choose him. Ah Choong was Sax Bee man."

"What d'you mean, Saxby man?"

"He was with Sax Bee a long time. Before Bukit Kallang. Before Kampong Malim. They were one. Very close."

"Did you report that to Major Turner?"

Wan Lo sipped more tea. "No, it did not seem relevant." He brought the word out rather proudly, as if he'd been waiting for an opportunity to use it.

"I see. Tell me more about Saxby then. What was he like? Did he still wear a beard?"

"Yes, he was very fond of his beard. He combed his beard every day."

"Did he? And did he go on a lot of anti-Jap raids with you?"

"He did not go on operations. While he was with us we were unable to make any attacks."

"Why was that?"

"We were under operational command of Kampong Malim group." He hesitated. "In later stages of war guerrilla attacks had to be made only when success was certainty. Arms, ammunition, everything was in very short supply. If we had plan of attack we would submit this plan to commander in Kampong Malim. There would be many considerations. Expected losses, reprisals on civil population."

"And while Saxby was with you Kampong Malim never gave permission for a raid?"

"Because of the considerations. Because of the difficulties."

"So things were pretty boring. How did he fill in his time?"

"He was very interested in things that grew in the jungle."

"Yes, he was a botanist. Did you know that?"

Wan Lo shook his head. "He did not say. But he was interested in trees and flowers. And mosses. Anything that grew."

"You say interested. You mean he collected them?"

"No, no. He did not collect. Sometimes he would draw them, sometimes he would talk to them."

Reid said, "*Talk* to them? He was off his rocker, was he, Wan Lo? Off his rocker? Mad?"

"No, he was not mad. Only, when he thought he was alone

he would sometimes talk to the things in the jungle. He was the only Englishman in the camp. Perhaps he got tired of talking only to Chinese. Perhaps talking to the things in the jungle was better than talking to himself, but the same."

"Yes, Wan Lo," Reid said, "but talking to *plants*!" Reid's eyes were black with fascination.

"It is an exaggeration perhaps. Perhaps only two times I heard and saw him talking to plants. He may not have been talking to them after all. He may have been talking to himself and happening to touch the plants at the same time. And I could not tell what he said. He was talking in a foreign language. He was talking in Hindustani, I think."

"Well, let's forget about his talking to plants," I said. "What kind of thing did he talk to you about?"

"Oh, all things. Everything. I think he was very religious man." Wan Lo paused. "Very religious man, but not I think Christian."

"Why not Christian?"

"He believed what old Malay people believe, old Malay people in jungle. Aboriginal Malay people. What are called Sakai. Such people believe everything has a soul, which perhaps is why when I saw him talking I thought he talked to the things in the forest. For old Malay people the trees would have spirits, some good spirits, some evil. And also they believe a man has more than one soul, five souls, perhaps more, but five main souls."

"And this is what Saxby believed?"

"Oh, yes."

"He *told* you that's what he believed?"

"Yes, he told me. He came one morning and said, Mr Wan, I am going into the forest because in the night the soul of my head went for a walk and hasn't come back. When I asked him what he meant, he told me that each of us had five souls, a head soul, an eye soul –"

He was counting by tapping each finger on the wooden table and there, for me, was Saxby, slapping the table in the upstairs room of Debi's, talking about the soul in the wood, the chip off the tree, and when Wan Lo hesitated, forgetting, I ended it for him. "A breath soul, a heart soul and a liver soul. I know. He mentioned it once before, years ago. But he didn't believe it then. Did he say why he believed it now?"

"No. Only that he believed and that sometimes his head soul would take advantage of the fact that he was asleep and go off into the forest."

"And then?"

"Then he must follow it, he said."

"And did he?"

"Yes, he would go into the forest."

"You mean go away for a bit?"

"Yes."

"For how long?"

"A few hours. Day."

"More than a day?"

"Sometimes."

"A week?"

"I think once nearly a week."

"And he'd go alone?"

"Sometimes he would take Ah Choong."

"And you didn't know what he was doing?"

"I assumed he told the truth, that going into the forest was something to do with his religion."

"But wasn't it dangerous letting him go off alone? I thought your people weren't keen on Europeans wandering about the jungle in case they were spotted and it led to your camps being attacked?"

"He never went out of camp looking like a European. He wore his disguise."

A tendril of excitement began to twist in the pit of my stomach.

"What disguise was this?"

"His Indian disguise. He looked like a Sikh because he stained his skin and dyed his beard, also he wore a turban."

"Did he wear his disguise when he left the camp to go to the beach rendezvous?"

"No."

"Why?"

"It was a long journey and there was possibility of being captured by Japanese. He said he would not like to be captured by Japanese except as himself."

"But wasn't there just as much danger of being captured when he left the camp for shorter periods?"

"No. Not so much danger and it was better for him to wear disguise if he was coming back here, otherwise if he had been seen he could have been followed."

"You were in favour of the disguise then?"

"Yes, I was in favour."

"What was the first occasion he wore it?"

Wan Lo said, "When first he came and told me of his dream. He said, Wan Lo, when I was asleep the soul of my head went into the forest so now I must get it back. I asked him what he meant and he told me of his belief. I said he must not leave the camp in case he was seen and followed back and then he said, Ah, yes, but I shall go as a Sikh. And so I agreed."

"And how long was he away that time?"

"Only until night. But next time it was longer. And he took Ah Choong."

"And you never asked Ah Choong what they did?"

"Oh, yes, but Ah Choong also believed in five souls and confirmed it was for religious purposes."

Reid said, "And you didn't think him mad?"

"No. Not mad. Only they believed in God. This is silly, not mad. One way is as silly as another."

I said, "So their trips were a mystery?"

"No, Major Brent. Not a mystery. They went for religious exercise. I was not interested in method of exercise. And I had not reason to doubt."

"Why? You say that as if there was a special reason not to doubt."

"He made many such trips, Major Brent, and always before going he said, Wan Lo, last night while I slept the soul of my liver or the soul of my head went into the forest. But once there was different trip. *Then* he did not say this about his souls. He said, Wan Lo, I wish to go into Bukit Kallang."

"*Into* Bukit Kallang?" Reid exclaimed. "You mean into the town itself?"

"Yes, into the town. He had plan. He would not say what his plan was, but he did not pretend he was going on religious exercise. He did not deceive me."

"So you let him go into the town?"

Wan Lo hesitated. "I did not give permission. He went without permission. But he had not deceived me. Simply he disobeyed."

"Did he go alone?"

"He went with Ah Choong."

"And when he came back did he tell you what he had done?"

"He told me that he had been to see Madame Chang."

I must have stared at him stupidly.

"Madame Chang?"

Reid said, "He means Teena."

Wan Lo nodded.

"Why would he go to see Madame Chang?"

Reid laughed.

"She was known to us professionally," Wan Lo replied, and looked at the table.

I looked from one to the other of them.

"What Wan Lo means, Brent, is that the guerrillas slept with the girls as well as the Japanese."

"That was pretty dangerous for her, wasn't it?"

"Also it was dangerous for us," Wan Lo pointed out.

"And the Japs never found her out?"

"No. Otherwise she would not be alive. The Japanese seldom went to her bungalow except to collect the girls. So sometimes we would call there. Our men were in the jungle for a long time. We had no girl soldiers in our group."

"And Saxby knew of this arrangement?"

"Oh, yes."

"And his plan turned out to be nothing more than visiting Madame Chang professionally?"

Wan Lo smiled. "It would seem," he said.

"How often did he go there?"

"Only once."

"And when? How long ago now?"

"Oh, long time. Nearly one year. Soon after he came to Bukit Kallang."

"And after his trip to Madame Chang there were more trips into the forest?"

"Oh yes. Many trips."

"It's a pity we don't know exactly what he did."

"It was as I said, for religious exercise."

"And you never once had him followed?"

Wan Lo shrugged. "In the jungle, Major Brent? You think it is possible to follow a man in the jungle? In Burma, I do not know. But in Malaya, this is not possible unless you know where the man is going and you are using well-worn tracks. Simply I trusted him and let him do as he wanted."

I thought: And it didn't matter a damn to you what happened to Saxby, so long as you got rid of him for a bit and had done with his interference.

"I suppose so," I said. "There's no more you can tell me?"

"No." He grinned. "Sorry."

For the moment I could think of no more questions. I grinned back at him. There was nothing sinister about Wan Lo. He knew nothing. He disliked admitting that Saxby might be alive because he would then have to adopt some kind of official attitude to the situation.

"Well, thank you. You've been very helpful."

Before we went he showed me round the camp. Behind the bungalow there was a clearing and three huts in which the men lived in what seemed to be a state of considerable squalor. There was a drill parade going on, for our benefit I thought.

162

Reid watched it with a paternal smile but it filled me with a kind of hopelessness and I was glad when it was over and the men straggled away giving us an unco-ordinated eyes right.

As we drove back, past Teena's bungalow, Reid said, "Are you going to call in?"

"This afternoon, perhaps."

"It's funny, Brent, but she never mentioned Saxby."

"Why should she? She didn't have to produce a list for you, did she?"

"I meant last night. I told her what you were here for and she just said, Oh, as if she wasn't interested."

"She wouldn't remember every visitor, would she? It sounds as if she had plenty of them. I gather you knew about the guerrillas."

"Of course I knew."

"So she doesn't exactly rank as a collaborator?"

"Not exactly, Brent. But she knew what side her bread was buttered, didn't she? Lie down for the hare, open up for the hounds, eh? I reckon she thought if you were always on your back nobody would shoot you down."

"I suppose so." I felt her lips on my shoulder.

"Oh, she's not slow in the uptake, our Teena. Mind you, I admire her for it. Know what she did? As soon as we got to Bukit Kallang? Dolled herself up and asked for an audience. What about that for coolness, Brent? What about that? She made no bones about it either. She admitted she and the other girls had been Japanese lays. She didn't mention the guerrillas, it was Wan Lo told me. I asked his advice. I didn't want to get mixed up in anything too blatant. So I made a bargain with her. She guaranteed a girl exclusively for each of us. She even agreed to a medical check. I guaranteed her and the girls protection and certain payments in cash and kind."

"She asked for protection?"

"No. But I thought it might be one of the objects of the exercise. So I threw it in *gratis*. Did you like her?"

"Yes, I liked her."

Reid glanced at me. I changed down to take the turn into the company area.

"Well while you're here she's yours. It all comes under the contract but you'll probably like to give her the occasional present."

"It's very hospitable of you. What about you?"

"I'll manage, I expect."

Manage! Of course he would manage. I hated his attitude and I hated his tin-pot little kingdom.

"It's funny isn't it?" he said. "Saxby and her? Eh? Saxby and her?"

"He may not have gone for that."

"Oh, Brent."

He may, I thought, have gone only to talk because he was tired of talking to plants. It was on the tip of my tongue to say so, but Reid would have seen at once that Teena had betrayed a confidence, and as he had implied by his exclamation: Oh, Brent! it was unlikely. Saxby and I had never shared a woman before, at least not to my knowledge, and that we appeared to have done so now was entirely Saxby's fault. He had not been content with his bloody plants, his five souls and whatever vision he had tricked himself into; and I felt he should have been. He had no business coming down from his holier-than-thou height, sleeping with women I slept with, making a situation untenable for me, denying me access to the dark room in which I could commit my mortal follies and delude myself into thinking they were not follies but acts, somehow, of faith. But faith in what, God knew, perhaps in there being room for tenderness, time for love, a moment for giving as well as one for taking even in places where lies were told, bodies claimed and people knew which side their bread was buttered.

Alone, in the veranda room, we talked and drank iced beer.

"I can't look at civilians in Malaya without remembering they lived with the Jap for over three years. I can't look at them without thinking they've got three years dirt on them.

164

I can look at the guerrillas though. And they can look at you. Have you noticed that, Brent? They can look you in the eye. They hardly know the difference between their right foot and their left foot, but what's drill? A man's either a man before he goes on parade or not at all. You can't drill guts into him."

He was sitting in his favourite position, leaning forward with his forearms resting on his knees, his glass of beer held in both hands, gazing into it. Without moving his head he raised his eyes to look at me. "They tell me you were wounded in Burma."

"That's right."

"Did you have a command?"

"Yes. A rifle company."

"So I was right. You're one of us. I thought so." He nodded. "It's the best command there is, isn't it? I wouldn't have changed it. How old would you say I am?"

"Thirty-seven."

"I'm gone forty. Forty-one soon. That's old for a company. It's too old would you say?"

"It doesn't automatically follow."

"No." He twisted the glass by rubbing his hands against it in opposite directions. "Once you rise above company level you're up against it, up to your neck in bumph and policy. That's an exaggeration, but you know what I mean. I've stuck to it here."

"How long have you had the company?"

"This one? Well it would be in the middle of last year. Before that I had B company of the second battalion, but we got smashed up in the Arakan. Shot to hell. I transferred to this battalion in the middle of '44, and I took over the company then. We fought all the way to Mandalay together. They're good boys." He looked up from his beer. "They deserve the fleshpots. What fleshpots there are in Bukit Kallang. It's not K.L. or Singapore. Trust us to get detached to a place like this. A muck job, they say. Reid and his boys'll cope with a muck job. So out we come, and we find we're still fighting, still geared up for punishment. But it's no bad thing, Brent. A bit of fighting, a bit of fleshpots. You weren't shocked, were you?"

"Shocked? At what?"

"Last night. She's got talent that Chang girl. She does that exotic stuff well and I like the boys to have it that way and not just a bang off somewhere when they can't get their minds off it any more. You see what I mean, you see what I'm getting at?"

"Not really."

"I've had to drive them, Brent. I've turned them from boys who wouldn't hurt a fly into men who'd as soon plug you as look at you. It was difficult at first, now it's difficult again. The war's over and yet it's not over. At any moment they might have to go off and shoot hell out of some bugger in the jungle, but they've got time on their hands and what I've done to them has turned them into men, men who feel their greens and need it often. What they know is fighting and drinking and whoring. It's not much for a boy. Not much, you say? Well, nothing's much in this world. What there is, do well, do damn well, and decently. Fight hard, drink hard, whore clean. That's why I want it done this way, each of them with his own girl, a girl he knows he can have any night of the week when he's off duty, a girl he knows some other chap isn't shafting."

He looked across at me. His eyes were dull again. He said, "But it's going, Brent. Going. Where'll they be a year from now? I'm a regular. They're not. You're not, are you?"

"No."

"What'll you do?"

"I've no idea."

"What did you do before the war?"

"Farmed."

"And it's lost its fire, then? Yes, that's what happens."

"I don't know. I've not decided."

"It's the same with the boys. Where'll they be a year from

166

now. And where will I be? When you're not sure what it is you've got, what it is you've *made*, how do you hold on to it?"

"Perhaps you shouldn't try."

"Ah then," he said, "you're nothing. Nothing."

5

LATE THAT AFTERNOON I WENT TO SEE TEENA CHANG. A storm broke as I reached the bungalow. Sheltered from the rain by the roof of the veranda I banged on the door for upwards of five minutes until it was opened by an old Malay woman who tried to tell me to go away, or so I gathered from the way she shouted at me and barred me from entering. Eventually she gave way and let me in. Barring the door again she told me to wait.

The entrance hall was dark, the two windows, one on each side of the door, being shuttered from inside. What light there was came through an open doorway in the wall opposite. It was hot and airless. The floor-boards were bare except for a square of rush matting in the middle. On the mat there was a bamboo table and on the table an indoor palm in a brass bowl. In one corner was a brass gong, waist high, suspended in a carved ebony stand, and in another corner a smaller bamboo table with an oil-lamp like the one in the pavilion. Apart from the open doorway there were several other doors leading off the hall but these were closed. The Malay woman had knocked at one and gone in, closing it again. Presently she opened it and indicated that I could enter.

Teena's room was lighter. It had two windows and only the one overlooking the front was shuttered. It was a large room, dominated by heavy Victorian rosewood furniture: dressing-table, chest of drawers, and wardrobe. An iron bedstead with brass knobs stood at one side of the unshuttered window shrouded in white mosquito netting. Beneath the shuttered window was a cretonne-covered sofa and an Indian coffee table inlaid with mother-of-pearl. A picture of the Sacred Heart framed in gold hung on the whitewashed wall above the chest of drawers opposite the bed. The bare boards of the floor were unpolished but looked clean, and there were two Indian rugs to soften the tread: one by the bed and one in front of the sofa.

Entering, she said, "Do you like it?"

Against its solid ugliness she looked enchantingly small, delicate, warmly fleshed. I said, "Yes, I like it very much." She was carefully made up and I assumed that I had been deliberately kept waiting while she got herself ready. She wore a dress similar to that of the night before. Waiting until she was seated I then placed myself at the other end of the sofa, away from the casual temptation of close proximity. She crossed her legs and leaned back at ease as if in her own drawing-room. Nothing in her attitude suggested intimacy of a more than social kind. The old woman brought in a tea-tray: silver plated tea-pot and porcelain cups decorated in the Chinese manner.

When we were alone she said, "You look very official."

"I am. A bit official, anyway. I'm going to ask questions. I'm good at that, aren't I? Did I ask too many last night?"

"Not too many. Ask more if you want to. Today's another day."

"I gather Major Reid told you why I'm in Bukit Kallang."

"Yes, he did."

"You said nothing to me."

"What should I have said, Tommy?"

"That you knew the man I'm looking for."

"This Saxby?"

"Yes, Saxby. He told Wan Lo Ping he'd visited you."

For a few moments I was lost in contemplation of her brows and eyelashes, of the intricate structure of the human face which at one moment seems to tell so much and at others so little.

She said, "Would you have wanted to talk about Saxby last night?"

"Perhaps not. But I'd like to now. Did he come to see you?"

"Yes, he came once."

169

"Only once?"

"Only once."

"Here to this bungalow?"

"Yes. He was here in the bungalow."

I kept my eyes on hers so that they would not be seen even to flicker in the direction of the bed; but the bed was there with the net hanging over it, the whole in a blatant state of preservation. A partly grown discomfort, the result of being near her, subsided.

"Was he wearing this disguise Wan Lo Ping has told me about?"

"Yes, he looked like a Sikh. I wouldn't have known he was English unless he'd told me, and then it was obvious. You know?"

"Was he alone?"

"He said he had someone at the back waiting for him."

"Was this day or night-time?"

"Day-time."

"He was taking a risk, wasn't he?"

"He didn't seem to think so."

"How did he arrive? Like I did? Knocking at the front door?"

"No. He was hiding in the jungle at the back. Anna went into the compound and he called out."

"Did he ask to see you?"

"Yes."

"By name?"

"I think so. He knew it, anyway. Anna told him to wait but he came in with her."

"And came into this room."

"Yes."

"Did Major Reid tell you why I'm looking for him?"

"No. Only that you were looking. I'd almost forgotten him."

"I'm looking for him because he seems to have disappeared. He's an old friend of mine. I knew him years ago, before the war."

"Well how can I help, Tommy? I only saw him that one time."

"Brian had got hold of some odd ideas from living with the Sakai. He had some odd enough ideas back in India, odd in the sense that he was an odd sort of fellow altogether, got odder when he came out to Malaya, and perhaps even odder when the Japanese invaded you. Anything you can tell me about what he said and the way he acted might be useful."

"Was that his other name, Brian?"

"Yes."

"But that's a nice name!"

"You make it sound as if he didn't deserve one."

"I'm sorry."

"What? Sorry for what?"

"For making it sound like that."

"But that's what you felt? He didn't deserve a nice name because he wasn't nice?"

She said, "It wasn't a question of nice. I thought he was crazy, that is all. I'm sorry."

"In what way crazy?"

"The things he said. The way he looked. Oh, everything about him."

"What sort of things did he say?"

"I can't remember. It was just all of it crazy. He was wasting his time, anyway."

"Wasting his time?"

I suppose the question, the way in which it was asked, surprised her out of a recollection of what had actually taken place into a consideration of what I was trying to visualize myself. Her eyes lost one kind of depth, but acquired another. I think she saw the combination of relief and perplexity in my own.

"He came to see me about the Japanese officers," she explained.

"See you about them? Why?"

She had taken a cigarette and I clicked my lighter on. She

held my hand in hers and when her cigarette was going she took the lighter and twisted it admiringly.

"Is it gold?"

"So they say."

She gave it back to me.

She said, "He wanted me to murder them."

After a while I said, "How was that to be done?"

"I don't know. We never got as far as working out the details."

"Why was that?"

I said it innocently enough but it ruffled her.

"Oh, Tommy, why was that!" She got to her feet. "Why was that! Because I told him not to be a bloody fool and that if he couldn't talk sense he'd better get back into the jungle."

She had gone to the dressing-table and now she returned with a folding paper fan. She sat close to me, flicked the fan open and waved it to and fro between us. I laughed, suddenly.

She said, "What are you laughing at?"

"The way you said bloody. And saying it to Saxby. The idea of your sitting here telling Saxby not to be a bloody fool."

She smiled. The fan made little phuffing noises. Outside the rain fell steadily. The wetness had drawn the smell out of green things growing, out of inanimate objects charged with the smells of what had touched them or lain close to them, of dust, of polish, of cut flowers, of hard wood, of cool silks and heavy smothering damask, and of the crushed rose petals whose scent sometimes crossed the space between Teena's body and my own.

"Oh, Sax Bee," she said, distorting the last syllable so that an element of play-acting was introduced. "He was a crazy old man."

"Well not so old."

"At least fifty. And his beard."

"Give him a chance! He'd be forty-one. Ten years older than me." I took her wrist and helped her with the fan.

"Was he very cross with you?" I asked.

"He said it wasn't the end of it. He said I'd hear more."

"Have you ever heard more?"

"Of course not. He was dreaming, that man." She pitched her voice higher to denote quotation marks. " 'You'll *do* this. You'll do it because I *control* the situation.' So I asked him what situation. But all he could do was go on saying he controlled it."

"Did he say anything about Wan Lo Ping?"

"What sort of thing?"

"About where Wan Lo Ping stood over this plan to murder the Japanese officers."

"Oh it was Saxby's idea, not Wan Lo Ping's. Wan Lo Ping would never have planned anything dangerous. The guerrillas in Bukit Kallang were just a joke."

"A joke?"

"They never *did* anything. Except sit about in camp, I suppose, and drill and sing songs and have political discussions. Saxby said he was going to change all that. He meant to start by getting me to murder the Japanese officers. And then he wanted me to make a list of collaborators."

I kept my hand from tightening its grip on hers. We were swinging the fan like a metronome.

"Did you refuse to do that too?"

"Yes, of course."

"Did he say why he wanted the list?"

"It was obvious wasn't it? So that they could be murdered too."

"By you?"

"Well it wouldn't have been me. I'd have been dead long before it was the turn of what he called the collaborators. The whole town would have been dead. That's what I told him. You're crazy, I said. If I murder only *one* of the officers they'll chop the heads off every civilian in sight. He went on and on and in the end he said he'd be satisfied for the time being if I agreed to send information to the guerrillas."

"What sort of information?"

173

"That's what I asked him. I mean what sort of information could I get that would interest the guerrillas? That one officer had a scar on his right leg, another did this and another that? He seemed to think Bukit Kallang was full of secret weapons or in the middle of important troop movements. He didn't have a clue."

I smiled, wondering from which of Reid's officers she had picked up that particular expression.

"Well, what was it full of, Teena?"

"It was full of people doing their best to get as much to eat as they could and of Japanese troops doing their best not to be bored or homesick. It was full of silly regulations and arrests when someone decided one of the regulations had been broken and then beatings up in the street or the police station, and executions. Oh, early on I expect it was different, worse I mean than that. I wasn't here. But it was different all over Malaya early on. It was all a shock then. You turned round, the British had gone and the Japanese were there and you were stuck with them. And you didn't *know* it was only going to be for three years. It might have been ten or thirty or three hundred and so there you were, and there *they* were, and that was it. So you decided. You decided what you were going to do. I told Saxby this and he said, Well what have *you* decided? I told him. I told him I'd decided to run a business. I said, This is it, this is my business. My customers are Japanese but the guerrillas are my customers too when they want to be and it's safe to let them. I won't turn a customer away unless taking him is bad for business. The guerrillas could be bad for business if the Japanese got to know, but if they don't get to know what does it matter? I said, I won't tell the Japanese about you but I won't tell you about the Japanese. That's what I told him. It makes sense, doesn't it? Now the Japanese have gone and my customers are the British. Some of the people in the town say I collaborated, but when you go into it all they mean is that I slept with them. Some people swept their floors, some cooked for them, some sold things to them from their shops. Oh, Saxby would never see a simple thing like that. You see it, don't you, Tommy? Would you have preferred it if I'd slept with the Japanese but cut their throats or sent silly messages about what time they called the roll to a lot of boys who lived in the jungle and drilled and sang songs?"

"No, but Saxby would have preferred it."

"I wasn't interested in what Saxby would have preferred. I told him to his face."

"How did he take it finally? Did he seem to accept it?"

"Oh, I don't know what he seemed to do. He said he'd give me a chance to come to my senses, and if I didn't I'd regret it later. I suppose he meant when the war was over. Well, it's over now and he was crazy. So crazy he's got himself lost."

"No, Teena. I don't think he's lost."

"Then why are you looking for him? Has he done something wrong?"

"He was supposed to get picked up by submarine in June. They wanted him back in India. He left Wan Lo's camp on May the second and that's the last anyone saw of him."

For a second or two she sat still, then moved the fan to and fro again.

"But May. That was ages ago. The Japanese were still here."

"I know."

"Then he must be dead if he disappeared ages ago – all that time ago."

I put my hand on hers. "Maybe. Or gone away to collect plants. He was a great plant collector too. He ended up by believing what the hill people believe, that a man has five souls. Did he tell you that? When was this visit?"

"It must have been a year ago. But don't let's talk about Saxby any more." She put the fan away. "Let's talk about you."

"All right, we won't talk about Saxby. We won't talk about me either."

"Who then?"

"You, of course. How long have you been in Bukit Kallang, Teena?"

"About two years."

"And the girls?"

"We all came together."

"Is this your bungalow?"

"No, it belongs to her." She nodded in the direction of the hall.

"The old Malayan woman?"

"Yes. Her two sons used to own the garage-lot, but they were executed for something before we came."

"Where were you before?"

"In Ipoh."

"Is that where you set up business?"

"Oh, no. I have been in other places. Taiping. Penang."

"What brought you to Bukit Kallang?"

"Some officers."

"Including Hakinawa?"

"No. Joe didn't come until later."

"Is that what you called him? Joe?"

"Yes, I called him Joe."

"Were you Joe's girl?"

"Yes."

"What was Joe's colour?"

"Yellow. I wore yellow too."

"But you weren't Yellow Blossom, were you, because you're never any of those names?"

"No, I wasn't Yellow Blossom."

"What was Joe like?"

"Not like you."

"Meaning?"

"He was not a bit inquisitive."

I smiled, not minding. "You talk about him as if he was better than most of 'em were."

"Is that another question?"

"Yes. Was he? Was he better?"

"Oh, it depends what kind you knew." And then her eyes fell on my shoulder and she flushed a little. "Yes, Tommy. Joe was better than most as you put it. After he came there were no more executions. People talk about things being before Hakinawa or after Hakinawa." She paused. "Poor boy. He committed hara-kiri."

"Why?"

She shrugged. "How can I tell you that? Perhaps some family trouble or some army trouble, some kind of dishonour. There are people who say this and people who say the other."

"What, for instance?"

"Oh, that he saw the ghosts in the garden of madness, or that he discovered Madame Chang was letting her girls sleep with the guerrillas."

"Would that be a reason for hara-kiri?"

"I suppose it might be."

"Was he in love with you then?"

"Perhaps he thought so. Who can tell? I did not see him for two days before he did it. I don't know what happened to make him do it. And on the third day he fell on his sword in the golden room."

"Did you get questioned?"

"No. I wasn't involved. And it was all hushed up." She lifted her shoulders fractionally. "Poor Joe. He was young, good-looking. You would have thought him happy. But his heart was too big for the small world we live in."

She made to get up but I restrained her.

"Why do you say that?"

"It's what I felt about him."

"Were *you* in love with him?"

"I liked him. Love is a different matter. What do people mean when they say love? There are different kinds of love. How do you know which kind is meant?"

I freed her and she stood up.

"Teena."

"What?"

"Did Saxby make love to you?"

I think I expected her to smile and say something like: Don't

be a silly boy; which would have told me nothing but everything. But she looked away from me, rubbed the back of her
hand again and said, "No. Perhaps at one point he wanted
to. But he was dirty. His skin was stained with some kind of
juice."

She went across to the chest of drawers and opened one of
the small ones at the top. Returning, she gave me a snapshot.

"That's Joe. It was taken outside the pavilion."

"By you?"

"No. One of his friends took it."

Hakinawa stood sufficiently within the shade of the veranda
to avoid screwing his face up. He had a friendly smile and
features unexpectedly occidental. He was wearing a kimono
which revealed a deep chest and a good breadth of shoulder. I
gave the snapshot back to her.

"He looked a nice fellow. It's a pity they take it so seriously,
this business of face. He had a good one. I expect he only
thought he'd lost it."

"Perhaps."

She glanced at the snapshot before putting it picture-side
down on the coffee table.

"You said you didn't see him during the last three days he
was alive. Why was that?"

"I don't know, Tommy."

I think she already regretted showing me the picture.

"Was it unusual for you not to see him for so long?"

"I suppose it was."

"So it might be true. He might have heard about the
guerrillas."

"Oh, well. He might."

"But how would he have heard? Nobody except the guerrillas knew. If someone in the town had known the Japs would
have been tipped off long before, wouldn't they? Is the old
woman at the bottom of it?"

She shrugged again.

"Or," I said, "might it have been Saxby?"

"Oh, Tommy! Saxby! How could Saxby tell Joe anything? And why would he do it, anyway?"

But she was busying herself over-much and too suddenly tidying an already tidy tea-tray. Again I caught her hand.

"We know why Saxby might have done it. To pay you out as he'd threatened. How is a different matter. When did Joe kill himself?"

I felt the slight pull of her arm and let her hand go.

"In May," she said. "On May the fifth. Now let's forget Saxby."

"He was last seen on May the second."

"I know, Tommy. You told me. And that's getting on for five months ago. Crazy old Saxby is dead. He got himself lost and bitten by a snake. Didn't he?"

"I expect so. Yes, I expect he did."

"So if he did inform it's all over, all done with isn't it?"

I nodded. She had seen enough shapes in the dark without my adding to them.

*

She showed me some of what she called her black-marketry.

"It's nice to have them. It's nice to have what has become rare and expensive."

"Why?" I asked, not disputing her statement but wanting it explained further in her own way.

"I don't know why. But it's nice. Don't you agree it's nice?" And she showed me more: boxes of sheer silk stockings, a roll of emerald coloured silk, a leather case containing lipsticks, powder, rouge, creams, eyebrow pencils; brand new, still wrapped in tissue paper.

"And these shoes." She opened the wardrobe and picked up a pair of high-heeled shoes made from soft, deep red suede. "Paris," she said, showing me the insides. "Have you ever been to Paris?"

"Once," I said. I described as best I could from such old memory the street whose name was printed on the labels.

Listening, she sat back on her heels with the shoes held in her lap. Once she shook her head to loosen the hair in her neck in the manner that was becoming familiar.

"Did you go to a night-club?"

"No, not a proper one."

"Or to the Folies Bergère?"

"Yes, I went there."

"And the women were naked?"

"Not all the time."

"Where also have you been in Europe? Rome? I have a handbag from Rome."

"No, not Rome. Only Paris."

"Have you been to a lot of brothels?"

I had to laugh because the question was so serious, so innocent.

"Why?"

"I am interested. I should like to own a nice establishment. What makes a brothel nice for a man?"

"I've not been to a lot of brothels. But let's say it must be the girls that make them nice, if 'nice' is the word we're looking for."

"The girls are important, naturally," she said, "but I think they should be friendly and not just sexy. They should have definite personalities. They shouldn't look or act like girls you only meet in bed. Then there are the arrangements. Clothes, colour schemes. All these are important, aren't they?"

"Yes, they must be. I've not given it much thought."

"What about music?"

"Sweet and low, I suppose."

"Oh, I don't know. I don't know about music."

"We had music last night."

"The gramophone is Mac's idea. I think it's a bit artificial."

"I like the music."

"Do you, Tommy?"

"I liked everything about last night."

"Thank you."

She tilted her head back and pushed the hair away from her

neck, first from one side, then from the other. She rose, put the shoes away in the wardrobe. I stayed where I was, crouched on the floor, watched her pack her black-marketry away.

When I got up she asked me for another cigarette. I watched her closely as I flicked on the gold lighter but for all the notice she took of it this time it might have been chromium, and then I wanted to give it to her; an irrational split-second impulse that had something to do with the way the tips of her shoulders curved barely away from the sleeveless mandarin-collared dress. I lit my own cigarette.

The impulse to give her the lighter there and then had gone but in its place was the intention to give it to her later on. It was a question of choosing the right moment, the right place. I thought I might give it to her that night in the pavilion. Saxby had never been to the pavilion and in Hakinawa's day she must have slept in the golden room. The scarlet room was ours because Reid only talked to her there. I put the lighter back in my pocket, conscious of seeking an occasion only Teena and I would share. She had crossed over to the tea-tray and was testing the pot for warmth and as she twisted round with the pot in her hands as if to say, Well, there's another cup, I remembered her as I had seen her the night before walking from behind the screen, barefoot in her red dressing-gown, without make-up; and with the stab of affection for the barefoot girl and the girl holding the tea-pot came the blunter thrust of Saxby threatening to ride roughshod over us with the mad assurance of five souls when she and I perhaps could scarcely muster two between us.

"What is it, Tommy?"

"What?"

I joined her, took the cup she poured for me.

"Is it your arm?"

"I expect so. It aches when it rains." I grinned up at her. In Teena's world and my world you had arms that ached when it rained, you poured luke-warm tea, you carried on your business, you surrounded yourself with objects of beauty like gold lighters, handbags from Rome, ornamental daggers; you kept the house inhabited and the fire going and used the darkness to make magic from and not to come at people out of.

"This list," I began.

"What list, Tommy?"

"You know. The one Saxby asked you to make."

"I didn't make it."

"Is there anyone else who might have made it? Anyone you know who harbours grudges?"

She had not joined me on the sofa but stood, frowning, smoking her cigarette without inhaling.

"How can you tell if people harbour grudges? Anyone might. It's not important. We all decide what we're going to do and then we do it. We can't tell what other people decide to do."

I put my cup down. It had stopped raining. "You're probably right. I'd better go now."

I stood up.

"Shall I see you tonight, Tommy?"

"Yes. I hope so."

She saw me to the front door and I helped her to draw back the bolts the old woman had shot home. It was, I felt, too early to kiss her and so I pressed her hand and said good-bye. The bungalow was made of wood and the walls, protected from the rain by the roof looked old and dry, dangerously inflammable. At the bottom of the steps I turned, but the door was shut again. I looked round the garden. Although the rain had stopped the sun had not come out to steam the moisture away. It dripped from the roof and the trees and I remembered Saxby standing in the hall of Mrs Ross's hostel with water falling from his hair down his face, into his beard, collecting in a puddle at his feet. I imagined him now, standing in the garden, watching the bungalow, his hands held out from his sides because they were stained with juice. He had come at her, not out of the night, but in daylight out of the jungle, drenched in sweat and dressed like a Sikh with a dirty rag round his head, and she had laughed at him and told him not to be a bloody fool. Perhaps he had touched her then, and shouted, You will do this thing because I control the situation; shouted because for all the burden of his souls the burden of his flesh was suddenly greater, and she shrank from him, wiped his touch away, left him with a memory of his moment of lust as indelible as her memory of his hand on hers.

I sat in the jeep with my hand on the ignition switch.

You poor, damn, bloody fool, I said to him, she's like me, not worth the killing, and this wasn't part of the plan, not part of the plan at all; I was supposed to help you; you weren't supposed to have to reckon with me.

The engine fired. I raced it, then let it idle.

If a man abandoned you to walk with God you could not let him go without a fight. You sought him out. But if you suspected him of coming back by stealth to warm his hands at your fire, steal your food, abduct your women, why then, you hunted him down. The fire might be but a flicker, the food rank, your women not worth the taking, but they were all you had, all that stood between yourself and the darkness into which you dared not follow him.

*

Calthrop said, "They want you to ring 'em in K.L. sir."

We were alone in the company office. I had called there on the way back to the house.

I put a call through to Turner. It took ten minutes. As soon as he came on he said, "Brent? Can you come to K.L. right away? It looks as if we've found him."

I sat down. I felt as if I had geared myself to take part in a contest only to find it cancelled.

"Are you there, Brent?"

"Yes. You've found him you said. Saxby you mean."

I saw Calthrop look up from his work.

"Where?" I asked Turner.

"I'll tell you when you get here."

"No, tell me now. Are you sure it's him?"

183

Turner hesitated. "Is there a situation at your end?"

"There could be. We were right, I think. There could certainly be a situation. I want to talk to Reid."

"Who's Reid?"

"The company commander here."

"No. Leave that. At least, it doesn't matter. Tell him if you like. But I'm sure this is Saxby."

"I'll come to K.L. But tell me now."

"All right. We're going up into the Sakai country tomorrow. Me and you and a chap called Walu."

"Who's Walu?"

"One of the Sakai. I've not met him yet but the military police say he's a young chap and speaks good English. He was with a mission before the war but went back to his people when the Japs came. It's one of these longhouse communities and Walu's the son of the headman."

"Where does Saxby come in?"

"I'm telling you. About a week ago these Sakai found a white man wandering in the jungle. At least, he'd been wandering, but he was unconscious. He's probably dying. The headman wants us to go and see him."

"Is that all?"

"No. Apart from thinking they ought to report the situation to us they also think it must be Saxby."

"They know about Saxby?"

"I gather they all do. All the Sakai. He's a legend apparently. This particular community's never seen Saxby but they knew about him and also knew he had red hair. This white man has got red hair. He's in bad shape. It's a four-day journey, Brent, and I want to start in the morning."

"Has this white man got a beard?"

"All white men wandering about the jungle have beards."

"What time d'you want to start?"

"Bright and early. You'd better come back straight away so that you can get some kip in. I gather the going'll be pretty tough. All right by you?"

"Yes."

"Am I spoiling your plans for the evening?"

"You are. But they can be postponed." I grinned into the telephone because I realized the weight had gone, the pressure had been eased by a man called Walu, the son of a headman, bringing tidings of a white man with red hair wandering in the jungle, and now lying ill and helpless.

"Good," Turner said. "I've roped in a medico and the long-house fellow can arrange porters. The Brig says we've got to have an escort because of bandits, so I've borrowed a few lads from one of the British battalions. All we want is you."

"I'll be there. Have a bottle ready. The kip can wait. I've got a lot to tell you."

"You've decided you like the idea?"

"Yes, I like the idea a lot."

"Good man. Don't clutter yourself up with equipment, by the way. I'm arranging for sleeping-bags and things like that. I hope your friend Saxby appreciates the trouble we're taking. If he's still alive when we get there."

For an instant the pressure came back.

"It might be better all round if he's not," I said.

"It *was* like that, then?"

"I think so. Yes, I think it was."

"Poor bastard," Turner said. "God rest his soul if he is and it was."

"His souls," I said, "not soul. Souls."

I rang off, looked up and found Reid had come into the office.

"Saxby?" he said, throwing his slouch hat on to his desk.

"They think they've found him. I've got to go to K.L. right away. I'll be away for something like ten days."

"Where have they found him?"

"In the jungle, with the Sakai. At least they're pretty sure it's him. We're going to find out. Will you give Teena a note if I leave one? I want her to know."

He nodded. For a few moments he watched Calthrop who

was signing despatch notes. "You'll miss the pavilion," he said. "Are you going to leave your kit?"

"Most of it, if I may. I gather we're travelling light."

He looked round at me. "I envy you, Brent. No room for me, I suppose?"

Calthrop stared at him, as though thinking for a moment he might have been serious.

"Not this time, I'm afraid. But if it's a false alarm you could help me comb the jungle round here."

"I might hold you to that," he said, and smiled, bending his head to rub his left eyelid. "I'll come up to the house with you. Bill, you coming?"

Calthrop said, "I'm not through yet, sir."

"Bumph," Reid said. "The bloody world's full of paper and people writing on it. Come on, Brent. Give me a lift in that jeep of yours."

We drove up the hill.

"I owe a mess bill," I reminded him.

"Ah, Brent, you're as bad as a bloody Scot. Neither borrow nor lend. It's on the house."

"What about Teena?"

"She's on the house, too."

"I pay for my own women."

"Then bring her back a present like I said."

"All right. I'll bring her back a present."

The occasion was there waiting. I would come back from the Sakai with the knowledge that she was safe from Saxby and I would give her the gold lighter.

Prabhu Singh brought me a pot of tea and some sandwiches. As I munched and drank I scribbled a note to Teena.

Dear Teena,

Sorry, I shan't be here tonight. They think they've found crazy old Saxby. I'll be away for ten days or so. Bless you meanwhile, and take care of yourself.

Love,
Tommy.

Putting the note in an envelope I gave it to Reid.

"I'll deliver it by the duty officer," he said. Our eyes met. I thought of the night that lay ahead of me and the night that lay ahead of Reid and his officers: of the dark garden, the feel of silk on the naked body. He only talks to her, I told myself. He only talks. But there was no way of knowing whether this was the truth.

He came down with me to where the jeep was parked.

"I'm going to tell you something, Reid."

"I thought you might be. I've given you every chance in the last half-hour."

"It's about Saxby," I said.

"Well?"

"Just for your information. Nobody else's."

"Go on."

I smoothed the steering-wheel with my left hand. The light was going, the night was gathering, the hour of ghosts approaching.

"We thought he'd run amok," I said. "We thought he'd stayed behind to attend to unfinished business. We thought he might have killed Cheong Poh Kwee." I looked at him. "Keep an eye on Teena and the girls."

"Why on them?"

"I think she was on his list. But don't tell her. There's no point in putting the wind up anybody, especially now."

"Wouldn't she have him?"

"He didn't go to see her for that. He wanted her to murder the Jap officers. She refused."

"Sensible girl."

"Keep it to yourself, Reid. At least until I get back. Agreed?"

I searched his face to see how he was taking it. I felt I had to leave somebody on the alert, I had to send in a nightwatchman and Reid was the best material that lay to hand.

He said, "I'm beginning to hope you don't find him this time. Then we could get up an expedition of our own, Brent. Couldn't we? What about that? That would be an end, wouldn't it? To go off into the jungle looking for a man who talked to trees."

"Why do you say an end?"

"Because it *is* ending. This, all this." He waved an arm indicating the garden, the house, the view over the hills. "Oh, it's all right when the muck's flying. They want you then. They need you then. You can stand up like a man, and fling it right back. But when it settles, that's different. There it is. You can't stand up like a man when there's muck settled up to your knees and it gets you in the end. But it's nice to give it a run for its money."

He lowered his head and considered me for a while. I almost regretted telling him. He was full of broken glass. If you shook him you'd hear it rattle.

"Ah, don't worry," he said. "I'll keep an eye on Teena."

"Thanks."

Awkwardly I twisted round to give him my right hand. He held it firmly for a moment and then released it saying, "Off you go. If he's alive when you find him and he can spare that liver soul of his, you know where to bring it."

"I might bag it first," I called back and he raised a hand both in acknowledgement and farewell and watched me all the way to the turn in the road.

6

ON THE EVENING OF THE THIRD DAY WE FOUND shelter in a deserted Sakai hut: ten of us, Turner and myself, Walu the son of the headman, three Sakai porters, a corporal and three privates from a British infantry regiment. At the last moment the medical officer had been unable to come. We had an uncomfortable feeling that the most important member of the expedition had been left behind.

The corporal and his men alternated between fits of gaiety at being released from regimental duties and bouts of gloom at the prospect, as Turner heard one of them say, of being murdered in their beds by the Sakai. We had begun with four porters but they had accompanied us only as far as their own village where Walu had recruited replacements. On this, the third day, we had our third set. It had occurred to us early on that Walu was the only man familiar with the whole route. I think we all prayed in secret for his safety.

At first I thought Walu's unwillingness to talk about Saxby was caused by shyness. It was Turner who put his finger on the trouble. "Walu's a mission boy," he said, after the second or third attempt to get Walu to talk. "He doesn't believe in a damned thing, does he?" It became clear that he resented the long journey back from what he would call civilization. He was dressed in shorts and shirt and sneered at the porters for wearing nothing but loin cloths. He had come only at his father's insistence and although he had faithfully delivered his father's message he was not to be drawn on the subject of the Saxby legend. "You ask my father," was all he would say. "It is old man talk." And Turner, on the last such occasion, grimaced and said, "He means us." We had to be patient until we got to the longhouse.

On the first and second days we had set off at dawn and marched until just after midday, a sensible arrangement that was, Walu explained, the Sakai way of doing things, but there had been trouble on the third morning over porters and we had got off to a late start. We had a much longer leg than usual to march if we were to reach Walu's longhouse on the morning of the fourth day as we wished and we were in a fair way to being exhausted when we did eventually find the deserted hut Walu had aimed for.

The corporal and his men made tea for us on their portable tommy-cookers. The Sakai boiled some rice and served up a curry. Then, dousing our fires, we all climbed up the ladder to the hut, curled ourselves into sleeping-bags and went to sleep, Sakai on one side of the room, the corporal and his men on the other, Turner and myself sandwiched between them.

That night I dreamt again of Teena. Turner was in the dream somewhere and I was in a valley: not quite Greystone's valley although I understood it to be Greystone's. It was one of those dreams that reaches a certain point in its development and then begins all over again with variations. I was walking out of the valley and Turner said, We shall be a long time on the march because it's the third day. We had to count the porters to make sure they were all there and then I went back to the beginning, but not to the valley. This time the valley had become a clearing in the jungle. Walu said, It is *ladang*, meaning a space cleared for cultivation. He bent down to pick a vegetable that grew fat, stood up and was Wan Lo Ping saying, Sometimes it is necessary to talk to plants. We set off along the narrow Sakai track. The trunks of the trees were tall and bare, standing high above the mass of jungle fern and creeper that flourished beneath them, and it was blue-green twilight in that place. For a moment the reality of the march entered the dream with Turner and Walu and the Sakai porters whose backs were familiar, pressing forward in front of me as I dropped behind, my body no longer tuned to so much exertion. But at the top of a steep, slippery incline there was a small clearing, not *ladang*, more like a glade, with the sun shining down through a hole in the tree-top ceiling and coming towards me was Teena dressed in long gold jacket and trousers. Again I went back to the beginning, and again, ended each time with Teena coming towards me dressed in this style that was wholly imaginary on my part.

I woke on the fourth day at first light. We were three to four thousand feet up and it was cold before the sun rose. I could tell that I had begun a bout of mild malarial fever. It was in my blood from the bad old pre-mepacrine days. It was the kind of fever that left me a bit light-headed but perfectly capable and with any luck nobody need notice it.

One of the Sakai was talking in his sleep. On my other side the corporal was undergoing his now familiar battle with some dream-authority of whom he seemed alternately contemptuous and afraid. Teena in gold jacket and trousers floated in and out of my day-time consciousness.

All at once there was a feeling of Saxby's presence, coming from outside up the ladder.

I turned my face towards the entrance half-expecting to see him framed in the doorless opening. His presence there would have been a shock but his absence did not help. I untied the top tapes of the sleeping-bag and sat up. Saxby was all over the room, filling it with the warm, sharp odour of things that are green and grow out of the moist dark earth. I wanted to say, Go away, but the words were irrelevant even if the need to say them wasn't.

My sitting up had shifted the hold the others had on their sleep. Presently the Sakai porters woke one by one. I lay back again and let the new day strengthen its grip on us. Within ten minutes we were all stirring.

*

There was a mile or two to go, Walu said, but we had had a similar experience on the previous day when he described the

191

deserted Sakai hut as just over the hill. Turner and I now adjusted our mental image of the last leg in the march to the longhouse as day-long, perhaps interminable.

The first stage was down hill. We followed the Sakai track through thick jungle and could not tell the position of the sun. The ground was slippery and in the very steep parts it was best to plant your feet sideways. I marched behind Turner and watched his tunic darken, felt my own begin to stick to my back. The slight fever gave me a sense of being about to become immune to the laws of gravity.

At the bottom of the hill we crossed a rock-strewn river that moved swiftly, waist-high. The sun sparkled on the water and a bird piped shrilly. From the opposite bank we entered directly into the forest again, the track leading upwards, gently sometimes but mostly steeply and on the steep parts I grasped the trunks of trees wherever they offered purchase.

And so to the top of the hill and down like a switchback to meet the river again at one of its many curves. This time it lay beneath us at the bottom of a ravine some thirty feet deep and ten yards wide. A Sakai bridge consisting of a single tree-trunk lay across the gap and by the time Turner and I reached it Walu was on the other side.

"Oh, well," Turner said, and went across. I followed him, kept erect over the last couple of yards by my own momentum. There were rocks in the stream below. We did not look down as we crossed but they were in our minds' eye and we could hear the rush of water against them. The corporal and his men came across one by one while the Sakai porters stood waiting their turn grinning at our clumsiness.

From the tree-trunk bridge the track veered left, following the high bank of the river so that the sound of rushing water stayed with us. At nine o'clock when we had been going three hours Turner called a halt. We smoked and brewed up. The fever had left me and my vision had sharpened so that every leaf, every pebble embedded in the earth, every hair on my own forearms and those of Turner who sat by me stood out in clear definition. The place where we halted was fringed with bamboo, green, delicate and graceful. Behind the bamboo were stunted palms, their fronded leaves oily and almost emerald green. Behind the palms reared the huge straight trunks of the primeval jungle. Below and in front of us the invisible river plundered its way through the sunless bed, but in our little glade the sun burned. Half closing your eyes the heat on your face was like the heat from a fire of green flame.

It seemed then that the forest came to me in the way the arid valley had once come, in a way that no jungle had ever come to me. I would have been content to stay there with the sun deep in my bones and the rushing stream echoing in my blood. But then I sat up, my back cold from the touch of Saxby's hand. All around the bright glade his smell was coming up from the earth and down from the sky.

"What's up?" Turner asked.

"What?"

"You look as if you've been stung."

"I must have dropped off."

He looked at his watch. "We'd better get on," he said.

From the glade the track continued to follow the river for several hundred yards, dipped sharply and brought us again to the bank. We waded across.

On the other bank there was a *ladang* reverting to secondary jungle. Walu said that his own people had once cultivated it. Heartened by this evidence of being in his territory we followed him at a rather sharper pace along the river-bank until some half an hour later the track turned off once more into the jungle and took us upwards a few hundred feet, down again through bamboo and then through tapioca and into the clearing where the longhouse was.

*

Built high off the ground and entered at three points by sloping ladders it was some fifty yards from end to end. Atap-thatched with plaited bamboo walls, sections of which were raised to let in light and air, its single roof gave shelter to the whole community.

The *ladang* was deserted except for a group of small brown-skinned boys and girls who seeing Walu and the strangers he had brought with him ran quickly up the ladders into the interior. Walu told us to wait while he went into the house. Presently he returned and asked us to follow him.

The longhouse was stuffy and dark in spite of its size and the several raised sections of wall. There was a pungent smell of tobacco, damp-decay and rancid cooking fat. It was all as I had imagined it from books I had read and pictures I had seen: the raised platforms on either side divided into family compartments, the wide communal area in the middle like a road running between terraced houses. In the centre of the hut a group of men and women sat in a huddle round a bamboo platform. On the platform lay a human figure beneath a blanket. When the figure twisted round we saw that it was a Sakai, an old wrinkled man.

Walu said, "It is my father. He is trying to get the white man well."

Turner said, "Where is the white man?"

"Over here."

We followed him almost to the other end of the hut. More used now to the light I saw that the platforms were crowded with men and women, the men naked except for loin-cloths, the women barebreasted or not as the mood took them or the cloth of their sarongs extended.

Walu stopped. "The white man is here," he said.

We stepped on to the platform and entered the compartment. There was a bundle of clothing in one corner, the sound of stertorous breathing, the sweet smell of sweat.

Turner looked at me.

"Well," he said, "you'd better take a look."

Walu opened a section of the wall. The cubicle was flooded with filtered light and fresher air.

"Look at that," Turner said.

On the floor beside the blanket-covered figure was an earthen jar, and in it someone had placed five flowers: pale, pink petals with tender green foliage, like wild roses. I knelt down. The sick man's face was turned away and the clothes so disarranged that I could not see him without pulling the blanket down. As I did so he turned his face towards me and I drew back because his eyes were open and seemed to be staring at me although in fact they probably saw nothing.

It was not Saxby. The shock of it not being him left me trembling. I looked at Turner and shook my head.

Turner said, "Oh," and then again, more resignedly, "Oh," and knelt with me.

"Poor devil," he said.

I felt round the sick man's neck for identity discs but there was nothing; nothing on his stick-thin wrists. The tips of his fingers were already blackening, his hands were cold and wet.

Outside the cubicle a group of men had gathered. Through Walu Turner asked whether the sick man had ever regained consciousness or spoken lucidly. He had spoken but not in a way they understood. Once he had shouted what might have been a name but it was not a sound any could put their tongues to. "Try, try," Turner said, but they only shook their heads. Turner pointed at me, "This is a friend of *Tuan* Saxby. He says the dying man is not Saxby." They turned to mutter amongst themselves. "Then there's nothing we can do," Turner said, coming back to my side.

Turner was aware, as I was, that shortly a man was going to die and go to his grave nameless. There was an immense sadness in this. On the four-day journey we had not thought of it in those terms. We had thought of discovering Saxby, of his being capable of recovery, of his responding to the medicines we brought. We had not thought of finding a stranger lying in an anonymous, lonely huddle of blankets. We had thought of it not being Saxby, of finding a stranger dead or dying, but the anonymity and the loneliness were things we thought of for the first time there in the longhouse where they were actual, capable of inspiring grief.

Under the blanket the man was naked.

"Where are his clothes?" I asked. Walu pointed to a pile of rags. Turner went through them: old, torn khaki shorts and shirt.

"Nothing else? No boots? No socks?"

"Nothing, nothing," Walu said.

And in the pockets there was nothing.

"Why are the flowers here?"

Walu said, "They have put them there thinking this man was Saxby."

"Why would they do that?"

"My father will tell you."

"What did you say your father was doing?"

Walu looked down at his feet. Western customs had already corrupted him utterly. Whatever his father was doing filled him with a certain shame.

Turner said, "You said he was getting him better. How will he get him better lying on a bed under a blanket?"

"It is his belief. He will tell you about it."

"Can't you tell?"

"He will tell," Walu said and then nodded at the dying man and asked, "Will your medicines get him well?"

Turner said, "No. He will be dead in an hour."

I looked at Turner, stung by the abruptness and bitterness of the way he said it, stung as though I had expressed or felt hope of the man getting better or living at least longer than an hour, and I looked at Walu who could be stung by nothing because he believed neither in the longhouse nor in our medicines.

But Turner was wrong. The man lived longer than an hour. He lived for five. Turner and I took it in turns to sit close by him. Our vigils began as a means of identifying him should he regain consciousness and the power of speech but they ended in simpler terms; in terms of holding his hand in case within his darkness he was comforted by that contact.

196

In the last half-hour the rhythm of his breathing changed and for moments at a time he would not breathe at all so that when the end came I did not know it until his stillness had lasted so long I realized it was forever. I said, "He's gone," and Turner came over. We straightened his limbs and tried to shut his mouth but when we did so his blackened tongue protruded. He had closed his own eyes long ago.

We pulled the blanket over his face. Turner said, "Poor devil. Poor bloody devil."

An hour and a half later we buried him in a grave the Sakai had dug beyond the *ladang* in a small clearing. They wrapped him in the blanket and the rush mat on which he lay and Turner and I carried him to the place. They brought his ragged clothing, the jar of flowers and the bowl from which they had tried to feed him during his illness and these were buried with him because he might need them on the journey he was taking. It was customary, Walu said, for the dead to be buried with their personal possessions.

Turner had remembered some of the words from the burial service and spoke them in his matter-of-fact way. The corporal fashioned a cross out of bamboo. When the grave was filled in we placed the cross at the head. As we went back to the longhouse the women set up a monotonous ritual wailing.

Turner said, "Was he English do you think?"

It hadn't occurred to me that he might not have been, but now that Turner had mentioned it the dead man's anonymity extended beyond the small matter of his name.

*

We had brought presents of tobacco for the community and they fed us with a stew of meat that Turner swore was rat. Walu said his father was resting and that if we wished to do likewise a place was prepared for us. His father would be better in the morning and would tell us what was known by the Sakai of Saxby.

"But we must start back in the morning," I said.

197

Turner put a hand on my arm and said, "Steady up."

"There's not time to steady up."

It had taken us four days to get to the longhouse. It would take four days to get back. We had given Saxby eight clear days in which to do exactly what he liked.

The headman still lay on the platform, his face ashen under the brown pigment. Walu said, "It is dangerous for him if a man dies while he is still trying to get him better." The old man had been in a trance, that much was clear. There was nothing to be done, nothing to be learned until morning.

Huddled together in an empty compartment at the end of the longhouse Turner and I and the four infantrymen prepared for sleep. "It's murder," I heard one of them mutter to his mate. "I never thought I'd see so many tits at once and not fancy 'em."

The rain thundered outside. I woke once in the darkness thinking that I heard a voice calling from beyond the *ladang*.

"We should have given him shoes," I said, "he can't go far without shoes."

The sound of my own voice broke the dream. I was sitting up and Turner was saying, "What? What's that, Tom?"

*

Next morning after we had eaten the old man received us and through Walu told us what we wanted to know.

Everything was learned in dreams, he said, for the dream world was wiser than the world which held a man a prisoner of his flesh. In dreams a man might send the souls of his head and liver adventuring, searching, but the souls of his breath, heart and eye would not depart from his body except in death. Sickness was caused by a giantess, who lay in wait for the wandering souls of dreaming men and it called for the power of one like himself, a *shaman*, to wrest the captive soul from her by sending the soul of his own liver out to find her and tickle her under the armpit so that she flung her arms up and the soul of the sick man could escape and re-enter his body. It was this service he had tried to perform for the white man. Perhaps he had failed because the soul he had been looking for was that of the man Saxby, the Dreamer of Flowers, The White Soul-Seeker, the Shaman of the Red Beard.

It was said by the hill people that the Dreamer of Flowers first entered the forest because the soul of his liver and the soul of his head had gone out in a dream and not come back and he entered the forest like a man still asleep. There were even some who said his other souls had gone out of his body and that he was like a dead man walking. It was told that he was found by men of a *ladang* far to the north and that they were afraid of him until the *shaman* of their village saw in a dream that the white man's souls were imprisoned in five flowers growing together in a place not far away. For many days the *shaman* tried to dream the actual location of the flowers but one day he learned, in a dream, that the white man must dream the place himself to recover his own souls. When the *shaman* told the white man of his dream the white man mocked him but that same night fell into a dream and saw the flowers quite clearly and how he could get to the place in which they grew. And in the morning he set off into the forest and returned at night with the five flowers he and the *shaman* had both dreamed. Only then did he tell the people that his name was Saxby, and afterwards they called him the Dreamer of Flowers. It was said that the Dreamer of Flowers found other flowers in the forest but that the five in which his souls had been imprisoned were planted in the *ladang* and he enjoined the people to let no man touch them because they were sacred.

There were many different stories of what had happened after the flowers were planted. Some men said that Saxby left the *ladang* and that the flowers stayed miraculously in bloom season after season. Some said that the flowers were pulled up by an enemy and that Saxby wandered through the forest searching for him to kill him. Other men said that the flowers were destroyed by the white men's enemies and that Saxby had sworn vengeance on them. Other men said that the flowers faded and that Saxby fell down dead with a cry that split the heavens.

"Five were burned that could not be moved," Turner said when we were alone. "We'd better get back, hadn't we?"

*

The sun struck hot as we crossed the river and the corporal raised his voice and sang.

> *I've got sixpence, jolly, jolly sixpence,*
> *I've got sixpence to last me all my life,*
> *I've got twopence to lend and twopence to spend,*
> *And twopence to take home to my wife.*
> *No cares have I to grieve me,*
> *No pretty little maids to deceive me,*
> *I'm happy as a king believe me,*
> *As I go rolling, rolling home.*

And the privates getting back their courage chorused:

> *Rolling, home, blind drunk,*
> *Rolling home, blind drunk,*
> *By the light of the silvery moon!*
> *Ha ha ha ha ha*
> *Oh!*
> *He he he he he,*
> *Rolling rolling rolling rolling home.*

It was now the fourth day of the march and we were remembering landmarks. That was why the corporal was singing. Within a couple of hours we would come to the wide track that led to the kampong where we had debussed eight days before. We would be in Kuala Lumpur by late afternoon if Turner could get the lorry sent up to fetch us.

Turner signalled a fifteen-minute halt. We sat down together and smoked. Walu had come with us only part of the way and now there were only two Sakai porters with us.

"You'll go back to Bukit Kallang?" Turner asked.

200

"Yes."

"Tomorrow?"

"No. Tonight."

He nodded. He understood because I had told him everything.

"Shall I come with you?"

"No, but you can come and see me. I'll ring you tomorrow if there've been any developments. Have you heard anything from Singaputan?"

"No."

"I may go up there."

Turner got to his feet, ready to move off. As he helped me up he said, "You want to go on with this, Tom?"

"I don't want to. I've got to. Why do you ask?"

"Because it's pulling you two ways, isn't it? I'm sorry."

"That's my look-out."

"Are you falling in love with this girl?"

"Don't ask such damn fool questions."

"You kept saying her name in your sleep."

I struggled into my pack and for once he did not help me, perhaps because I looked determined to do it alone. "One thing," I said, turning on him, "no more of this walls-have-ears business. I ought to tell her what's on our minds, oughtn't I?"

"It's up to you."

"I'll think about it. She has an inkling, I'd say."

"I know, you told me."

I said, "He's mad isn't he? He's been round the bend since 1939. The Japs made it worse and Wan Lo worse than that. You understand that, don't you? He never talked to plants in Kampong Malim. The guerrillas there said nothing about talking to plants did they?"

"No, Tom."

"And he never had to tell them he'd lost one of his souls. He never had to dress up like a bloody Sikh, and go looking for it. They didn't know about that ever."

"If they did they didn't tell me when I was with them."

"No. He had Lieu Lim then. It's Wan Lo Ping you see. Bloody Wan Lo Ping with his damned singing and drilling."

Presently Turner said, "You can't blame Wan Lo, Tom. It's Saxby who's the danger."

"I know. I know it really."

We set off on the last leg. I could still smell Saxby. He was everywhere in the jungle. Each night, in sleep, I had gone on journeys in search of him and had woken shivering because in dreams Saxby was the giant who captured the wandering souls of the forest. It was he who had captured one of the souls of the unknown white man and kept it until the white man died. Then he had released it and it had come that first night in the longhouse and called out from the edge of the clearing.

So went the dream. Once in the dream I met this Saxby standing taller than the tallest tree in the forest, so tall that he had to part the canopy of branches far above me and peer down through the gap before he could see me where I stood calling to him.

"Why did you do it?" I shouted. "Why did you take the soul of the unknown white man and keep it until he died?"

He laughed, the sound like that of thunder in the forest, and said, "Because I control the situation. Because he was on my list."

7

"YOU BRENT? YOU IS IT? WHERE ARE YOU?"

The line to Bukit Kallang crackled with atmospherics. I told him I was speaking from Kuala Lumpur and would be with him by half-past seven that night.

"Come on, then. Come back. Nothing's happened. It's like the grave here. You can see the ghosts. Did you find him, Brent? What was he doing? Talking to it? Swapping yarns with the jungle?"

"No, it wasn't Saxby. You sound as if the sun's gone down early."

"Oh, it's gone down, you bet your life. So it wasn't Saxby."

"It wasn't Saxby. Is Teena all right?"

"I told you. Nothing's happened. There's been no change. At least, not of any importance. You can have back your little Madame Ching-Chang. If it wasn't Saxby who was it?"

"Nobody we knew. Nobody anyone knew. I'll see you at half-past seven."

*

Reid was drunk. He stood in the veranda room at the head of the stairs and watched me come up, shook his head as if in amazement, as if needing to clear it.

"What's this? Jungle green? Where's your khaki?"

"Coming up behind."

I was still wearing the uniform Turner had given me for the trip.

"How come, Brent? I'm used to you in khaki. My little pigeon-hole picture of you shows you dressed in khaki."

"I will be when I've had a shower."

"What? Haven't you bathed? Not changed? Straight out of the jungle sweating like a pig? Lucky, lucky man, that calls for a drink."

But his speech was not slurred and when he walked to the veranda where his officers waited, you would have thought him quite sober. Bidding them good evening I saw the stranger with them, the green lad, the student soldier whose father might be Colonel Sutton or a draper in Purley, who had come to take Ballister's place. And the coincidence of Sutton's arrival with Reid's drunkenness made it impossible not to wonder whether they were connected. I say Reid's drunkenness but it was more the nervous disorientation of a man trying to get drunk and failing.

Sutton was a good-looking boy of nineteen or so with fine, straight fair hair, cropped at the neck but growing long on top. It was inclined to flop over his forehead and then he would bring up a surprisingly smallboned hand and push it back into place. His face was shiny with heat and brick-red with sunburn: so fierce a colour that when I first saw him I thought him painfully shy.

"So it wasn't Saxby," Reid said, handing me a generous drink, topping up his own. "You had your journey for nothing. Did you see any plants you knew? Know any trees to talk to?"

"We weren't on speaking terms. Cheers."

"Cheers." He swung round at the others. "Sit down, for God's sake." When they had done so he said, "No need for ceremony, Major Brent's one of us. We all know each other here." He paused. "No, that's not quite right, is it? Sutton!"

Sutton got to his feet again.

"Brent, you've not met Sutton before, have you?"

We nodded at each other across the width of the drinks table. Once more he sat down.

"They have sent me Sutton," Reid said, "to take the place of Ballister."

I said, "Well, good. Good for Sutton." I swallowed my drink.

"Are you going?" Reid asked. "Getting out of all that mucky clobber? Then wait. I've got something for you."

He went over to his bedroom. MacAndrews, filling the gap, said, "Who was it, sir, if it wasn't Saxby?"

"We never knew. We got there in time to bury him."

"Brent!" Reid's voice interrupted us. "Hang on there."

He came out with the red dressing-gown.

"Here," he said. "This is for you. This hasn't changed. Nothing's changed, I told you that, didn't I?"

*

"You have walked with us in the valley and stood with us on the hill. We ask for Your blessing on the living and for Your mercy on the dead."

He dipped his spoon into the soup. At the other end of the table Ballister's place was still laid, the chair still drawn up, empty, dominating. Sutton had not been allowed to sit there. He was in a seat of questionable honour, on the ghost's right hand.

"So it wasn't Saxby," Reid said. "So Saxby is still at large." He looked from one to the other of his officers, finally at me. "I broke my word. I told them. I told them what you suspected Saxby of."

"I see."

"They think you're potty."

Calthrop said, "We said it was a potty idea, sir, not that Major Brent was potty."

"You spend too much of your time with words, Bill, words on paper. Now you play with them. So the idea was potty, so Major Brent had the idea."

I said, "Has it gone further than this room?"

Calthrop said, "No, sir."

I turned to Reid. "Not to Wan Lo Ping?"

"Not to Wan Lo Ping. Not to Teena Chang. Only to my lads, my boys, my brave bulls. And they said you were potty. They don't see that you can't leave a man in the jungle. They don't believe this man's there, anyway. They think the war ends when the brass hats sign their names to something."

Suddenly he snapped out: "What do you think, Sutton? How do you think the war ends?"

Sutton paused, soup spoon half-way to his mouth. The others looked at their plates.

Sutton completed the movement with the spoon, swallowed, and said, "I don't know, sir. I've not thought about it."

"You've not thought about it. You ought to have thought about it. But I'll tell you. The war ends when the last shot's fired. D'you see the catch, Sutton?"

"No, sir."

"It's plain enough. You ought to see the catch. But then you've never been under fire, have you?"

"No, sir."

"So there are things you don't know about yourself. Things *you* don't know, but the rest of us do, know about ourselves that is. How we act when the muck's flying. Your father was a regular, wasn't he?"

"Yes, sir."

"And you say you're not?"

"No, I'm not, sir."

"Are you going to be?"

"I've not decided, sir."

I broke in.

"Well, what is the catch?"

Reid looked at me. "*You* ought to know. That surprises me, you not knowing. The catch is you can't tell where the last shot's coming from, or when. That's why you can't leave men like Saxby wandering about the jungle talking to trees. It's men who talk to trees who're the danger. They're the chaps who come out at you sticking a round up the bloody spout when the rest have packed in."

"So what do you do?"

"You hunt them down. Shoot them if necessary."

"I don't see it like that."

"No?"

"Not when the chap sticking the round up the bloody spout is a friend of mine."

He put his spoon down.

"You've got to choose, haven't you?"

"Choose what?"

"Between shooting and being shot."

"Not if you haven't got a gun to shoot with."

"Brent. Brent, oh, Brent. You're a fool, aren't you?"

"And you," I said, "seem to be as pissed as a newt."

He stared at me, his mouth open. He swung in his chair, challenged his officers. "Well? Do you take that? Do my brave lads let a stranger tell me I'm as pissed as a newt? Do I hear no sound? No snarl? Are my young lions silent?" He pushed the soup plate away. "Mac!" he shouted.

"Yes, sir."

"Am I pissed?"

"Yes, sir."

Holmes laughed. And then Reid leaned back in his chair and roared with laughter, too. "You see, Brent? You've subverted my officers. You've alienated their affections. You ought to be ashamed, after all I've been doing for you."

"What have you been doing?"

"Why," he said, "looking for Saxby, what else?"

"How have you done that?"

"By asking questions. I've had patrols out every day, Brent. Think of that. Slogging through the jungle on your account. A fine circular tour it's been, combing the villages, searching the old clearings, asking questions."

"What kind of questions?"

"About an Englishman dressed up like a Sikh, travelling alone or accompanied by a Chinese."

"I see."

"Ah, but do you? Do you understand what it means to order patrols out when your second-in-command thinks you're wasting the company's time. No. Worse than that, making it a laughing stock."

"Well, you're the officer commanding," I reminded him.

"Am I?" He looked at Calthrop. "Well so I am. Don't forget that."

"I don't forget it, sir. But if battalion knew they'd think we'd gone crazy."

"We've never cared what battalion thinks. We don't start caring now."

I said, "Have the patrols discovered anything?"

Calthrop answered before Reid could do so. "Not a thing, sir. That's the point. But when you ask questions like that you start a rumour going. It goes ahead of you and before you know where you are you're being sent off on some wildgoose chase by a village that doesn't know anything but wants to be helpful. Like yesterday. Like the day before. And the day before that. We'd be better off chasing that bandit camp in the Sungei Malim area, if you don't mind my saying so."

"And coming across Chinese boys bathing in rivers," I said. "Yes, I agree. I agree with you, Calthrop."

Reid frowned. "Why?"

"I'd rather you didn't send patrols looking for Saxby. I wouldn't like one of them to find Saxby bathing in a river."

I felt MacAndrews shift a bit in his chair.

"Is that a criticism, Brent?" Reid asked.

"Yes and no. No, because what Mac did was obviously nothing more than a reflex. Yes, because I think his reflexes are too quick."

"It's because they're quick that he's alive."

"I know."

"So how can they be too quick?"

"They were too quick from the Chinese boy's point of view. He isn't alive, is he?"

"That was his look-out."

"I wouldn't want it to be Saxby's."

208

MacAndrews said, "Not even if he'd killed Teena, sir? Would you mind if I found him bathing in a river then?"

"Take this damn soup away," Reid shouted suddenly. The mess-waiter appeared from behind the half-closed kitchen door. While he removed our plates and the knife, forks and spoon from Ballister's place and then served us with M. & V. stew we sat in silence.

When we were alone, Reid said, "You'll apologize to Major Brent, Mac."

"Oh, for pete's sake," I began.

"I said Lieutenant MacAndrews would apologize to you."

"He's entitled to his say."

Reid ignored me. He said, "MacAndrews, did you hear?"

There was nothing for it. MacAndrews turned to me and said, "I beg your pardon, sir."

"For that matter I beg yours."

Reid said, "Right. Now we forget it."

The meal came awkwardly to its end. The apology had sobered him. On his face was an expression of almost startled misery. After Ballister perhaps it was MacAndrews he had been fondest of, Calthrop who least commanded his affection because Calthrop was older, ambitious enough to be a challenge to the authority Reid set himself out to exercise. I wondered what was in store for Sutton. He could not, surely, go on forever being punished for not being Ballister? Sooner or later Reid would have to decide whether utterly to reject or partly to accept the new face; if only as that of an unwanted cub whose shape would be licked out with a tentative, bitter and exploratory tongue.

I watched Sutton. My first impression of him had been wrong. He was not shy. He had the tight-wound, unresilient look of someone packed with explosive and there was the ghost of a smile on his lips, a smile not of amusement but of recognition. A picture was forming, and Sutton saw it.

I was uneasy. Saxby came into the picture somewhere. Saxby was being used by Reid in a way I thought must be clear but which for the moment I could not fathom. It was like a game of chess, Reid my opponent, Saxby a pawn which Reid held suspended over the board, myself waiting to see what square Reid put him on before I could tell where the danger was going to lie. It would have been better if I had known where I stood myself, what square I was on, whether it was for Saxby or Teena I was really playing.

You want it both ways, Brent, I told myself; you've always bloody well wanted that. You've got to make up your mind.

But it was no good telling myself that. It was not my mind that had to be made up. It was my heart, and not my mind, that knew you did not leave a man to the mercy of plants and yet could not let him come at you.

And that heart was, in its complexity, as strange and mysterious as the pavilion with its chambers of different colours, its doors to come in by and its doors to go out of, its strong supporting pillars awrithe with dragons. But within it there was always the illusion of the occasion found.

*

She was in her Chinese mood. "Tonight I am Madame Ho," she said, kneeling upright on the cushions. "Please to inform Mac." But Mac had gone to the jade room with Lily, Holmes to the golden room with Suki who by European standards was no more than a child and looked absurdly fragile in his beefy arms.

"Forget Mac."

"Yes. I will forget," she said.

Her red silk dress was embroidered with red silk dragons and in the yellow light of the lantern her cheeks looked almost sallow. Her brows slanted upwards and a daring stroke of the pencil shaped her eyes like almonds. Against her Chinese mood I had no defence. I joined her on the cushions and gave her the tiny package in which I had wrapped the gift. She took it from me slowly and held it between the fingers and thumb of each hand with her other fingers arched stiffly but delicately like the wings of a bird arrested in flight.

"Aren't you going to open it?" I asked after a while.

She turned the box over and began to pick at the string.

"Let me," I said, and leaned towards her. Our eyes met. I could not help kissing her. When I had the string off I gave the packet back to her. She took off the paper, folded it neatly and placed it on the chest. Then she lifted the lid of the box, twitched at the cotton wool until the gold lighter was revealed in its soft white bed.

She lowered the box to her lap, keeping her eyes on it. She said, "Is it for me always, Tommy?"

"Yes, for you always."

"It is very beautiful." She kept her eyes down. "Very beautiful, rare and expensive."

I said something about not having bought it.

"But it is beautiful," she insisted. "Also it was expensive. It was yours and you have given it away and that makes it rare." She looked up now. "Doesn't that make it rare? There is only one such lighter in the world. No other lighter of this make and price has been yours and given to me." She put the lid back on. "It is the rarest thing I have."

I offered her a cigarette.

"Let's christen it," I said.

"You christen it. Tonight I am not smoking."

I took a cigarette, waited while she opened the box again and held the lighter up in two hands. The small flame glowed steadily as I bent towards it.

"There," she said, "it is christened. It is called Bright Flame." It lay now on her palm. "Bright Flame is a friendly spirit. Whenever I want to see you I can summon Bright Flame."

"What'll you say to her?"

"Oh, it is not a her. Bright Flame is a man spirit."

"How'll you summon him?"

"Well. I shall say, Ho! Bright Flame –"

"Go on."

"Bring Tom Brent."

211

"What if he can't?"

"Oh, he will always bring you."

"How?"

"In his eye. In his one golden eye." She clicked the lighter on and we stared into the flame together. "There you see. You are always in his one, bright golden eye."

"You can see me there?"

"Yes."

"But not now. Look!" I blew the flame out and at once she uttered a cry, snatched her hands away and pressed them to her cheeks so that the lighter fell between us on to the scarlet cushion. I shivered. The movement had been so swift that my apprehension had to fade before I could entertain the suspicion that it had been as artificial as a piece of theatrical business. I picked the lighter up and put it in the pocket of her dressing-gown which lay folded on the chest. She had told me on the first evening that she was Madame Ho when she felt drawn to her mother's country by her ignorance of it, her wish to know a lot about it. I wondered whether this was only part of the truth or even whether it was the truth at all. Enchanted, willing victim though I was, the worm was there, the thought that Madame Ho came out on nights when men like Brent were likely to remember that in the interval there had been other men, men like Reid. Perhaps Madame Ho was only a device to make such men forget such men.

She said, "What is the matter?"

"Nothing, nothing." I seized her almost angrily, crushed her like the petals her hair smelt of. When I opened my eyes I found that with her free hand she had lowered the lantern to a pale, blue glimmer.

*

The lantern shone again, she sat naked, moving the palm-leaf fan to and fro. I watched her shadow on the wall. Between us the shadow of the fan was magnified to the size of a giant moth. I turned back to her.

"Are you still Madame Ho?"

"Yes. And no. Half-way Madame Ho."

"Why *were* you Madame Ho?"

"Because I felt like it. My mother was Chinese. I told you this."

"And you've had more of your mother in you tonight than usual?"

"Yes, Tommy."

"Was she a Catholic, Teena?"

"No, why?"

"You have a picture of the Sacred Heart."

"I was brought up in a mission school."

"Where?"

"In Malaya."

"Where in Malaya?"

"Up-country."

"And your mother is dead."

"Yes."

"How old are you?"

"Twenty." She added, "Did you think I was older?"

"Yes."

"How much older?"

"I thought you were more like twenty-five."

"Is that a compliment?"

"Yes, it's meant as a compliment. Did you like the mission?"

"I liked it very much. When I was fourteen the Father allowed me to teach the small children."

"Is the Father still alive?"

"No."

I turned my head to watch our shadows. Her mother's death and the priest's death had the same anonymous quality as that of the unknown white man.

She said, "Did you find Sax Bee?"

I shook my head, looked round at her, reached under the net for my cigarettes. When she saw what I wanted she gathered up her dressing-gown from where it lay at the foot of the mattress and felt in the pocket.

She clicked the lighter on and said, "I can only use it when I'm with you or when I'm alone. If another man is with me and wants a cigarette and I summon Bright Flame he won't come. So I shan't summon him."

I said, "I shan't hold you to that."

She put the lighter back carefully into its box. She said, "I shall hold myself to it," and took up the fan again.

"I only meant that the present has no strings."

"You would not mind if I lighted Major Reid's cigarette with your gold lighter?"

"No. It's yours now, not mine."

"Then why do you look so cross?"

I did not answer. She leaned forward and kissed my right shoulder. I caught and held her face with my left hand, the thumb supporting her chin, the fingers pressed to her right cheek. She drew her brows together in a mock frown, pulled away, sat upright again but I stopped her from waving the fan. Waving the fan gave her an advantage over me.

She said, "How long will you stay this time?"

"I don't know."

"Are you still looking for Sax Bee?"

"Yes, still looking."

I released her hand but she let the fan lie still in her lap. She said, "Will Sax Bee be in trouble when you find him?"

"Why should he be in trouble?"

"I don't know. Only you talked about him as if he might be."

"It depends what he's done."

"What might he have done?"

After a bit I said, "He might have killed somebody."

She picked the fan up, looked at it, began to wave it above us.

"We won't talk about Saxby," she announced.

"What then?"

"About the pavilion."

"Tell me about the pavilion."

"A man from China built it," she said.

"What was his name?"

"I don't know. It is written in a book but I have not read it yet."

I said, "Written in what book?"

"The book of eternity. It is what my mother called it. The man who built the pavilion is dead."

"I know he's dead. The Japanese killed him, didn't they? They stuck his head on a pole and made everybody in Bukit Kallang march up the hill to look at it. After that they called it the garden of madness because men lost their heads in it and when there's a full moon the ghosts of all the people who lost their heads come out of the pavilion and stand in the garden remembering and looking for their shoes."

She had put her head on one side. She said, "Why should they look for their shoes?"

"Because they need them. They have a long way to go. All the way to Heaven. They can't go until they find their shoes. That's why they're ghosts."

She smiled.

"Go on," she said. "You never talk. You only ask questions. Tell me more about the pavilion."

"It's a magic cave."

"Yes. I like it to be that."

"Ah, but do you know why it's magic?"

"No."

"It's magic because the sun sleeps here."

"Here? Here in this room?"

"Yes. You can see the sun set from the window. At least you think it's set. But that's where you'd be wrong. It falls out of the sky and tumbles into this room. Then it curls up and goes to sleep. That's why the room is scarlet."

"Has the room got a name?"

"Yes, it ought to have a name. What though? You're good at names."

She reached for her bare ankle and clasped it, still waving the fan with her other hand. Presently she said, "I've thought of its name. It is the Scarlet Room wherein the Setting Sun lies sleeping."

I ran my finger along the soft crinkles on the sole of her foot. "Yes, that's a good name."

She frowned. "But what happens in the morning, Tommy? How does the sun get out of the Scarlet Room?"

"Well, not many people know about that, but actually, just before dawn, it walks in its sleep and wakes up looking through the window of the Golden Room."

"Yes. Ah, yes. And it stretches its arms through the window and says, Golden Room you are mine."

"And that room's called the Golden Room Enslaved of the Rising Sun."

"Yes."

She had stopped fanning. She was a child, enraptured by a fairy tale; or a woman storing up enchantment for men. "And the Jade Room," she said, "that is called the Jade Room of Day long Happiness because outside it the sun is shining in the sky on to the green trees."

She smiled, waved the fan again.

"What about the ante-room?" I asked.

"Yes, we must think about the ante-room."

"The room of the Dancing Dragons?" I suggested.

"Why Dancing Dragons?"

"There are dragons dancing on the floor."

"Also there are fish swimming."

"And birds singing without making any sound."

"The Room of the Swimming Fish?" she asked.

"The Room of the Tongueless Birds?" I countered.

After a while she said, "There is no name for the ante-room, but I've thought of names for the two doors. The door that only open inwards, that is called the Door by which men enter in anticipation of Desire. But the little door that opens outwards, that is the door by which men go in memory of loving."

Was she cautioning me, warning me that however often a

216

man entered the pavilion he could not stay there, that the time would always come when he had to go?

"Must a man go out by that door, Teena?"

"There's no other door."

"He could stay here. He need not go at all."

"You said it was a magic cave."

"Yes."

She smiled again. "You would have to be a magician always to live in a magic cave."

I caught her arm. "Ah, but I am," I said. "I am. Watch."

*

We went out on to the veranda to see whether the night had cleared. A young moon had climbed above the garden and hung there.

In the moonlight the red silk of our gowns gleamed like gun-metal and against it her skin was white and luminous. Transparent scarves of mist lay motionless just above the ground and across the garden the house floated on the mist like one built in a dream. The dark pavilion was a boat and we were lovers standing by its rail.

She asked me the time. It was one o'clock. I said, "Let me take you back alone, Teena."

"There is no need. Duty officer will see to it."

"Damn the duty officer. You'd think it was a kind of parade."

"But I don't want to go back yet."

"I didn't mean yet. I meant when it's time. No, a bit before it's time. Before it's morning. While it's still like this. We'll find our own harbour."

"Harbour, Tommy?"

"It's not a cave any more, it's a boat. Look, the garden is a lake. There's been a storm but now it's calm and we're drifting in the middle of it."

She said nothing for a while and then, simply, "I should like that."

217

8

I COULD NOT SLEEP AGAIN BUT LAY LISTENING TO THE quiet rhythm of her breathing. Mist seemed to have entered the room through the open window: an effect of moonlight but curious, unsettling because of its stillness. I wanted to move, to sit up and smoke, but that would have woken her, so I lay cramped and hot, held restlessness in as the silent hills in whose arms we sheltered held in their restlessness.

Between three and four I dozed fitfully. I woke chilled. The night had changed its shape. Now the pavilion was restless and I was alert and did not want to move because I was aware as I had been that morning in the deserted Sakai hut of Saxby coming in from outside, of his entering and filling the room, burgeoning in it until I felt the words, Go away, forming hard in my chest, so hard that suddenly they released themselves. For a few seconds whatever spirit lived in that room paused in surprise and then Teena moved and said, "Is it time?" She entered wakefulness as easily as she entered sleep.

"It's just after four."

She raised herself and said, "Oh," and then, "Do you want to go?"

"Yes, we'll go now."

I reached out and raised the wick of the lantern. The room became the image of itself the night before, untouched by the passage of the last few hours and yet reflecting them.

As we dressed we talked in whispers like conspirators but the expected magic of the moment was quite absent. In her voice and the things she said she showed none of the soured irritability I was conscious she ought to feel and which I felt myself. She wrote a note to Anna and left it on the chest weighed down by a dirty glass. The whole arrangement was furtive and unreasonable; but still important.

We left the dark pavilion and walked over the wet grass. The moon shone intensely. I thought of the scene that would be enacted there in an hour's time, of the two girls shepherded across the garden by a duty officer booted, uniformed, conducting the night's operation to its close, wrapping it up, while the young lions slept on in the pavilion, satisfied, smug.

The fifteen hundredweight truck stood solidly in the way of the jeep in the porch. To get the jeep out I should have to move the truck. The duty officer might have slept through the softer noise of the firing of the jeep engine. The noise of their own truck would be sure to wake him and bring him out to see what was up. With two arms I might have pushed it out of the way. With one and a half I should probably fail. I moved to open the cabin door.

She touched my arm. "You'll wake them up."

"Well, does it matter?"

"It would be a pity."

I said, "I'll try and push it then."

"No, let's walk."

"Your shoes."

"I can walk in them."

"You'll ruin them."

"I have other pairs. I won't ruin them. And I should like to walk. It doesn't take long."

"All right, if you're sure. I'm sorry. It was meant to be nice taking you home alone."

"It is nice for me."

Arm-in-arm we set off down the drive.

"You've walked before, then?"

"Why?"

"You said it doesn't take long."

"Yes, Tommy. I have walked before."

"With Reid?"

"No. With Joe."

219

"Hakinawa."

"Yes. Hakinawa."

We came out of the drive. The trees let moonlight through their branches like pale sunshine. We stopped to light cigarettes and then walked on down the curving road like lovers strolling on a summer night. But we were not lovers. The picket guards at the company and platoon headquarters challenged us half-heartedly, grinning at us, showing their white teeth. At the main guardhouse they had to raise the white pole to let us through and a sepoy called out, Shabash! meaning, Bravo!

Leaving the shadows, coming out into the main road my own shoes made no sound but the heels of hers tapped on the metalled surface, sharp and clear.

"He was a brave chap," I said.

"Who?"

"Hakinawa. Or did he always carry a pistol?"

"Why should he carry a pistol?"

"Wasn't it dangerous for him, alone like this?"

"He was not afraid."

"But he was afraid in the end. He committed suicide."

She did not reply.

We would not talk about Saxby but he loomed everywhere. He had lain in wait watching the bungalow, discovering the way Teena came home alone with Hakinawa. And one such night, the night he disappeared perhaps, as Hakinawa began the journey back to the house on the hill he had come up behind him, held a gun to his back, or a knife, and whispered that the girl he slept with carried information to the guerrillas, and then he had melted into the shadows and left Hakinawa alone to think about it. How long, I wondered, had it taken Saxby to discover that Hakinawa had taken his own life instead of Teena's.

We walked beneath the triumphal arch. The stucco of the buildings shone moon-bright and the sky here seemed paler. Coming to the bungalow we entered the deeply shadowed compound.

"There you see," she said, "it took no time."

She knocked on the door with what I imagined was a distinctive beat.

"Come in and have some very early morning tea," she said. I accepted her invitation. Impatiently she knocked again. A thin wind stirred the bushes in the garden. They rustled dryly. She shivered and leaned closer to me.

We were let in by the old woman who carried an oil lamp. She was muttering to herself. Teena spoke to her harshly and took the lamp to light us to her room. She set it down on the chest of drawers beneath the picture of the Sacred Heart.

"Tea won't be long," she said.

She left me alone for a bit. While she was away the old woman came in with the tray. Her sons had run the garage and the bungalow was hers but she was treated like a servant. I wondered how much of the girls' earnings she received. She did not speak to me or acknowledge my presence in any way. She set the tea-tray down and walked out as though the room had been quite empty.

And it was empty. I stared at it, understanding its utter emptiness. The drawers and cupboards were crammed with Teena's black-marketry, but when she was not in the room to be adorned by them they lay in their hiding places lifeless. When she was not in the room the room itself was lifeless. She carried everything in her, left no impression of herself behind and this, I saw, was because she laid no duty of reflection upon the things surrounding her or upon the people who knew her. But when she returned to them she illuminated them with her own presence.

"Have you poured yourself a cup?" she asked.

"No, I was waiting for you."

She came to the sofa, sat with me and poured tea. She had taken off her dress and wore an English-style housecoat that had nothing to do with the pavilion. It was a neutral grey-brown shade. Her hair was freshly combed. She wore no make-up. She was hard and ambitious and would sleep with any man

221

prepared to pay the right price at the right time, and if there were no right price or time she would move heaven and earth to find or make them. She had driven a Japanese officer to suicide and outplayed Saxby here in this room. She had offered herself with Anna, Lily, and Suki to Reid, submitted them to inspection like cattle. She had brow-beaten the old woman under whose roof she lived and the spoils of her profession were packed away in a chest beneath a picture of the Sacred Heart. She had laid deliberate siege night after night not only to men's lust but to their sense of the strange and colourful and had transformed what was common or garden into an illusion of beauty and wonder by a series of simple primitive tricks.

And she was warm and beautiful and magically innocent and seemed to be afraid of nothing. I was sick with jealousy at the thought of another man touching her, but even as I let the jealousy erupt I could not become blind to the possibility of her deliberately provoking possessiveness in the men with whom she slept. She was leaning back on the sofa with her eyes half-closed, the corners of her lips turned up. I could almost feel her stripping the layers of jealousy from me to see how deep they went and saying to herself: This is good, this is good for business.

It was good for business, perhaps, to pretend that Reid only talked to her, good for business to allow the legend of a love affair with Hakinawa to grow, because it presented her as a woman capable of passion outside the contract. Perhaps she told Reid *I* only talked to her. Perhaps she still opened her doors, opened her legs, as Reid would say, for the guerrillas. Perhaps one of Wan Lo Ping's flat-faced henchmen sometimes knocked and entered. Perhaps Hamsher with his mad eyes cold and penetrating had fumbled with her bare breasts in this room and straddled her for a couple of dollars and a few cigarettes. She had cheated the Japanese like that. There was no reason why she should not similarly cheat Reid.

I rose and she said, "What do you want, Tommy?"

"It must be nearly light. I'll be going."

"What is wrong?" she asked.

"Nothing," I said. "I must go."

"You've not spoken to me."

"Sorry. I'm tired I suppose. We didn't get much sleep."

"You can sleep. You can sleep here."

"No, I ought to go."

"Haven't I pleased you tonight?"

"Would it worry you not to have pleased me?"

"It would always worry me, tonight especially."

"Why tonight?"

"You gave me Bright Flame and he's a happy spirit who only comes out on happy nights."

Briefly there was an echo of her Chinese mood. I wondered what her third and private mood might be. I wondered whether there was a Teena none of us had ever seen, neither Hakinawa nor Reid nor myself, a Teena who in the privacy of this room forgot what was good for business and surrendered herself to the passions she knew so well how to kindle in others.

"Was it a happy night for you?" I asked her.

"Yes."

"Because of the lighter?"

"Because you gave it to me and we were on a boat drifting on the lake."

She had remembered that.

She said, "And we walked home and didn't come back in the truck."

"Shall we always walk home?"

"No, you need to sleep."

"What about you?"

"I can sleep all morning. I'm going to sleep soon." She hesitated, repeated her invitation. "You don't have to go back if you'd like to sleep too."

Did she mean outside the contract, as a friend? I wanted her to say it, to say: As a friend. But she simply stood there waiting for my answer and I was too proud to say: Do you mean outside the contract, do you mean as a friend? because she would have had to say yes. It would have been bad for business to say no.

"No, I ought to get back."

She said that I should at least wait for the truck and go back in it, but I wanted none of the truck. She became resigned to my going. I asked her to light my way to the front door but instead she took my hand and led me from the room and through the dark square hall.

She unbolted the door. Before I opened it I said, "Take care of yourself, Teena."

"Yes, Tommy."

From another part of the bungalow a voice was raised, the old woman's I fancied. Teena called back in English, "It's all right."

I said, "Is there anything you haven't told me about Saxby? Anything that might help me to find him?"

She did not answer at once.

"No, I don't think so."

She opened the door a foot or two keeping herself in its shadow in a way that made me think of her as vulnerable in spite of everything. I bent and kissed her.

*

I waited for a moment on the veranda, listened to the sounds made by the bolts as she shot them home. What I first thought of as the thin light of morning was the diffused silver-grey light of a moon in a sky that had lost the dark bottomless look of night. The garden compound was still in deep shadow. Through the trees and shrubs which partly hid the bungalow from the road the buildings opposite stared flat and blind. The road where it was visible at the end of the curving drive had the lonely, waiting look of all roads that are empty in a town that sleeps.

But it was not quite asleep. As I came to the end of the drive I heard a scuffling, clacking noise from higher up the road near the junction; distant, but quite clear, and, I thought, coming nearer, echoing on the hard surface: someone walking at a leisurely pace, someone wearing sandals, the kind of sandals that are held to the foot by suction and a single strap over the big toe.

I went out and stood in the middle of the road.

I could see him quite clearly. He was perhaps thirty yards away. Apart from the sandals his feet and legs were bare, blue-black in the moonlight. He wore a pair of shorts that flapped baggily above his knees and an old khaki shirt hanging loose outside his belt. A haversack was slung over one shoulder, the strap aslant across his chest. A turban was wound round his head.

He continued walking towards me with a slow slack-kneed Indian gait but when we were ten feet apart he stopped.

Beneath the turban his face and beard looked as if they were carved from ebony. He stood quite still but I could see the slow heaving of his chest as he breathed. At first I could not make out any expression on his face, but then the features began to take shape and I saw that he was smiling. Neither of us spoke for a long time and then he said in Hindustani, "Greetings, brother. God go with you."

I replied in the same language, "And with you also." The language fell like music, lost, sad, reminding me of the valley where he had taken me.

"What would you with me, brother?" he said.

I was silent. I did not know. There was an air about him so remote and yet so gentle I fancied that were the moon to shine more clearly on his face I should have seen upon it an expression of beatitude.

"Have you no words, brother?" he asked.

"No, Brian."

The smile faded slowly.

"What name was that?" he asked, still in Hindustani.

"Brian."

The ten feet separating us grew intolerably long. It was he who lessened them. He came towards me, close enough to put his hand out and take me by the chin which he did with the quiet, unhurried gesture of a blind man. When he let his hand drop I did not wipe away the feel of it.

"What is your name?" he asked, and when I had told him he remained silent for a while. Presently he repeated the name, "Tom." And then again, as if nearer to remembering, "Tom." The smile returned. "Ah," he said very quietly in English, "so it is you. It is you, coal-heaver."

"Yes."

He glanced towards the house I had just left, and then, as if considering, at my waist, my side, to see perhaps what arms I carried.

"I came to find you, Brian."

"Why would you do that?"

"In case you needed me."

"I do not need you." He looked round again. "And you have come alone?" he asked.

"Yes. I've come quite alone."

He brought his hand up to his chest.

"The moon is bright, so you are not alone. If you look down you will see your shadow."

I looked down, froze for a moment before twisting round to ward off the man who had come up behind me and whose shadow made a third with mine and Saxby's, but too late to avoid the blow from the shadow's raised arm. Falling I felt the jarring shock of my body's impact with the road and then the road began to spin and, spinning, flung me weightless into the featureless landscape of space.

PART III

The Flower Dreamer

I

"IT WAS SAXBY, WASN'T IT?"

"No."

"Who then? Who was it, Brent?"

"I didn't see. He came up behind me."

Reid lowered his head because he wasn't focusing properly. Behind him I could see the picture of the Sacred Heart but there was no scent of rose-petals now, instead, Reid's smell, the acid drift of his stale, alcoholic breath. The room was darkened because Teena had closed the shutters, but mid-morning sun made the spaces between the slats incandescent like wire-thin strips of lighted neon. The mosquito net was bunched and tied above my head and when I shut my eyes its white chrysalid form came with me into the rosy darkness behind my lids.

"You're a damn' poor liar, Brent."

I kept my eyes shut.

"It's a different tale to what you told young Sutton."

"What tale was that?"

"You said it was Saxby then."

"I was concussed. I'd got Saxby on the brain."

"Sure."

"It wasn't Saxby." I opened my eyes. "D'you think Saxby would beat me up like this? Bastard."

"Saxby? A bastard?"

"No, the fellow who did it. That bastard."

"You're in bad shape."

"I'll be all right."

Reid leaned forward. "And then you'll go after him?"

"After whom?"

"Saxby. For giving you a hiding."

"It wasn't Saxby. I've told you. I give up telling you."

He grinned and put a hand on my arm. I moved it away.

"You're lying, Brent, because you don't want me to send out a patrol."

He stood up, still grinning, and began to prowl round the room with the shambling dignity of an animal that has been in a cage for a long time and has developed sores it scorns to lick.

"Are you going to stay here?" he asked, coming to the bottom of the bed.

"For a bit."

"Does Teena mind?"

"She hasn't said so."

"Shall I get the M.O. down from Kampong Malim?"

"Don't bother. The local fellow's been. But perhaps you'd ring Turner in Kuala Lumpur."

He took out a cigarette and threw me one. I let it lie and he did not offer me a light.

"I suppose you take it for granted she won't come to the pavilion while you're here? I suppose you just assume she'll stay and nurse you?"

"I take nothing for granted, Reid. I don't assume anything."

"It's as well. Yes, it's as well never to assume anything, never to count on anything." He chuckled. "But I'll let her stay. You can have your Madame Chang."

I said nothing.

"You're scorched by it, aren't you, Brent?"

"By what?"

He sat on the end of the bed.

"Scorched worse than those lads of mine," he said. "I'll tell you something. They don't give a damn for me really. They'd let Calthrop dish me at battalion if it wasn't for what I let them do in the pavilion. You can see it on their faces, the way they look at me in the morning after they've had it and in the evening when they start wanting it again. A new O.C. mightn't tolerate it, so they grin and bear me and tut-tut amongst themselves when I hit the bottle."

"Why have you hit the bottle?"

He said, "For the pleasure of getting tight. But do you know, Brent, I can't get tight any more?"

"Bad luck." I shut my eyes, hoping that he would take himself away, but his voice crackled on. He couldn't get tight but his vocal chords were beginning to seize up.

"Yes, bad luck. I can't get tight and I can't do *it* any more. What about that, Brent? Eh? Isn't that mug's luck?"

I opened my eyes again and watched him.

"Mug's luck. Reid's luck. You've not heard that, have you, not heard about what was called Reid's luck?"

"No. I've not heard."

"Reid's luck." He said it to himself, and sat for a moment or two staring at the lump in the bedclothes where my feet were. "Yes, Reid's luck. All the way to Rangoon and not one platoon commander lost. Reid's luck, they said. Don't cross the bugger or you'll cross his luck, so the old man tried like hell not to cross me, tried not to bitch me like he wanted to in case he bitched my luck and bitched his own. He didn't bitch it but, by God, he pushed it. He pushed my luck from one end of Burma to another and if we'd had any proper fighting to do in Malaya he'd be pushing it here, too."

"Perhaps it wasn't just your luck, Reid. It could have been everybody's."

"Ah! No, Brent! Mine! My luck! Let me keep my own bloody luck! No other bugger would want it. It *wasn't* luck, you see. I had it on me as a punishment. When you're really being punished, punished by somebody clever, at first you're made to think it's something else, something good. It's like what they say about the gods making men mad before they destroy them. That's what I was in Burma, mad. They made me think I'd got luck. Everyone of us could have died a score of times, died clean like proper soldiers. But we were spared. They punished me by sparing my officers and then taking Ballister and filling his lungs with salt-water while he waded ashore from a landing craft to a beach where nobody was firing at us."

"What do you think you're being punished for?"

He began to chuckle. "Why that's it! I don't know! None of us knows. We just know I'm being punished. The others don't say anything, but they can *see*, because it's there, like a mark on me." His smile faded. "Now I'm being submitted to some sort of test. Whoever it is that's punishing me, they're playing cat and mouse now. Take Sutton, for instance."

"All right. Take Sutton."

He got up and walked about the room.

"I've got to stop being a bastard to Sutton, haven't I? I thought I was being pretty canny when he first arrived. I thought, well, now, this is interesting. They want me to be nice to Sutton so that when I've been nice long enough I'll find that was the very thing I hadn't got to be."

"What's made you change your mind?"

He swung round. "Nothing. Except what's in here." He tapped his chest. "But if I play into their hands by not being a bastard to Sutton any longer I can't help it."

"Into whose hands?"

"Ah, Brent! *You* ask that. *You*. Don't try to kid me! You know what things are about. I can talk to *you* without you thinking I'm round the bend." He glanced up at the ceiling and twitched his thumb to draw my attention, as it were in confidence, to the sky we couldn't see.

"That crowd," he said. "Up there. *Their* hands."

"Oh. Them."

He came back to the bedside and looked down at me.

"Brent, you don't think you fool *me*, surely? If you weren't scorched by *them* as well as by what you've got between your legs you wouldn't give a fig about Saxby would you? Not a bloody fig. The only difference between you and me is that *they're* not punishing you yet. They still let you get tight, they still let you lose yourself in women, they still let you throw off some of the load. You're not a Holy Roman, are you?"

"No."

"It's easier for the Holy Romans. It's all right for them.

They think they can take their putrid little souls to the confessional once a week and squeeze them out like boils. But you and I Brent, we know we have to take the muck round with us, we know that if there's a God he's not likely to be interested in mumbo-jumbo, and if we commit a sin he's going to mark it down for eventual reckoning and not let us squeeze it out by repenting here on earth. You've seen that, haven't you? Seen that repentance is something we're only going to be allowed to do on the other side when He's added it all up, the good and the bad, with everything recorded and nothing erased, debit and credit and a balance struck at the end. And that's the sum total of our soul, isn't it Brent, what's left at the end? What's *left*! That's funny! Mine must be in the red already because they've already begun to punish me. *Nothing* left and no more credit, eh? The overdraft's at its limit."

"It's nice to know there's a limit."

"What?"

"To know they don't let you go on and on building up the debit balance."

"Ah."

He came round to the other side of the bed to stub out his cigarette in the ashtray.

"Is that what the punishment's for, do you think, Brent? To reduce it? Does the punishment you endure go down to your credit? And how did I get so badly in the red? What did I do *wrong*?"

"Reid, I don't know. I won't say I don't care but my head hurts like hell and I want to go to sleep."

"Brent, I'm sorry. Yes, I'm sorry."

He went over to the chest of drawers for his slouch hat.

"Brent?"

"What?"

"I'm having the town patrolled at night. They'll have orders to keep a special eye on here. And from now on the duty officer will be armed."

"Thanks for telling me."

"But I'm doing it for *you*. I can't have an officer beaten up in the streets of Bukit Kallang without making a bit of a show! Even Calthrop can't object to that. Besides –"

"Well?"

"In your present condition you'd make a poor business of guarding Teena if Saxby came back."

"It wasn't Saxby."

"Why are you so stubborn? Why do you try and protect Saxby? They've made *him* mad too. They won't mark it down in your favour if you go out of your way to save him, will they? Will they? They've put the finger on him, Brent. That's what they've done. Put the finger on him."

He raised a hand in farewell and left me.

*

It must have been Ah Choong whose shadow made a third with mine and Saxby's, Ah Choong who struck the blow I saw coming, but Saxby had done nothing to stop him; on the contrary, he had timed his warning nicely to enable me to see the threat but not avoid it. He had tricked me, lulled me into a sense of security knowing that at any moment Ah Choong would come out from wherever he had been hiding; and judging by the state of my head and face two, possibly three blows had been delivered although the first had been enough to knock me unconscious.

Because there had been these other blows it was difficult not to suspect Saxby of having taken the stick and given me what he thought of as the *quietus*, difficult not to believe they had left me for dead or been disturbed before they could finish a business they had a mind to. It was not until some fifteen minutes later that Sutton, driving the girls back in the duty truck a bit earlier than usual, caught sight of my prostrate body and so it could not have been the sound of the truck that saved me. Perhaps in a room above one of the shops opposite a lamp had been lighted or a woman had called loudly to rouse her family for the day. But whatever it was that had disturbed them

I could not get the picture out of my mind of Saxby standing over me bringing the stick down or of Saxby standing there letting Ah Choong do so. The beatific expression I fancied I might have seen on his face if the moon had been brighter was, like everything else about Saxby, a mockery. With a blinding headache, and the less acute but more insidious ache of slow deep anger at having been on the receiving end of what Reid called a hiding, I realized that what had looked like a complex situation had, in the space of a few minutes, become simple.

Flat on my back, weak as a kitten and with only one good arm at the best of times, I knew the day would come when I must put on my sahib's face, spit on my coal-heaver's hands and go after him to teach him that he could not have his head in heaven and two feet on the ground, have me beaten up and get away with it, attempt to kill me and not answer for it.

Bastard! I muttered, Bastard! May trees suck you dry, plants choke you and God turn his back on you, but not before we've met again, face to face, not before I've tried to make you pay for every moment you've come at me, every twitch of conscience you've ever made me feel, every prick of fear you've made *her* bear, every dishonourable hour that passed for Hakinawa before he fell on his sword, every Jap you burned alive in revenge for a burnt flower.

And it was my job, not Reid's, not Turner's. In those first few hours I wanted only to recover quickly and go after him alone.

*

Anger was followed by calculation. While I was in the bungalow I felt, in spite of Reid's jibe, that Teena was safe, but I did not object to his decision to have the town patrolled at night; it was an extra precaution against the possibility of Saxby still being in the area. I felt it more likely, though, that my presence in Bukit Kallang must have come as a shock to him. He would see that his game, if not exactly up, had been got on to. He would retire, to live, to fight another day. This meant a period of safety for Teena. During it we would mount a proper expedition to smoke Saxby out of his hole and then I would face him. I would make it clear to Reid and Turner that Saxby was mine to bring in. If he had committed crimes, the courts of man and not the courts of heaven would exact the penalty.

And as the expression "courts of man" passed through my mind I seemed to hear Saxby saying, Ah, courts! You reduce it to this at the end? It comes down, does it, to this? What else? Aren't you forgetting something? The bowl of water? Have you forgotten that? For it is, isn't it, a question of water? For your hands? To wash them in?

*

Sometimes on that first evening as I woke from fitful sleep I would feel her presence in the room but the muscles of my neck had stiffened and I could not move my head towards the source of lamplight where I guessed she sat. I had no sense of time. It was not dark enough to see the luminous hands and numbers of my wristwatch yet too dark to see them without bringing my wrists closer and the effort was out of all proportion to the need.

I slept deeply through whatever noise was made by the girls' departure in the duty truck, and the local doctor, an Indian called Pannikar, finding me asleep, did not waken me on his evening visit. He told me next morning that i-sleep was the best i-cure and that I had greatly resolved myself by being left to it. But between his visit at night and the return of the truck which fully woke me up I dreamed.

She was alone in the pavilion.

She was alone, but not alone because I was there, although invisible and inaudible to her. She sat on the scarlet cushions in front of the scarlet chest brushing her hair with a brush that turned itself into a palm-leaf fan so that then she was not sitting on the cushions but on the mattress, waving the fan backwards and forwards. The fan was getting bigger and heavier and all at once the room was filled with giant birds that had burst the stone bonds of the mosaic. They dithered about in corners, clacking their heavy yellow beaks, half-spreading their green pinions to get momentum for short lumbering runs across the scarlet tiles. She had to beat one back with the fan and then its open-billed mate *came at her* hissing in its throat because it had no tongue. She was running bare-foot down the veranda steps through the lake-mist of the garden and I was calling with this voice of mine she could not hear and running after her on legs that would not cover distance. I had to warn her that Saxby waited quietly on the deserted road as invisible to her as I was, and as she fled towards him he towered skywards and blotted out the moon. I cried out: Teena! Teena! and she grew out of night to lamplight with her real hand on my hot real forehead and, knowing her safe and real, I let the dream spin and whine away like a top, back where it belonged in the dark, frosted world of sleep, a twisting, diminishing fragment of ice.

*

Turner came on the second day. Reid accompanied him because he had gone first to company headquarters to ask the way. It was curious to see them together.

Reid said, "I'm not staying, Brent. There's a lot to do. We're getting reports in, but *he'll* tell you. Are you feeling better?"

"Thanks."

"Good."

When we were alone I said, "What does he mean?"

Turner sat on the bed.

"He means reports of a Sikh accompanied by a Chinese. Is he mad by the way?"

"Why do you ask?"

"He's marking up a map, sticking it with pins and flags wherever the Sikh's been seen."

"It's his way."

"But the flags show that Saxby would need wings on his feet to have been in all those places at the times he's said to have been. It's a waste of time going on with it. *Was* it Saxby?"

"Yes."

"Reid says you got round to denying it."

"I wanted him for myself. For giving me this."

"It's not a one-man job."

"I know. But he's still mine. I still owe him something personally."

He got up from the bed. "I've brought you some sick-bay comforts. I left them with Teena Chang." He held my eye steadily. "I like her. Does she know it was Saxby who clobbered you?"

"She was in the room when I came round. She must do."

"You haven't discussed it since?"

"No. I can't in cold blood. He was here to get her. Ah Choong must have been hidden in the garden waiting for him to rendezvous."

"D'you think you've scared them off?"

"For a bit."

"Tell me about Saxby."

Afterwards he said, "Strange, strange meeting. Let me know when you're fit. We'll plan something. My guess is you've scared them off altogether."

"It could be."

"And it's a long way to the Sakai."

"Which Sakai?"

"The ones he was with before the Jap came. I think he'll have gone back to them. I'll do what I can to trace just where that was."

"Check in Singaputan too."

"I'll do that. But he won't go back there now that he's seen you. Frankly I think we've lost him for good. And I wouldn't be sorry. You saw him. We know we were right. But the consequences of being right were never very nice to contemplate, were they?"

"You're forgetting. He probably thinks I'm dead. Oh, he'd lie low for a bit but I think he'll be back."

"I can't believe he meant to kill you."

238

"I've got a broken head to prove it."

He grinned. "Better than a broken heart."

On that ambiguous note he left me. When he had gone Teena came in with the cigarettes, whisky and fruit he had brought. She was in her Chinese mood, her armour against Saxby, talk of Saxby, thoughts of Saxby: her armour against so much.

*

While I was at the bungalow she did not go to the pavilion. I had her to myself. I could observe her at all hours.

I could not talk to her about Saxby. Sometimes I lashed myself with the suspicion that she had lain, still lay with him, because he exerted hypnotic influence over her, that it was to cover her with his black hairy body he had walked clacking down the road; that she was in the habit of receiving him on her return from the pavilion and he in the habit of waiting in the undergrowth of the garden until the duty truck had come and gone; that it was to free herself of his influence that she had invited me to stay that morning.

And yet it is wrong to call it a suspicion. It was no more than a far-off drum beat of doubt, less even than that: an anticipation in silence of the note of a drum because at that time, that joyful, sad and mysterious time, the sound of drums, of gongs, was not to be unexpected.

For this surely, was the occasion of love, long sought, now found, presenting itself like a flower that opened its petals to the moon and bewitched with its perfume the sense that otherwise would say the moon must wane, the petals fall. Jealousy, suspicion; these were only the measure of love. There was always an inner stillness. Closing my eyes when she left me alone for a while I could conjure it. There might be footsteps, the sound of girls' voices, laughter; but mostly the restful quiet of a house in which there were rooms where people liked, sometimes, to be alone, and none of these sounds and silences was strained, or imposed by my presence there.

A single, narrow bed had been brought into the room and there, for the first two days she would sleep at night, and rest during the day. Waking once between lunch and tea I caught her sleeping, caught her unawares with her mouth a little open, her hair tousled, her face as creamily smooth and inexperienced as that of a child.

Why, I thought, this *is* the occasion, *this*, and why should you have always thought it would be an occasion shared?

Watching her I felt that it was enough to have found the occasion in her, and that it was too much to expect that she should find it in me at once, if ever. And yet she had a capacity for it, surely?

When she woke and came to me, sleepily, sat on my bed and smoothed my bristly chin, a hard streak of male vanity persuaded me it was only a question of time; that whatever she felt or did not feel for me at the moment was unimportant. She was a woman, one whom I loved, desired, was jealous of, and could in time be conquered, translated into the image of the woman she really was so that knowing herself wanted she would respond, capitulate and want me, only me, in return.

It did not matter who else had touched her, it only mattered if someone other than myself should touch her now. A hollow would form in my chest at the sound of the duty truck and only her reappearance when it had gone again would fill the hollow in.

"Where did you get to?"

"To see the girls off. Didn't you hear the truck?"

"I was asleep. Who was duty officer? Young Sutton again?"

"Yes, Toby was duty officer."

"Is that his name? I don't call that a name."

"It's a nice name."

"When's he going to get a girl of his own?"

"He hasn't got any girl, Tommy. Major Reid won't let him go to the pavilion. That's why he's always duty officer. He's been duty officer ever since he came."

"He wants to be, I expect."

"Why should he want to be?"

"So that he can come here and see *you*. How long did he stay this time?"

"Only five minutes."

"You were gone longer than that."

"I thought you were asleep."

"Does he behave himself?"

"Silly Tommy."

"Well, does he?"

"Of course."

"Swear it."

"Seal it."

"How?"

"Like this."

Sometimes this possessiveness would squander itself in the face of her Chinese mood.

*

On the third day Pannikar let me get up and late in the afternoon I rose and shaved with the soap, brush and razor Sutton had brought down from the house the previous day. Shaving left-handed had once been an awkward business but I was now adept at it and getting rid of three days' growth afforded a sensual pleasure of its own. I was back on my feet. Going into the bedroom I found her standing with her back to me looking out of the window. She had changed into a Chinese-patterned dress.

I said, "I see you're Madame Ho. Shall I tell Mac?"

Turning, she smiled. "Yes, please to inform Mac."

I went over to her.

"On second thoughts I won't."

"Mac must always be told when I am Madame Ho."

"No, he mustn't."

The Chinese mood was an artifice and she could use it to hold me off. I rubbed my cheek against hers.

"How's that? Better?"

She leaned away, touched cheeks and chin with her sorcerer's hands.

"It is very clean, very smooth."

Very beautiful, rare and expensive.

Before I shaved she had let me make love to her in the locked, shuttered bedroom. The shutters were open now, the room full of light and air. If I tried the door I should find it unlocked. I felt she had begun the process of trying to ease herself away from me. If you are well enough to make love, she had said, you are well enough to shave. We had made a joke of it, and if she had still been in her European mood when I came out of the bathroom with my smooth, tingling, satisfied face, I could bave bullied her a bit, treated her with that tough-tenderness which comes naturally to a man after love-making; but the Chinese mood, at once submissive and remote, demanded a subtlety of attitude I could not call up at such short notice.

She gave me my first cigarette and offered me my first whisky.

They're not punishing you yet, Reid had said, they still let you get tight and lose yourself in a woman.

She sat on the edge of her own narrow bed.

"Teena?"

"Yes, Tommy?"

"I'm falling in love with you."

She looked across at me. I forced her to speak by saying nothing further myself. Eventually she said, "You are like Lieutenant Hakinawa."

"No, I'm not. And I'm not hara-kiri prone."

"I did not mean that."

"What did you mean?"

"You think the world is big. But it is very tiny. For us it is no bigger than the pavilion."

Standing near her I put my hand under her chin and tilted her face towards me.

"Wait," I said. "You'll find it gets bigger every day."

2

ON THE AFTERNOON OF THE FOURTH DAY PRABHU
Singh drove to the bungalow in my jeep and asked to see me.

"You've got the wrong afternoon," I told him when I went
into the hall. "I'm coming back tomorrow."

"But it is a message from Major Sahib," he said, in Mahratti,
rolling his eyes lewdly, trying to catch a glimpse of the women.

"Well what is the message?"

"He has written it. It is here."

He gave me a folded piece of paper torn from a field-service
notebook. It read,

> Dear Brent,
>   Come at once. I have seen the movement of a man or an
> animal.
>   Ted Reid.

"Wait here."

In the bedroom Teena was still asleep. I collected my shaving
kit and wrote her a note.

> I've had to go back to the house. You were sleeping. Today
> is no worse than tomorrow to leave you, and tonight I'll
> wear scarlet.

*

High above the garden of madness jutting out a bit from
the tangled precipitous face of the hill there was what looked
like a natural, rocky platform.

I gave Reid back his binoculars.

"Did you get it, Brent?"

"I think so. But no movement."

"No," he said, looking again through the binoculars himself, "it was only once. But I saw it. The movement of a man or an animal."

He lowered the glasses. His face was brick-red and streaming with sweat, his lips parted.

"How long have you been out here in the sun, Reid?"

"All day. Ever since it came to me."

"Since what came to you?"

"That Saxby used to watch the pavilion from somewhere."

"You'd better come in. You'll get heat-stroke."

"That's right. Heat-stroke. I'll come in."

He let me lead him back to the house.

In the cool of the veranda room he sat slumped in a chair. I gave him a glass of water and a salt tablet.

"You're a good chap, Brent. The others leave me to it. They're not interested in Saxby. I'll be all right in a minute. I've got to be fit, Brent, haven't I? We've got to find that platform. We'll go together. Be a good chap and get the map-case from my room. It's marked with all the places he's been seen."

I found the map-case on his bed. The talc that protected the map was covered in red, green, and yellow chinagraph markings, and in one corner he had written in block capitals: *Operation S.*

Operation Saxby.

He was calling to Prabhu Singh. When I went back into the veranda room the orderly was coming up the stairs.

"Go to Lieutenant Sutton," Reid told him, "and ask him to come up to the house on his motor-bike. There's a job for him."

We pored over the map, pinpointed the place where the rocky platform would be, but there were no tracks leading to it.

"It's where he used to go, Brent. You see. Where he used to go when he told Wan Lo he was looking for the soul of his liver. And I swear he was there today. Watching me, probably. Watching me through binoculars behind the cover. Grinning at me thinking I couldn't see him."

"You may be right."

I studied the map. He told me he had another on the wall of the office into which he stuck pins. The one in the map-case carried the same information.

"If he's been seen in all these places he'd be a magician, Reid."

"That's why I used different colours. Look at the colours separately, follow the marks colour by colour, patterns form."

"None of them go near the platform, though," I pointed out.

"The red markings aren't too far away."

He took the map from me.

"Will you come with me, Brent?"

"To the platform?"

"On a search party into the jungle. We could go to the platform first. We could crack this business together, crack it once and for all. You want that, don't you, Brent? You want to get Saxby over and done with, clear your plate of him and take your bearings?"

I nodded. He was a shrewd judge of men.

"A small patrol," he said. "Small and mobile. Four or five strong. We could cover a lot of ground."

"I ought to ring Turner."

He looked disappointed.

"There's no definite objective," he said. "You can't drag a man all the way up from K.L. to beat the jungle as if he's beating for game. And I want to start tomorrow. You're fit, aren't you?"

"Fit enough."

"Ring Turner and tell him you're going. He won't want to join us unless Saxby's reported in a definite place."

"You reported him on the platform."

"Three majors on one patrol is dam' silly," he said.

"But Turner's got to have the chance of being one of them."

I went down to the hall and put a call through. It took five minutes.

"You win," I told Reid when I joined him again. "Turner's in Singapore for the rest of the week."

He had the whisky bottle out and a glass held ready.

"Then that's settled," he said.

"You'd better lay off that whisky, Reid. Lay off that if you're going to command this patrol."

He paused. His hands were quite steady. He was about the toughest man I had ever met. He could go on the bottle for days, spend hours in the broiling sun and end up like this, his hands as steady as a rock.

"You're right, Brent, I'll lay off. I *can* lay off. I don't need it now." He put the bottle and glass down with a slam. "I'm better now. I'm ready to show 'em. God! I'd have no other life than the one I've had. I'd do it all over again. Look, look at that, feel that."

He pushed his sleeve up, flexed the bicep hard.

"How's that for muscle, Brent?"

"Good enough."

"I've lived a man's life," he said. "Lived a man's life since I was a boy. I was in the army as a boy. Not many people know that. I did boy-service, Brent. *Boy* service! God, they called you boys but you had to live like men. In those days all I wanted to be was a sergeant, a little tin-god. Stripes on your arm, we used to say, instead of on your backside. I was in a British battalion up near the Khyber. I shot my first man when I was eighteen, picked him off clean as a whistle from two hundred yards. And old Sergeant White said, Good man! He'd always called me boy before. Come here, boy; do this, boy; bend over, boy. Now it was good man. It was a golden day, Brent, a golden, iron-hard day, with a kind of haze coming up from the rocks and a puff of wind blowing the sweat cool on your face. Just rock, and hill, and the sky a sort of purple, and the chap I'd shot lying almost invisible, just the flip of his long robe when the breeze caught it. We were spread out in a thin line behind cover, taking it in turns to pick 'em off if they showed so much as a finger. The lieutenant always made a kind of game of it. It was my first action, my first time as a full private. I was third along. The first fellow had scored a hit but the fellow

246

next to me missed. I was trembling like a leaf, Brent, afraid I'd miss too when my turn came. But when it came, ah, I was steady, yes, my hand steady, steady as this, like this, look. I remembered everything I'd been taught, everything they'd drilled and yelled and belted into me, the way to control your breathing, the first gentle pressure on the trigger, then squeeze, not pull. And there he was, dead as yesterday's mutton and White saying in a voice so gentle, so mild, so unlike his other voice, Good man, Reid. I felt like a giant."

He took out a cigarette but seemed to think better of it, let it roll away on the table.

"Is that why I'm being punished, Brent? Is that it? Oughtn't I to have felt like a giant? Was it the devil that made it a golden day and not God like I thought?" He swung away towards the veranda. "Ah, then, why did they *teach* me that?"

A motor-cycle was coming up the hill. It throttled down in good time for the turn into the garden.

"We're taking Sutton with us, Brent."

"I thought we might be."

"I can't change what's in here, Brent," he said, turning again towards me and hitting his chest. "If what's in here is rotten, if it's why I'm being punished then all I've got to look forward to is more punishment. Like I said the other day, I can't go on being a bastard to young Sutton. I must treat him like I treated Ballister, like I treated all of them, like I've always treated men the army's given me to command. You see that, Brent? Do you see what that way is? I've treated them as men who might one day look up themselves and feel like giants. That's the only worthwhile thing I've got to offer anybody, that feeling, that you're a giant and could punch a hole in the sky."

"Is that how Ballister felt?"

"I don't know how Ballister felt. The men who trained me never knew how I felt. I was a spotty face they'd shouted at, a shiny seat they'd lammed with a pace-stick, a body they saw prone behind a rock getting a tribesman lined up in his sights. What did they know of *my* golden day. Or I of Ballister's?"

The motor-cycle died with a phut somewhere near the garage.

"And what shall I know of Sutton's if he ever has one? All I can do is put him in the way of it. We can't keep these things to ourselves, Brent. Whatever's important to us, why, we've got to share it, haven't we? I've got to start sharing it with Sutton. And if it's the devil's work there's nothing I can do but wait for the flames."

Sutton's boots rang out on the stone floor below.

"Reid," I said.

"What?"

"If we find Saxby, he's mine. Not yours. Not Sutton's. Mine. Saxby's not going to be shot so that someone can feel he punched a hole in the sky."

*

That night before he said grace he told Sutton to move into Ballister's place.

"You're a bit crowded on that side," he explained.

With the soup cooling we watched Sutton change over.

"You have walked with us in the valley and have stood with us on the hill. We ask for Your blessing on the living and for Your mercy on the dead. Amen."

"Today," he said, drinking soup, busying himself breaking bread with his free hand and dropping pieces into the plate, "I saw the movement of a man or an animal on a platform on the hill behind the pavilion. Tomorrow I'm leading a search party consisting of Major Brent, myself, Lieutenant Sutton and two guerrillas provided by Wan Lo Ping. Sutton?"

"Yes, sir?"

"Did you remember to ask that they should speak English?"

"Yes, sir."

"And will they?"

"Yes, sir."

"Good. You're making progress. A few days ago you would have said you expected so or thought so."

He dropped the spoon noisily into the plate.

Calthrop said, "What's the search party for?"

Reid broke more bread, rammed a piece into his mouth like gun-cotton into a breech; and began to laugh.

"Yes, what's it for? What's it for, young Bill? What do you think it's for?"

"Saxby, I suppose."

"You suppose correctly."

"Just for the day?"

"No, Bill. We take three days' rations with us, but we might call up more. It depends, yes, very much depends. We'll base ourselves on that Chinese vegetable grower's place the other side of the hill, the one where the river runs."

"How long do you think you'll be away though, sir?" MacAndrews asked.

"Two days. Three. Five. A week. It's not exactly in my hands."

Calthrop looked from MacAndrews to Holmes and then to Reid.

"Does battalion know, sir?"

"No, Bill. Battalion does not know."

"Oughtn't you to tell them?"

"I don't know, Bill. Ought I?"

"Well, yes. Otherwise if the old man rings through when you're not here what do I say to him?"

Reid leaned back as the mess waiter removed his soup plate.

"Bill, you say to the old man what you've wanted to say this last four weeks. You say: Sir, my company commander's got quite out of hand, I can no longer pull on; and the old man will say, Calthrop, it was only a question of time, you will assume command of the company and send Reid back to me in chains as soon as he condescends to reappear."

It was M. & V. stew again. The waiter put the plates down one after the other until they were lined up like little round tombstones.

Calthrop said, "Is that what you think, sir?"

"Push the salt along would you, Mac?" Reid asked. When he had finished sprinkling it on his stew he said, "One thing you will do and that's maintain the town patrol. There'll be three of you left to share the duties of duty officer which means only two girls will come to the pavilion. Madame Chang will naturally not come to the pavilion at all. The bungalow will therefore be closely guarded. Is that understood?"

Calthrop had not begun his stew. "It's understood, sir."

"And will be done?"

"It'll be done."

"Then that's settled."

"Not quite, sir. You still haven't answered my question."

"Remind me of it."

"I said, is that what you think, sir?"

"Yes, it's what I think, but thoughts can be treacherous, can't they, Bill? Thoughts can lead us into all kinds of nasty little misconceptions. Have we been together too long, would you say? It could be. It certainly could be. People are like cheese, you know, and what you learn about them is like a piece of wire. It's tempting to pare them down, to cut them down to size, and that's wrong, yes, that must be wrong. Think of it, Bill, if we all looked round this table and saw each other as little squares of dry, stale cheese, none of them worth eating."

Later he said, "I apologize for my thoughts. It's my deeds that count. I leave you in command. I've written to the colonel. If you looked in the company office you'd find a sealed envelope waiting for tomorrow's dispatch-rider. You'll not be embarrassed by questions you don't like answering. I was pulling your leg, Bill. The joke misfired and nobody felt like a giant."

He got to his feet, although the meal was not yet over. We rose to ours because this was a mess and he its president. Such military niceties gave a closing dignity to a disreputable scene.

"Continue," he said, "dinner's not finished and your appe-

250

tites are younger than mine. Sleep is what I need, gentlemen. The old sod needs his kip if he's to go marching tomorrow."

He walked over to the archway, paused, turned and stood there with his hands held a bit away from his body, his head lowered as though focussing us against the concentrated blaze of the hurricane lanterns.

"0700, Brent. All right?"

I nodded.

"Sutton?"

"Yes, sir."

"An early night for you, too. Ask one of the others to take duty officer from you."

"There's no need, sir."

"I said an early night. Sound sleep. Bed. Straight after your dinner."

Calthrop said, "I'll do duty officer, Toby. You've had more than your whack."

Reid smiled.

He said, "Anna will be disappointed."

*

They went when they had finished dinner, Holmes and Mac together, then Sutton. Calthrop stayed on. Our eyes met over coffee, met, that is to say, on the understanding that something had to be said.

"There's nothing we wouldn't do for him, sir. Did you know that?"

"I didn't know."

"It's true, though."

It was the last thing I had expected him to say, and yet it fitted in, it made sense.

"Can you persuade him to call it off, sir?"

"I don't think so. And I've got to find Saxby. I can't do that alone. You don't really want him to call it off, do you?"

"He's set his heart on it, I know that," Calthrop said.

"That's what I meant."

"But I think it'll finish him."

"He's tough as old boots."

"Physically, yes. I meant finish him – emotionally." He flushed, but stuck to his guns. "He's not well emotionally, sir. I don't mean mad."

"What do you mean?"

"A lot of things. For one, he's taken to walking in his sleep."

"Oh?"

"You've never seen him then?"

"I've never slept in the house."

He glanced up. "You wouldn't need only to sleep in the house to have seen him, sir." He hesitated, but there was no drawing back for him now. "He comes and stands outside the pavilion."

"Asleep?"

"Yes, sir. I've seen him three times now. Sometimes when I'm restless I go out and have a quiet smoke. The first time I saw him I thought he'd come over to rouse us up for something but when I spoke he said nothing. I went down the steps and right up to him and then saw he wasn't awake. After a bit he said something in his sleep and walked back to the house."

"Were you able to make out what he said?"

He traced square patterns on the table-cloth with his coffee spoon.

"It sounded like, Good man."

"Oh."

"He's got no idea of it. No memory of it or anything like that."

"How do you know?"

"I don't know. I just feel he hasn't."

"Do the others know about this?"

"No, I haven't told 'em. I don't think they know. They just know there's something killing him. We all know that."

"Ballister?"

"It started before then, sir. It started when the Japs packed in. He walked into my tent and said, Bill, the buggers are finished and that means I'm finished too. He's always done odd things, said odd things. He got away with murder where the colonel was concerned. But saying he was finished hit me because he looked it. Ballister being drowned was the last straw."

"What was Ballister like?"

Calthrop completed a complicated design, began another.

"He had a mean streak."

"Mean?"

"Yellow."

"Reid seems to take the opposite view."

"He didn't when Ballister was alive, sir."

"And now he's suffering from remorse, for treating him badly?"

"He didn't treat him badly. He was never anything but fair to all of us and that included Ballister. He made us be fair to Ballister too. Holmes was the worst offender in the beginning." He smiled faintly. "As perhaps you'd guess. He once took Holmes on one side and belted him across the ear for needling Ballister. He made us see we had to help Ballister act as much like a man as he could. Don't get the wrong impression. I don't mean the rest of us thought we were any great shakes. But Ballister was one of those imaginative chaps who think they've got two shadows, one in front and one behind. The trouble was he didn't look like that. He looked about as rough and tough as they come but given the sort of situation where the rest of us would have been too bloody ashamed not to have a go old Ballister would usually find a way of sitting his platoon on its arse and waiting for the situation to change. The only thing poor Ballister ever volunteered to do was lead the way on to the beach when we landed in Malaya."

I offered him a cigarette.

Taking it, he said, "Keeping his place laid, building him up as a kind of hero wasn't remorse, sir. It was his way of trying to keep Ballister in our minds as someone we'd had to be decent to and ought not to forget or stop being decent to now that he was dead. But it's been killing him. He thinks he's being punished but hasn't worked out why. You know he's not really the least bit interested in Saxby, don't you, sir?"

"I think if you say so I'm prepared to believe it."

"It's Sutton he's interested in." Calthrop paused, then continued, "He's only using Saxby as a way of getting Sutton into the jungle. When he first saw Sutton I thought he was going to hit him. Now he's come round to the other way and poor old Ballister's ghost has been laid. Why? Can you tell me why?"

"No, Calthrop, I can't."

"It's not easy, sir. He's turned right against us in one way, since the Ballister business. And something's killing him. We have scenes like tonight and the night you came back from your trip into the Sakai country. And I have him laying into me most of the day. He thinks we're plotting against him, just waiting for the chance to dish him at battalion as he calls it, and he does and says things that make you want to dish him. But only at the time. It's beginning to kill *us*, now, because we never know when he's going to treat us like dirt. But even so we can't forget what he was like in Burma. I can't. I don't think the others can, either."

"What was he like?"

Calthrop trailed the spoon away in a diminishing line and laid it down. "It sounds a bit silly, but one day when I was on my beam ends and the Japs had been pasting us for twenty-four hours I found him just standing watching me, knowing exactly what was in my mind, and if he'd said, Come on, Calthrop, we've got a date with the devil, I'd have got up and followed him. The point was he looked ten feet tall."

He raised his head and looked me straight in the eye.

"Whatever else you sometimes think about him, and some of the things you think are pretty odd, you never forget *that*. And it doesn't matter what made him feel big enough to look ten feet tall because at the time you didn't care. It made you feel six feet tall yourself, and that's a *healthy* feeling."

He lowered his head again, gave me no chance to judge how subtle his use of the word healthy had been. But he was older, shrewder than the others and I guessed that he saw explanations of Reid's obsessively masculine behaviour which had not occurred to Holmes and MacAndrews, which almost certainly he had not discussed with them, which he dared only hint at to me but which having hinted at he defended as though to ensure Reid's safety from a disgrace he guessed might always be round the corner.

He had volunteered to relieve Sutton of the role of duty officer. He was no longer so keen on going to the pavilion. Perhaps the thought of Reid coming to the edge of the veranda and exploring in dreams the obsessions he was not wholly aware of in waking, perhaps the muttered exclamation in the darkness, put him off. Perhaps he had been too long one of Reid's young lions not to feel unmanned by the revelation of one and one together sometimes making three.

*

The *kris* lay hidden in the folds of the scarlet gown and when I took it out and put it on the mattress with its handle towards Teena and its blade towards myself I remembered the impeccable *makan-walla* and the piece of scarlet brocade that I had lost long ago. She would have looked well in a dress made from it.

She sat within the net kneeling upright, her pale skin golden in the light of the lantern. Although as always she had removed her make-up she was still in her Chinese mood. I carried in my mind's eye a picture of the way her brows had slanted upwards, outwards to the temples. Her hair fell to her shoulders, hair and shoulders that had touched my hands with joy. The firm gold fruit of her breasts still warmed and shaped the palm of my hand and the ball of my thumb still prickled from the touch of her rouged, tender, erectile nipples. I looked from her to the *kris* whose jewelled handle glinted. Her hand lay close to it. She said, "It is very beautiful, very valuable. Why do you give it to me?"

I reached out and touched her hand. "Because I love you, Teena."

She did not look at me but slowly took her hand from mine, picked up the *kris* and kissed the handle. Then she rose, lifted the net and went to the scarlet-lacquered chest. She knelt on the cushions, lifted the lid and put the *kris* inside.

She turned the lamp down and came back to me. The palm-leaf fan stirred the air faintly. Drops of earlier rain still fell outside. We lay on our backs side by side in the darkness.

I felt her move. Her hand touched my chest, glided slowly, lightly down to my stomach, rested there.

I said, "The *kris* is a man spirit like Bright Flame. He wears silver armour and has jewels in his helmet."

"Has he got a name?"

"Yes," I said. "He's called Shining Dagger."

She said, "I like that name."

"You must say, Ho, Shining Dagger –"

"And then?"

"Put your hand in his."

"And then?"

"No one will harm you. He's a tough fellow. A mighty warrior."

Her hand moved up to my chest, higher, over to throat and chin and cheek. She turned my head towards her.

"When must I call Shining Dagger, Tommy?"

I tried to make out the expression on her face, but the darkness covered it. Her fingers began to move over my cheek and lips as if exploring their secrets.

"When another man wears scarlet," I said. "If another man puts on scarlet."

"What will Shining Dagger do to the man who wears scarlet?"

"He'll extinguish the fire in his blood and make him nothing."

After a while I said, "What'll you do when I've gone?"

"I shall stay in the bungalow until you come back. I'll be safe in the bungalow. I'll take Shining Dagger with me."

"Yes," I said. "You must always have it. It's my love. I've armed you with my love."

3

REID CALLED ONE OF THE GUERRILLAS CHOP AND the other Suey. I never knew their real names. Both of them were thin as rails. Their English was adequate but by the end of the first day their incessant chattering in their own language had begun to get on my nerves, more so than their habit of leaving their rifles with the safety catches off, more so than their apparently abysmal ignorance of the jungle. As we set up camp on the first night we did so in the knowledge that we were lost, not in the desolate, final sense, but in the sense of having been led so far in the wrong direction by Chop and Suey that even they admitted we should have to go back to the track intersection in the morning.

We had been looking for a track to lead us to the rocky platform. We had set up what Reid called base camp in a clearing in the jungle, in the house of a Chinese vegetable grower who had supplied the guerrillas with food during the war. The vegetable grower knew nothing of a track leading to the face of the hill overlooking the garden of madness but he certainly set us off in the right direction to strike whatever track might do so. Once we were on a track which according to the map passed within a mile of the platform we hoped to find another unmarked track. In the event we found too many unmarked tracks. In three years the guerrillas had veined the jungle with them, with far more than either Chop or Suey could distinguish. Half-way through the afternoon we reached a place where three tracks met. Instinct told me which would be the most profitable to explore but Chop and Suey swore that the track I favoured went nowhere near the platform or the place where the platform would be.

Reid gave Chop and Suey his casting vote. "After all," he said, "they've lived in the jungle."

Afterwards we found that this, though true, was misleading. They were not experienced guerrillas. They had only joined Wan Lo Ping in March. They said they knew what Saxby and Ah Choong looked like. I told Reid I should have preferred them to know the country but nothing could diminish Reid's good spirits. The prospects of bivouacking in the jungle because it was too late in the day to turn back merely made him grin and whistle. We built little platforms to keep ourselves off the ground, roofed them over with branches covered in ground-sheets, and hoped for the best. Chop and Suey talked far into the night. I gritted my teeth and prayed for sleep. When I woke on the morning of the second day I was light-headed with fever. It was this that led to the quarrel –

*

– this, and the fact that, as Calthrop had warned me, Reid was not engaged in a search for Saxby but in an initiation ceremony. The initiate was Sutton, and the S in Operation S did not stand for Saxby at all.

I began to wonder whether Reid had really seen the movement of a man or an animal but instead, discovering what looked like a platform, had placed Saxby on it to give himself an excuse, a valid reason for doing what he was determined to do. It seemed to serve his purpose just to be in the jungle and to watch Sutton responding to it. And yet he seldom talked to him. And Sutton himself marched in stolid, stoic silence, his fair hair flopping down beneath the brim of his slouch hat, his mouth open a bit, his eyes quite blank when they looked at you.

The fever worked its mild but penetrating way through my bloodstream. At times I had difficulty in not letting my teeth chatter. My jaws were clamped together. I marched between Reid and Sutton. Reid whistled. Ahead of us were Chop and Suey hotly disputing a point that had arisen at breakfast and that would go on being disputed until sleep overtook them.

The jungle was thinner than Turner and I had encountered on the march to the longhouse. The tracks were wide. We could have walked two or even three abreast had we had a mind to do so. Leafstrewn they curled gently through the feathery, silver-green forest. Sometimes the forest thickened and darkened. Sometimes it fell away down a hillside to a clearing that showed signs of abandoned cultivation.

When we arrived back at the junction of three tracks it was noon. I pointed at the track Reid had given his vote against the previous day.

"That one," I said, determined.

"No, no," one of the guerrillas said.

"No, no," said the other. "We go back to the vegetable garden."

"You can go back to the vegetable garden if you like, but I'm going by that track."

"They seem pretty sure, Brent," Reid said.

"They were pretty sure yesterday and they were wrong yesterday."

"They weren't wrong," he said. "It was a question of trying a track they weren't familiar with. *It* was wrong. The one you want to try is one they say they are familiar with."

"They're not familiar with any bloody track," I said, raising my voice.

Reid stopped smiling. "Neither are you for that matter." He turned back to Chop and Suey. "Major Brent thinks that's the right track. You say it's wrong. Where does it go?"

We waited until they had reached agreement between themselves.

"It goes back to the vegetable garden, but by a different way."

"I wouldn't say by a different way so much as in the opposite direction."

"It turns back. You go one mile that way, then it turns back."

"A mile isn't far," I said. "We'll soon be able to see. We could go back to the vegetable garden that way as well as any other." I jerked my pack up. Normally Reid helped me. Now he stood and watched. I was sweating heavily before I had finished.

"It's a waste of time, Brent," he said. He came closer and lowered his voice. "And I'm in command, Brent. I've only got three men beside yourself. If you make an issue of it and it turns out you're right the Chinese will lose face. They've got to be considered. We've got to take it at their pace. We've got to make them see we trust them."

"I don't trust 'em a bloody inch," I snapped. "And I'd rather watch 'em lose face every ten minutes than go taking the wrong turns every half-hour."

"They've only taken one wrong turn, Brent."

"It's about to be two."

He put his hand on my arm. I jerked it away.

I said, "I'm going to try it, anyway. I'll go alone. If you want to save their faces tell 'em I'm recceing it to satisfy my own silly curiosity."

Without waiting for his reply I set off along the track. He came after me, calling. I stopped and turned round.

"Are you ill?" he said.

"No, just cheesed off with being messed about by those two chattering bastards."

"You're in a muck sweat. It's a touch of fever, isn't it?"

"Just a muck sweat."

He watched me, waited for me to look away first and admit the lie. It was difficult to decide which was worse: to admit the fever or have him thinking I endured rather than admit; either way would attract his solicitude, his obsessive tenderness. Even holding his eye long enough would do it. I turned away, said over my shoulder, "If I'm wrong I'll be back in an hour. If I don't find you here I'll take it you've gone back to the vegetable garden and follow on."

"All right, Brent," he called. "But supposing we find Saxby while you're not with us?"

I stopped. "He's mine. Remember that."

But in what way "mine"? I did not mean "mine". I meant not Reid's, not Sutton's.

*

The guerrillas were wrong. The track did not turn back. It veered gradually, as far as I could tell, in the right direction but after an hour's going it came to an abrupt stop on the edge of a tumbling hill-stream and there was no visible continuation on the other side. I swore and looked at the map. The stream was not marked on it. This gave me heart.

The bed of the stream was thick with rocks and boulders. At this point it descended steeply, too steeply, I thought, for a continuation of a track leading round the spur of the hill to the platform to be found downstream. Entering it I climbed up through the cascading water, putting my weight on to my left arm, pausing every few feet to examine the other bank.

I found the track some hundred yards on, hardly a track at all in comparison with those we had used so far. The forest was thicker too and soon I was moving through twilight in a world where a sense of direction was impossible to maintain. Wherever the track widened I paused to examine the ground for signs of recent use because in the wider parts there were patches of damp earth showing through the carpet of leaves. I wished I had been the kind of fellow to whom a bruised or broken leaf was a sign as clear as could be wished for but I was soon reminded I lacked that kind of talent and pushed on without looking for evidence.

But then in spite of the thickness of the forest it became evident that the track was bending quite sharply to the left, turning the spur of the hill. When it seemed to have reached the limit of its turn it began to descend. Slowly the ground fell away ever more sharply to my right, rose ever more steeply to my left, and I guessed I was moving along what appeared from the garden as the precipitous face of the hill.

The track became a ledge. I halted for a moment, my back able to rest against solid ground. In front of me the trees that grew out of the hillside below reached up above my head. Behind me the earth was knobbly with the half-bared roots of more trees. The ledge was completely hidden from observation.

*

Almost without realizing it I reached the platform. A bulge of rock on the face of the hill erupted like a bone thrusting through flesh. Dizzy from the sudden revelation of height and distance I squatted on my haunches and looked down in astonishment at the pavilion. From here it looked like a doll's house. The garden was empty, the house stood blind in the sun. It was half-past two by my watch. The journey had taken me two and a half hours. I decided to give myself a quarter of an hour's rest and then start back. I should be back at the track intersection just after five and should have my work cut out to get back to the vegetable garden before dark.

I lit a cigarette and after a moment or two began to study the platform. It had a frontage of some four yards. It was about the same in depth. To one side the foliage spilled over and gave cover. I moved across and lay on my stomach. There was a more restricted but still clear view of the garden and I saw that Reid had been right. A man could lie here and watch all that was going on and not be seen even by someone looking for him through binoculars.

I found the broken twigs first. A hole had been made in the thick part of the foliage and the broken-off twigs lay shrivelled on the rock. A hole had been made so that no twig or leaf should obscure the lenses of a pair of binoculars. I shoved my face closer to the hole.

"Perfect," I told myself.

And then I smelt Saxby. He put his hand on the small of my back. I twisted round, my mouth open to cry out, but there was nothing there. Saxby was no longer on the platform but he had been there and left the smell of his soul. I sat up. Looking again at the twigs I counted them. There were five.

"There's something else," I said aloud. "There must be something else."

I cast about. What I found was a heap of stones. I had looked at them several times before realizing there was something unnatural about them. They had been piled together by hand.

Inside this pile of stones I found his sandals.

On the inner side of the soles, smooth polished by the press of his feet, words in the Hindi script had been cut by a sharp pointed instrument. The inscription inside the right foot ran:

These are the shoes of Putan Singh. Let them rest undisturbed, for this is the shrine of the soul of his liver and of the soul of his eye.

And that on the left foot:

He sent the soul of his liver walking abroad and with the soul of his eye he learned the secrets of the garden of madness and made his list.

*

Ripples spread out. *Putan Singh*, they whispered, lapping softly round the name. Putan Singh. His Sikh name. The ripples quivered, died suddenly, because I had got it, the derivation, the twist: Putan Singh, *Singaputan.*

Singh meant the lion and was a name all Sikhs bore although it did not in itself denote membership of the sect. They were enjoined to keep on their persons *five* things. Five. *Kirpan,* the warlike dagger, *kaccha,* the undergarment of modesty, *kangha,* the bangle, *kankan,* the comb, and *kes,* their hair kept long. Over all these was the vow to purity, *Khalsa.*

In my haversack I had a field-service notebook. I took it out and copied the inscriptions into it, making an English translation below. Then I put the sandals back in their haven of stones and covered them.

It was two days ago that Reid had seen the movement of a man or an animal. I did not doubt now that he had seen a man. But which man? Had Saxby himself inscribed the shoes and put them under stones or had it been Ah Choong? Had Saxby died and left Ah Choong to set up his shrine? If so, there would be other shrines for the souls of his head, breath and heart.

I opened the notebook again and read what I had copied into it. With the soul of his eye he had learned the secrets of the garden of madness and made his list. Here on the ledge he had lain and watched the movements not only of the Japanese but of those civilians who had shown evidence of their guilt simply by being there. He must have spent hours on the ledge. He must have holed up for the night somewhere.

I put the notebook into my haversack, strapped it and rose, swinging it on to my left shoulder. I had been over an hour on the platform. I would have to hole up for the night myself.

At first glance the ledge had seemed to peter out but this was due to the shape of the rock and presently I found that it continued.

It led me in twenty minutes to the cave.

*

The cave was a dreadful place of shadows. It lay where the face of the hill turned and hid itself from the arc of the sun. It was dark and damp, loud with the dripping of unseen water. I rested in its mouth, lighted my tommy-cooker and as the water boiled in the mess-tin melted two tablets of malted milk. I opened a tin of bully and munched it drily while I waited for the drink to cool. I counted my cigarettes. Three for tonight, two for tomorrow. Sutton was carrying the spare rations.

I grinned into the cavernous dark to keep my spirits up, found myself whistling *I've got sixpence*, longed for a pint of cold, foaming beer to take away the cloying taste of the malted milk.

When my eyes were used to the gloom I lighted one of the night's ration of cigarettes and stood up to begin the search. Within a few minutes I found his satchel hidden beneath stones. In the satchel was an indelible pencil, a pair of binoculars and his book.

I took the satchel into the open and sat there outside the cave.

All but a few leaves of the book had been torn out, but on the remaining leaves in Saxby's still recognizable hand, in English, was the following:

I am wounded and losing blood. There is discoloration.

It was this way. In the year that I call the year of the orchids I saw in a dream five flowers and the path to take to reach them. I woke, followed the path and found the flowers there. I gathered them with their roots and carried them back to the longhouse. The people called me the Flower Dreamer, the *Shaman* of the Red Beard, and told me that the five flowers were the sign of my five souls.

Once I lived with a woman in a place called Singaputan. I went back to her after the year of the orchids. Nothing had been touched, no bench, no book, no flower, all, all as I had left it. Why? I asked, and she said, Because you are my beloved and a holy man. You went into the forest gathering the green things of God's heart in silence. What is silent is sad and what is sad is holy. God! I thought, I have been holy, then, in my time, so holy, sad and silent and empty of dreams and visions. She was a good woman.

I attended to business and returned to the longhouse. There they were still, those five, rooted, set apart, guarded by a little thicket. Why? I asked, and they said, Because you dreamed them and they are your souls. To dream all your five souls is the most powerful dream you can have and shows your greatness in the eyes of your heavenly father. And you are our *shaman*.

Lover to a woman, *shaman* to a tribe. But what to God? I had thought of myself once as a vessel, empty, waiting to be filled. Half-way would have done. I did not ask to brim over. There was also a time when I looked for Him and a time when I no longer looked, no longer believed in Him or in myself. Now I saw that I had been wrong. I saw that we were, indeed, both of us there, waiting, eyeing each other. He had planted the flowers and shown me how to find them. He had instructed the woman to do as she had done. He had done these things, while my back was turned, and then coughed, as if to have my attention. It was a very quiet vision, not at all what I had thought a vision would be like. It had a tentative air about it. I think we both felt it. I had to stay still, be very quiet. He may have been filled with curiosity that a man could stand so still. I could almost feel him edging up to me as if, having granted this man a vision, He wondered, Well now, is it? Is it He? The man Saxby? And would have touched me. Which would have been a beginning. A touch can excite the senses to violence and what a touch that would have been, rock against rock, steel on steel, blue flame crossing blue flame!

But he did not touch me and I continued quiet. I felt that the next move had to come from Him. If He meant business. If He wanted me. Why should we come easily to Him? What was claimed as His, why, He must take it, surely? I felt that it was not, after all, given to us to search for our image, but only given to God to search for His in us. And here was one waiting, yes, ready for finding; as he knew, having seen me wandering in the forest, having made that small sound, that clearing of the throat, to let me know He was there.

And so we remained.

*

The flowers were burned by the Japanese and the people were afraid to catch my eye when we returned there and saw the ashes. They thought it an omen of bad luck, death. They wondered why I did not fall down with a cry, having my souls burned like that right from under my nose. They said I must entreat God to restore them. Entreat? Yes, they said: Pray. They were very interested in the white man's God. I think they wanted to see what I looked like on my knees. *But in all this business I have never prayed.* I have never gone down on my knees. If we are made in His image it seems better that we should not kneel. He would not, would he, enjoy eternity in the company of angels unused to standing upright? He would get sick of bowed heads and moth-eaten wings.

So I did not pray, I left the charred clearing, I left the ashes to grow cold. I walked in the forest for many days and met a band of Chinese soldiers. Amongst them was one, Ah Choong, a young lad who bore on his body the marks of a hundred cigarette burns. He had been in the hands of the Japanese and his hatred of them consumed him. He despised his fellows who would never go with him or let him go alone against the invader. There was no one in control. They argued amongst themselves and watched each other to see what move was made. Ah Choong was too young to be taken seriously by them even though it was said he had been stoic under pressure and had divulged nothing.

The way they sat in their clearing watching each other was the way He watched me and I watched Him. I thought the next move had belonged to Him and I couldn't tell whether his move had been to have the flowers burnt and bring me here or to bring me here because someone had burned the flowers and must be punished. I could not tell whether he had made a move at all.

And all at once I realized he was watching me no longer and had not been from the day they burned the flowers. He had gone. It is worse for a blind man to be granted a few days sight than to know nothing but continuing darkness. I could never again persuade myself that neither of us existed because for a short time I had proof that we did. I found this comforting. After a while I was able to think things out more calmly.

At the root of the trouble was this business of the flowers being destroyed by fire. They are your souls, the people of the longhouse said, and, when they were burnt, You must pray for their return. I had refused to pray, and if the flowers had been a vision of my souls and nothing more then things would have been all right, yes, all right, because having been granted the vision, I would not lose my soul simply because the flowers in which the vision had come were destroyed.

But the flowers were more than a vision of my souls, *they were the medium through which He and I were able to watch each other*. Through them I could see Him and, worse, worse, through them he had chosen to see me. And he had chosen flowers because who would have expected a plant to be molested? Who would think of destroying a plant by fire? I have my soul, my five souls which make up my totality of soul, but I cannot see God any longer, and He cannot see me. It is to burn away this darkness that I have done what I have done. I know that with one finger he could revive the flowers, but I don't think it was easy for Him to grow them in the first place, no, not easy, for He had His own pride and having swallowed His pride once to grow the flowers only to have them thrown back in his face by the devil, *it has been up to me*. He swallowed His pride, and I have swallowed mine to punish the devil. But neither of us has been down on his knees. In the darkness we have stood eye to eye and breast to breast. We have been together in this business. He would not let me avenge the flowers and burn the darkness away only to reveal that in the light of day there was only myself at work. It is a cause for regret that the business must go unfinished, that I must go out with the darkness still intact. But He will know that I tried, that when I saw my responsibility I also took the opportunities which offered to punish the devil and the devil's comforters.

*

The devil has found me a worthy opponent. I have matched his cunning. He has been forced to scrape the bottom of his barrel for means to make the work difficult. Each time I killed he has whispered the word "remorse" into my ear, trying, you see, to put the idea of remorse into my head, to get me down on my knees where, in the darkness, God would only stub his toe on me. The devil was never interested in the killings. Those of the dead whose souls belonged to him he kicked into the pit with a backward thrust of his heel. He was only interested in me. He assumed many forms: once, the form of a woman, the woman Chang, and, for an instant, I was in danger, for this was a terrible form to come to me in. I drew back in time. She should have been dead by now, but the devil has looked after her well.

Yes, he found me a worthy opponent. He knows that now. Did he think he tricked me in the matter of Ah Choong? Did he think I would not notice that, in the body of Ah Choong, he came one night to walk by my side? I had been with Ah Choong for a long time. I too have had helpers. There was one, Lieu Lim, a simple man, an honest man who had courage but no notion it was to punish the devil that we lived in the forest. With Ah Choong it was different. He knew well enough what we were doing but in the end the devil had him.

We had gone one night to a place called Bukit Kallang where, but a while before, having freed ourselves of difficulties, we had taken the life of the devil's lickspittle, Cheong Poh Kwee. We had planned to hide in the garden of the bungalow of women and, when they returned from the pavilion in the garden of madness, kill them. I had failed once in this for reasons I cannot fathom.

But on the road I met a man speaking with the tongue of the past. The devil had put him there. The devil, in his time, had put many men in my way, Wan Lo Ping to name only one, but has not entered them. The devil had not entered the man we met on the road but he had entered Ah Choong. Ah! Did he think he fooled me, tricked me? That I would have on my hands the blood of this coal-heaver? Why were you there, coal-heaver? Why had you come to find me? In the end we have secrets from each other. I do not know why you were there, that night, on the road. You do not know that when I saw the devil had entered Ah Choong I laid hands on him saying: *Nahin, nahin, wuh mera dost hai;* which is to say, Be still, he is my friend. For you were my friend in the day when I needed friends, comfort.

*

The business goes unfinished. We came into the forest and there I turned to Ah Choong and said, Here in the forest are all the images of God and Heaven, but the devil has entered you. And I told him to go from my side so that I should not be hindered in the matter of burning away the darkness, and was not hoodwinked when the devil made Ah Choong cry out and pretend to be afraid and beg not to be left alone, and the devil, seeing that he had failed, and hoping to have my life if he could not have my soul, snatched the *kirpan* which I always carried with me and we fought together, struggling for possession of it.

I fell, bleeding, and called, God! God!

And then, oh, then, although the darkness had not been burned away someone cried out in a loud voice and I think it was You, because the devil – his hand raised to dispatch me – fled in terror. I felt myself raised up and heard a voice whisper: Your time has come, see to your shrines. And I was led to the place above the garden and bid leave my shoes and hide them under stones. And then I was bid come to the cave and write my book. Which I have done.

*

It is very quiet in this place, as quiet and still as it was when You cleared Your throat and we looked at each other. In this place I shall set up the shrine of my breath soul and head soul and then go barefoot and blind, which, since the darkness has never been burned away, is fitting, and, carrying with me the soul of my heart lay down to sleep where other flowers still may grow. For it was, oh, I think it was You who cried aloud and You who raised me in Your arms? You who will lead me to the house of flowers where once I was thought holy? In the end, having been proud, having each been proud, I must go proudly and You, if You want me, must reap my soul proudly.

But if this is not to be I am not ashamed to die alone.

*

It was almost dark when I had finished copying his book into my field-service pad. I returned the book, pencil and binoculars

to the satchel. Then I changed my mind and took the binoculars out thinking that he had forgotten they should lie in the
place of the soul of his eye. I replaced the satchel in the shrine of
stones and walked to the platform, perilously because of the
gathering night. There I collected stones and built them in a
mound over the field-glasses.

And then I lay huddled on the platform, chilled by the thin
wind that blew in with the night over the restless hills. I
opened the map I carried in my pocket but found it too large
scale to include Singaputan. Damn her! I thought, for losing
faith. Turner had said there were no flowers left.

I watched the deep velvet sky and then, as the night grew
older, and the time came, the tiny pinprick of light that glided
like a firefly over the garden towards the candleflame of the
pavilion. Did I catch a glimpse of red as well as yellow and
green? Or were there only the two colours? I closed my eyes.

A kind of peace and comfort entered my body from the
rocky earth of the platform, as though I found myself welcome
there, and from over the years I seemed to hear Saxby saying: I
have always been accommodating to my friends.

4

REID SAID, "WE'D GIVEN YOU UP."

I jerked my head at the half-dozen sepoys who sat on their hunkers with their rifles stacked and their equipment piled in the middle of the circle they made.

"What are they?"

"Reinforcements. Some of Sutton's men."

"Were you coming out to find me, then?"

Reid laughed. "No. As I said. We'd given you up. You went your way. We thought we'd better go ours."

He was taking it easy in a rattan chair on the narrow veranda of the Chinese vegetable grower's house. It was midday. I slung off my pack and lighted the last of my cigarettes.

"Where's Sutton? I've run out."

"He's around."

"And Chop and Suey?"

"Bathing. Grub'll be up in an hour. Then we move off."

"Any particular place?"

He scratched at his groin. "A disused guerrilla camp. About two hours from here. We leave at 1400 hours."

"May I look at your map?"

"Help yourself."

But it was the same as mine.

"Has anyone got a smaller scale, Reid?"

"No. Why?"

"I want to check the direction of a place called Singaputan. It's roughly east, but how far I don't know. It's where Saxby lived before the war."

"Never heard of it, Brent."

"Well, if it's all the same to you I think I'll go back."

"Back where?"

"Home. I can get to Singaputan by jeep in a couple of hours."

"You think he's there?"

"He could be."

"Suit yourself."

I bent down, unstrapped the pack, took out towel and soap. The notebook was safe. I could feel its shape underneath the pair of spare socks. Standing, I found Reid watching me. He would be glad to see the back of me. He had not asked me where I had got to or whether I had found the platform. He was not interested in Saxby. That was why I would not show him the notebook. You did not show notebooks of that kind to men who were in the jungle to play soldiers.

I said, "Why the reinforcements?"

"We think there are bandits. We don't know how many."

"In this old guerrilla camp?"

"Yes."

"So the search-party turns itself into a bandit patrol?"

"That's it, Brent. Any objections?"

I shook my head.

"By the way," he said, "did you find the platform?"

"I found nothing. I just got lost."

He grinned. That pleased him. Almost, he liked me again. I went down the steps. The sun was very hot. I wanted to get away from Reid. On my way to the stream I met Chop and Suey. They paused and made jerky little bows, saving their faces or saving mine by saying nothing.

In the stream the rocks formed a natural pool and behind the rocks where the water forced itself through a narrow channel bright daggers of light glittered. There was a hole in the tree-top ceiling above the stream. Stripping, I entered the water. On an overcast day the water would be black, chilled by its tumbling run down the stony hill. I practised my peculiar one-armed swimming, then stood in the shallow, soaped and rinsed myself.

From the cave the ledge had continued into the hills, going, I guessed, in the direction of Singaputan. Waking that morning after the sun was up, the pavilion and the garden of madness empty, I had thought of carrying on alone beyond the cave, at least for an hour or so. There would always have been a chance of coming upon him, a chance of finding his body, but in the end to go as quickly as I could to Singaputan had seemed the wisest course. It was now half-past twelve. I could be back on the road by half-past two, back in Bukit Kallang by three, in Singaputan by five or six. I could ring Turner and, if he were back from Singapore, arrange to meet him at the junction I remembered noticing on the map in the veranda room, and we could go the last leg together. Turner was the man to go with, not Reid.

I turned, making for the bank, and paused. Sutton was watching me. He had come down to bathe and had a towel round his middle. He was staring at my right shoulder but did not seem embarrassed to be caught doing so. As I waded towards him he simply lowered his eyes politely.

"Hello, Sutton."

"You're back, then, sir. Did you find the platform?"

"Not a thing."

He had dropped to one knee and was scrabbling for pebbles. He began to play ducks and drakes while a few paces behind him I dried myself. His body was slim, a bit like a girl's from the back. His skin was very white as if he had been dipped in bleach up to the neck where the brick-red sunburn began. There was a mole, the size of a half-penny, on the left shoulder-blade.

Without looking over his shoulder he said, "Is it difficult swimming with that arm, sir?"

"More or less. But I was never a good swimmer, anyway."

"Swimming's one of my favourite things."

"You'd better get in, then. I gather you're leaving at two."

He had his arm drawn back, a flat pebble held between finger and thumb. After a second or two's hesitation he sent it rippling across the surface of the pool.

275

"Aren't you coming with us, sir?"

"No."

He got down on to the other knee and remained, his trunk held upright, his hands unclenched but stiff as though restrained from making fists.

"Where are you going then, sir?"

"Back to Bukit Kallang."

He looked over his shoulder now.

"Then you don't think it's Saxby?"

"Don't think what's Saxby?"

"The Sikh, sir."

"What Sikh?"

"The one we're going after. The one they say's in this old guerrilla camp."

I moved closer to him. He brought up his hand and pushed the lock of hair back into place.

"I don't know anything about a Sikh, Sutton."

"Then you haven't seen Major Reid yet, sir?"

"Yes, I've seen Major Reid."

His lips were parted slightly. Now he closed them firmly and looked back at the stream, feeling for another pebble.

"He said nothing about a Sikh," I went on. "Should he have?"

"You'd better ask him, sir."

"I'm asking you."

He wiped his mouth with the back of his hand.

"You'd better ask Major Reid, sir."

He threw another pebble. It hit the water with a vicious little splash.

I said, "What's wrong?"

"There's nothing wrong, sir."

I went back to my pile of clothes and finished dressing.

"I'm out of cigarettes," I called.

He got to his feet and went to his own discarded jacket and trousers. From the pocket of his jacket he took a flat red tin, opened it and held it up.

"The spare are in my pack, sir, but have one of these meanwhile."

I took a cigarette, lit it with the old cartridge-case lighter with which I had replaced Bright Flame.

"Thank you, Sutton." I considered him for a few moments. "When I ask Major Reid about the Sikh," I said, "he'll know I've heard about him from you, won't he? Will you mind?"

He had a strange, innocent, violent face.

He said, "I shan't mind a damn, sir."

"I see. I wanted to be sure."

"It's coming to me, anyway."

"What's coming to you?"

"A beating."

"What are you talking about?"

"Nothing, sir. He reminds me of someone, that's all. Someone I used to get beaten by."

"Not your father."

He smiled. "No. A chap at school. A prefect."

"And?"

"That's all. I always knew when I was in for a beating because I knew the ways he had of making it so that I was due for one. After I'd had it he'd be all right again. For a bit, anyway. Until he thought I ought to get another."

"Major Reid can hardly take a cane to you," I smiled at him.

"No, sir. He can't use Ballister either. I've had that one. But I'm due for another. I'd rather get it over so there's no need to cover up for me, thanks all the same."

He turned abruptly and walked back to the stream. I disliked him for his intelligence, his knowledge of the world, and because he had resisted its corruption but let his innocence go sour. I thought to myself, What a dangerous young man you'll be once your innocence has gone.

*

Reid leaned his head to one side and rubbed the eyelid. "What an extraordinary fellow you are, Brent. First of all you

277

muck us about over which track to take, then you decide to opt out, now you decide to opt in again. Sometimes I feel you're not being wholly open with me. Is that what it is, Brent? Are you keeping something from me that as leader of this patrol I ought to know?"

"Well, it could be, Reid, couldn't it? On the other hand you're keeping something from me. Like a Sikh reported in this guerrilla camp."

"Ah."

"Why didn't you tell me?"

"Because you said you were going home and then to this place Sungei Pootan or whatever it was. It seemed odd to me, Brent. You disappeared for nearly twenty-four hours, and when you came back it was just to say kiss your arse. You found the platform, didn't you?"

"Yes."

"You lied to me."

"Yes."

"You found some clue to Saxby's whereabouts."

"Yes."

"Why did you lie?"

"Because Saxby is my affair and we don't go after him with rifles."

"You were keen enough to come on patrol. It was I who found the platform. I have a feeling you owe me some sort of apology, Brent. After all, I've taken you a lot into my confidence."

"Too much. You've told me more than you should. You don't give a damn about Saxby as long as you can make what you'd call a man out of Sutton. I warned you before we started. I'm not having Saxby hunted by men who want to feel like giants. That's why I'm opting in again, in case this Sikh *is* Saxby. I don't think he is but I can't rule it out."

"Brent, I'm beginning to think this friendship with Saxby is a bit odd. After all, he gave you a hiding and constituted a threat to your girl."

278

I clenched my teeth. I had to stand there taking it. It was essential for Saxby's safety not to let Reid reach boiling point. The whole damned patrol was becoming like a row of kettles under which you had to keep turning down the gas. I had to bite back the reply that would have made Reid bubble.

"You can think what you like, Reid. But I'm coming with you and Saxby is mine."

"You've made that clear."

"Good."

"But let *me* make something clear, Brent. This is an armed patrol. If we run into trouble the Sikh takes his chance along with the rest of us, whether it's Saxby or an Indian wandering round spare. If you've got no stomach for it, stay out of it. If not, you'll come on the same footing as the rest of them. That's to say under my command."

Stomach! Run into trouble! Was there no end to this man's capacity for melodrama? I opened the pack, rummaged in it and gave him the notebook.

"Read that," I said. "A madman wrote it. He lived in a world of his own, but it was a dam' sight cleaner than this one."

I went inside where the Chinese and his wife were putting the finishing touches to the tiffin they had prepared for Reid, Sutton and myself from our own rations. I was not sure whether I really knew what I meant by saying that to Reid. But it was a question of warning him, of letting him see for himself that the patrol as such had no significance whatsoever, *that you did not enter Saxby's world with sten-guns and rifles and make any impression on it.*

Reid came in presently, threw the book on the table. He did not need to ask questions because the copies of Saxby's book and the inscriptions of his shrines were headed with details of the time, place and manner of their discovery.

"I have two things to say, Brent."

"Go ahead."

"Saxby's either dead or it's a trick. If he's dead that's that. If he's not, watch out."

"What do you mean?"

"You can be simple at times, Brent. If I saw him on the platform he probably saw me. In that case his so-called shrines and his so-called book are red herrings. He wanted you to find them, to think he was dead and to think he saved your life instead of trying to murder you. He may be waiting somewhere to do it properly next time."

He stumped out again. His heavy boots made the wooden steps creak. He yelled for Sutton.

I put the notebook back in my pack.

In Reid's world and my world nothing was too mean or vicious for a man to be thought capable of. You could not rule it out. You could rule nothing out.

After tiffin, as we made ready, I found Sutton cleaning and oiling his sten-gun.

"Where did Reid hear about this Sikh?"

"From the Chink, sir. Someone told the Chink last night there was a Sikh hiding in this camp. He was full of it when we got back."

"Who was the someone else who told him?"

"Another Chink."

"Do you have to call 'em Chinks, Sutton? You sound as bad as Holmes."

"What else can you call 'em, sir? That's what they are. Chinks. The Indians are wogs, the French are frogs, and the Germans are —king huns." He bunched the piece of cotton waste in his fist and threw it away. His blue eyes glinted. "I come of a long line of soldiers, sir."

"And now you're one yourself."

"That's it, sir."

"And you don't want to be."

"Yes, I do, sir. Major Reid wants me to be too. But I've got to go through it first." He smiled to point the sarcasm. As I walked away he called out, "Look at this, sir!" and hefted the sten-gun. "I've made a good clean job of that. I've never done *that* before."

"Done what, Sutton?"

"Pickled a switch for my own butt."

He waited for me to laugh, to be amused. When I did not laugh he turned his back, began to walk over to where his sepoys rested on their rifles.

5

MY WATCH SHOWED FOUR-FIFTEEN. AHEAD OF US was the sound of a waterfall. We had left the track and taken cover in the jungle because we were near the disused guerrilla camp. I did not like the sound of the water. It disguised the noise made by men. I felt it was typical of the guerrillas to have set a camp up there. From where I crouched I could see ahead of me the crown and brim of Reid's slouch hat and behind me a section of Sutton's face and the barrel of his sten-gun. Chop had gone on ahead. We were waiting for ten minutes. If he had not come back by then we were to follow him. Suey stayed with us.

When the ten minutes were up Chop had not returned. Reid got to his feet and we moved back to the track. Suey went ahead. We followed, spacing ourselves out some fifteen feet apart with the sepoys bringing up the rear.

The track led us to the bank of a swiftly flowing stream. The fall was some two or three hundred yards to our left by the look of things. To our right the track continued at right angles, following the line of the stream. We found Chop sitting on a rock, grinning.

"No one here," he said.

"No," said Reid. "Not here. Where?"

"Perhaps further on in old camp."

"I thought we had come to the camp."

"No." Chop's wisdom was allowed out to dazzle us. "Old days we bathe there." He pointed up-stream. "Man guard this rock. Others bathe. Man shoot warning Japs come."

"Good," Reid said, "only don't shoot warning now."

We continued the march up the bank of the stream. The noise

282

of the waterfall diminished as the stream took us in a slow curve.

"Path still used," Suey said, bending to point at damp earth. There were footprints in it.

"Recently?" Reid asked.

"Oh, yes. Today. Yesterday."

Chop lifted a hand. His thin face seemed to grow tauter and bonier. A hundred yards ahead with his back towards us a man sat fishing a pool from a flat rock. One doubted he would find fish there. Reid signalled us to move from the track to the jungle. Chop edged towards Suey, touched his shoulder. A look of understanding passed between them. Suey handed his rifle to Chop, unsheathed his bayonet and held it like a knife on the flat of his palm.

I pointed at it, raised my eyebrows and said in a low voice, "Why?"

Suey grinned. "Frighten," he said. "Frighten, bring him."

I said to Reid, "I'll go with them."

"No. Leave it to them. They know what they're doing."

"No bloodshed, Reid. Tell them."

"They know. Calm down."

Chop gave Reid Suey's rifle. Then the two guerrillas turned away, the one with the bayonet, the other with a rifle. They disappeared into the jungle.

From where we crouched we could still see the back of the man who was fishing. He was brown and half naked. On his head was a wide-brimmed straw hat. He was so still that presently we guessed he was dozing. The line hung slackly from a short length of cane.

The sweat began to trickle into my eyes. I wiped them carefully with my left hand. Sutton knelt beside me. I could see the beads of perspiration on his nose and upper lip. He was breathing through his mouth, his eyes unmoving from the back of the brown fisherman. My own view of the fisherman was bounded on the one side by the trunk of a tree and on the other by Sutton's cheek. As a drop of sweat fell from his upper lip and he

283

put out his tongue to taste the salt of it we saw Suey come out of the jungle a few yards behind the man on the rock. Chop lay hidden somewhere giving him cover.

Suey went forward inch by inch. The sun struck at the blade of the bayonet as he levelled it in his hand. I stood up. I wanted to shout, but no sound came. I had been trained too well. The daylight was suddenly veiled with blue and violet as my eyes rebelled against the glare and then they re-focused and the bright colours of the day became separated, all the detail of rock and river, tree and sky, sharpened, purified.

Suey was now but a leap away from the man on the rock. Staring at that brown back my own back crawled, aware of the sharp sunlit blade so close to it. Suey did not leap but in a movement too quick for my scorched eyeballs he had his left arm round the man's throat and the dagger outstretched where the man could see it as something the sky had bred: a gold, sharp glint out of the blue.

Suey swung the man round. The fishing line had dropped and the hat fallen off. He looked like a Chinese. He had both hands clawing at Suey's arm and we could see from the angle of his head that he looked nowhere but at the bayonet.

Chop came out of the jungle, his rifle levelled. Suey lowered the bayonet so that the man in watching it became aware of his other adversary. Chop went up and jabbed the muzzle of the rifle in the man's stomach. Suey had one hand over the man's mouth now. Gently they slid off the rock. With Suey's hand on his mouth, the knife pricking his side, Chop's rifle levelled like a final argument, the fisherman was led quietly off the path into the forest.

*

We waited for five minutes and then for another two. I looked at Reid. He refused to catch my eye. Sutton knelt as before. Once I thought I heard a cry, but it might have been a bird. The waterfall thundered. It had thundered through a million such afternoons.

284

Suey appeared and motioned us forward. He said, "He say four men only in camp."

Reid said, "Including him?"

"No. Four other men. One Sikh, three Chinese."

"Does he know names?"

"Said no. They come short time. He here long time."

"Is the Sikh wounded?" I asked.

"He did not say."

"Are they armed?" Reid asked.

"He say no, no arms."

"He's lying," Reid said.

Suey turned away and led us through the forest. In a small clearing Chop stood over the fallen body of the Chinese. I recognized the look.

"Is he dead?" I asked Chop.

Chop moved away from the body. I bent down and turned the head. The eyes stared. Blood covered the chest. They had used the bayonet. He was quite an old man, with wrinkled skin, and looked like a tortoise no longer protected by its shell.

"He would make noise," Chop explained.

"At least," I said, "you were quick."

I turned away making for the track. I heard someone behind me. He took my arm.

"Hold on," Reid said.

"No," I said, "I shan't hold on. I'm going to the camp. I'm going by the track. I'm going in the open. The war's over. We're not patrolling for Japs. We're looking for a man who blacked his face and lived in the jungle like a poor mad bastard with another poor mad bastard called Ah Choong. We're not looking for Japs or thin old Chinamen sitting on rocks fishing."

"Keep your voice down."

"Why?" I shouted. "Why?"

I turned on to the track where the clean sun burned the earth and as I went I wrenched the lanyard from my belt, drew the pistol from its holster and, pausing, threw it far out into the stream, glad because I had one arm still capable of throwing. As I went on I jerked the pack from my shoulders and left it lying on the ground, pulled the belt from round my waist and threw it into the jungle. Then I marched free, unweaponed and unequipped. I began to run and call for Saxby as loudly as I could.

*

I came to a clearing and stopped on its edge. Around it the forest was emerald green and the blue of indigo. The grass was trodden and the air was heavy with the scent of the juices of the bruised stems. At one end of the clearing, a hundred yards away, stood a hut built high on stilts, its atap thatching ruinous, its walls bulging with age and damp.

I cupped my mouth and called, "Saxby!" and in a moment or two three men appeared from where they had been hiding in the jungle a few yards from the hut. They were Chinese as far as I could tell and they held rifles ready. I began to walk slowly towards them. One of them shouted then and when I did not stop cocked his rifle up.

It was important not to stop walking or to stop thinking. Every step of the way I was going to have to think: That fellow will probably shoot me. Every step of the way except the last I was going to have to take another step. I was going to have to do this without flinching because Saxby had held out his hand and said, *Nahin, nahin, wuh mera dost hai,* and if Saxby was somewhere at the other end of the clearing I had to get there and not be stopped by a man cocking up his gun. I had to get there before Reid got there, before Chop or Suey or Sutton got there. I had to sweat and walk and think because years ago I had shrugged my shoulders, packed my bags and said: To hell with him then. And I had to sweat and walk and not be afraid of the man cocking his gun up because of a wrinkled old Chinese who had sat half-naked on a rock dreaming of fish. I had to walk and not be afraid so that in that clearing, in that green-blue place, under the hammer blows of

286

the golden sun, I could offer from my world something clean. I had to walk and not be afraid in order to ransom for just a few seconds of time the soul of my liver.

When the firing started my feet were still propelling me forward. Reid had opened up from the edge of the clearing down to my right: Reid with his revolver, Chop and Suey with their rifles and Sutton with his sten-gun. The man with the cocked up rifle went down like a stone. I saw him going down with my eyes but not with my comprehension. I think his companions spun round intending to fire but the bullets whipped round them, dancing in the grass, and I had an impression of bodies, bullets and grass dancing together, and of the end which was sudden and quite still, and I was reminded of how death has a habit of never arriving but of having come and gone without your knowing.

I had started from the other end of the clearing knowing that for once I had to walk and sweat and not be afraid, but when I arrived at the place in which the three bodies lay I saw how useless the effort had been and how it might have been better if I had not cast my revolver away and run to the encampment shouting for Saxby, making them think I came alone, because if we had come in strength and surrounded them, then, even if they had resisted they would have had a chance.

Reid was at my side.

"You're mad," he shouted. "Mad! Mad! I ought to have let him shoot you. You asked to be shot. You deserved to be shot."

Chop was kneeling by the man who had cocked his rifle up, whose chest was shattered. He stripped the man's shirt away and turned the body face down. All over his back and arms were tiny white stars of scar-tissue, minute explosions of dead pain under the skin.

"Ah Choong," he announced.

"Yes, yes. Ah Choong," Suey said.

"You fool, Brent. You bloody fool!"

I went up the rickety ladder into the hut. In one corner a

Sikh, his long hair unturbanned and streaming over his shoulders, began to blubber.

"Sahib! Sahib!" he cried.

Reid was behind me. "So that's Saxby," he murmured.

"It's not Saxby," I said.

"It was Ah Choong down there."

"But this isn't Saxby."

Reid pushed past me, making for the Sikh. I grabbed his arm.

"If you touch one hair, Reid, I'll bloody murder you."

He hesitated. I kept my grip on his arm until I could feel the tension going out of him.

"What's got into you, Brent?"

"You don't know, do you? You haven't the faintest idea."

"I saved your life," he said. "That's what I know."

When I got out into the open again Chop and Suey were searching the bodies and finding nothing. Sutton was stumbling away towards the edge of the forest, dragging the sten-gun by its sling. Before he got to the cover of the trees he fell on his knees. You could hear the noise of his being sick from fifty yards away.

*

Before night fell I hunted for and found my pack and belt. Reid refused to go back that evening. It was a four-hour journey to the road and he thought we would lose our way in the dark. We buried the bodies and stayed the night in the clearing. At six the following morning, taking the Sikh prisoner with us, we set out for home.

The Sikh offered bribes, wept, begged for mercy and finally for a quick death there in the jungle. He was one of the policemen from Bukit Kallang who had run away when the Japanese surrendered and left them unprotected. He had spent the night tied to a tree. Now he was made to march with his hands bound behind his back.

Before we began the march home I apologized to Reid and

thanked him. He had saved my life. He had saved it in the only way he knew. Whether the whole business was his fault or mine was neither here nor there. What I had done was foolhardy. It could have endangered the lives of us all if the clearing had been well-manned. It was useless to attempt to deny it.

My apology put him back into his good humour. When he had been back in it for an hour or two he began to refer to my exploit with affectionate amusement. He would look at me with the gleam in his eye, shake his head and say, "Mad!" Then he would chuckle and say it again, "Mad!" He had saved my life. I was in his debt. He liked that. For him, it created between us a powerful male intimacy.

He asked me what I proposed to do about Saxby, but he was not interested in my reply. The patrol had achieved almost more than he could have wished. It was over for him now. He had saved my life and Sutton had smelt the bitter, exciting smell of cordite and had seen for the first time what sten-gun fire could do to the human body. He had been sick at the sight but that, perhaps, for Reid, since Sutton had taken himself off to try to be sick in secret, was no more reprehensible than it would have been for a boy who, having taken his beating well, shed a few tears in private.

Once, when we halted, he came and sat beside me.

"Brent," he said, "do you know what was in that letter?"

"What letter?"

"The one I wrote to the colonel."

"No, I don't know."

"My resignation. My formal application for a posting back to India. I'll climb on to the dungheap before they throw me on it. I'll dish myself. I'm still good enough for that. I'll bring my own curtain down, bring it down on *this* note."

He had a kind of courage. He was consistent, but then a man so single-mindedly obsessed was bound to be. One day, I thought, he might wake up and know why and by whom he was being punished. Would he be able to face that, or would he crack then and, as Calthrop may have feared, bring disgrace upon himself? For the truth was he was punishing himself for sins only his subconscious mind had knowledge of. They were sins he had been brought to by other men who lived and died in the monosexual world of military splendour, where seduction was a matter of pace-sticks, coupling a business of bullets, and lying with women merely a reward for passing more important tests than those of natural love.

He did not immediately show Sutton that Sutton had passed a test. For the whole length of the march back he hardly spoke to him. We emerged from the jungle at a quarter to ten. There was a fine smell of morning in the air and the metalled road was mottled with shade and sun. Pausing there Reid offered us cigarettes. When Sutton took one Reid laid a hand on his shoulder in a brief gesture of acceptance.

A look of relief came on to Sutton's face but then, as he held Reid's eye, the look changed to one of renewed wariness.

"Have you got a light?" Reid asked him.

Sutton fumbled with his lighter. His hands were unsteady and when he had lighted Reid's cigarette he moved away to the side of the road. Perhaps, up to that moment, he had forgotten that he had to go on living with Reid, that the patrol was not an end, but a beginning, that there might be other tests in store.

*

Reid had sent a runner ahead an hour before and we had only a few minutes to wait for the transport: the beef wagon for the Sikh and the guerrillas, the thirty-hundredweight for the patrol. Reid elected to go in the beef wagon and I in the front seat of the truck. At the road junction in Bukit Kallang wagon and truck parted company and as the truck drew level with Teena's bungalow I told the driver to stop. Going round to the back where Sutton and his sepoys stood strap-hanging I said, "Will you do something for me? Check that the jeep's got a full tank? I'll be back in twenty minutes."

"Yes, sir."

He jumped over the tailboard and went to the driver's cabin. He was not meeting my eye.

*

"You are shaved," she said, feeling my cheek.

"At dawn, in cold water."

I felt dirty, disreputable, but she submitted to my kiss.

"You're safe," I said, "safe because of Shining Dagger."

I held her away from me. She was all the refuge and wonder I could want. With her, now, the world came back into shape, back into drawing.

"Did you find Saxby, Tommy?"

I gave her the notebook, and made her sit down and read it there and then, and each turn of her wrists, each flexible movement of her fingers was a kind of anguish to me in case those hands should prove ready for only one kind of giving, one kind of taking. She gave me back the notebook.

"Poor Sax Bee," she said and rose from the sofa, stood for a moment with her back to me. "Where is the house of flowers?"

"It used to be in Singaputan. I'm going there now."

She turned round. For once she had achieved her Chinese mood in her European make-up.

"Are you coming back?"

"Yes."

"When?"

"Tonight."

"It may not be tonight, Tommy. If he is not there or if he is there but not yet written in the book then you would stay until he is there or *is* written in the book?"

"I'd only stay if he's there but not yet written in the book."

"So you may not come tonight?"

"I suppose not. Why? Have you got to know absolutely?" I held my arms out to her again, but she moved away to get cigarettes. "If I'm not coming back tonight I'll send you a message. Otherwise I'll be here. And then I shall ask you a question."

"What question, Tommy?"

"Whether the world has grown larger."

I took the cigarette she offered and wondered whether she had understood that I was asking her to come away with me. She produced the lighter and clicked it on.

"There," she said, "there is your one golden eye."

"I've got two, not one. And they're not gold. Look."

She smiled, let the flame out, put the lighter back in her pocket. She said, "If you find Sax Bee your job'll be finished."

The Chinese mood had gone, gone out with the flame. I was glad. I was afraid of it.

"Yes, it'll be finished."

Her eyes seemed to deepen as I watched them.

"But there are other jobs," I said. "Jobs of all kinds in all kinds of nice places, like Singapore, or Bangkok."

"Or Batavia? Surabaya?" she asked.

"Yes, anywhere. Lots of jobs, lots of places. But we'll talk about jobs and places tonight." I took her hand. *She had understood.* "I must go. See me to the door for luck."

She came with me. As I pulled the bolt back she said, "Tommy?"

"Yes?"

"I haven't thanked you for Saxby."

"What do you mean?"

"For looking for Saxby."

And then she reached up and took my face between her hands, drew it down to hers and kissed me tenderly, lovingly on the lips.

"Good-bye, Tommy."

"Until tonight," I said.

I left her and set out for the house on the hill, walked under the triumphal archway from which the bunting had been removed. It was being got ready for dismantling. I walked on down the road, into the turning that led in slow S-bends through the tall, straight trees.

Calthrop was waiting for me on the veranda of the wooden hut.

"Major Turner rang half an hour ago."

"What did he want?"

"He asked me to tell you to go to a place called Singaputan at once if you got back this morning. I said we'd already sent transport to collect you. Does the message make sense, sir?"

"Yes, it makes sense. But I'll want a new map."

I followed him into the office.

6

IT WAS HALF-PAST ONE WHEN I PASSED THROUGH what, according to the map, was the last kampong before Singaputan, and on this stretch of road, familiar because it was like so many other stretches and not because I had driven along it once before, I met the motor-cyclist.

Rounding a bend we each had to pull in. For a moment I thought he was losing control of his machine but he was only waving his arm to get my attention. I stopped the jeep. He swung round, behind me, and drew up level, twisting the throttle. He was a military policeman.

"Is it Major Brent, sir?"

"Yes, corporal."

"You've saved me a job, then, sir. Major Turner told me to try and find you."

"You want me to follow you?"

"If you would, sir. It's not much ahead."

He gunned the machine and swerved away, steadying himself with his boots which scraped the road surface. He looked over his shoulder once.

My mouth was dry, my stomach empty. I had eaten nothing for six hours.

The gap between jeep and motor-cycle shortened; the corporal was flapping one gloved hand slowly up and down. He went out of sight round a corner. Turning it myself a few seconds later I rediscovered him riding slowly through Singaputan. It was the same but not the same. I had imagined it more straggling altogether. The huts on stilts were closer to the road, the compounds smaller, the whole hunched together with the jungle pressing in. At the end of the village there was a fifteen-hundredweight truck with M.P. markings, and a jeep that looked like Turner's because the plate on the back was of the same colour and design as the flashes he wore on his sleeves.

Nearby, the people of Singaputan were gathered together, watching the bungalow outside whose compound the truck and jeep were parked. The corporal stopped there. I drew level with him as he manhandled his machine on to its back-rest.

"Why here?" I called. "It's wrong. There's a road leading off to the left somewhere."

The corporal jerked his gloved thumb at the bungalow. "You'll find Major Turner there, sir."

I got out.

"What's up?" I asked him.

He unstrapped his crash helmet. "This bloke Saxby, sir."

"Is he here?"

"Yes, sir."

"Alive?"

He pulled the crash helmet off. He was sandy-haired, red-faced, far younger than he looked with the helmet on.

"No, sir."

He began to get out his cigarettes. I walked up the wide path to the veranda, paused, said aloud, "But it's wrong. This isn't the place at all."

Turner came out and, seeing me, came to the head of the steps.

"It's wrong, Turner," I called to him without greeting. "This isn't the place."

I climbed the steps.

"I know," he said. "It's where we made a mistake. You'd better come inside."

Over the threshold I stood still. It was wrong, but it was right. In the middle of the room there was the low table where once I had eaten mounds of saffron rice and pulao chicken, and the two wicker chairs on one of which he had sat dressed in his bright sarong. But the walls were bare. There were no plants.

295

"Sit down," Turner said. "I've got something to tell you."

"I know. The corporal beat you to it. Saxby's dead."

"There's more to it than that. And we need you to tell us that it *is* Saxby." He hesitated. "If you can." He took my arm. "Sit down, Tom."

I moved away. "Not for the moment." I could not sit on either chair.

The corporal coughed. He had come to the doorway.

"Anything I can do, sir?"

"Yes, you might relieve your pal, corporal."

"Right, sir."

He went. Turner produced a flask of whisky, uncorked and gave it to me. "You haven't eaten, I suppose. Have some of this."

I took the flask and tilted it, glad of the rawness and heat of the spirit.

"Right," I said.

"He got in yesterday, Tom. God knows from where."

"Not only God. But go on."

"You've found out something?"

"I've got it written down. I'll show you in a moment. How did you find out he'd got in yesterday?"

"From the M.P.s. You know they had orders to keep an eye open? Well, they've not got much to do round here and got into the habit of riding over quite often. Probably had their eyes on some of the girls. But they got interested in Saxby too. Being policemen they have a nose for anything that's being kept from them. Nobody in Singaputan was really forthright about him. Until today. The corporal who brought you in came over yesterday evening. He thought something was up from the way they all acted. This morning one of them went down to the police post and told them Saxby had come back, and was dead. I think they were on Saxby's side while he was alive, Tom, especially with the police showing an interest, but when he was dead they thought they'd better let us know."

"When did he die? Last night?"

Turner had taken out a cigarette. He lit it before answering.

"Tom, if it is Saxby, he looks as if he's been dead for more than twelve hours. But they swear he only came yesterday."

"And they must be right. He came from the jungle above Bukit Kallang, and he was there only four days ago."

"Tell me what you know."

I gave him the notebook and waited while he read it. Before he had finished the man whom the corporal had relieved looked in at the doorway, and withdrew. His cheeks were muddy yellow. Turner gave the notebook back to me.

"I understand better now," he said. "Come on."

I followed him through bead curtains into a narrow passage. The same but not the same. It began to be different in the compound behind the bungalow. I could see no bath enclosure, and the ground was tilled, fecund with vegetables. He led me along the narrow paths which separated the beds and, reaching a clump of bamboo where the jungle began, he stopped, took me by the shoulders, and turned me round to face the back of the house.

"Is *that* what you remember, Tom?"

"No."

"Look underneath the stilts. Look at the path that leads to the house from the road. You can see where it used to continue, *under* the house, into the garden. It only stops there because the ground has been dug up."

I was stupid with raw whisky on an empty stomach. I shook my head.

He said, "She had the new house built across the track that used to lead to the old one. When I came here first I simply wasn't to know, was I?"

"Why did she do that?"

"You'll see in a moment. You'll see her, too."

He pushed through the clump of bamboo and I followed him into the close, hot smell of green forest, and presently, beyond the bamboo, into the dark cloister of an overgrown path that had once been a track curving continuously so that

297

you drove head-on towards a thick curtain of leaf and frond. Where the path stopped there was the ruined, four-posted shelter struck by a shaft of sun that filtered through the forest ceiling. From here a new path stood at a right angle.

Coming on to it Turner stood aside.

There seemed to be nothing left of the bungalow that had stood there, fifty yards ahead, only a hint of the solid shape of roof and wall behind the entwined stems of the plants and vines and creepers that grew up round it, spilling out from inside, twisting up from below, hanging down from above: a riot of green leaf, white, red and purple flowers whose scents, rich with both life and corruption filled the air.

To one side the corporal stood on guard. The woman was kneeling on the ground, her head bowed, one hand on the lowest step of the short flight which led to the place that had become a shrine of flowers. The handrail was preserved, perhaps held together, by the tenacious grip of root and stem and, if you climbed the steps, you would have to do so without touching the rail because it was thick with blossom.

Approaching her I knelt and put my hand on her shoulder, but she buried her ugly face deeper in her arm and moaned. The hand that rested on the lower step was deformed and stiff, gnarled, hopeless and misshapen; a bulb, a tuber, fit only for planting.

I straightened, found Turner watching me, and then, conscious of his eyes on me, I walked carefully up the steps.

I entered the plant room and then he seemed to rise from an invisible chair by an invisible table and cry: And oh! a rock that moves, a plant that talks, wouldn't that be a monstrosity? And, wiping from his face the outer skin of feeling, turned and clacked his way through the swinging bead curtain that still hung in the open space, with his hands clutched to the label he would not allow God, let alone other men, to see. Mildew patterned the bulging plaited walls and in here there were no flowers, only thick, green, white stems and the dropped, decayed leaves of the seasons scattered like bits of paper to mark the way of his going if God should ever wish to follow him. And, if God should ever wish, I thought, then, oh, then he must tread carefully for the floor was ruinous, laid over in the most dangerous places with bamboo poles that the woman must have hacked and sawn with her own hands and carried breathlessly up the steps of the shrine so that she still could enter the holiest place of all, the place of his sleeping.

Entering it I smelt the death smell that is like the smell lime trees make when their pale, creamy flowers turn brittle and yellow. It was dark, for here the plants choked the windows, clawed at the walls and ceiling as though to break through them and burgeon upwards, higher and higher to face heaven proudly. I cried aloud when I saw him resting on his bed of flowers and hid my face, sickened by his smell and the look he had of being shaped from earth.

But when I looked at him again I saw that it had indeed been he, the flower dreamer, the *shaman* of the red beard, the man who had scattered earth in front of me but never dirt, who had held out the hand I was always late in taking, but had still held it out when *I came at him* out of the past on the road to Bukit Kallang. His long hair streamed over a white pillow, and what had been those hands were folded, what had been those eyes were closed. The stain had washed itself from his skin and the roots of his hair and beard were red and living. He had lain down to die naked and on his left shoulder there was a crust covering the wound – the same crust on the soles of his feet.

I stumbled out of the room, through the plant room, down the steps and for one moment the eyes of the woman were raised to mine, and then I was walking down the path only half aware of Turner coming behind me. When I got to the ruined shelter I turned in there and was sick.

*

"We can only burn it," Turner said, "burn the whole lot."

I stayed to see it done. The woman shrieked and would have thrown herself into the flames, but the corporal held her back, his face as white as a sheet, muttering over and over, "Steady on, mother, it's all for the best."

And at five o'clock I drove back to Bukit Kallang alone.

7

THERE WAS TO BE A *TAMASHA*, WHAT REID CALLED
a bit of a show. The dressing-gowns had been sent down to
the bungalow. "It means they'll bring them and lay them
on cushions, the old way, the Jap-yap way. And when a man
picks one up they'll know which girl he's chosen."

He caught my arm. We were on the stairs, coming away
from the veranda room, the last to leave. He had been drinking
again. "Ah! I know what you're afraid of! Forget it. I've told
those young pups of mine no cheating. Pick your own girl
is what I told them, not some other blighter's." He swayed.
"Brent," he said. "Brent, I'm sorry. God, yes. Sorry about
Saxby," and went to the bottom of the stairs into the naked
light of the hall, pulled himself up short at the entrance to the
mess where half an hour before I had eaten my dinner alone.
The mess was in darkness.

"But it's over now, Brent, isn't it? Over for both of us.
We've cleared our plates. Now we take our bearings. Do you
like that?"

"It depends."

"Ah, what's wrong with you, man?" He slapped my right
arm, above the elbow, then dropped his hand as if he had been
stung. "I'm sorry, Brent, I forgot your arm."

"It doesn't hurt. Come on, Reid, if we're going."

He caught my other arm.

"No. Wait a bit. I want you to *know*. I want you to know
just how I feel." He hesitated, looked puzzled, let go of my arm.
"What's wrong? You closed up on me then. You shut me out.
I always know when a man shuts me out. Aren't you interested
in how I feel?"

"Feel about what?" I asked cautiously.

"About going. Tomorrow's my last day. I go tomorrow."

"Is that when it is?"

"That's when it is, Brent. Indecent haste would you say? Indecent haste on the part of my colonel?"

"You asked for it, didn't you?"

"Ah, I'm not complaining. It's what I've been telling you. I feel alive again. And I think I've stopped being punished. What about that?"

"They're letting you get tight?"

He laughed.

"So you've noticed it."

If he wants Teena, I told myself, I'll fight him for her.

"I'm getting a bit tight, yes. I've cleared my plate. Perhaps I've wiped the whole slate clean. That would mean I was right. I had to stop being a bastard to Sutton and what's in here isn't rotten. Come on, Brent." He put an arm over my shoulder, flicked on his torch and trundled us both to the door. "What a time we had. What a bloody wonderful time. And you! Mad! Mad as a bloody hatter, walking across that clearing not giving a damn for their bloody rifles, and young Sutton letting 'em have it cool as you please. Shall I forget that, Brent? Ever? It was another day, I tell you, a green, golden, wonderful day."

His arm which had been resting lightly tightened briefly. He meant nothing by it, but I had had enough of him. I twisted away and faced him. He had his back to the lighted porch and I could only see his shape, his lowering bulk. I said, "It was a day when bloody murder was done. That's what I shall remember."

Half-way across the garden I waited for him to catch me up. "I'm sorry, Reid."

"That's all right, Brent. You've had a bad day, I know."

We walked the rest of the way together, but silently. I dared not quarrel with Reid. He had the authority to turn me out of the pavilion. Tonight, I was determined, should be my last time in it, but I had to have tonight.

Calthrop, MacAndrews and Holmes got to their feet as we

climbed the steps. It was strange to see them there in uniform. They poured us drinks and offered us chairs and eventually Reid sat down and, in two short sentences, fixed the evening in our minds indelibly.

"Well, lads, the end looks like this. Lanterns in a Chinese love pavilion and our time together at the bottom of a glass."

He looked from one to the other, his glass raised, toasting each of them separately. In silence they raised their own glasses to him and drank, thinking perhaps that because of his luck they owed him their lives and therefore their present pleasures, their future happiness.

I shivered, turned in my chair to face the house from where the *tamasha* would begin. In the darkness the world was big because its horizons were limitless. I wondered whether Teena, walking towards the pavilion, would understand this, and entering, tell me with her eyes that *our* time together had scarcely begun. The restless hills which I could not see were waiting too, holding their breath.

*

The *tamasha* began with the explosions of Chinese crackers. They leapt out of the darkness over by the compound wall.

Sutton said, "That means they want you to go into the ante-room, sir."

We were still on the veranda. The girls had reached the house half an hour before and had sent Sutton over to warn us there would be a bit of delay, to tell us to cover the window between the two doors with a curtain and to take the gramophone outside where it could produce invisible music. Reid had said to him, "Stay and watch. Stay and have a drink. Forget the 'phone." And Sutton had stayed, booted, gaitered and armed with his duty officer's sten-gun, which, with Saxby dead, he really no longer needed.

Now he moved towards the steps and Reid said, "No, hang on, Sutton. You might as well come inside and watch the show. See a bit of life."

In the ante-room there were three cushions on the mosaic floor. Further back, in accordance with Teena's instructions, the wicker chairs were set in a row and we went to them now and sat down. Sutton picked up a spare chair and joined us. The two doors were propped open.

There were fresh bursts of crackers; a staccato series of reports which continued uninterrupted and came closer until the sound enveloped the pavilion. Acrid smelling smoke rose thinly and hung outside on the veranda and through the smoke Suki came with tiny, stylized footsteps. She was dressed in black silk pyjamas and wore a wide-brimmed pointed straw hat on her head.

Holmes called, "That's my girl!" but she took no notice. She came and stood behind the three cushions, knelt, made obeisance. Reid led the applause.

Straightening up but staying on her knees she said in a clear, high voice, "Tonight I wear black because I am the spirit of the night and black is her colour. I welcome you to the sun pavilion. The spirit of the night is guardian of the three spirits of the pavilion and I carry them in the sleeve of my garment. So. One, two, three."

She drew from inside the wide sleeve of her jacket three silk handkerchiefs: yellow, green and red. She put one on each of the three cushions, yellow to her right, green to her left and red in the centre. Then she arched her arm and pointed at them in turn.

"This is Yellow Blossom, the guardian of the golden room enslaved of the rising sun. And this is Green Lotus, who keeps the jade room of day-long happiness."

She extended both hands, dipped her body and said, "And this is Red Jade, keeper of the pavilion and of the scarlet room wherein the setting sun lies sleeping."

She stood up, looking childlike in her plain black jacket and trousers. Pointing at each of the three doors in turn she said, "In that room the sun wakes up and stretches his golden arms. In that one he is happy and playful through the day. But there in

304

the third room he burns up the memory of the day and falls into a dream and while he dreams, I, the spirit of the night, guard the pavilion and the spirits who wake when the sun sleeps."

She held her right hand to the brim of her hat as though shading her eyes and looked into all four corners.

"The spirit of the golden room is shy as dawn," she told us, "And the spirit of the jade room is mischievous as the day is long." She put her right hand to her face, thumb beneath chin, fingers spread away from her cheek and called, "Yellow Blossom!" Then, with the left hand, "Green Lotus!" Spreading her hands at us she said, "You see? They do not come when I call, and so –"

She clapped her hands, mock-imperiously, and at once there was a thin, melodious sound, high-pitched on a quarter tone. It dipped, rose again, dipped, rose, became patterned by a quick soft drumming and then by a deep contrapuntal melody, not Chinese music but Indian: the music of the valley. Had Teena chosen it for me?

Suki picked up the yellow handkerchief, rose and went to the left-hand door. She held the handkerchief out and Yellow Blossom's hand appeared from behind the door-frame and caught the other end, so that when Suki came back into the room she brought Yellow Blossom with her, the handkerchief held between them at arms' length. Yellow Blossom came reluctantly, keeping her face hidden behind her free hand, the rouged palm of which was turned towards us. In the crook of her left arm she carried the yellow gown. When they were near the cushion she let go of the handkerchief and sank down, still hiding her face.

Suki said, "This is Yellow Blossom, the spirit of the golden room. See, she is putting the gown on her cushion. The man who desires to know the secrets of the golden room must choose the yellow gown."

She came to the other cushion and picked up the green handkerchief. When she got to the doorway on the right she did not hold the handkerchief out but rolled it into a ball and flung it into the darkness. At once there was the close explosion of a cracker and Lily, dressed as Green Lotus, twirled into the room, laughing, evading capture, uttering little cries whenever Suki seemed about to touch her, until, breathlessly, she sank to her knees, laid the green gown archly on the cushion and said, "I am Gleen Lotus. I am the Spilit of the jade loom of daylong happiness. The man who – the man –"

Mac called helpfully, "– the man who desires to know the seclets of the gleen loom –"

Lily covered her mouth with both hands and then, flinging them out, declaimed, "The man who desires to know the seclets of the gleen loom must choose the gleen gown!" And she struck an attitude while Mac led the applause.

Now Suki picked up the red handkerchief and stood between Yellow Blossom and Green Lotus. At the touch of her hand on their shoulders they rose and said in unison, their voices sounding no older than those of children reciting in a schoolroom, "We, the spirits of the night and of the golden and green rooms speak for the spirit of the scarlet room, Red Jade. Red Jade wears the mask of silence because she is spirit and guardian of the room in which the sun lies sleeping and cannot speak for fear of waking him before morning."

They moved backwards to the door, turned, pressed their bodies together and raised their arms, locking themselves into a yellow, black and green curtain from behind which Red Jade would appear. I caught a glimpse of red and white and knew that she had entered the pavilion.

The music had quickened. I thought that when they lowered their arms I would see the answer in her eyes. The two melodies met, merged; sprang apart, moved to meet again.

The three spirits said, "And the words of Red Jade are spoken in silence but shall be made known to the man who wears her colour."

They moved away from her.

She was magnificent, and terrible: dressed in a long, wide mandarin robe of deep red brocade patterned with green and

306

gold embroidery. Her arms were held stiffly, bent at the elbows with the forearms extended in a straight line in front of her to hold the scarlet gown which lay across them. Her white hands were bent at the wrists, palms outwards, facing me, holding me off.

But the most terrible thing was her face. She had no human face. Her face was hidden by a chalk-white expressionless wax mask and the only recognizable feature of her head was the dark soft hair that framed it. There were slits in the mask for her eyes, but through them I could read nothing. She moved to the middle cushion, knelt by it and placed the scarlet gown on it. Anna and Lily joined her. They knelt by their own cushions. The timing and execution had been perfect. As they settled the music ended. I heard the others applauding but I felt readier to cry out, to get to my feet and go before she could hurt me more. She had used the words and symbols of our private joy for what I suppose I had always known but always hoped they would not be used. And on her face was the white mask of rejection.

Suki said, "Now choose your colours in this order, yellow, green and red. But I first, for I am the spirit of the night. He who would know the secrets of the night must put his hand in mine."

Holmes got up, put his hand in hers, removed her wide straw hat and kissed her. In turn Calthrop and MacAndrews knelt, picked up their gowns, held out their hands for Anna and Lily to take, and when they had been taken bent forward to kiss the girl of their choice. They rose and moved away from the cushions leaving Teena there alone.

I was conscious of their eyes, flat fish eyes like the dead eyes of the fish in the mosaic; their eyes, but not her eyes. If she looked anywhere through the narrow peepholes of the mask I fancied it was at the space between Reid's chair and mine. Tommy, she had said, I haven't thanked you for Saxby; and took my head, kissed me, and said, "Good-bye," because I was too much like Hakinawa, too fond, too foolish, my heart supposedly too big for the small world she was content to live in and in which she had already made her choice, a choice she had reaffirmed in a masque that both encouraged us to business and to forget that it was business we had come together to transact. But my forgetfulness had gone beyond the bounds of what was good. The wax mask was a reminder. I felt that beneath it she was in her European mood, hard and calculating.

At last I got to my feet, intending to go to her, kneel and say, "Is it no, then?" She would not have lied, I would have got a straight answer. From behind the mask the most unpalatable truths could be thrust home.

A voice said, "Hold on!"

It was Reid. He had risen with me, held me lightly by the wrist.

"It must be done properly," he said, and went to her, knelt, almost fell, picked up the scarlet gown and said slowly and carefully, "Red Jade. You are number one girl and I am number one man. I choose your colour to give to another." He paused, lost his balance, steadied himself with one hand on the cushion. "To give to another who's proved himself worthy."

He got to his feet with some difficulty, stumbled over the trailing end of the gown. She put out a hand to help him and he muttered hoarsely, "Thanks," stood above her, his head lowered, searching the room. He caught my eye.

"You," he said. "You, Brent. Not you. You're lucky to be here at all, not to be dead, six feet under, not that we dug 'em as deep as that, only our lives get buried that deep, not our bodies."

He swung round, breathing heavily, searching I knew now for Sutton and, seeing him where he sat, bunched the red gown into a ball and threw it at him. One of the girls, Suki I think, stifled a cry of "Ah!"

"Well, Sutton. There's the gown. Here's Madame Chang."

Sutton stood. His lower lip was trembling. I think he had been expecting it, gearing himself to meet it when it came. The sten-gun which he carried by the sling clattered against the arm of the chair and he held the red gown as if it were somebody else's dirty washing.

"Well, go on, Sutton. I'll take over duty officer." He began to chuckle, came and grabbed Sutton by the shoulder. The bones of his hand showed through the skin, he held him so tightly. "Come on, young Sutton, kneel on the cushion. Don't tell me you don't know what to do."

Sutton, forced to it, knelt, and his hand, pushed out by Reid, waited for Teena's. For one brief, heart-hammering moment, I thought: She won't do it, she'll get up and come to me.

And, for another instant, the white mask was turned to me and then she raised her own hand and placed it in his. She was saying it again; Good-bye, good-bye.

As I left the pavilion I heard Reid calling, "Brent! You're a bad bloody loser! A bloody bad stinking loser, Brent!"

But he did not understand, really, what it was I had lost.

"Finished," I said to myself. "Finished, finished."

*

The house was empty but the lights had been left on in the veranda room and there was a scent that showed the girls had been there. I wondered whether it was in that room or in another that Teena had put on the robe and the mask. I opened the door of my own room and switched on the light, but it had the feeling of my own emptiness in it. I switched on the fan, poured myself a drink. It wouldn't take me long to pack. I found and unrolled my canvas holdall, opened the chest Prabhu Singh had scrounged for me that very first day. Packing was a bloody, a thirsty business. I carried the bottle to my bed and poured another glass.

I drank to the brocade gown and recalled how like it had been to the brocade that had once taken my fancy in Singapore. I drank to the shoes from Paris, the stockings from New York, the handbag from Rome; to her bare shoulders gleaming against the material of a sleeveless, high-necked frock and to

309

the dark curling hair she sometimes shook free from her neck. I drank to her European mood and to her Chinese mood, to the palm-leaf fan and to the slender, red-nailed fingers that waved it. I drank to each of her pointed golden breasts, each rouged nipple, and to the soft, warm curve of her stomach in which the navel was set like a whorled shell. I drank to the way you could press your ear to the shell and hear the singing of the sea. And I raised my glass and drank to that other enchanted place which your hand, moving over velvet surfaces, would feel under it suddenly as a foot walking from marble might feel the springiness of turf.

I drank to Bright Flame and his one golden eye, winking perhaps at this moment in the darkness of the scarlet room between two other pairs of eyes which would not notice him there because for them his eye was not to look at but to see by. I drank to Shining Dagger who had not been summoned but lay most likely wrapped in tissue-paper in the depths of a drawer with other rare and expensive things. I drank to Teena Chang because she was beautiful and had given me pleasure, and finally I drank to myself because I had been a fool and fools should be drunk to.

At eleven o'clock I heard Reid coming upstairs, closing the door of his room. Ten minutes later he opened it again and went downstairs to sleep in the bed in the duty officer's room so that the phone if it rang would ring in his ear and wake him from dreams of old battles or of other conflicts unresolved. At half-past eleven I heard Holmes and Suki come up to bed, borrowing MacAndrews' room by the sound of it, not wishing to disturb me in Holmes's which was next to mine.

At midnight I drank to the day that had ended and to the day that was beginning, turned out my light and lay on the bed fully dressed, intending only to doze the whisky away, to be up again and gone before morning. But just before I fell asleep I changed my mind. I would not slink away in the dark. I would see her once more before I went, see her once more and wish her good luck.

8

IN THE DREAM THE MOON HUNG IN THE SKY OVER THE garden of madness like the waxen mask of Red Jade and as the ghosts of those who had suffered death walked down the steps of the pavilion, I, who seemed to be amongst them, looked up at the sky and watched the mouth of the mask curve into a smile of contempt. I put out my hand and another was placed in it and when we turned to each other, two poor ghosts looking for our shoes, I found that my comforter was Teena Chang.

Teena, Teena, I cried, and she was gone then, pursued by the giant stone birds, and by dragons that hung in the air like sea-horses, whirring their suddenly tiny wings, darting at her when she passed them, blowing silken streamers of fire down their green, shining nostrils. Teena, Teena, I cried, and found that the streamers had led me to a bower of vines and creepers that had so far defied the laws of nature you could see them growing, breathing, pulsating in slow, rhythmic, predatory motion. I dared not look away because then I should have seen the monstrosity, the earth-man, slapped and patted into dark, moist shape as though haunted long-haired children had shaped him on a black-sanded beach and left him to the moon and the murmur of oily water.

I was out of the bower now, walking in a clearing towards the place where Reid and Sutton stood cocking up their guns. Behind them in the ruined shelter the earth-man waited. When Sutton began to fire the woman started screaming far away in the forest, but she must have been running through it towards us because her shrieks were suddenly close by.

Light expanded, glowing, translucent, just beyond my eyelids. A man's voice broke in, harsh and commanding, but the shrieks went on and someone was pounding on a door. At once I was awake. It was broad daylight. The knocking was real, the shrieks were real. I staggered out of bed, my crumpled uniform and the realization that I had slept fully dressed increasing the foreboding that came with me like the tail end of the dream into the day. I crossed to my own door and opened it. The door of MacAndrews' room was open. The voice I had heard was Mac's. He was yelling, "Stop it! Stop it!" and Holmes was saying, "What is it? Christ, what's wrong with her?"

There was a splash of water and the shrieking changed to a gasping, spluttering fight for breath.

"What's wrong with her? What's wrong?"

She began to moan and sob.

I was at MacAndrews' door now. Holmes was standing by the bed, clutching a towel to his middle. Under the net Suki, her mouth open, covering her breasts, shrinking against the pillow, was staring at Green Lotus who knelt on the floor in her pavilion finery, swaying backwards and forwards with her head in her hands and water dripping from it. In MacAndrews' hand there was an empty carafe.

"What's wrong?" I said.

MacAndrews swung round. He said to Holmes, "Look after her, Nick." Then, joining me, shutting the door, he said, "It's Sutton, sir. He's gone off his rocker. He won't come out of the pavilion and he's holding us off with the sten." He moistened his lips and I turned, making for the stairs, knowing the other thing he had not told me; and as I ran down them he called out, "She must still be in there. He says he'll only talk to you, only come out for you," and I heard him coming down behind me.

I saw Anna first. She was kneeling on the gravel path at the end of the compound wall. Calthrop stood near her and when he saw us coming he said, "Take her back to the house, Mac." She twisted round, pressing her shoulders against the wall. "No," she said, "I must wait for Teena."

I pushed past Calthrop. Reid was standing alone, a few yards away, facing the pavilion. The sun was well up but the grass was still wet and behind the pavilion a layer of mist lay trapped at the foot of the hill. There was no sign of Sutton but when Reid lurched forward a few paces, his limbs heavy, unco-ordinated, a report shattered the stillness and a bullet kicked up a plume of dust in the middle of the garden thirty paces away and looking again at the pavilion I saw a whiteness, a pale fleshiness as if someone had moved in the room behind the open window.

Reid turned and saw me. His face was brick-red and streaming with sweat.

"Get him out, Brent," he said hoarsely and then took my arm, restraining me, as if first there was something he had to explain. "I let them sleep in a bit. No harm, I thought, no harm for once. I knocked them up half an hour ago. He called out then. He seemed all right then. But he didn't come out when the others came and when I went back to shake him out of it he fired, Brent, he fired, fired at me."

He pushed my arm away and faced the pavilion, cupped his hands to his mouth and cried, "Sutton! Major Brent's coming over like you wanted. He's coming now."

He looked at me.

"He wanted you. Go on, then. Get him out. He wouldn't be there if it hadn't been for you. If you'd had any guts you'd have fought for her last night. Get him out! Get the poor bloody boy out!"

It was like the day in the clearing, but this time I was afraid. I was afraid because each step brought me one step nearer to a bullet in the chest or nearer to knowing with every sense what only one sense so far told me. I was too late. I had begun to be too late from the moment I walked away from the pavilion the night before and walking back to it now I was finally, irrevocably too late. I had walked away from the pavilion just as, six years before, I had walked out on Saxby. The pavilion was the place which seemed to have been waiting for me all my life, the logical end to days and years spent looking for a sign that God had touched me in some fashion.

When I was twenty yards from the steps he pushed through the scarlet door and came on to the veranda. He was barefoot and wore only his jungle-green trousers. He brought the sten-gun up with a jerk, warning me to stop. I stopped. The sweat was trickling into my eyes. I dashed my hand across them and saw him more clearly. There was dried blood on his chest.

My breathing had gone all wrong. I had to suck the air in and the air was stale, rank with gunsmoke and a nightmare smell of dead flowers. I wanted to call out to her but did not do so in case she did not answer, in case there should be nothing in reply but the echo of my own voice from the high hill behind the pavilion.

I started forward again but he shoved the gun out, pointing it at my stomach, and told me not to come nearer. Then, gripping the gun with one hand he put the other in his trouser pocket and pulled out a piece of paper which he crushed in his fist and worked into a ball. He flicked it at me.

"Read it," he said.

I picked it up.

"Read it," he repeated.

I smoothed the paper out. On it she had written in pencil:

It is written in the book of eternity that when the man asked her to go with him because he loved her she did not know what to say. There are many kinds of love and she could not tell what kind of love was meant. So she summoned Bright Flame and Shining Dagger and looked at them and saw that in one was the golden eye of his heart and in the other the strong arm of his faith and then she knew what her answer had to be.

I turned the paper over but the other side was blank. I looked up at Sutton.

"It was for you," he said.

The muscles of his throat were working. He wasn't off his rocker. He was frightened. He nodded at the paper, jerked the

314

gun at it, as if trying to get me to say something about it. At the back of my mind I was conscious of some kind of omission, a gap, something puzzling to do with the letter but I could not think properly about it. I could only think that she was hurt and that he had hurt her and that I must get my hands on him.

"For you," he repeated. "It was meant for you."

I walked to the bottom of the steps. He backed away.

"It's no good," he said. "It's all up with her. You're too late. You shouldn't have left her. You asked her to go away with you and then walked out on her. Why? I ask myself why?"

It was like Reid talking.

"Why?" he said. "Perhaps I didn't *count*? Was that it?"

I climbed the steps. His back was pressed against the wall.

"You thought I didn't count as a man? You were wrong, wrong. I did. I had her twice. What about that? She was just a bang-off to me, just a bloody Chinese whore, but at least I didn't lead her up the garden like you did. You did, didn't you? *Didn't you?* She thought you were taking her away. It's proved. That's the proof there, that letter. It was in the pocket of the dressing-gown and she must have put it there so you'd find it, only you didn't find it because you ran out on her. *I* found it. I asked her what it meant but she wouldn't say, she just lay doggo and let me do it to her, lay doggo like she hated it and when I woke up I wanted her again and *touched* her and that's how there's blood on me. She'd killed herself while I was asleep. She killed herself because you ran out on her, killed herself with your bloody *kris*, and I wanted to kill *you*, Brent. It made me sick, seeing her like it, thinking people might think it was me that did it to her."

He was shivering but still keeping me covered with the gun. Suddenly, from quite close behind me I heard Calthrop say, "It's all right, Sutton. Nobody's accusing you of anything," and Sutton showed no surprise to hear Calthrop's voice. He had watched him come up behind me. He had raised his voice so that Calthrop could hear.

I held the letter out and said, "Where's the rest of it?"

I had to repeat it but he shook his head as if not understanding.

"The rest of it," I said. "The part that told me what her answer really was."

For a few moments he went on shaking his head and then became still. In a clear, low voice, he said, "That is all there was," and lowered the gun; stood there with a curious air of defencelessness, strength and innocence.

He moved aside, leaving me free to go to the scarlet door, even put his hand on it to push it open for me, and as I came close to him I smelt the metallic odour of the gun, the acid, offensive stink of his body and I hit him hard across the mouth. His head jerked to one side. He kept it there, eyes averted, and a thin trickle of blood appeared on his chin. The sight of his blood made me tremble and I hit him again, smearing the blood across his face. He made no move, uttered no cry. I got him by the shoulder and thrust him at Calthrop who stood on the steps watching.

"Get him out of here. Get him out and keep him out. All of you keep out."

I pushed through the door. The door leading to the jade room had been left open and the mosaic glowed with pale green light. There was too much light, too much air. I closed the jade room and then moved to the other door.

The scarlet room was dark, the shutters closed. She lay on the mattress as though asleep. I knelt by her. "Teena," I whispered. "Teena? Teena?"

I went back to the door, locked it, moved the lacquered chest against it and went back to the mattress; covered her pale, unclothed body with the long mandarin robe.

I wanted nobody there but sometimes they came to the door and called out and I answered them so that they would not try to get in by force.

After a long time I went to the window and opened the shutters. I took the chest away and opened the door and Anna was there in the ante-room. I told her to go away and she covered her face with her hand, and went, and when I knew that I was alone in the pavilion I turned back into the scarlet room.

I knelt and gathered Teena into my arms and paused there; weeping suddenly because I only had one proper arm with which to carry her and there was nowhere to carry her except away from the pavilion.

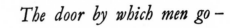

The door by which men go –

PART OF HER MAGIC NOW IS THAT SHE IS TWO PEOPLE and there is no telling which is the reality.

When it was all over the *kris* was returned to me. For a long time I could not touch it. I could not look at it. It was my guilt, my love, my despair, my relic of years of futility; and there were things I knew that I could not put my tongue to, could not press down into those deeper layers of knowledge where you find conviction. Time has not changed that, but what was a doubt, a tendril of suspicion sometimes as slender as a thread, sometimes as thick and twisted as the stems of the plants in the house of flowers, now finds expression in the mood that settles on me when the hungers are dull and it seems that we are all deluded, sick and dangerous, that, living, we are a danger to each other.

In this mood, a mood informed by knowledge of the world and its ways I think that Sutton lied.

She comes to me then in her European mood and I watch her throw off the mask that has served its purpose, shake her head a bit to rid it of the constriction imposed by the tapes the mask was tied with, loosen her hair from the back of her neck and lean forward to accept from Sutton a light for her cigarette. She straightens then, supports an elbow in the palm of her other hand and smiles at him encouragingly because she thinks that he is young and nervous and needs putting at his ease.

She shrugs when he finds the *kris* and the letter in the pocket of the scarlet dressing-gown, resists the temptation to say, Oh, it was Tommy, he was in love with me a bit. She does not tell him that the *kris* is an object she no longer wants, having no use for something that will make other men nothing when they put on scarlet, or that the letter is deliberately vague because she needs to be mysterious even in the way she rejects a man. But she puts her hand on the lapel of the gown he has on and gently draws it down. She cannot twist her fingers in the hair growing on his breast because he is hairless, like a girl, but she takes his hand and puts it on her own breast; hesitates then, because his hand is cold and weightless.

I tell myself that it was a sound Green Lotus heard in the night which, remembered in the morning, sent her hysterically into the house when Sutton began to fire. She never explained. She retreated into silence and with her companions did what the *tuans* told her, said what they said she should say. I do not forget the way they sat together, waiting to give their evidence, their pretty faces as hard, as unforgiving as stone.

The story Sutton told was never questioned. He said he lost his head, wanted to kill me because of what I had done that had caused her to take her life rather than go on with the kind of life she was living. He was young and looked untried, unused. He gained a certain sympathy. He said that she must have had the *kris* hidden somewhere because he had not seen it before, except that once, in my room, the day he had to collect my shaving kit and bring it to Teena's bungalow.

The fact that the other girls knew nothing of Teena's plan to go away with me was considered unimportant; but I can still hear myself saying: Bangkok, Singapore: and her reply: Batavia? Surabaya? as if intending to convey that in such exotic-sounding places the end of our affair would be additionally squalid.

Perhaps the suspicion that Sutton lied was entertained by a few people other than myself, but it was only over the dead body of a prostitute the lies, if lies they were, were told, and I had no evidence to offer, beyond my intuition and my suspicion, that could stop the affair being rushed swiftly to its furtive, hushed-up conclusion.

But in this mood, this certain mood, I think he killed her; killed her in order to destroy the only person in the world who could betray him afterwards to others with a smile, a shrug of the shoulders, a whispered confidence that he had not proved himself a man. Perhaps it was the thought of Reid waiting for that proof that most unmanned him. Perhaps he had seen him, as Calthrop had, watching over the pavilion, and, on that night with Teena, felt his presence there, just outside in the darkness beyond the scarlet room. Perhaps when she lowered the lamp and he lay there impotent and ashamed, the black, violent shapes he was no stranger to burst in and filled the room as the stone birds had filled it in my dream; or he may have slept and, waking, turned her to him in a last attempt to defeat the ugly monster of perversion that gibbered on his shoulder. And afterwards, whatever the manner of its doing, I think he would have crouched in the farthest corner of the room, waiting for morning, abject and terrified until he hit upon an explanation that absolved him; and all that then remained was to walk into the morning, armed, to test the edges of his story on the only man who could prove it wrong.

For in this mood I do not see her, I do not remember her, as a woman who would have loved me without my knowing it, or killed herself in sorrow. I do not mean that I think of her as a woman with no capacity for sorrow. She was sad, for instance, the night that I gave her the *kris;* sad, come to that, whenever I gave her what was rare and expensive. She received such gifts in her Chinese mood, as though, knowing they must outlast us, they were reminders to us of our mortality. Perhaps she saw them too as symbols of the parodies of love. She said: For us the world is no bigger than the pavilion. She may have meant: The world is no bigger than that for me. Perhaps the magic lamps she lit for us and the spells she wove owed something of their splendour to a fear she felt of the world outside, and the enchantments she conjured were conjured not only for us but for herself as well.

Perhaps she felt herself incapable of love, or thought its counterfeit a less exacting, more rewarding joy. Or she may have dreamed of entering the pavilion and of seeing there a man to whom her heart and blood would leap; if so, then even if the story that was told and the legend that grew up around her are untrue, they are her best memorial.

If they speak still in Bukit Kallang of the woman of the world who died for love, then that would be true, for she died, we must admit, for love: for love of her own that never came, or for my love that came and went unwanted; for love of freedom, for love of dignity, for love of greater riches or possessions than I could give her; for love of sorcery, for love of love.

And when the hungers are sharp I sometimes feel her presence and look up, half expecting to see her come to the open doorway of the bungalow to watch me as I trudge back from the fields of the new valley I have found; or, if it is night, and this other mood is on me, an elusive fragrance of rose petals may come drifting in with other and familiar scents, and I will pause and wonder, become sensitive to the texture of the known objects that surround me as if aware of a hidden gift they have revealed of being able and about to transform themselves. And at such times I have, once or twice, gone to my room and seen her standing there, or kneeling with her back to me, her head a little bent, waiting to enact the scene she had devised with skill and tenderness.

And then I tell myself that Sutton spoke the truth; that he woke, indeed, and found her lying there. Nothing helps, then; least of all the knowledge that the mood must pass, the hungers be assuaged, the press of heaven lightened, the certainty return that Sutton lied.

But in this scene she kneels on the scarlet cushions in the scarlet room, dressed in the mandarin robe, refusing to take off the mask that hides her face until I have found the letter and the *kris* in the pocket of the scarlet gown. The mask is worn to hide her face from everyone but me, the *kris* returned because she has her lover to protect her. And when I find the letter and the *kris* and ask her what they mean she raises her

324

arms and unties the mask so that it falls away and strips with it all the defences she ever had and I remember that the words of Red Jade are only to be spoken in silence to the man who wears her colour.

But then, before I can take her in my arms the scene begins again, as scenes will do in dreams I have, and this time I am not there at all and Sutton kneels where I am kneeling. She turns the lamp up high, moving stiffly, encumbered by the heavy folds of the brocade. The walls gleam as red as jade, as red as blood, and, with her back to him, she takes the mask off and places it quietly on the lacquered chest, turns then, with a face paler than the mask and smiles with her lips because she must be careful not to weep, or anger the boy, cheat him in any way. Each small movement has become studied, as delicately controlled and artificial as the way in which she sometimes holds her hands to make them look like the wings of a skylark, motionless in the sky, high above its nest. And when time has run out and there are no more small duties to perform she leans over the lantern and lets the long night slowly take possession of the room.

*

Sometimes I think that Saxby, in the end, did not fail in the business of killing her. Sometimes I think she was doomed in that few seconds it took me to unbolt and open the door of the hostel in Bombay to which Saxby had come to find shelter, or even in the fewer seconds it took me to accept his invitation to eat curry with him. There are so many occasions to which you could point as the one decisive moment for Teena: the occasion when I thought, To hell with him, when I bought the *kris*, when I gave it to her, when I fell in love with her or felt the first pang of jealousy and began to demand more from her than she was willing to give, when, if it was true that she loved me, I failed to see it in her eyes.

But none of these occasions was significant in itself and they only arose because Saxby was what he was and I am what I am, and they are only fallacious arguments that would produce a pattern out of the sad jumble of our dreams.

One thing I am certain of. I would have had Saxby no different. He seems still to tower up in the darkness to which those times have gone and I would not have spared God a single jab from that hard elbow, one tap on the shoulder from that peremptory finger. Knowing him, I feel myself to have been with him if only for a short time and vicariously in his business of importuning Heaven, of not being prepared to accept that showing you believed had to be a one-sided affair. I would rather have had Saxby's brand of doubt than my own brand of faith which is, perhaps, no more than the belief that in the love of one human being for another, whether that love be returned or no, there is all the glimpse on earth that God will grant us of our souls before the time comes for us to go barefoot to hold them to the light and see what's left of them.